Metropolis

ALEX JANAWAY

Published by Browncoat Books 2015
Copyright © 2015 Alex Janaway
Map illustrations by Laura Watton-Davies
Author Picture by Claire Moir
All rights reserved.
ISBN: 978-0992813765
ISBN-13: 099281376X

THANKS TO

Andrew Ruddick, Will Darbishire and Helen Lawrence for their support, enthusiasm and most all, good advice!

ALSO BY ALEX JANAWAY

Redoubt
The Coming of Night
Tangier
End of Empire

Go to www.alexjanaway.com to find out more about the author and his upcoming releases.

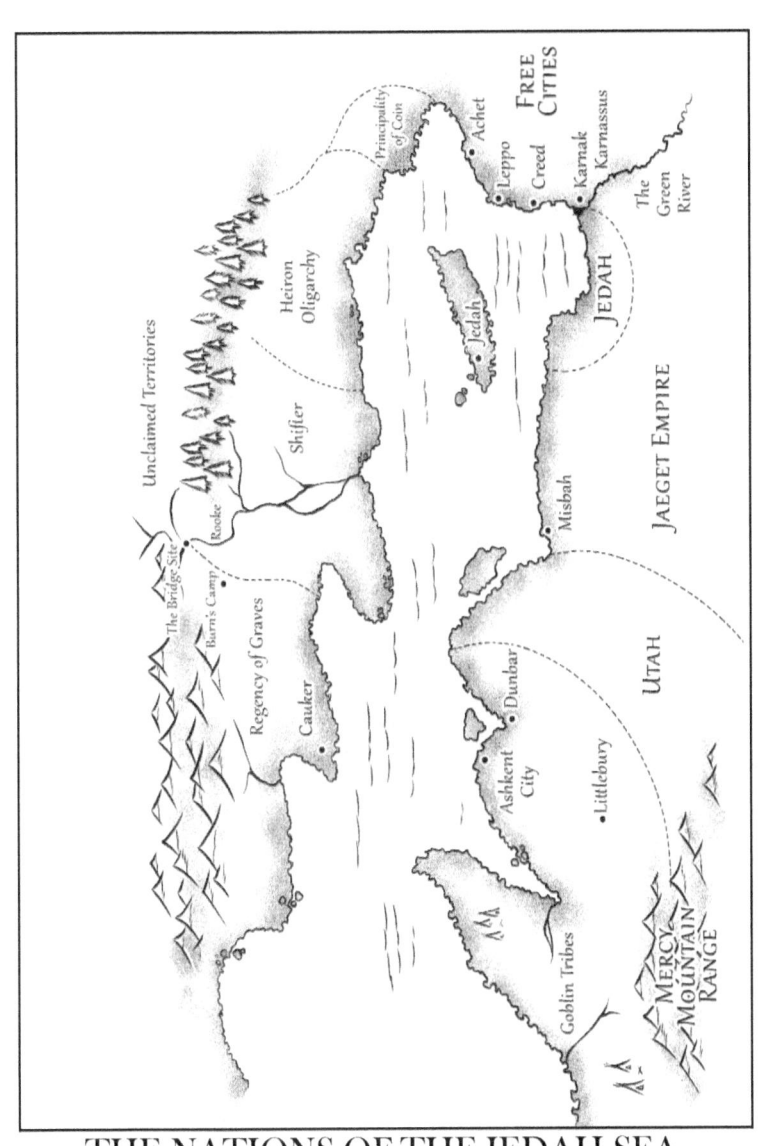

THE NATIONS OF THE JEDAH SEA

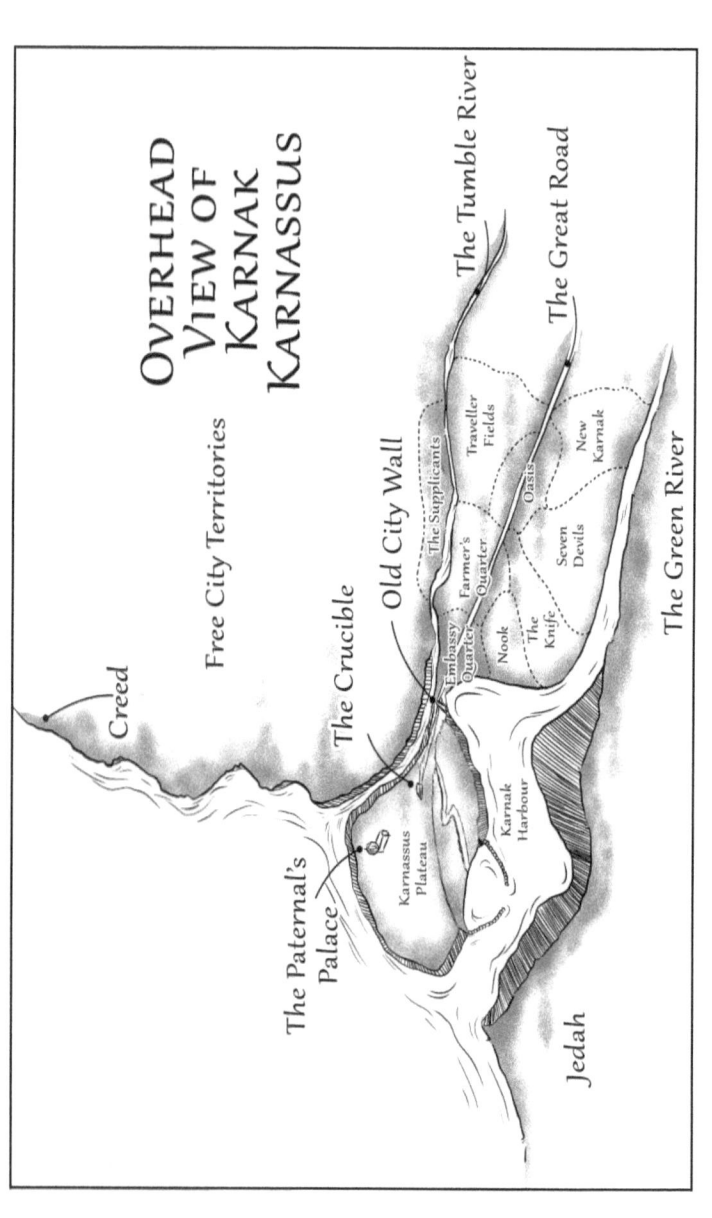

Overhead View of Karnak Karnassus

Chapter 1

A man of middling intelligence but impressive physique walked along the alleyway. He appeared in no hurry. In one hand he carried a sack of food and in the other a bottle filled with ale. Sustenance for a job that was far from done. Halfway along the alley, he stopped by a nondescript door that was reached by two steps made of crumbling clay house bricks. No light filtered out from underneath the door jam. His companion must still be in the cellars at the back of the building.

He placed the jar on the top step and reached up to retrieve the key hanging from a piece of string tied around his neck. He inserted the key into the lock, turned it and pushed the door open just a crack. He pulled the key back out but kept it in his hand as he knelt down to collect the bottle. He stood up and took the next step pushing the door wider with his shoulder. An arm appeared from the darkness, the faintest flash of moonlight glinting from a blade as it was buried into the man's neck. He stood there for a moment, swaying gently, hands still gripping the sack and the bottle. Then the same arm took hold of his cloak and pulled him inside. Moments later, the door was shut.

Major Dav Jenkins burst from the doorway and staggered

down the steps into the alley. The door slammed against the side of the wall with a thud. Dav hissed. It was too damn loud. Surely someone must have heard that? He blinked, wiping blood from his forehead with the hand that still clutched the knife. His right eye was beginning to swell shut. He clutched his left side as he took another ragged breath. Everything else was a dull ache or just plain numb but the pain coming from his ribs was sharp, and it made him want to throw up. They must have cracked at least two. He'd taken his knocks in the past but he had never had to endure a broken bone. He'd been lucky like that. Fighting in a battle, stood shoulder to shoulder with your comrades, you became so flushed with energy and awareness you lost a sense of the pain you were enduring, you never noticed the cuts or the bruises. It was only after, when the veins no longer coursed with energy born of fear and anger, that the body broke down and you'd feel sore for days, in places you didn't even know you had.

And he could feel it all now. They had done a real number on him. A good, solid working over. Just to get him in the right frame of mind. And wasn't it just his luck that they had not moved him to the Ministry for interrogation, that no one had been able to worm their way into his mind. Lucky indeed. Lucky that the two thugs left to soften him up had made one simple mistake, they had not tied one knot tight enough. Lucky that one had gone for food and left the other to take of care business. Who did they think they were dealing with? He might be getting on but he was still a damned officer in the finest army in all the Jedah.

They should have shown him more respect.

He stumbled from the alleyway and made his way down a quiet street towards the quayside. This far from the main berthings there were not many folk about. Anyone with any sense would be asleep at this hour. He was certain that dawn was not far away but there was no sign of it in the sky above his head. It was still a dark blanket studded with bright, twinkling stars. He could name many of them. At least he used to be able to. It was strange, a lifetime of marching underneath them, of navigating by their fixed points, he should have no trouble recalling their monikers. But this night, as his life was drawing to an end, his thoughts started to focus on a certain matter, crowding out all else.

He thought of old friends he'd left behind. Most of them in the grave, and one or two he would have liked to say goodbye to. But that's not how it worked. Only families had the luxury of being with folks who cared when they passed, gathered around the sickbed as the last ragged breathes are exhaled. His family wasn't like that, not the one he had chosen for himself. As for loved ones...well, that was the real kicker. He had never expected to meet anyone. Hadn't planned for it, had never really been looking for it. And yet here, in this distant place, it had happened. He had fallen in love and nothing could ever be the same again. And wasn't it just his fucking luck that he had no choice but to turn his back on it all? He had no chance to explain, to say goodbye. *And what would I have said?* Sorry didn't have the weight. No words did. How could you explain to someone that you would happily give your life for, that you had no choice but to leave them? That it was the only way to keep them safe? No doubt they'd argue, come up with a hundred reasons not to and a hundred more how they could get out of the situation. But there was just one. The only sure way he could think of to guarantee that his secrets were never dragged from him. *As long as the bastards don't have a necromancer.* But he intended to be far too long dead for them to access his

3

memory.

His path had taken him to the far western docks, where the ships were mostly owned by local companies. As such, they were empty of crews and had only roving guards. He turned onto a quay and walked down along the wood-planked path, barely hearing the gentle creaking of the ships moored to either side, or the lapping of water against the stanchions. He reached the end of the quay and looked out into the harbour. The water was dark, almost black, except for the reflected light from above. It was quiet, but in a sleepy, peaceful way. It was, all things considered, a nice spot. He looked at the knife he still carried, the one they had been using to cut little red lines down his back. He let it fall into the harbour.

He lowered himself down onto the quay and put his legs into the water. As it quickly filled his boats and soaked into his trousers, he was pleased how warm it was. He reached into his jacket and withdrew a small vial. They had frisked him for weapons but had never thought to check the lining of his clothes. Another reason why he suspected they did not realise who and what they had. His was a routine taking.

He could not see it in this light but he knew the liquid contained within the vial was dark purple in hue. The day he had been issued it, he had been assured that it was fast acting and painless. He would fall asleep and his body would just... stop working. Not a bad way to go. If it wasn't so prohibitively expensive, this could have been a perfect way to chose one's own death when old age and infirmity took hold. He broke the wax seal, pulled out the little cork stopper and poured it into his mouth.

Oh. It was quite sweet. He hadn't expected that, he would have thought it would be a bitter, acrid concoction. He swallowed it down and let the vial float away. He braced his arms to either side, ignoring the pain coming from his chest, and lowered himself off the side and into water. He kicked his legs out beneath him and let go. He sank briefly into the water before he started a gentle paddle, moving his arms in a wide, sedate fashion. He could already feel his eyes getting heavy. He felt tired. All he wanted to do was sleep, to rest. He'd earned that much, he'd done his duty. He looked up into the night sky.

'I'm sorry,' he whispered.

All things considered, it truly was a pleasant way to die.

Chapter 2

It was the middle of the night. There was a loud knock on the door. In three years there had never been a loud knock on the door in the middle of the night. Jon Forge stared at the door with one open eye, the other squeezed tightly shut to compensate. The door was knocked again.

'Shit.'

Forge pulled the blanket off and swung his feet onto the floor. He stood up and walked stiffly away from his cot towards the source of the noise. He stopped by the door and picked up the wood-axe resting against the frame.

'What?'

'That Forge?'

'Yeah.' The voice sounded familiar.

'You gonna let me in?'

'You gonna give me a reason why I should?'

'Captain Jon Forge, you might be retired but I can still get your arse kicked back into service.'

Yeah, that voice was very familiar.

'You got company?' he asked.

'Two men. They're with the horses. I want to talk to you alone.'

'Right.'

Forge stepped to one side and reached for the bracing bar one handed. In the other he held the axe to the side and horizontal so he could get a good swing going.

'You gonna put whatever you are holding down before I walk in?' the voice asked.

'Right.'

Forge lowered the axe and opened the door. Before him stood a well-built man, wearing fine riding leathers and a black cloak. Black gloves rested casually against the pommel of his sword. The cloak's hood was pulled back yet the face was still indistinct in the darkness. But Forge knew it anyway. Features that were so craggy they could have been chiseled from granite, a well-kept beard, long turned grey and blue eyes that were as bright as they were cold.

'General,' he acknowledged.

'Captain,' said General McKracken, late of the Ashkent Army.

The General stepped through the doorway and into Forge's one-room cottage.

'It's a bit dark in here,' said McKracken.

'It's the middle of the night.'

'Jon, put a light on, would you?'

'Right.'

Forge went to the stove, there was still a small red glow emanating from the remaining pieces of charred wood sat among the ash. He reached for a thin reed taper, touched it to one of those chunks and blew gently. The wood flared brightly and the taper caught flame. He withdrew it, cupped a hand around the flickering light and lifted it towards a candle resting on the shelf behind the stove. The flame transferred easily to the wick and the room lost a little of its gloom. Forge snuffed out the taper and laid it on the shelf next to the candle. He picked that up and took it over to the small table that sat opposite the stove. McKracken had already made himself comfortable on one of the two chairs, his cloak draped over his legs, the gloves placed on the table top.

Forge took the other chair and sat back. He scratched the crotch of his woollen undergarments. He didn't like wearing them but winter had only just passed and the nights were still cold. And he wasn't getting any damned younger. He rubbed a hand through his thick beard and up over his head, moving some of that hair away from his vision. At least he still had good sight. He blew air out through his nose and studied the General. The General looked right back. Forge hadn't seen the man for years, not since he'd retired from the army.

'Heard you quit,' said Forge.

'You might say that. But a man like me finds it hard to let go.'

Right. Forge knew that. McKracken had turned sniping and rib-digging of the Ashkent Assembly into an art form. No doubt the powers-that-be thought pensioning him off might stop that. Fucking idiots.

'Speaking of which,' said McKracken, 'how's civilian life working out for you?'

'It's quiet,' Forge shrugged. 'I like that.'

'Sure you do.' McKracken pointed at a bottle that was sharing the table with the candle and a crude leather tankard. The light reflected off the glass, its bottom half almost black thanks to the red wine it still contained.

'You drinking that?'

'It's the middle of the night,' said Forge.

McKracken grunted, reached over and helped himself to the tankard and the wine.

He took a gulp and made a face.

'Doesn't your pension pay for better than this shit?'

Forge took the tankard out of McKracken's hand and threw back a generous mouthful.

'I don't get a general's pension, Sir.'

McKracken rubbed a hand across his chin and smiled. It was thin-lipped.

'Fair enough. What about business? Somebody actually paying for your crap?'

'Axeheads always need sharpening, arrowheads need replacing. I get by, but I'll never be a proper smith. '

'Still, *Forge's Forge*. I can't decide whether it's clever or sad.'

Neither can I. Forge put down the tankard.

'General, let's cut to it, shall we?'

McKracken nodded and leaned in close. Forge could see the flickering light, reflected in his pupils. The first warmth he'd ever seen from the man.

'I left my command two years ago. Strange as it may seem, I'd grown tired of the constant travel and nights spent in a tent sleeping on a bloody cot. Looking at your face, I think maybe it's not so strange. Fact of the matter was I needed a change but, like I said, it's hard to let go. I've been keeping busy, working on the fringes, getting involved in some of the more... delicate operations of government.'

Forge nodded. The spy service. The Assembly called it the Diplomatic Corps. He knew better. It was where all the dirty work was done. Bribery, extortion and assassination; it was where conflicts were started, avoided and ended. Everyone forgot that the military played a part. At least war-fighting was cleaner. Usually.

He sat back and folded his arms. The General made a face and followed suit.

'I'm not directly involved, I don't handle agents. I tend to act as a third party, a go-to man when something needs to be done outside normal channels. It doesn't happen that often and don't make that face, Forge. I've been engaged by the Executive Member of the Corps, directly. That means this is important. It means that the Corps don't trust their own people to handle this.'

Forge experienced a mild sensation of interest. It was unusual to hear of anything which the Assembly couldn't deal with directly. They were masters at politics and business alike.

'Have you ever been to Karnak Karnassus, Forge?'

'No, don't think we've ever been at war with them. Heard a lot about it though. Dav sent me a letter a while back – said he was getting posted out there to our embassy.' Major Dav Jenkins, one of the few friends he had left. The man had come through for him when it looked like the game was over.

McKracken leaned forward. 'Karnak Karnassus is the largest of the Free Cities, and that's not doing it justice. The place is huge. It has more souls living in its walls than the entire populations of some middling-sized countries I could name. It would take some effort to hold it. There's plenty who have tried in the past and plenty who would like to try now. It sits on a huge wedge of rock between two rivers, controls a vast part of the trade routes from the East to the Jedah Sea. It also has two nations sharing land borders and another half dozen free cities able to reach it with their navies.'

'They must feel a little out on a limb,' Forge observed.

'That's not the half of it. Karnak has high walls and the will to defend them. It likes its independence. But the real way it keeps the peace is not through its strong defences but through mediation. Their rulers decided that the best way to keep safe was by a policy of divide and conquer. Or in other words, they set themselves up as the arbitors for all disputes, disagreements, arguments, agitations and conflicts. Karnak became the place to settle scores, placate friends and turn enemies into even better allies. And you know what? They all bought into it, every damn nation, city state, kingdom and tribe with delusions of grandeur. Karnak is home to embassies, envoys, deputations and consulates from every single country you and I have heard of and a dozen or more we haven't. And it's not just governments that use the place; all the major trading concerns have offices there. If you want to talk, if you want something agreed or you want to avoid going to all the expense of a war, then you go to Karnak.'

'It would've been nice if we'd used it more often then. It might have meant a few less battles me and my lads would've had to fight,' said Forge.

'Oh we did, we do. You have no idea just how much gets done and sorted before the Army get called in. Fighting is always a last resort,' replied McKracken.

'Then it scares the crap out of me to think how much worse it could've been,' said Forge.

McKracken picked up the tankard and took another sip.

'I knew and it scared the crap out of me on a daily basis. Now, the thing about Karnak - and what gives them the edge - is that all negotiation is handled in one place, a palace, and within it resides a room where all the threats and violence, all the deals and the dirty secrets can be aired without anyone knowing about it. A magically shielded room called the Chamber. No one gets in without an invite. What goes on in there stays in there and between whoever's been doing the talking. I said there was arbitration, so there needs to be someone who can listen to it all then devise a means of charting a way through the dispute.'

'The Paternal,' said Forge.

Mckracken slapped his hand on the table.

'That's right, the Paternal. A man who knows more about the plans, schemes and strategies of governments than even the finest spy ring, including ours. Makes him the most important and well-protected individual within a thousand miles. There are any number of folks who'd love to have him as much as they'd like to hold Karnak. The thing about the Paternal, and what makes him so popular with everyone, is that he is completely objective, incorruptible and utterly discrete. He never discusses what he knows outside of the Chamber and carefully selects what he says within it.'

'Powerful man.' *And probably the only honest one in all of the Jedah.*

'He's a prisoner,' replied McKracken bluntly. 'It's the price he pays for his knowledge. The Paternal is selected from among the relatives of the ruling council and sits for five years. He and his family are moved into the Paternal's palace and treated like Emperors, or very well looked after hostages. They want for nothing. Yet the Paternal can never leave. And when the five years is up, he is put down, his secrets taken with him to the grave. His family are given a handsome payoff and moved out the palace to make way for the next bunch.'

'Can't imagine there are many who want the job.'

'You'd be surprised. There are any number of families who are happy to send a son to take the position. Makes them important in the local scene. And who wouldn't want to live like a King for five years? Plenty would trade their lives for just that much. Even so, they are still a prisoner, and there is a small army dedicated to protecting and guarding him. He is never allowed outside his walls, he will never walk free. You get to my age you appreciate the little things like fresh air.'

'Won't argue with you there,' Forge ran a hand through his own, rather less well-kept beard. 'So what happened? Someone try to kill him?'

'If they had, I wouldn't be here,' McKracken sighed heavily. Forge caught a glimpse of the old man under that iron exterior. *That'll be me soon enough.* 'Some time ago a message was passed to Councilman Trajan, a long standing member of the Ashkent ruling body, and also the Executive Officer of the Diplomatic Corps. A day later he called me in. The message had come a long way and had been exchanged by a number of hands. This had been sent outside all the normal channels. The message was for Ashkent and for Trajan. It told us three things. Firstly, that the man who originated the message felt he could trust no one. Secondly, that there was a traitor buried deep within the Ashkent government. Finally, it said only one man could tell us who it was. In exchange for that information we have to guarantee safe passage and protection for him. That man is the Paternal.'

'Shit.' Forge didn't need to hear any more to know where this was going. He had no link to the man, no knowledge of Karnak. He was just a simple soldier, and that was the problem. 'Why in the sweet seven hells do you want to be telling me that?'

'Because you are like me, Forge. You're retired, no longer beholden to the Ashkent government or military. You are a free agent, able to go wherever you want, whenever you wish.'

Damn, was that a twinkle in his eye?

'I'll make this simple. We want to know who the traitor is. So we get the Paternal out.'

'You have sorcerers, can't they find that out for you?'

'Normally, yes. They form part of our normal security protocols. Fact of the matter is, we can't afford to let on we know. The traitor might try to commit suicide, and we don't want them dead until we've found out what they've shared. There's still a chance we can turn this to our favour.'

Forge snorted. Politics. It was enough to make a grown man spit.

McKracken scowled at Forge. 'Anyone that deep in the organisation is probably protected against magical interference. This has to be done the old way, by being smarter.'

'Then that rules me out. '

'Don't be so optimistic. We get the Paternal, we get more than the just our traitor. We get everyone. We get everything. It'll screw over our enemies and make sure our allies keep playing nice. Only for a short while, but it'll be fun.'

Fun?

'This mission doesn't exist. You and I never had this conversation, but the result is this: you are going to Karnak Karnassus and you are going to get the Paternal out of the city and bring him to me.'

'Bollocks I am.'

McKracken stared hard at Forge. Forge stared right back. There was no way he was going to let McKracken win this pissing contest; he had no power over Forge anymore.

'I thought you might say that. It still stands. You'll do this.'

'Why?'

'Because I can trust you. Because you don't want to do it. Because you are a godsdamn stubborn son-of-a-bitch when you put your mind to it.'

'And I'm expendable?'

'That too. You can be traced back to Ashkent if they put

14

you under the knife, specifically they'll trace you back to me. And they can't touch me. All they know is I'm a retired general. I don't make policy. They can never prove it was the Assembly that sanctioned this.'

Forge wasn't impressed with the argument. 'Is that all you got? If so, I'll kindly ask you to leave. I'm tired and I've got more important things to do.'

'No, that's not all I got. I know you won't do this for Ashkent. When you rode into Shifter you did that for your friend, just to avenge him. You shouldn't have come back, it was a suicide run.'

'I had help.'

'That you did. This time it's not so different.'

'Really?'

'Jon. Who do you think sent that message in the first place, who died to get it out.'

No. Forge felt ice travel up his spine.

'Major Dav Jenkins wasn't just a military representative. He was working for the Corps.'

'No.'

'I'm sorry, Forge. '

Damn it all, Dav. What had you gotten into? 'How did he die?'

'His body was delivered to the embassy. He was beaten up, but what killed him was poison. That's all I know. Who did it? Could've been anyone, but the Paternal reached out to him and somehow Dav got the message out before he was caught. That, considering the security apparatus around the Paternal, is a major feat.'

Forge wasn't listening anymore. Dav was, had been, his oldest friend. They had joined the army at the same time, worked their way through the ranks. But Dav was the smart one, the one who realised that when you get to a certain age, you shouldn't be out in the front lines anymore. And now he was dead, doing his duty until the end. That's how they all died, everyone he cared about, fought with and bled with. *And here I am. Still alive. How does that work? Because I got out, you idiot.*

General McKracken stood up and threw his cloak about his shoulders.

'I won't see you again before you leave. Head for Dunbar - there will be a ship waiting for you, it's called the *Crimson Shore*. Its captain will tell you everything you need to know. If you set out in the morning you'll be there in six days. Three if you go by horse.'

Forge remained in his seat and kept his arms tightly folded. If he didn't, he was liable to stand up and strangle McKracken.

'Why would you think I'm going to do anything? Dav's already dead, there's nothing I can do about that.'

McKracken finished adjusting his cloak and started to pull on his gloves, right hand first.

'You'll do it. Because you'll finish what your friend started. Because you owe it to him. And because you are a stubborn bastard who'd die trying rather than give up. You think it was Dav who sanctioned that little jaunt into Shifter years ago? I knew what you were up to and I approved. I know what you are capable of, Forge'

McKracken finished putting his left hand glove on and stepped towards the door. He hesitated for a moment and Forge watched him fish around at his waist. He turned back to Forge and threw a small pouch onto the table. It landed with a solid 'clunk'.

'Consider this an advance. Get yourself a horse, anything

else you need for the trip. There will be more when you get back. I know you don't want money but put it this way - you get the Paternal back to us, that pension of yours will look a damn sight healthier.' McKracken looked around the cottage. 'And you can get yourself a better place, employ an apprentice or something.' He turned, walked to the door and opened it. A gentle gust of wind blew into the room, causing the candle flame to gutter and die. Forge looked at the general, a black figure silhouetted against the faint glow of the night.

'I came to you, Forge, because as I've already said, I trust you. Do this for Dav or do it for Ashkent. I don't really care. In the long run, you might save some lives.'

McKracken closed the door and Forge was blanketed by darkness. He sat there for a long while, just tapping his fingers against the tabletop. *I haven't said yes to anything but that doesn't really matter. That bastard knew. As soon as he mentioned Dav, he knew he had me.* Forge reached under the table and pulled out a drawer. He retrieved a small pile of papers. They were all from Dav. His friend had never stopped writing to him, even though he knew Forge would never reply back. It didn't mean Forge didn't read them. He did, every one. Dav had told him that he was going to Karnak Karnassus and had asked him to come along. A fresh start, back in the military but away from all the campaigning, a nice easy job that meant he could wear the uniform but not see anyone get hurt. It was a better way to spend his retirement. Forge had wanted no part of it. He'd made his decision.

He picked up the letter on the top of the pile. He had received this one a month ago. Dav had written that things were getting on top of him, that he needed a friendly face, someone who had his back. Someone he could trust. He had just dismissed it, just put it down to Dav still looking out for him. Now he realised. It was the best Dav could do in a letter that had every chance of being intercepted. *Damn me, Dav. You were in trouble. And I was the one you turned to.* And Forge was too wrapped up in his own misery to have seen it. His friend had needed him. *I should have been there to look out for you. Just like you did for me.* And now his friend, his only true friend, was dead. Forge felt a tear roll down his cheek. He felt ashamed.

'Dav.' *I let you down.*

He reached out and found the pouch. He lifted it up, tested the weight, felt for the coins inside. It was heavy, the discs felt thick. Gold pieces. Hells, he could run now with this, get across the border and start again. He could. But he wouldn't. He had failed his friend in life; he had turned his back on him. But he would honour Dav in death. He would avenge him and make the bastards pay. Because there was no one else who cared.

Forge left the pouch on the table and groped his way back to his bed. He was tired and it was still the middle of the fucking night.

Chapter 3

Forge emerged into the sunlight a couple of hours after dawn. He squinted as he gazed at the sun, a haze obscuring some of its power. The ground was covered in a light frost and it felt hard beneath his feet. He lifted the backpack onto his shoulders, slipping his arms through the straps. His sword was wrapped in cloth and held in place against the centre of the pack to keep the weight distributed equally. His hand-axe was tucked into his belt on the right hand side and on his left, his knife sat in a leather scabbard. Over it he wore a long leather jacket, mostly dark brown with patches of mottled black and green. A pocket on the inside of the jacket held the pouch and most of the gold McKracken had given him. The rest was hidden in the lining of his boots. It paid to have back-up.

He stood by the door, trying to get used to the weight that was settling onto his back. It had been a long time since he'd had to hump so much shit, yet the familiarity of it rolled back the years. As he had packed he had looked in the small piece of broken glass that served as a mirror. The brown-eyed man staring back hadn't aged much since he had left the military. The Army had aged him long before that anyway. He stretched and felt his stiff muscles complain. His brown hair, no longer a crew cut, had grown out and was tied back, though that couldn't hide the streaks of grey. Either way you looked at it, he wasn't a soldier anymore. Yet here he was, just about to march off on another mission like he hadn't been away. That made him angry. What had been the point? He had retired for a reason. But when you got right down to it, you carried your sins with you. And you couldn't turn your back on what you were.

Forge reached out and closed the door. He turned the lock, pocketed the key and stepped off the porch. All his tools were inside the workshed abutting the main building. The furnace and anvil were still sat under the covered awning behind the house, if anybody fancied taking the anvil, good luck to them; the thing weighed a ton and wasn't worth the effort. He walked along the path that led out of his clearing in the woods upon the hilltop. He glanced at the bent and stiffened grass that marked the presence of the horses and riders from last night. Three sets of hoof prints just like McKracken had said. He made his way along the trail and listened to the birds in the trees to either side. A squirrel bounded across his path. He skirted round a pile of horseshit.

The trees thinned out and he emerged in the shallow valley that held the village of Littlebury. Two dozen houses clustered around a central square and a mill which sat on the far side of a solid wooden bridge. There were another score of families that lived close enough to call this place their home. Folk were up and about their business. A few acknowledged his presence with a curt nod or brisk 'good morning'. He responded in kind. He wandered past the local inn. The yard looked empty so probably no one was staying, or at least had already left. He liked the inn: they brewed their own beer and made half-decent scrumpy. He stopped at the barn next to the inn. A wagon was parked outside and two young lads were lifting sacks off the back and carrying them inside.

'Morning, Jon. Going somewhere?' asked a man emerging from the shadows of the barn. He was balding, with thick grey and black mutton chops and had hands the size of Forge's anvil. He wore a think woollen jumper and had a leather apron wrapped around his stomach.

'Red,' responded Forge.

Red folded his arms and studied Forge. Red was the inn's owner and one of the few people Forge liked in Littlebury. If you had to make friends with someone, make sure it's the man who pulls the pints. Red was also ex-military. He got it.

'You're packing an arsenal, Jon. And I know you don't like hunting. So tell me you ain't decided to re-enlist.'

'Like shit, I have,' replied Forge. He'd have to keep telling himself that, just to keep a sense of perspective. 'I've got an errand. Might be gone a while.'

'Uh-huh.'

'You still got that old nag of yours?'

Red ran a hand over his head and frowned.

'Yeah, she's out back.'

'Need to borrow her.'

'Right. Where's she going?'

'Taking her to the coast.'

'You bringing her back?'

'Probably not.'

'Then you can't have her.'

Forge chewed the inside of his cheek and cocked his head.

'Let's put it this way. I only need her to take me there.'

Red looked at him, his face neutral. The two lads had stopped work and were watching the exchange. Forge shot them a glance then raised an eyebrow. Red got the message.

'You two, bugger off. Don't go far, you're not done yet,' he ordered.

21

They ran off past Forge and into the inn's yard.

'You were saying,' said Red.

'I don't know when I'll be back. I have to leave her there.' He thought for a moment. He fished into his jacket and pulled out the pouch. He opened it and produced two of the gold pieces. Red's face was a mixture of surprise and interest. 'You get this for the hire of the horse. I'll pay for stabling while I'm gone. Then I bring her back.'

'Hells, Jon. I don't often get to see gold around these parts. These will help with my retirement pot.' He held his hand out and Forge dropped the coins into the palm.

'I thought you were already retired,' Forge said.

'Nah,' said Red, examining the gold. 'This is for when I really retire. There'll come a point that I won't want to run this place anymore.'

'Does that mean I can have her, then?'

Red smiled.

'Sure you can. Anything to help a friend out.'

Funny how money always greased the wheels.

'I get a saddle, right?' Forge asked.

Red laughed and slapped him hard on the shoulder then gently guided him into the barn.

'You know, Jon, living up that hill all by yourself isn't helping with your social skills.'

'Yeah, whatever.'

Ten minutes later Forge climbed onto the bay mare. The saddle was worn, the leather cracked. The horse was at least ten years old. No galloping on this one. At least he knew the shoes were in good nick. He'd made them barely a month ago.

Red finished tying off the backpack and stood back.

'There you go. All done. You got any food?'

Forge had packed some bread and a piece of cheese. It's all he'd had in.

'Not really.'

'Thought not. I'll put some ham and a flagon of beer in your saddlebags. Don't say I don't look after you.'

'I won't. Here,' Forge reached into his jacket and retrieved two folded parchments sealed with wax and passed them over. 'Thought I'd better write and let those that care about me know that I might be gone a while.'

Red looked over the scrawled writing and nodded. 'No problem, I'll pass these over to the next Messenger passing by. Who knows, they might even get them before you've come back.' Red offered his hand to Forge.

'Keep safe. Since you came here my profits doubled. I can't lose my best customer.'

Forge took Red's hand and squeezed it. 'Will you keep an eye on my place?'

'Sure.'

Forge nodded and released his grip.

'Thanks, Red.'

He took the reins and squeezed the horse's flanks.

'Hey, Jon,' Red called after him. 'You gonna be okay?'

Forge smiled.

'I'll be back smellin' of roses.'

He heard Red snort.

Yeah. Who am I trying to kid?

Chapter 4

Nazar the Lucky stepped out of his cabin onto the deck of the *Crimson Shore*. He stretched and breathed deeply of the chill evening air. His nostrils were filled with the familiar smells of the sea. Salt and sweat were the main constituents mixed with a dose of rotting fish and sour wine. A heady mix and one he would be hard put to forsake if he ever had a mind to. He walked along the deck to the prow of the ship and placed a hand on the small figurehead of Merine, the Goddess of the sea and of good fortune. She was the patron for many merchants who plied their trade around the Jedah Sea, and even though she was particularly capricious for a deity of luck, it paid to at least try and stay in her good books. Though, in truth Nazar, doubted she cared overmuch. He had seen both good men and bad, devout and heathen, taken into her loving embrace. She could be a right bitch.

Nazar looked to his left out into Dunbar harbour. There were only a few vessels berthed out there, small coastal fishermen by and large. Most of his fellows had left when the first winds of Spring had begun to play across the water. Along the wharfside, his was but one of only three trading ships still tied up, and he knew for a fact that one was due to leave with the tide first thing in the morning, while the other was subject to a small dispute about ownership. That was something he need never worry about. The *Crimson Shore* was his, his alone and he was indentured to no one. He turned around and looked over the deck. *Ah, but by all the Gods of the Sea, the Crimson Shore is a pretty maid.* A trading dhow of a classic design, with a single triangular lateen sail, a curved prow and a long, thin hull, painted red. The addition of a cabin at the far end behind the wheel was a personal consideration; while many ships of this type might have a wheelhouse, he had decided to go a little further. At his age he felt he deserved this luxury. Had he not earned it after a long and occasionally successful career?

Everything was in order: the ropes were stowed, the wood was scrubbed, and barrels were lashed to the side, just as they should be. Below him, the hold was fully stocked with cargo and supplies. The ship was ready to sail. Yet there were two very important, no, *critical*, elements missing from this scene. One was their passenger - and who knew when he would turn up – the second was his crew. He had elected to take a short nap earlier in the day, and that nap must have been a long one because he could swear the sun was barely at noon when he had closed his eyes. Now the sky above him was black and only the faintest of glows could be seen turning the clouds to the purple and red far to the west. The *Crimson Shore* was bereft of life. He was the only soul upon it and had been for many hours if he was any judge. *The bloody bilge rats!* He stalked over to the gangplank, placed a hand on the rail and tapped his finger against the wood. He knew what this was. It was boredom. It happened to all of them. Stay too long on land, have nothing to do but watch your fingertips grow. *This wouldn't do.*

Nazar strode down the gangplank, his body bobbing as the

wood flexed under his weight, and gained the wharfside. He turned left and marched the few dozen yards to the nearest hostelry. He opened the door and stepped into the gloomy taproom taking in the atmosphere of stale beer, old tobacco and the acrid odour of tallow candles. Even after so many years plying his wares, he had never grown accustomed to the rougher scents of the western countries. He was from the east and was used to the finer aromas of incense and a multitude of spices. Back home such substances were commonplace but this far west there were plenty of folk willing to spend good money on the mysterious and the exotic. Such was the nature of trade, supply and demand.

He cast a suspicious eye over the clientele, more out of habit than anything else. He was a regular in Dunbar and knew all the faces before him. *Ah!* And there they were. His crew were ensconced in a corner table nearest the counter. He walked over and stood with his arms folded, looking over his loyal and trusted colleagues. Medhji, his first mate and longest serving crewmember, of an age with Nazar, his skin tanned and leathery, with a scarred jaw and overlong ears. Rabi, the bold and brazen loudmouth from Jedah Isle who boasted long black hair worked into a single braided ponytail and dark-brown eyes threaded with red veins from too much drinking. Benji and Bors, the two brothers who had begged passage from Cauker and then never left, both well-built young men with fair hair and deeply tanned skins, they could have been considered handsome if not for the angry red birthmark on Benji's left cheek and the lack of front teeth in Bors's mouth. Then there was young Hassan who had been a wharf rat before Nazar had taken pity on him, he had dark skin common to the eastern nations and an open face and a wide-eyed innocence that his life should have crushed from him years ago. And finally Wenham, a quiet ex-soldier from Shifter, he kept his brown hair short and spikey and sported a raggedy beard that failed to hide the scars on his face. He had something of the hair trigger about him but was dependable enough. He also doubled up as the ship's cook and showed some skill in producing food that was almost palatable.

They all went silent at his approach. *That's right. Look guilty.* They shared looks with one another. It fell, naturally, to Medhji to mediate. He stood up and smiled happily.

'Captain, glad you finally woke up, we were starting to worry. Here, shift up lads, make some space.'

'And just why would you expect me to sit here drinking with you? I have an unguarded ship out on the wharf full of cargo that, I might add, represents any future pay you might expect to earn over the next nine months.'

'It was guarded,' said Bors, a look of complete sincerity on his face.

'After a fashion,' added Benji.

'Was it indeed?'

'By you!' said Hassan, his youthful face full of bright shining teeth.

'That's right, Captain. And thanks for letting us off, duty,' said the booming Rabi waving his tankard vaguely in his direction.

'Did I?' Nazar asked, directing his gaze squarely at Medhji.

'Yep, the First Mate said so, Captain,' added Rabi.

Medhji put his hands on his hips and cocked his head thoughtfully.

'I could've sworn I checked with you earlier, Captain, but you were sound asleep when we decided to come ashore. I knew you wouldn't mind, besides we are virtually right next to the ship and we could probably hear of there was any ruckus.'

'We'd come running, Captain,' said Bors.

Nazar seriously doubted that any of them were in fit state for running. Except maybe Wenham, who was nursing a half-drunk tankard and just shrugged when he looked at Nazar.

'The lads really needed this time off. They all appreciate it,' said Medhji.

'It gets mighty boring waiting on a ship that ain't sailing,' said Benji.

'That it is. Mighty boring. Folk are liable to get bored and get into trouble,' said Medhji. He raised a knowing eyebrow at Nazar.

He's right on that front. Damned boring. Nazar sighed. Medhji was probably right. No one was likely to come robbing along the wharf front of Dunbar. The place was too small. Everyone knew everyone and the Watch knew those who liked to cause trouble. More importantly, everyone knew Nazar. There'd be no acts of piracy in these waters. *Oh well...*

'All right, then, who wants another?'

There was a cheer from his crew.

'I'll help you get them in, Captain,' said Medjhi.

As they moved to the counter Nazar nodded at the barkeep.

'Another round, Rafe, if you will.'

Rafe, the proprietor, smiled at Nazar and got to filling tankards. He was no doubt happy to have paying customers stay in port a while longer.

Nazar looked hard at Medhji.

'Two hours in twelve. That's all I ask of you lot. Two hours in twelve to stand at the top of the gangplank and keep a watch on who passes by. '

'And very reasonable that is too, Captain,' replied Medhji. 'But we've been waiting for more than a week for our passenger to turn up. That's a mighty long time to do nothing.

We should be out there by now, heading east with thoughts of profit, wine and women. Though I wonder if in Rabi's case, it might be goats.'

Nazar slammed his palm onto the counter. 'You think I don't know all that? Damn it man, I want to be well rid of this place. Our cargo is not unique, we have plenty of competitors who will shift theirs first and drive down any prices we might care to ask for.'

'Then let's be off, Captain. Leave this fellow to his own devices. He can find passage with some other ship. He can pay a fisherman, Hells he can ride all the way east for all I care,' said Medhji.

'You know I can't do that,' replied Nazar, even though he was precious close to following his First Mate's advice.

'Not like you to be beholden to anyone,' observed Medhji.

Nazar smiled. *And that's one or the reasons I never became a success.* He raised his hands, 'I told you, this is a big player. We do right by him and he says we'll never have to pay mooring fees in any port of Ashkent again.'

'And if we just cut and run?'

'Then we never have to pay mooring fees in Ashkent again, because we'll be hounded across the Jedah Sea until we are caught and fed to the fishes.'

'Sweet deal.'

'And sour.' Nazar added. All he had received was a letter bearing the seal of Ashkent. It told him to wait in Dunbar until a passenger arrived. They were to take the passenger to Karnak Karnassus as part of their usual trading passage. More often than not he would have ignored such an entreaty, but for the warning and the small diamond that had accompanied the letter. He had neglected to share that last piece of information with his crew.

'So we wait and then go back home, again.'

'Aye.' They both hailed from Karnak and Nazar had no doubt that was the reason why he had been selected for this task. It intrigued him a little why someone would even know of him. He made it a point of never making himself too big a target. Not since it had all gone horribly wrong for him. Rafe placed four tankards in front of him. Nazar pointed at the tankards. 'Here, Medhji, take these to the table. I will bring the others.'

'Yes, Captain.'

Nazar leaned against the bar and wondered how much longer he could wait for his passenger. There was business to attend to and the winds of the Jedah Sea waited for no man. He really didn't want to have to pawn that diamond to compensate his crew for their losses.

'I heard you talking,' said Rafe, as he filled another tankard. 'You waiting for someone, are you?'

'That I am.'

'Might be your wait is over. Just had a rider turn up an hour ago. Looked like a man who could handle himself, judging by the amount of sharp stuff he was carrying. Paid me to lodge his horse for six months. Paid with gold. I think that means he plans on being away for a while.'

Nazar stood straight. Behind him he heard the door open and shut.

'Sounds like my man.'

Rafe tilted his head .'Then look behind you.'

Nazar turned around. Stood by the entrance was a man taking off his cloak. He walked towards the bar and nodded at Rafe.

'I found that ship I was after. Nobody on board.'

Nazar coughed politely.

'That is because we are all here, my friend!' he announced.

The man cocked an eyebrow. He walked to the bar and stood next to Nazar. His eyes were sharp and clear but also a look of sadness about them. Nazar knew that look well, it told of great loss. And there was something else too, there was steel. It was not hard to see why. Rafe had been right about the weapons he carried. This man had come prepared for a fight. And though he had grey in his hair, and his beard was flecked with sliver, Nazar had no doubt this person was accustomed to hardship.

'You from the *Crimson Shore*?' the man asked.

'I am its captain. And whom, might I enquire, is asking?'

'The name's Forge. I was told to find your ship.'

'And you know where we are going?'

'I'm going to Karnark Karnasuss.'

'Then it sounds like we are both who we say we are. I am Nazar the Lucky, and it my pleasure to meet you.' He put out his hand and after a moment's hesitation, Forge took it. 'Would you like some ale?'

'Wouldn't say no.'

'Good. Rafe, one more please.' Nazar turned to his crew, who, to a man had all been watching the exchange.

'Men, our passenger has arrived. Master Forge is no doubt tired from his travels and would appreciate a good night's sleep. To that end consider this your final night on land. Enjoy the evening and lay your heads where you will but,' he waggled a finger at them, 'we will be leaving on the morning tide. If you are not on board then consider yourself out of a job and out of the profits.'

Benji and Bors touched their tankards, Rabi gave a cheer.

'We'll all be there, Captain, not to worry,' promised Medhji.

31

'Who's worrying?' responded Nazar. He looked at Forge. The man was already drinking deep.

'You have a room here? This might be your last night before enjoying the comfort of the Jedah Sea.'

'Won't be the first time,' Forge replied.

'I don't doubt it.'

Forge gave Nazar an appraising look.

'Do know why you are taking me to Karnak?'

Nazar shook his head.

'No. Nor do I know who it was that commissioned me and my crew to do so.'

Forge grunted. 'Trust me, that's for the best.'

'Oh, of that I am convinced. All I have been told is to take you into Karnak as quietly and without fanfare as I can manage.'

'Nothing else? No other orders?'

That's interesting, thought Nazar. *Orders is it?*

'No. My mysterious employer left me nothing more than promises of reward or punishment for failing to take you.'

'Sounds like him,' muttered Forge. He finished his ale and placed the tankard firmly back on the bar.

He fished in his pouch and retrieved a silver piece.

'Here, another round for your lads.'

Rafe pounced on the coin and had spirited it away with moments. He then refilled Forge's tankard.

Nazar smiled. At least this Forge had some manners about him. 'With any luck we will reach Karnark in a month.'

Forge stared at him. 'A month? Why so long? It should only take us a couple of weeks.'

Nazar suppressed a smile. It wouldn't do to unduly upset this man. 'I am sorry, but while I have been commissioned to carry you, there was no indication of when we should arrive. I take from that that I am free to conduct my normal business. I have goods to deliver and more to buy. It is, after all, my livelihood.'

Forge took another long drink. 'Fine.'

'I am glad that you consent to this. Do you understand the trade winds?'

'A little. I've spent my fair share of time aboard ships.'

'Good. The trade winds begin to blow after the cold months, or at least, the conditions are better to sail by them then. The storms have abated and the risks are reduced,' Nazar raised his hands and described a circle in the air. 'All merchants are governed by the winds; they travel in a circle around the Jedah Sea. We will pick up spices from the eastern ports, stopping at Karnak and then north to the other Free Cities and Coin, and then head west, landing at The Oligarchy, Shifter and Graves. And finally, we arrive back where we started. We wait out the winter months and set sail once more.' He lifted his tankard in salute and Forge made a sour face at him. 'Thank you for the ale. Let us drink to your health and a swift and successful journey.'

'It better be,' said Forge, tilting his own tankard in response. 'Your boat's only got the one cabin. Guess I'm sleeping down below?'

'If you wish. It is a little...cosy down there, not much room what with our cargo taking priority. Many nights the lads sleep on deck. Though the evenings are still a little brisk.'

'And I am not getting any younger. I can do without being cold and wet,' replied Forge.

Nazar laughed and clapped him on the shoulder. 'And that is why I am the captain and not a crewmate!'

Chapter 5

The soldier stepped out into the courtyard of the Palace dressed in the uniform of the Paternal Guard. He took a moment to adjust his gauntlets. A bell tolled high above him, coming from the Silver Tower. It rang three times, indicating the change in shift. He hurried across the courtyard and joined the other twenty men who were falling into two lines in front of the shift commander.

'Come on, don't dawdle,' he admonished the late arrival, who joined the end of the front row. As tellings off went, it was perfunctory at best. The shift commander was an old sergeant who had spent most of his career at the Paternal's Palace. There was very little that bothered him or excited him, as long as everyone did what they were supposed to do.

'Sorry, Sergeant,' replied the soldier. He stood to attention. He and the rest of his shift all had their helmet visors raised, enjoying a cool breeze playing across the marble flagstones. The courtyard was in the rear of the Palace and used solely by guards and staff. No visitors ever came this way. As soon as they were dismissed, the visors would come down and they would become faceless guards. Their armour was well-forged steel, without embellishment but burnished to a high gleam: helmet, breastplate, greaves, and gauntlets. Beneath was a jerkin of ring mail, similarly buffed to reflect the light. On their backs were cloaks, made of fine, golden silk. Their visors were made of silver; they covered the entire face with a smooth plate, blank and featureless with slits for eyes and the mouth. When the visors were down, the looked less than human, more like statues. But then, that was the idea. To wear such armour all day in the heat of the city would exhaust most men but the Paternal Guard were conditioned to carry the weight. It helped that within the halls of the Palace it was always cool, often shadowed. Even those stationed at the entrance could find relief as those passing into the Palace walked under a broad portico before the bronze-clad doors. Each guard carried a seven foot spear, and a longsword buckled to their waist, sheathed in a silver scabbard. Everything was designed to impress, yet remained functional - they were still charged with defending the Paternal after all. Each guard drilled for an hour each day, usually before their shift started. Though, in living memory, no one had ever drawn a blade in service to the Paternal. In fact, the Paternal's Guard had never ventured beyond the walls of the Palace. Theirs was to defend and protect. And to ensure the Paternal never left.

'Alright then, listen in. We have two deputations visiting the Paternal today. The first is due to arrive before the fourth bell, a collection of mercantile concerns haggling over rights. At the sixth bell, the Jedah ambassador and his staff are arriving. They are expected to remain within the Chamber for some time. They will be meeting a deputation from the east. Chances are they'll be in and out all evening so keep that in mind. Remember, you are faceless and should not be seen. Now then, no change to the usual routine. Half of you at post, the others walking the halls. Listen in for your names. Boulas, Gad, I want you outside the Chamber. Mallick, Najor, you two outside the Paternal's private chambers.'

The soldier half listened to the orders, his mind drifting off. Suddenly the sergeant's voice broke him out of his reverie.

'Calill! Are you bloody listening to me? That's the worst thousand yard stare I've ever seen,' the guard sergeant barked.

'Sorry, Sergeant,'Calill replied.

'You look like shit, Calill. Been burning the midnight oil? Save it for your day off. You and Barakee are walking the halls. Maybe that will wake you up a bit.'

'Yes, Sergeant,' replied Calill.

The sergeant scowled at him for a moment longer then continued with the dispositions. They would only be on duty for two hours and then they would report back to the sergeant to be told who to relieve. Once the briefing was finished, the shift was dismissed. The men split into pairs and lowered their faceplates into place before moving off to their assigned positions and patrol routes, their pace even and in step. Barakee joined Calill and leaned close, speaking quietly through the thin mouth slit.

'You still not sleeping?' his voice sounding dull and muffled.

'Not much.'

'Well don't damn well fall asleep on me or I'll kick your arse.'

'Get in line.'

As they left the courtyard and walked thorough an archway leading to the public area of the palace, both fell silent. Guards were not allowed to speak unless spoken to. Only the shift commanders were allowed to communicate to their men.

Together, they marched at a slow and steady speed towards the administration wing of the Paternal's Palace. While the ruling council had their own impressive edifice not far from the Palace, the art of politics was conducted here, and there was a large staff of scribes, lawyers and librarians. In support of them were servants, cooks, and bottle washers. The proceeded along wide corridors where men and women of all nations and races negotiated their private business, flowing around and past the guards as uncaring as river water to a fish. A few minutes later they passed a pair of guards walking the other way, neither pair acknowledging the other. Those two would return to the rear of the Palace and go off shift. Now it was the responsibility of Calill and Barakee to provide the silent, watchful security for the administrators.

This section of the Palace had only two levels and a few minarets which were mostly for show. The lowest floor was broadly made up of large, airy chambers full of functionaries set at desks producing all kinds of records, manuscripts, agreements, contracts and lists, usually in multiple copies. Along the connecting corridors were a number of storage rooms, where the documents produced in triplicate or more, would have be placed for future reference or insurance. Each of these rooms was locked and their keys were kept in the watch commander's office. Only two people were given the rights to sign out the keys, the clerk who was allocated to that room and the Master of Clerks. The Paternal Guard walked along this warren of offices and industry with impunity. They were seldom looked at and the civil servants they encountered never bothered with greetings or small talk. It wasn't as if they knew who it was they spoke to. Each Paternal Guard was chosen with a view to the size and shape, they needed to be broadly similar in stature; it helped enhance their image of anonymity.

Their passage along the upper floor was somewhat different. All the guards, although Calill knew that not all would admit it, experienced a certain level of tension when they ascended one of the stairs. This floor was reserved for the Ministry of Relations. The place looked similar to the floor below in design and decoration, yet the rooms here were used for private offices and...other things. It was, as the name suggested, the place where Karnak Karrnassus conducted its foreign affairs. And indeed there was a foreign secretary in place. But that secretary was not the one who ruled this place, they were there purely to state the position of Karnak Karnassus in any discussions. It was the Minister of Relations who was the power and the relations he presided over was nothing like what a newcomer might believe. The Ministry's true role was to manage the darker side of politics, the shadow wars, the deeds and designs of those who wished to gain advantage outside of the normal political channels. It was a place where a thousand agents were controlled and coordinated, where secrets were gathered, analyzed and manipulated. Just as Karnak had become the hub of the political world for many nations, so it made sense that here was where deals were made and information fought over. Every embassy and consulate had their agents and negotiators out on the ground and they all needed to be watched. Gaining that information was critical for the Paternal's negotiations and the Ministry ensured that that it was gathered by any means necessary. What made the guards so uneasy were the lengths that were gone to go gather it. The nights were the worst. You could hear the screams coming from behind doors that looked innocuous and no different from any other in the administration wing. You could never tell whether the poor unfortunate was being tortured or whether one of the Ministry's mages was inside their mind. They called it Ripping. The process of extracting knowledge was such a terrible affair, it left those who had been Ripped diminished. He had seen a few led out of rooms by Ministry men. Their eyes were lifeless, there was no spark of awareness. Calill felt his heart race a little when a door ahead of them opened and out stepped the Minister and his clerk.

The Minister stood waiting patiently as his clerk fussed with the door. The Minister wore loose fitting cream linen trousers, a purple silk shirt and a red sash tied about his waist. His robes of office, a fine cloak of ermine sat upon his shoulders. Of average height and unimpressive build, his head was shaved, although one could trace the shadow of his hairline. He sported a light moustache and his skin about his face bore marks of aging. All in all he was a man that did not stand out in any way, except for his eyes. A rich emerald green that had a way of boring into your soul and making you speak of things you had no business saying and damning yourself in the process. Despite his stature, his reputation made him seem like a giant.

He had seen the man a thousand times before and he knew what to do. *Step sure, step quietly. Look to your front. You are nothing. You are the silent guardian. You are not human.* Even as he passed, Calill caught the briefest of sights of the room within: white walled, white tiled and in the centre was a chair. Strapped to that chair was a man. His mouth was open in a silent scream. Another man, a Ministry mage, was bent over him. The mage's hands were placed on the head of the captive and his fingers, his fingers were inside the man's head. And yet there was no blood. Ripping. It was the most civilized of tortures.

Minister Swarbreck stepped from the room and waited for his clerk to close the door behind them. He watched the two guards walk by then turned to the clerk.

'What do you think, Orlaise? I am not sure I trust the manner by which we came to this. It seems contrived.'

Orlaise took a moment to lock the door and place the key in his pocket. The clerk was a short, stocky man in his fifties. He had a shock of thick, grey hair that was pulled tight against his scalp and tied into short ponytail. His brown eyes flashed with caution as he watched the guards move further down the corridor, ever mindful of loose talk. He wore a simple white shift tied with a brown leather belt and soft camel hide sandals upon his feet that ended in a sharp pointed upwards curve, which was the fashion of Karnak. Swarbreck, being of Heiron descent, chose to dress a little more adventurously, it also reminded him where he came from and why it was better to stay here than there.

Swarbreck was content to let Orlaise chew over his response. He always enjoyed the clerk's painful attempts at phrasing his responses diplomatically. He was always so... *precise*, it was a matter of pride with the man. Everything had to be tidy, everything ordered. An appropriate mannerism considering the particular work the clerk was asked to undertake. Though it made him rather less than human in Swarbreck's eyes.

'The source has always been reliable,' started Orlaise.

'But you have your doubts too,' stated Swarbreck.

Orlaise bit his lip before nodding.

Swarbreck shook his head. 'Come along, Orlaise. Speak frankly. We are alone.'

'I think it is a lie. The fellow has been compromised.'

Swarbreck frowned. He had his suspicions and they were seldom ever wrong but it was simply good policy to review what he believed. *Nothing assumed. Nothing to chance.*

'Go on,' he urged.

'It was in the wording, just little things. He used the word *"must"*. That is an entreaty. Our contact has never demanded or expected anything before. He has always stated facts, never emotions. I think that message was written with someone else in mind. They want us to jump left.'

'Then we need to jump right,' stated Swarbreck.

'I would consider it,' agreed Orlaise.

Swarbreck nodded and then started moving along the corridor, going the same way as the guards, walking steadily, matching their pace. Yes, they could just finish this game quickly. Call the bluff and shut the whole operation down. Yet there was an opportunity here. And he did so enjoy exploring just how far he could go.

'I wonder. Is there value in playing this out a little further? We know who the likely perpetrators are, but I want to know who they are working for.'

Orlaise shrugged. 'It may be one our neighbours that is behind it? If so it will be hard to bring them in.'

'I know. But I think this is an occasion where a message needs to be sent. Once we have evidence the deal has taken place, we take the front men and their handlers, make an example of them and make it clear that the players in question now owe us for not going public.' Swarbreck always made it a point to garner leverage. Especially with those powers who he could not see easily brought to heel.

'And our informant?' asked Orlaise.

'As you say, he is compromised. You know how I feel about trust. He's a broken asset now. When we close down their operation, I want him disappeared.'

'Ripped too?'

'No, we save that for those that turned him. We can learn

more from them. We can be magnanimous in our actions. Call it a small token of gratitude for services past rendered.'

'I'm sure our asset will be grateful,' replied Orlaise.

'Is that sarcasm I detect?'

'Minister!' said Orlaise, clearly affronted at the notion.

Swarbreck raised a hand in apology. 'I leave the details to you, Orlaise, just make sure there is nothing left once you are done.'

'There never is.'

'Very good.'

They reached a corner. To their left a door sat in the wall while the corridor turned sharp right and continued on.

'I will be in my office if you need me,' Swarbreck said.

'Very good, Minister.' Orlaise bowed deeply and continued on.

Swarbreck reached into his robe and withdrew a small iron key. He placed it into the lock, turned it right until it clicked and then softly uttered three words. This released the seal that his mages had placed upon the door. He pushed against the red lacquered wood and the door swung inward without a trace of resistance. Stepping into the office he closed the door and took a moment to survey the scene. It was a sparsely furnished room, with just his desk, a solid looking block of wood, carved from mahogany that had come from the jungles far to the south. A few chairs made of the same and a small table sat to one side which held several glasses, a decanter of water and another of wine, both of which he personally collected from the kitchens each morning. The walls were washed with lime but held no decoration. His room was in the corner of the wing, affording him more space and daylight. The far wall was almost all glass from the mid-point to the ceiling. From there he could look out onto the busy street fronting the palace, watching the world go by. Some would consider that a risk, but considering whom he was and where he was, it hardly seemed as such to him. He was in the most protected building in Karnak Karnassus, there were magical wards aplenty set upon this room and indeed his very position as Minister would make most shirk at the very thought of making an attempt on his life. Woe betide anyone that tried and especially if they failed. Besides, he spent so much time in the Palace, he needed to see the daylight, indeed, to see the city. It was easy to forget what his job was and why he needed to do it. This was his city and it forever stood upon a precipice, always fighting to stay upright. The citizens thought that their city was impregnable, that war would never come to them again. That was not true. War was with them all the time, Swarbreck and his people fought it daily, maintaining the balance, never giving an inch, never showing a sign of weakness. The Paternal may be the symbol of Karnak's preeminence in the world, but he was just the keystone in the arch. Beside him, men like Swarbreck strived to hold him in place, lending their strength and support to hold the entire edifice up.

Any number of states and powers would like to see Karnak fall, would love to get their hands on the information that he and his forebears had garnered and sworn to protect. It was a solemn duty, and one that he had chosen to fulfil for as long as he could. He was the son of a Heiron merchant who had made Karnak his home and the city had given him everything. The Families knew the value of driven men, no matter what their provenance. A man could rise to great power and even become a Minister if he was loyal and able enough. He lived and breathed his job and in his seven years he had never once been found wanting. He did what he had to, when he had to, and no one questioned his methods. *I do this for us, for Karnak Karnassus. For the peace and prosperity it brings.* It was a prayer of devotion he said daily. A reminder, a way of keeping him focused on what mattered. He would do what he must.

He walked across to his desk, past the two cushioned chairs sat in front of it and moved behind it to settle down into his own, high backed, leather bound seat. On the left side of the desk was a small bottle of ink and two quills, on the right was a three-pronged candlestick. Before him was a leather-bound satchel. He pulled it towards him and undid the cord that held it shut. He reached inside and pulled out a thick sheaf of papers. These were the collated reports, facts, missives and analysis from the various departments within the Ministry. He had people working on the embassies, the trading blocks, the visiting deputations, the merchants and the crooks. What he had to do, what he was good at, was looking for the links, the subtle connections between and within each group, trying to decipher and discover who was reaching out to who and for what reason. He played this game well. He had to because those outside these walls were also adept. He couldn't hope to control or contain every machination, only the ones that could threaten the city or the brokered alliances it had forged or assisted in supporting.

He took his time, reading each page then reading it again, within his mind he cross-checked with facts he had already marked, then committed to memory any new details, filing it away in discrete corners of his brain. This was perhaps his greatest skill, his ability to mark and remember information at will. Once he was satisfied with each page, he took a quill, dipped it into the ink and scrawled a short message directing what should be done with it: where it should be filed, who else needed to know, what action must now be taken and who must do it. The storerooms of the palace were full of such pieces of paper, compartmentalized and kept for future reference or use. He moved to another page, this one regarding the investigation into the death of an Ashkent officer. That had been an unusual incident. The man in question, Major Jenkins, was a military attaché to the ambassador, and there had been nothing in his previous history to suggest any clandestine work. He had been in post for a year and had gone about his business with nothing untoward. Yet three months ago he had been flagged, his behavior had become unusual and out of character. He was seen by agents spending more time in and around the environs of the palace. They had checked for appointments and found none. When followed he was seen going down to Karnak harbour. He read that Orlaise had personally sanctioned the arrest and detainment of this individual. A day later he was found dead, floating in the harbour, bereft of all valuables and his face and body marked from a beating. Before his body was returned, an inspection by the Ministry physicians had made it plain the major had died of poisoning.

It was clear to Swarbreck that his death was made to look like a simple robbery gone wrong. That in itself was hardly news, this was Karnak Karnassus. Yet it was also clear to him that Major Jenkins had taken the poison himself as soon as the Ministry had made a move on him. It was a clumsy attempt at hiding his tracks, especially when matched against the Ministry. It was untidy as far as he was concerned. Swarbreck didn't like loose ends. The good major had ensured he had taken his secrets to the grave with him. The Ashkent embassy had taken receipt of the body and naturally claimed they knew of no reason for why their man was murdered. As was the usual protocol, Swarbreck had his people keeping a close watch on the affairs of the Ashkent diplomats and staff but as yet there had been no correlating evidence. If they were wise, they would have shut down whatever operation they were engaged in. If they were wise... it was a loose end he needed to ensure it was tied up one way or another.

He continued his work, moving from page to page until each one had been logged, marked and placed on the completed pile. At some point during his work, day had moved to night and his room was in shadow. He put a thumb and forefinger upon his eyelids and squeezed them tightly, finally feeling the strain of trying to read in the dark. He stood up and leaned over the candlestick, each prong holding a short red candle, their wicks a clean, unburnt white. There was a small box of lighting fuses next to the candlestick, he took one, struck it and allowed the flame to build before lighting each candle in turn. As the candlelight grew, his room brightened and he watched the shadows flicker and dance across the walls. It was a semblance of life, and he enjoyed watching them play. He turned his back on them and looked out of the window onto the street below and the city beyond. From his vantage, looking west, he could see the rooftops of grand houses, temples and municipal buildings, all bathed in the glow from a thousand fires. It was a beautiful sight. On the street, the people moved about their business. The Paternal's Palace had many braziers set before it and illuminated the way for passers-by. It also chased away any helpful shadows for the more optimistically minded interloper. Out there right now, there should be at least two of his people watching who was coming and going. Their observations would be checked and tallied with the clerk posted inside the entrance to the palace.

He placed his hands behind his back and hummed. *I do this for Karnak Karnassus.*

Chapter 6

Another crate was pushed up out of the hold and into the waiting arms of Forge and Wenham. Together they walked it across the deck and negotiated their way down the gangplank and onto the wharf of the small coastal town of Misbah, located in the middle of the Jaeget Empire. Nazar watched them with arms folded and a stern expression. A man wearing a thickly woven purple robe made a mark in a ledger and nodded. With that he handed over a pouch to Nazar who, instead of opening it, weighed it in his hands, gave his own small nod and walked back up the gangplank.

'That's our business done,' he announced. 'Now let's be moving on. Medhji, the tide is with us. I want the *Crimson Shore* on its way.'

'Yes, Captain!' responded Medjhi, running down the gangplank past Forge. 'You best get back on board, the Captain doesn't like to tarry in this place,' he said.

'No shit,' replied Forge, perplexed. This was unusual. Normally they always spent an evening in harbour if they could. He looked at Wenham.

'Why the hurry?'

Wenham wrinkled his nose and spat into the water.

'Captain doesn't like it here. So we go.'

'Right.' Together they made their way back on board. Forge let Wenham go first and watched the man start stowing kit. He had gotten enough out of him to know Wenham had been a soldier for a time - you could always tell. And Wenham had him pinned in turn. There was no need to go into specifics, considering Forge had been picked up in Ashkent, it was obvious to which army he had belonged. As for Wenham, Forge was pretty certain he came from Shifter. It was the inflection in some of his words and the odd comment. There was no need to push it. Wenham wasn't one of the forgive-and-forget types of professional soldier who wanted to swing the lantern and trade stories of the life. Especially considering it was Forge and his men who had kicked Shifter's arse in the last war. He was trying to escape his past and Forge had no reason to dredge it up. He could well understand Wenham's point of view. He'd been trying to do the same.

An hour or so later they were ready to leave.

'Captain, ropes off,' Medhji called.

'Very well. Let's be on our way,' Nazar called back.

Forge stood by and watched Hassan and Medjhi scuttle up the gangplank and pull it back on board as the *Crimson Shore* slowly moved away from its berth. Nazar let the retreating tide take hold of the ship while the crew readied the sails. After a few minutes the sails had a little wind in them which took them out of the small harbour, past the mole and into the Jedah Sea proper. Once there, they gathered speed and moved beyond Misbah and Forge walked over to join Nazar. They stood for a moment in companionable silence. Up above the sky was darkening, the moon was full and the sky was clear, countless stars twinkled brightly. There would be plenty of light to see by tonight.

'Never seen you in such a rush,' he said.

Nazar ran his hand along the tiller and smiled.

'You may not believe me but there will come a time I no longer wish to pursue this life. One has to make deals and decisions that do not always sit well with one's conscience. Yes, I see your face is making an expression of doubt. But I have always tried to be fair and moral in my business affairs.'

'Tried?' responded Forge.

'Yes. As much as I can. But it is sometimes necessary to sail close to the edge. That man has bought a shipment of weapons. He is neither a merchant, nor a noble, nor a member of the government. He is a crook.'

'Then why sell to him?'

'There is only ever one reason. Money. He pays well.'

'Fair enough. If he is a crook, nine times out of ten he'll probably use the weapons on other crooks,' Forge surmised.

Nazar nodded. 'That is what I tell myself. And in so doing I sleep at night knowing that I am one more step towards a time that I may live comfortably in my dotage.'

Chance would be a fine thing. 'Believe me, I'm still trying to enjoy my retirement,' he muttered.

Nazar's eyebrow rose. 'I had you for a man who was fully engaged in whatever your chosen work is. A soldier, yes? Or at least a man that fights for a living. Your trip to Karnark is surely not part of your retirement?'

Forge realised he was probably giving away too much. There was still a need for secrecy. 'Let's just say that my continued retirement depends on the outcome of this little jaunt.'

Nazar grunted. 'Hah. Very good.'

Forge scratched his beard and studied Nazar. 'Why are you

called Nazar the Lucky?' You didn't get a name like that without a story behind it and Forge always liked to hear them; it told you a lot about the type of person you were dealing with.

Nazar whistled. 'Now there is a sad tale or a happy one, depending on your disposition. One moment,' he paused and squinted. 'Medhji, I am thinking we should continue on tonight. The wind is blowing fair and we can gain some time back.'

'As you say, Captain. You want me to take the tiller?'

Nazar shook his head.

'Not now. I am content for the next few hours,' he looked back at Forge. 'Now then, why am I called "Lucky"? It is a simple tale. When I was younger I had proven to be most adept at the business of business. I sailed the Jedah Sea first as a young lad, not unlike Hassan, learning how to sail, to read the water and the winds. I also found that I had some talent in understanding the notion of trade, of barter and how to make a profit.' Nazar stood up and slapped his chest proudly. 'I was the youngest captain to come out of Karnark in living memory. It was not surprising that my ambition grew. I started up my own merchant company and acquired stakes in other ships and started to build a reputation. But for some reason, and I have examined this question many times since, it all started to go wrong. I lost one ship to storms, another to piracy. I had purchased my goods with my own capital, and without them I had no means of recovering costs. I borrowed heavily from lenders, men I should have known not to trust. They crippled me with repayments. My remaining concerns were not bringing in enough profit; I blame the worry, it blinded my business instincts. When the dust settled, well,' he smiled, his face shadowed in the twilight. 'I had to give up my remaining ships. I was left with nothing. Except my life. And I was lucky to keep that. It took me another ten years of grafting for others before I had enough to put a downpayment on the *Crimson Shore*. It took another ten years before I had paid off what I owed. Now I am master of my own destiny once again. I think that that is why I am called lucky. There are not many who get a second chance.'

'Sounds to me like you earned it,' replied Forge. 'You worked your balls off to get back to where you were.'

'The best kind of luck is the kind you make yourself, my friend,' said Nazar.

'I'll take any kind I can get on this journey,' said Forge.

Nazar inclined his head. 'As you say.'

Don't want to know any more, do you? Forge looked along the coastline to the south. There were lights not far away, some burned solitary and alone, others were grouped together, creating a bright, inviting glow. There were countless hamlets, villages and towns along their route. Mostly Nazar ignored them, saving his stops for the larger settlements. The lands were changing too, they were not as green for starters. The trees were different, not as strong or as thick, their branches more skeletal. The soil looked less healthy, rockier, the colour was leached from the surroundings. It wasn't a place that he felt comfortable with. He understood that the temperatures during the summer months were so high, a man could die of thirst in just a day or two. It was only along the river valleys that cultivation and life still had a firm grip. They had already passed several, and the waters had been full of fishermen and trading barges. It was all new to him. Forge had never been this far east; his campaigning had been to the west of Ashkent or along the northern nations across the sea.

'Nazar, you come from Karnak, right?'

'I do indeed.'

'Will you tell me of the place? '

'I could. What would you like to know?'

'Everything. I need to know the people, the politics, the streets themselves. A friend of mine once said that a city is like a living, breathing animal. It was alive. I need to understand it.'

Nazar whilstled. 'I think what you mean to say is that you wish to know how to survive it. Yes?'

Forge smiled. Nazar was a smart one.

'You got it.'

'Well, then. Where should I start? What do you already know? Shall I treat you like the newcomer you are? Assume nothing?'

'Works for me.'

'Karnak Karnassus. The jewel of the Jedah! They say it has stood for a thousand years and I have no reason to doubt it. It was a free city before such a thing existed, before any of the other city states declared their independence. It sits upon a great promontory of rock, a great plateau that rises above the water. On two sides it is bounded by water, one wide channel the other little more than a chasm. Its inner walls describe a great arc across the landward side. But do not let that fool you. The city is far greater than that. Once the Paternal was established and Karnark did not have to worry so much about armies trying to take it over, the city started to spread. There is nothing like the allure of peace and prosperity. The old city is on the plateau, but the new city, the great city, that has grown far beyond the plateau and outwards into the hinterlands.' Nazar spread an arm wide. 'Suburbs, industry, agriculture. And slums. Plenty of slums. The last census said there were three hundred thousand souls crammed into the city. And that does not include those just passing through. Can you imagine such a thing?'

'I'd rather not. I've never liked big cities. Too damned tight, no room to breathe,' admitted Forge. He had enough trouble with Littlebury. When he was younger he could tolerate it, now though, he didn't see why he should have to.

'Hah, then you'll have no love for Karnark. Trust me though, you grow used to it.'

Forge doubted that. Nazar was still talking, clearly warming to his subject. 'Now where was I? Yes. The southern side is the larger channel. It is where the shipping goes and where the great harbour is based. I did not describe Karnak clearly perhaps, because the great plateau does slope down to meet the sea on this side. The northern channel is thinner, more like a large canal, cutting its way through the rock. It's a sheer drop down to the water. You could navigate through it and join the river beyond Karnak, but the way is blocked by a gate; the authorities do not want any possible access routes around the city unguarded. That way they can also control the flow of traffic and goods.' Nazar reached down, picked up a small waterskin and took a swig before passing to Forge. Nodding his thanks he put it to his lips. *Wine?* He raised an eyebrow. Nazar grinned. 'They say one should never sail drunk. I disagree, never sail sober.' Forge shrugged. *Fair enough.* He took another large swallow and handed it back to Nazar, who took another swig before placing back on the deck.

'Karnak Karnnassus is so named because it was once two villages. Karnak was centred on the harbour, inhabited by none but fisherfolk. At the top of the plateau was Karnassus. At first it was a keep, home to a minor noble, with a few hovels clustered around it. Then the noble built a temple. Then a few more. And more people came to visit them and more began to stay. Karnassus grew and Karnak found itself supplying a whole horde of priests, functionaries and servants. Karnak had to expand to accommodate the merchants and supply ships that were coming from all around. I am glad to say that the profit motive finally won over the religion and the powers that be realised that Karnak Karnassus was ideally placed to make a lot of money. And so it has. They say it is the wealthiest city in all the known world.'

Forge picked up on a certain tone in Nazar's voice. 'You don't sound so sure.'

'What? Oh, no, I am sure,' he said, shaking his head. 'I believe it is. But also believe me when I say that wealth is not shared out so well amongst the populace. The ruling families keep the money close to their chests and live on the plateau. But whole areas of the wider city are little more than slums. The sorts of places where you can get into a lot of trouble if your face doesn't fit and you are walking down the wrong street at night. Come to think of it, I know a few streets you wouldn't want to be walking down during the day.'

It sounded to Forge just like any other city he'd been to or heard of. Each one had its wealthy quarters, its merchant districts, industrial areas and slums.

'What about the Paternal? How does the politics of the place work?' he asked. In truth he had a decent understanding of what the Paternal was for but not necessarily the mechanics. And that was what he really needed to know.

Nazar sighed theatrically and raised a finger into the air. 'And there lies the reason why Karnak Karnassus has become the legend it is. The city provides a unique service, the Paternal, the ultimate arbitrator. In matter of great delicacy, parties can come together and air their grievances in front of the Paternal. He does not judge, he only weighs factors and offers solutions. Anything and everything can be aired in his presence and he guarantees absolutes trust and secrecy. The Chamber, you have heard of it? The Chamber is shielded by powerful magics, the best money can buy, and the Paternal is incorruptible.'

'So I hear. What is he, a saint?' asked Forge. 'The way it sounds to me, the Paternal has all the cards. You telling me he never lets on? Never screws over one side if it helps him or Karnak?'

'I cannot say whether the present or any of the past Paternals were good men or bad. It doesn't matter. The Paternal is chosen from the population of the city. He is ensconced in the Paternal's Palace, treated like an Emperor, and no earthy pleasure is denied them. Yet, the Paternal is a prisoner, a slave to the system that has created him. He can never leave his palace, never walk the streets and he can never, ever, talk to anyone about what he knows, what he has heard, what he has seen. After five years, they are killed. Just think, the amount of knowledge in their heads? They could topple kingdoms if they wished. The ruling council knows better than to let anyone have so much power. To be chosen as the Paternal is to have a death sentence placed upon you.'

'Sounds like a shit job. Why not just refuse?'

'Then you die and your family dies with you. Not just your immediate family. Every single member of your extended family: brothers, sisters, aunts, uncles, cousins even. The council have refined this system over many years; they know how to make it work. They don't just pick anyone, it's not a lottery. They choose carefully. They pick a man they can control. Inevitably they pick a man with a family. It gives them the leverage they need. A man chosen to be the Paternal has a lot to lose, and remember, we have had a Paternal for a century. Generations have grown up believing and buying into the myth that to be the Paternal is the greatest gift a citizen of Karnak Karnassus can be given. There are great houses, inside the council and out, who volunteer their sons. It's all politics and power. When a Paternal's time is done, he is accorded every honour and his family is moved out of the Palace and given enough riches to keep his children's children's children in luxury for all of theirs days. Just think, if you were offered such a deal, would you at least not consider it?'

Forge thought for a moment. If he'd have a family, would he have said no? He'd like to think he'd tell them to shove it up their arses and go down swinging. But then, what if he'd had a chance to save the lives of his men, just by giving himself up? What would he do?

'I have pondered that same question many times,' said Nazar. 'As luck would have it, I was never blessed with a family. The Sea has always been my mistress, fickle bitch that she is. But at least I am free.'

'Freedom? There's always some bastard thinks they own you,' said Forge.

'Hah! Yes, you are right! But they have to catch us first, yes?'

In Forge's case it had been too difficult. He'd let himself be caught. Still, there was a son of a bitch somewhere out there who had killed his friend. And even if he was not his own master, even if it was not part of his mission, he was going to find that son of a bitch and tear him apart.

*

'Captain?'
'Yes, Medhji?'

57

'There's a red sail to the north of us.'

'Oh.'

Forge looked up from where he sat with his back to the mast. There was a certain tone to Nazar's voice. He watched him gesture for Rabi to take the tiller. The crewman, his face sombre, quietly took it and Nazar walked to the port side of the ship. The other members of the crew drifted across to join him. Forge's interest was piqued. He pushed himself off the deck and walked over to stand by Medhji who pointed his finger northwards. 'There. I'd say about a mile away.'

Forge squinted. He saw the red sail. It was off to port. Judging by the wind direction he reckoned it must be angling towards them. He looked at the faces of the crew. Most of them looked worried: Wenham was tightlipped, Medhji looked confused and Nazar was thoughtful. *Trouble, then.*

'This is what happens when you leave it too late to start the journey around the Jedah,' remarked Medhji.

'Red sail,' said Forge. 'Could be Heiron?'

'No, it ain't them,' muttered Bors.

'Pirates,' spat Medhji.

'How can you be so sure?' asked Forge looking at Nazar. The captain was chewing his lips.

'Merchants speak to each other. There was talk of a red-sailed ship preying on the smaller ships last season,' said Nazar, after a few moments of silence.

'These waters are not patrolled,' added Medhji. 'That's why you want to be part of the main wave following the trade winds,' he added, pointedly.

'Saftey in numbers,' said Forge.

'Less chance of being noticed,' agreed Medhji.

'What do we do, Captain?' called Rabi from the tiller.

Nazar made fists and bounced them on the railing top. 'The

wind is coming from the northwest. They are running with full sail and have the speed. We cannot outrun them unless we make for land.'

'Then what?' asked Forge.

'We try and ground the ship,' replied Nazar.

'And how does that help us?' asked Medjhi.

'It keeps us alive,' he replied, his voice sombre.

'We get on the land. They'll just weigh anchor and wait for us,' said Bors.

'Probably. But maybe they'll get bored and move on,' said Medjhi.

'Or maybe they'll come after us on the ground,' said Wenham.

'Captain? What do you want to do?' asked Medjhi.

Nazar met Forge's gaze.

'These pirates do not like to leave survivors. I will not risk the lives of my crew.'

'And if we can get to land, they'll strip the *'Shore* and leave us with nothing,' said Medjhi.

Forge was still looking at Nazar. He knew what the unasked question was. *Fine.* He nodded. 'If we don't land the ship, then we are going to have to fight,' he said.

Nazar nodded. 'My crew are good lads. Every one of them. But apart from Wenham, we aren't fighters. Bar brawls don't count.'

'Depends,' muttered Benji. 'You get the first punch in, most folk lose their appetite.'

'He's got a point,' said Forge. 'Don't suppose you know how many there are?'

'Not sure,' said Medjhi. 'They have been picking off dhows and smaller traders. Ones that have a crew about our size.'

'Ones that can't put up much of a fight,' added Bors.

'Then they won't be expecting one,' said Forge. He looked at Nazar. 'What weapons you got on board?'

'We have hooks, cudgels, an axe or two and our fists,' replied Nazar. He smiled. 'And we have you.'

'Then let's get ready,' replied Forge.

*

The pirate craft was now only a hundred yards off the port bow, still angling in towards the *Crimson Shore*. The dhow was keeping to its course, heading east. Nazar was back at the tiller and the rest of the crew were carrying on with their duties. Forge stood inside Nazar's cabin, he had donned his leather jacket and wore his weapons. His knife was in his left hand, the hand axe in his right. His sword was still strapped to his back. He took a deep breath and rolled his shoulders. It had been a while but he could feel the tension building up inside of him, the inevitable nerves that came before a fight. It was normal and it was only human to feel them. What surprised him was the undercurrent of excitement. Had he missed this? Perhaps his life has gone too far the other way, that he had missed a sense of purpose. *Is killing all I'm good for?*

'Ahoy the ship!' came a shout from the deck of the red-sailed ship.

'What do you want?' shouted Nazar.

'We want what you got. Don't try and run.'

'We have nothing of value!' replied Nazar.

'We'll be the judge of that.' The voice sounded a little closer now. 'Run down your sails or we'll ram your sorry arse.'

Nazar was silent for a moment, playing the part of a worried sea captain, considering his options. 'Very well. Medhji, do it,' he ordered.

Forge listened to the activity outside. 'They are thirty yards away,' said Nazar, quietly. 'I count ten men. They are all armed. Two have bows. Three are carrying hooks.'

Forge nodded but said nothing. He and Nazar had considered a show of strength - that by having Forge stand front and centre the pirates might consider an easier prey elsewhere. But Forge had suspected that any bowmen would have put paid to his display pretty rapidly. He reached out and pulled the door towards him letting it open fully. Light spread into the cabin and he moved further back into the shadows.

He could hear laughing and joking from the pirate crew – their spirits were up and they were feeling confident. The Crimson Shore shuddered and creaked as the other ship made contact, sliding against the hull with a thud.

'Take what you want but leave us be,' said Nazar.

'Maybe,' said the pirate that had been doing all the talking. 'Now step back.'

Forge watched the crew move to the starboard side of the ship.

Another, quieter thud signalled the landing of a pair boots onto the deck not far from the tiller. Forge strode out of the cabin and towards those boots. The pirate who owned them was pointing a sword at Nazar. He was bald and was missing his ear on the right side. He was also unarmoured. The man barely had time to register his arrival before Forge thrust his knife deep into the exposed armpit of the pirate. He continued on as Nazar rushed forward, pulling his own blade from underneath his shirt. The next pirate in line was already turning to face Forge when he raised his axe and swung it in an arc, burying it into the pirate's collarbone. Shouts erupted around him as the crew of the *Crimson Shore* took their cue, retrieving their weapons from under sailcloth, boxes and clothing.

Forge quickly assessed the situation. Two more pirates were on the deck. The crew would have to deal with them. Looking across to the other ship, he saw faces stunned into inaction. That was the key – put them off balance and take advantage of it. The two bowmen were amidships and had yet to react to the change in circumstances.

'Take 'em down!' cried the familiar voice of the pirate ship. Forge had hoped he had already killed the leader. Either way, he had to deal with the bows. He placed an arm on the railing and leapt over and across to the other ship. He gained his feet, reach up and pulled his sword from the behind his shoulder. Ahead of him the two bowmen loosed, aiming at the *Crimson Shore*. A pirate carrying a sharp scimitar and wearing leather vambraces stood in the way. The pirate raised his blade high and Forge moved in close, striking him in the mouth with the pommel of his sword. He pushed the pirate to one side and made for the bowmen. The one nearest lost his arm to a two-handed downward cut. The second turned to face Forge who leaned forward and extended his arms, thrusting his blade point into the bowman's belly.

Forge turned and parried a horizontal cut from the scimitar-wielding pirate. His mouth was a bloody mess and it looked like he had even fewer teeth than when he started. The pirate followed up quickly with another attempted overhead strike. As he blocked the cut, Forge saw another man running up to join the first. The scimitar came down again, attempting to beat him into submission. The metal rang as the two blades met and Forge kicked out hard. The scimitar wielder squealed, dropped his blade and staggered backwards. Forge faced off against the second pirate. This one was the leader. His skin was swarthy and weather-beaten, his neck covered in a web-like tattoo. His fingers were covered in rings of all kinds in an ostentatious display of wealth. His hair was tied back into a long ponytail and it swung behind his back as, two-handed, he made to swing his tulwar in a diagonal downward cut. Forge stepped back and the weapon's arc sliced through air. Forge had to stay focused. The surprise attack was over and now he had to rely on his dueling skills. They were out of practice. The stepped back again and bumped up against one of the archers. He felt a hand grip his leg and he lost his balance, tumbling back. He hit the deck hard as the pirate captain followed up his tulwar raised above his head. The one-armed bowman, his face a picture of agony, was scrabbling to hold him down. Forge tried to squirm free but it was too late. The pirate captain was ready to strike. Then a look of surprise passed over the man's face and he stumbled. His legs gave way and he fell to his knees as the tulwar dropped from his hands and he pitched forwards onto the deck. Nazar was stood behind him, bloodied knife in hand. Forge kicked out against the bowman. His bootheel connected with the bowman's face and he fell away. Forge pushed himself up and shuffled backwards. He looked around. The battle was over. Benji and Bors were setting about the scimitar pirate with clubs turning him into a bloody mess. Forge looked away. Wenham scurried past, carrying a hatchet and buried it into the head of the bowman.

Nazar offered a hand and hauled Forge up.

'That was exciting!' shouted Bors, with a feverish gleam in his eye. Forge snorted. He knew that look. Bors had that heady condition brought by battle, he'd probably be throwing up in a minute.

'We get them all?' asked Forge as he surveyed the scene. Nazar nodded. 'Any casualties?'

'Just Medjhi. Took an arrow,' replied Nazar. Forge spotted Medjhi, clutching his right arm, the shaft was embedded just above the bicep. He was white-faced but standing. 'We were fortunate. You cut those men down so fast they didn't know what was happening.'

'That was the plan,' said Forge. The remaining crew of the *Crimson Shore* were gathered by the railing, their faces flushed with success.

'My lads made short work of the remaining two boarders and we followed you over. Quite a vault over the railing. I didn't think you had it in you.'

Forge hadn't been sure himself. The fight, such as it was, had taken moments, but he'd had no awareness of time or that he'd had support so close. The years of drill and combat conditioning had just kicked in. His instincts were still sound, it had just been a while since he had used them. He looked at the knife that Nazar still held. 'You did alright too.'

'I am not a fighter but I know the dangers the seas hold. I will defend what is mine when I have to. The crew know that as well.' Nazar smiled and slapped him on the back. 'I think you just made up for making us wait for you back at Dunbar. I believe we may profit from this.' He tucked the dagger into his belt and clapped his hands. 'Let's pick this boat clean then we'll set it adrift. Wenham, go and help Medjhi pull that dart out of his arm. And make sure it is properly washed out.'

'Hey, Captain. Are we the pirates now?' called Rabi.

'Heavens no,' muttered Nazar and looked at Forge. 'It's far too dangerous a profession. Who knows who you might end up meeting.'

Chapter 7

'Well, sister? What did you see?'

'I saw the same as you, sister dear.'

'And what was that?'

'Well, you would know.'

'Yes, I suppose I would.'

'Exactly.'

'Good...'

'Care to share your thoughts?'

'Oh, yes, sister, I could do that.'

'Then, sister dear, I feel myself ageing with anticipation.'

'I must say, you are looking a little peaky. It is this dry climate. I myself have no such issue.'

'That's because you are a dry and barren hag held together by sorceries and incantations, and a thousand bargains with who knows what demonic forces.'

'That's true enough.'

'I myself stay looking this good through rigorous exercise and healthy eating.'

'My way is better. Less effort.'

'And that, my dear Taimsin, is why I get all the men.'

'Hardly, Tailsin. I get my fair share.'

Tailsin sniffed and inspected her sister critically. It was like looking in a mirror. If that mirror was one of those found in travelling fairs that deliberately distorted the picture. Her twin sister Taimsin had the same lustrous red hair, the same cute button nose and white skin speckled with freckles. But whereas Tailsin's body was lithe and flexible, Taimsin's carried some extra weight about her person that some might describe as curvaceous. 'You get your share, sister dear, by bewitching them and sucking them dry of their life energy. Haven't you ever thought of pacing yourself?'

'I think about it all the time, sister. But why on earth would I want to? I'm very much the wham-bam type of girl. Get in, get it done and get out fast. You are the one who has to pace yourself. Without my skills you are always slower.'

'At least I get to savour what I do...wait!' Tailsin raised a gloved hand. 'We are getting off the point here. We do have a pressing matter to discuss.'

Taimsin sighed. 'Very well, at least sit down, or you'll start pacing. I hate that. It gives me a crick in my neck watching you.'

'Very well.' Tailsin sat in the chair opposite her sister. 'While you have been taking your ease, I appeared to have picked up a shadow or two.'

'What kind?' asked Taimsin. Her face had lost its smile.

Tailsin rocked back and steepled her fingers under her chin. She smiled benignly at her sister. 'That's better. Always the professional.'

'It is our creed, is it not?'

'I think in our case it is more a guideline.'

'Speak for yourself. The watchers, sister,' prompted Taimsin.

'I am not certain. They look rough, but I don't think they are gangers. I would vouch they are government men.'

'What do you think tipped them off? Was it your leathers?'

'I shouldn't think so. I wore a cloak.'

Taimsin nodded her head. 'That will be it then. It is far too warm out there to be wearing a cloak, you should have dressed down. Or at least let me put a glamour on you.'

Tailsin scowled at her sister.

'No glamours, concealments or befuddlements unless absolutely necessary. You know how many mages they have looking out for any kind of sorcery? You said it yourself, there is an unusual number present in the city. No. The best place to hide is in plain sight. You should have learned that by now.'

'Didn't work for you did it?'

'Whatever, sister dear. Can we just go and sort this out?'

'Usual method?'

'That alleyway we spotted by the old warehouse should do perfectly.'

'Right.'

Tailsin sat back and took the mug of wine her sister had been nursing, placing her back against the wall and drinking deep. She stopped and raised an eyebrow at Taimsin.

'Still here?'

'Off I go, then,' grunted Taimsin. She stood and walked away from secluded booth at the back of the inn and walked past the innkeeper. Taimsin beamed at the man.

'Off out for a stroll. Don't wait up.'

The innkeeper nodded vaguely, his face confused.

Taimsin halted by the door and collected the green cloak hanging off a peg. She looked around once more, nodded in a satisfied way and ducked out.

Tailsin continued to drink deep of the wine. If she was forced to admit it, her sister was probably right, the cloak was too much. But the leathers weren't a problem; the amount of bravos, mercs and outlandish foreigners made for a heady mix of outfits, styles and attitudes. She waited a few moments more, threw some coins onto the table and followed her sister out. She nodded at the innkeeper. He wore the same vague expression. The 'necessary' glamour was holding very well, just as it should. Ask this man anything about his guests and all he could recall was a single woman, not two, staying in his place.

Tailsin stood by the door and adjusted her belt. It held just the one visible knife. That would be all she needed. Stepping out onto the street, she lifted her head up, letting the sounds of the harbour wash over her. She looked right, then left, and then turned in that direction, following the harbour wall south and east. By now, her shadows should be well ahead, following her sister, the woman wearing the green cloak in the hottest part of the day.

She strolled along, taking care to enjoy the sights, a slight smile on her face. Around her, stevadores, officials and sailors mingled together, going about their daily routines. She was just one more face in the crowd. After a minute or so, she spotted one of her shadows. A thin-looking man with long greasy hair wearing a ragged poncho over threadbare trousers, she called him Shabby. She increased her pace a little until the distance between them was only a few yards. The man was intent on his target. And why wouldn't he be? Ah, and there was the other one, another twenty yards ahead. She caught just a glimpse of him, dodging along, just in front of a small cart being dragged along by a miserable-looking mule and his rider. That one was a little larger, balding wearing only a frayed woollen waistcoat and breeches down to his knees. She called him Baldy.

She was content to follow on, letting the game play out. This far along the harbour, the nature of the business changed;

large weather-beaten warehouses replaced the mix of drinking dens, residences, brothels and shopfronts. This was where the larger cargos were brought and stored before shipment. The crowds had started to lessen significantly and she dropped back a little. They were reaching a left turning and both men headed in that direction following a smaller lane, no wider than a wagon, up a slight incline. At this point Tailsin stopped her tail and waited on the corner, watching their progress. They passed more structures some of which had only small spaces between them, most butting up against their neighbours. Fifty yards ahead on the right hand side of the lane, a warehouse with a faded hanging sign pronounced the Nazar Shipping Line. If it had been great once, it certainly wasn't anymore. The building was empty of everything but rats and their droppings. The windows were boarded and the doors sealed with chains and padlocks. Baldy crossed the street and turned down an alleyway between the warehouse and the one further on that also looked like it had seen better days. Shabby stopped and took a moment to look behind him. Tailsin ducked back behind the corner, waited three seconds, then peeked round. She saw Shabby following his comrade into the alley. In response she stepped smartly into the lane and jogged up it, reaching the warehouse, stopping at the alleyway and taking a further look.

Shabby was at the far end, where the alley finished at the back wall of another building. He was scratching his head and looking at something to his right. He moved out of sight, entering another space, a second alleyway. Tailsin followed on, drawing her knife into her left hand as she moved. At the end she looked right down the alleyway and saw nothing, just shadows fading to darkness as the walls loomed in. She took another step forward and the picture changed. Directly in front with his back to her was Shabby, a little bit ahead was Baldy. Baldy was turning around with a look of confusion on his face, which turned to alarm as he spotted Tailsin.

She reached out, grabbed the hair on the side of Shabby's head, and violently slammed it into the plaster and brick wall on the left: once, twice, three times. He crumpled to the ground.

She stepped lightly over Shabby as Baldy let out a gurgled yelp and charged at her. As he drew near she swiftly extended her arm out at shoulder height and the blade slid into Baldy's throat. He stood transfixed, his eyes wide. She pulled the blade back out then thrust it into his left eye. She withdrew the blade once more and Baldy fell. Tailsin turned and stalked back to Shabby. She knelt down and listened to his ragged breathing. She leaned in close and started to whisper in his ear.

'Has he got anything to say?' asked her sister.

Tailsin looked up and shrugged as Taimsin emerged from the shadows at the end of the alley. Tailsin lifted Shabby's bloody mess of a head and cut this throat. 'Said he was Ministry.'

'Hmm. Should we be worried, sister?' asked Taimsin.

'Should we?' replied Tailsin. She wiped her blade against Shabby's poncho.

'If you had just let me use my magic on him.'

'That would have been too much,' Tailsin replied.

'I suppose so, I am very artful at concealment, very hard to detect.'

'That's the idea. No reason to draw attention.'

Taimsin spread her arms and looked up at the walls. 'And no reason to poop on our own doorstep.'

'Quite right, sister dear. These fellows shouldn't be missed, and if they are, there's nothing to tie them to us.'

'We should probably ditch the cloak though.'

'Agreed. Here, give it to me. I'll get rid of it.'

Taimsin handed over the cloak and stepped lightly by Tailsin. She stopped and gave her a kiss on the cheek.

'I'll take the long way round. Twins walking together in the warehouse district will draw far too much attention.'

'Indeed.'

Tailsin watched Taimsin make her way along the alleyway and back onto the lane. She held out her hand palm up and a small bird landed on it. Taimsin tilted her head, leaned in close, nodded and called back, 'No one else was following these two. I do hope this man turns up soon. I am getting quite bored of waiting. I fear that only more needless mayhem will ensue to brighten our days.'

'Me too, sister dear, me too.'

Chapter 8

The *Crimson Shore* entered the waters off Karnak Karnassus
a little before midday. The sun was set high in a clear blue sky
and was starting to become more than a little uncomfortable.
The weather had been growing warmer for the last two weeks
as they had sailed east, and Forge was finally starting to feel his
burned and weather beaten face calm down a little. He'd been
in a bad mood the last few days on the water but it was finally
starting to lift now the end was in sight.

He stood at the bow of the ship, hands resting lightly on the
rigging, watching the city grow before him. He had to admit,
he was impressed. Medjhi had been the first to sight the
plateau, emerging from the haze. That had been an hour ago
and still they were nowhere near making the harbour, the
wind kept them mooching along at a steady five knots. At least
now he could make out the landmarks. The great plateau
towered over the water, the cliff face a stark, glowing white.
On the top, a multitude of buildings the same colour as the
cliff, beyond that were towers, both curved and straight. He
noted that from the part of the plateau he could see, there
were no walls, no battlements. Only balustrades and gardens
looked out over the water below, the site clearly a preserve of

the wealthy and powerful. Any defences against seaborne assault had long been removed from the cliff edge, not that it was a viable place to attack anyway. He wouldn't want to try and scale that thing. But a hundred years of peace had not completely dulled Karnak's need to defend itself. Built into the rock face were a number of large platforms and upon them, though he could not make them out clearly, were artillery pieces: ballistae, catapults, and firepot launchers. From those platforms, accessed by tunnels in the rock, they could command the entrance to the harbour.

His professional eye considered how he might lead an assault on such a place. First up would be to take out the platforms, so that meant sorcery, it was the cleanest, safest way. You could get into a shooting match with a suitably armed fleet but the potential to lose manpower was too much. *Yeah, just blast 'em. Get some Ashkent combat mages on the job.* Then it was into the harbour. And that would present another big bag of problems. He had no sight of them yet, but Nazar had already intimated that the defences were considerable and effective.

And what of an assault by land?

It had been tried before and all attempts had failed at great cost to both sides. Looking towards the coast to the south, he could see why. The spit of land that Karnak Karnassus sat on was now surrounded by a sprawling mess of humanity. They were still on the western side of the harbour mouth yet it was clear to Forge that this newer city was vast and apparently surrounded by another wall. Try fighting through that lot. A mass of low-roofed, poorly-maintained houses, their owners leaching off the wealth on the heights, taking what they could to survive. It was no life.

Forge shook his head. *Fuckin' city folk. You are welcome to it.* He smiled and he felt his brow crinkle painfully. *Damn, am I missing Littlebury?*

As the minutes passed and the *Crimson Shore* made its sedate passage into the wide river channel that ran along the southern edges of the plateau, they passed numerous fishing ships. Some were little more than rowboats, holding one man and a rod to larger, others were industrial trawlers, where bare-chested, burly looking men threw out large nets and then hauled them back on board. They were constantly calling out to each other, sharing stories, passing the time of day and occasionally trading insults. Moving beyond them, the view of the rest of the city finally opened up. From Forge's position, he could see the slope down from the plateau towards the dockside. It was a patchwork of streets and buildings, all sharing the same white and cream colouring. These houses marched north and east covering the slope and no doubt meeting the river chasm on the far side. He could also see the old city walls, though much of them were swallowed up by the sprawl of the new city, as it continued to spread outwards and beyond.

'Heads up, here comes the mighty navy of Karnak Karnassus,' called Nazar. He pointed at a ship emerging from the harbour. It was twice the size of the *Crimson Shore* with a wooden firing platform fitted to its prow and a larger two-storey platform to its rear. It had one sail, slightly larger than theirs and bearing the symbol of Karnak Karnassus, a black bull's head against a white background, surrounded by a garland of green laurels. It was running against the wind and was currently being powered by oars, twenty to each side.

'Everyone be friendly, there's no point giving them a reason to stop and inspect us,' advised Nazar. He adopted a wide, beaming smile and waved energetically at the oncoming ship.

'Come on, join in, you bastards,' he said through his gritted teeth.

'Bloody hell,' muttered Rabi. He started to wave as well. 'Hello, yes, lovely to see you.'

Forge didn't wave. As the naval ship swept by, he took note of the ballista mounted to the front and the rear of the craft. Both were armed with large projectiles that had grappling hooks on the end. He had seen this type before, called a Harpax, designed to be loosed against an enemy ship, the grapnel snaring the craft and then winching it back ready for the taken ship to be boarded. Speaking of which, someone over there had finally decided to wave back.

'There you go,' said Nazar smugly, 'it pays to be persistent.'

Forge walked along the deck to join him.

'Small ship,' he said.

'Oh, that's just one of the coastal craft, they look out for pirates, smugglers and the like. You wouldn't get them involved in any major tussles unless they had no choice. It's just for show, to make the innocent feel safe and the guilty try harder to look innocent.'

'Ever been boarded?'

'Oh, many, many times. I am known as being a reputable trader so I am left alone these days, mostly. It depends who the captain of the other ship is. Some of them can be vindictive.'

'How large is the actual navy, then?' asked Forge. He was looking at the approaching harbour wall. The mole extended out from the side of the cliff, just where it met the lower south-eastern slopes of the plateau and formed a crescent, cutting out into the main channel then curving back in. It was at least twelve foot in height, had battlements crowning the top and was punctuated by a squat towers, each with an emplacement on top. At the end of the mole, a larger blockhouse marked the entrance to the harbour. The gap was a hundred yards or so wide before a second mole started its sweep back towards the land, finishing the near encirclement of the seaward side of the harbour. There were not so many fighting positions on the further mole but they probably didn't need to be so concerned about a fleet coming along the river from the south. Definitely another job for the battle mages. Last thing he'd ever want to be doing was to be part of a troop ship trying to get into that harbour. He realised Nazar was still talking.

'They have have deliberately running the Navy down, there hasn't been much point in recent years. I believe they only have three of the larger galleys left. You'll spot them in the naval shipyards to the left as we enter. They are the first you encounter. Over a hundred years ago, the Jaeget Empire launched their surprise assault coming along the river and burned most of the fleet. No one had expected that, so the defences were never really up to the mark on that mole.' Forge raised an eyebrow. *So much for my tactical nouse.* Nazar went on speaking. 'That also coincided with the institution of the Paternal. After that the Government never saw much reason in maintaining a large fleet. The whole point was that they no longer wanted to *stop* nations coming to them anymore.'

'Right,' said Forge, stepping away and returning to the prow. They were in the harbour proper now, having gone beyond the moles, and the true scale of the operation became apparent. On the left Forge could see the naval shipyards, which were quite small, only a half dozen slipways, three of which held the larger galleys Nazar had been on about. You could see it had been bigger once, the shipyard next to it shared the same construction and the naval building was demarcated by an additional wall built outwards towards the water, effectively splitting it in half. On the other side, a collection of fine-looking ships were moored up on quays with companionways leading back to shore. They all appeared to be of differing styles and designs. Only one was out of the water, on one of the slipways, being fussed over by a crew of workers cleaning the hull.

'That's the diplomatic dock,' said Benji, who stood next to Forge readying a mooring line. 'All the bigwigs have ships here. They don't like them being out of the water for too long. I guess it's so they can make a sharp exit if needs be.'

'Like they'd get out of the harbour before someone took a shot at them,' added Bors.

'Reckon so,' said Benji. 'Less'n you do it right at midday, the locals are all asleep then. I think you could make a fist of it.'

The *Crimson Shore* found itself one of many ships entering the harbour, jostling for space. Beyond the diplomatic dock, a network of wharfs and piers spread out across the water, servicing all manner of ships. Many resembled the *Crimson Shore*, but there were also barges, huge trading galleys, and smaller sailing ships. If he wasn't mistaken, that was a Harradan longship tied up over there. *Hells, that must have been a trip.*

Nazar was steering the ship towards a quay with a number of spare berths, about midway along the harbour but at the end of the quay, nearest the channel.

'It's a pain in the arse having to haul the cargo to the dock but the fees are a little cheaper,' explained Bors.

'Medhji, get the sail up, we'll run her in slow. Benji, Bors, you get ready to tie us off.'

'Right, come on, Wenham, give me a hand hauling her up,' shouted Medhji. His arm was still stiff and sore but was healing well.

As the crew worked around him, Forge was looking forward to getting off the ship. But there was something else playing on his mind now. He had to work out what he was supposed to do next. He had no orders, no plan, no direction. All of these things were guaranteed to vex him at the best of times. But considering what he was being asked to do...well, the sea voyage had been a nice way of avoiding having to face up to what his mission was. He crushed down hard on the rising feeling of hopelessness. He had faced impossible odds before and somehow made it right. *For Dav.*

Nazar guided his ship up against the quay, the two brothers jumped off the ship and tied her off and moments later the gangplank was run out. 'Hassan, go along and find the Clerk of Shipping, usual place. Let him know we've arrived and I'll be along later to settle with him.'

Forge watched Hassan tear off over the gangplank and along the pier. He turned to Nazar. 'What's the rule on weapons here? Am I allowed to carry?'

Nazar was turning towards the cabin door and stopped. 'What? Oh, no, no rules as such. You'll see plenty of people armed around here. Just keep it... discreet. That way you won't draw attention to yourself.'

'Good,' said Forge, and started across to the entrance to the hold. He could do discreet.

'Forge?' called Nazar, 'are you heading into the city straight away?'

Forge shrugged. 'I figured I would. No point in hanging around waiting for something to happen.'

'Fair enough. I'll accompany you to dry land.'

Forge nodded and entered the hold to retrieve his things.

'You can leave your rucksack,' Nazar called down. 'We won't be leaving for a couple of days. You are welcome to stay or find lodging as you wish.'

Nice of him. 'Appreciate it.' It would be better to have a friendly base to operate from until he found his feet.

He retrieved his sword belt, climbed out of the hold and followed Nazar onto the quay. He buckled on his belt settling the weight on his hip and tying off the knife sheath on his left side tight against his upper leg. Nazar, now dressed in a fine white cotton robe cinched in the middle with a piece of rope, strolled alongside him. There was a ledger tucked under one arm and he was smiling in a distant kind of way.

'You happy to be home?' asked Forge

'Happy?' Nazar replied, his face screwed up in thought. 'I'm not sure if that is the right word. This place has many memories, good and bad. But like most of us, I allow the bad to outweigh the good. Still, we have completed our arrangement to our mutual satisfaction. No one permanently hurt and no one out of pocket.'

Forge knew that did not apply to him. His task was just starting and someone, at some point in the future, was definitely going to get very hurt.

'Oh look,' exclaimed Nazar, pointing at a galley berthed just ahead. Every inch of its hull was painted blue, the finish was sleek and smooth, and on its prow was a figurehead of a mermaid drawing a bow. The detailing was as near perfect a work as he had ever seen. 'An elf-ship,' continued Nazar, 'you don't see many of these this far east.'

They walked past the ship's gangplank, a grand affair more like a ramp, lovingly crafted with railings on either side that bore little carved details of sea creatures.

'Don't they have an embassy here?' asked Forge.

'No, they don't see the need. They are travellers, are they not? They don't like to spend so much time in one place. And they never let anyone on board they do not trust. So that excludes humans, naturally,' replied Nazar, drily.

The elves had been driven from the mainland centuries ago, leaving their settlements to the advancing wave of goblin tribes, who were themselves pushed westwards with the progress of humankind. They had taken to the seas, creating their own floating towns and villages, trading with nations of men but never getting too close. And Forge knew well enough the grudge they bore the goblin nations.

They saw no elves aboard the ship as they carried on past, reaching the end of the quay where it joined the wharf running along the front of the city proper. It was essentially a long platform of rock, made flat through the tools of man and constant use. The back of the wharf was taller than two men and on top of that was a waist high stone wall. There were also several cranes and hoists dotted along the top of the wharf wall.

They met Hassan coming down one of the many steps and ramps leading from the street above. 'I saw the clerk – he's got a letter for you. Said you had to collect it. No one else.'

Nazar looked at Forge and raised an eyebrow.

'Very well, do we have an unload time?'

'Stevadores are all busy. Won't be until tomorrow morning now,' replied Hassan.

'That is fine. Tell Medhji the crew can finish up the chores and stand down for the evening.'

'Yes, Nazar.'

'Hassan?'

'Yes, Nazar?'

'Also tell Medhji, I want a watch roster. A real one. And I am not to be included in it. Am I clear?'

'Yes, Nazar!' Hassan said, with a cheeky grin.

Nazar sighed.

'It is like herding cats sometimes. Have you ever had to do that?'

'Once or twice,' replied Forge.

'Yes, I imagine you probably have,' said Nazar, indicating the stairs Hassan had just descended.

Together they climbed up to the street level. At the top, the vista that greeted them was both familiar and unusual. Forge had heard a word for it once: cosmopolitan. The street was wide and cobbled with drainage channels on other side that looked like they actually worked. Set back on pavements was a frontage of buildings that included inns, a coffee house or two and several larger and imposing edifices that bore the names, in several languages, of the merchant companies that owned them. Most nations clustered around the Jedah Sea shared a similar language, having adopted the trader's tongue many centuries earlier. And it was that which allowed him to read the names: *Al Rashid Traders to the Paternal, Markesh and Sons Shipping, Rocksea Circle Line.* They were grand buildings, with wide open doors framed with porticos and faux columns holding up engraved marble archways. Small windows looked out over the water on the higher levels and the roofs had small carved sea creatures set on each corner – they looked like kraken or sea serpents, neither of which any of these folk would want to encounter for real. This scene stretched to the left and right, curving gently round the edge of the harbour.

'Believe it or not, I had myself one of these, once, many years ago. Not on the waterside, not so close to the wharf, that is reserved for the serious players, but I was quite proud of it,' said Nazar.

'I guess you'd like to see some of these guys suffer, no?' said Forge, his attention drifting to the crowds.

'Oh, it's not their fault. But I must say, if you have a spare moment and the inclination, I'd happily pay you a small fee to wrap up some unfinished business.'

'Maybe next time.'

'Oh well, it was worth asking. Quite the crowd, isn't it?'

He wasn't wrong. Here locals mixed with every creed and nation from the Jedah Sea. Forge could spot at least six countries that he knew represented, be it in their dress or features. Blue-eyed northmen, the sharp featured Heirons, more than a few from Ashkent, the tell-tale green headscarves of sailors from Graves, the curved falchions carried by the men and women of Jaeget. And there, sliding down the street, were two elves. They wore lose fitting linens under leather waistcoats and carried thin rapiers at their waists. They carried themselves with an odd grace and wore a look of detachment. It was their eyes that always got Forge. The ears he could live with, but those eyes, almond shaped and set to close to one another, they belied the alien, *other* quality of elves. You couldn't trust them, capricious and wilful bastards.

'Have you ever dealt with elves, Forge?' asked Nazar, his hands clasped behind his back.

'Not really, never at my level. We got relations with 'em, least the Assembly has. But I've heard enough about what they are like and I don't think I'd get along with them very well.'

'Doesn't that apply to everyone regarding you?'

Forge shot Nazar a dirty look. The bastard had a point though. 'Where's this clerk's office?' he asked.

Nazar indicted to a small blocky building set behind railings to their left.

'Just over there.'

Nazar led the way to the Clerk of Shipping's office, past two bored looking guards and into the cool shadowed interior. Forge took a moment to size up the guards as he walked past. They wore white cotton leggings and tunics under stylised leather breastplates, gauntlets and grieves. Wrapped over and around their heads were lengths of white cotton and on the crown a steel skullcap with a small spike. For weapons they carried spears and shields. Overall, he didn't rate what he saw. Neither man looked like he would be interested in getting into any serious action. At least it told him he wouldn't be getting any trouble from harbour guards.

Inside they encountered a high countertop upon which sat, looming over them, an officious looking fellow with a large book and quill poised over it. He had grey tufts of hair growing out from the sides of an otherwise bald head and a short grey goatee.

'Nazar,' he said, without looking up.

'My old friend, Abir, it is good to see you. Has it been another year? You have not aged one bit,' replied Nazar.

Abir looked up, his dark brown eyes shrewd and sharp, his face narrow.

'I've aged many lifetimes since I started this job. I am a withered husk of a man because of it.'

'But you do it so well!'

'I am the only fool who will. Having to deal with the likes of you has made my hair fall out. Can you believe it?' he was looking at Forge now, 'I used to be complimented on my hair, long and lustrous, thick and flowing. Where has it gone?'

Forge held back on what he felt was the most suitable but

least diplomatic answer.

Abir shook his head, thankfully not expecting a response, and dipped his quill into an unseen pot of ink and made a mark in his book.

'Hassan tells me you are berthed out at the end. Doing it cheap these days, hmm? It'll be the usual charge, thirty for three days.'

'Usual? It used to be twenty-one!' cried Nazar.

'It got changed last year, just after you left, so it's been usual for quite a while now.'

Nazar, instead of haggling, retrieved a small pouch from around his neck and counted out three coins.

'I am bled white and not a thing sold.'

Abir lowered his quill and scooped up the money. It disappeared into a compartment on the other side of the counter with a tinkle. Abir then turned and picked up a letter and passed it down to Nazar.

'This has been waiting for you for three weeks.'

'Thank you, Abir,' said Nazar.

Abir waved his hand away, took up his quill and started to mark his book once more.

Nazar nodded to Forge and led the way out.

'Short and sweet' said Forge.

'Oh, Abir and I go way back, good of him to do me that nice berthing deal.'

'Really?'

'Yes! Normally you have to pay thirty-six for three nights.'

They walked a short distance back along the street before Nazar leant against the railing and broke the plain wax seal of the envelope, unfolding the single piece of parchment. Forge stood next to him, watching the world pass by, trying to get a sense of the place. It was damn busy and folk were not dawdling much. He watched a street hawker pass by pushing a cart loaded with small amphorae and a mismatch of glass bottles.

'Water?' the hawker shouted. 'Anyone want water? So much about but not a drop to drink!'

After him came a cart slowly pulled by two oxen. On the sidebar sat a large, sweaty fellow berating the beasts and encouraging them to greater efforts. He was failing miserably. His cargo was a number of rickety cages carrying multi-coloured birds of varying sizes. They all looked mighty agitated. Forge didn't approve of caging birds or animals, just like he'd grown to have a healthy dislike for slavers. He'd made it one of his last acts as a serving officer to hunt down the group who'd caught and trapped some old friends of his. Last he heard they'd all died pretty quickly in the penal arenas he'd sent them too. He supposed having lopped off their right hands prior to shipment wouldn't have helped their chances much.

'Well, there we are, then,' said Nazar. He had finished reading and held the parchment in his hand. 'It seems that I have some fresh orders, courtesy of our mutual benefactor.'

'And?' replied Forge, immediately on edge.

'I have been requested to remain in Karnak for two weeks. I am then to transport you and any cargo you might have around the Jedah Sea and deposit you back on Ashkent soil.'

'Nice to know,' said Forge, mollified. He was relieved to find out that there was actually an exit plan in place.

'There are also some words for you. I paraphrase slightly but you are to make contact with a man called Fahad Fudail. He can be found in a hostelry called *The Moon of Karnassus*. He will be there at midday for one hour, every day, until you arrive. Here.'

Nazar handed over the letter and Forge scanned it. There was nothing else in it that Nazar had not already told him.

Forge looked at Nazar. 'What do you think?'

Nazar's face took a resigned cast.

'It seems that the crew of the *Crimson Shore* are embroiled in your affair more than I was aware. Yet there is little I can do about it. There is at least a period of time for us to work towards - two weeks. Not so long that people might start asking questions and taking notice of our lingering here,' he stood up straight and pulled down on his robe. 'We have goods that need to be unloaded and the business of business must carry on regardless. That is what should happen and what will happen. And you will need to go to the hostelry - I know of its whereabouts - and find this Fahad Fudail. But not today, I think. It is well past midday and I find myself thirsty. I will stand you a drink. '

'That sounds like a plan. You not worried about the crew?'

'What, my crew? I have my complete faith in them. If they give me cause for disappointment, I would ask a boon of you. Perhaps you would deliver some re-education to them on the concept of keeping watch.

'I can do that.'

'Yes, you do seem to have the fists for it.'

Chapter 9

Forge took another sip of his ale, tried to ignore that it tasted like weak piss, and wondered what time it was. He was sure that he'd been here more than an hour and that midday was about to hit. The hostelry of *The Moon of Karnassus* was a middling sized business of three floors that specialised in giving errant sailors a bed for the evening when they had had their fill of shipboard living. The entrance led into a room that was plain, unadorned and poorly kept. It had a small bar with several tables scattered around the dimly lit space. Thus far he had seen a sum total of three residents come by. Two looked like they had just gotten off ship, the third was accompanied by a women who had even less teeth than the sailor she was with. The owner didn't bat an eyelid - it was that kind of place.

Forge had not asked whether the owner knew this Fahad Fudail. If this man had been coming in for what must have been at least a couple of weeks, then he should do, but he didn't want to immediately make himself known. He'd rather get to see who he was dealing with first.

'He'll be along in a minute,' said the owner.

Forge looked at him.

'Your mate. Comes in at the midday bell as regular as you like. I imagine you guys haven't seen each other in a while.' The owner, a man in his forties with greasy black hair and a large mole on his left cheek, had not stopped rubbing a tankard with a rag, and had not looked up.

'I can't wait,' muttered Forge.

At that he heard the midday bell sound out across the city. Nazar said it was a huge beast, mounted atop a platform in the centre of the plateau. Its striker was the size of a battering ram and was operated by a series of complex gears, counterweights and pulleys. The smith in him was keen to see it at some point but for the moment his attention was drawn to the opening door in front of him. Stepping through was a well-built man wearing a yellow cloak over brown linen trousers, leather boots and white tunic open wide at the neck.

'There he is,' said the owner. 'You want two fresh ones?'

'Sure,' said Forge.

The man closed the door, looked at Forge and took a seat at the table sat in the middle of the room facing the wall to the right of the bar.

Forge waited for the two tankards to be poured, nodded his thanks to the owner, put two coins on the counter and then carried the drinks over to the table. Forge stood behind the chair opposite the man.

'Fahad Fudail?'

The man opposite him looked up. There was no doubt he was a local. His head was completely clean-shaven and marked with tattoos of twisting dragons: tails entwined, claws spread and snarling mouths. His skin was swarthy, his face covered with stubble, his ears elongated by heavy gold earings. A jagged scar ran down his left cheek. He placed his hands flat on the table revealing a collection of large gold and silver rings, at least one to a finger. Around his neck he wore a small bronze medallion that hung low on his bare, hairless chest. He looked up at Forge, his eyes dark. He indicated the chair in front of Forge, who duly sat and pushed over one tankard.

'I was told to look for a man from the west. You fit that description,' said Fudail. 'I was told that you could tell me why you are here.'

This was it, the point where he had to start coming clean. If this went south, he expected he'd have to fight his way out of the building.

'I came here to repay a debt,' he said. 'Though there won't be any appreciation for it.'

The man inclined his head, pulled his hands from the table and gathered up the tankard.

'I was told to expect you might say something like that. You are at least trying to maintain some kind of secrecy. I was told you are here to free a prisoner. A prisoner you have never met who is kept in a prison that you cannot enter. And if you were to ask me, you are a damned fool.' Fudail raised the tankard to his lips and drank deep.

Forge reached for his tankard and copied the manoeuvre. It hadn't escaped his notice that having the pair of them sat in the middle of the bar did leave them open to observation. But then, maybe that was the point. 'I think I'm a damned fool,' he agreed.

'There, at least, we have common ground. I am indeed Fahad Fudail, and I have been engaged to assist you in your enterprise. I am someone who knows things. I am someone who knows people. I am someone who can get things done.'

With that head, he looked like someone who stood out in a crowd. 'You a ganger?' asked Forge.

Fudail nodded. 'I was, a long time ago. But I grew up, I

moved up. Got myself a nice place in the Nook. '

'What are you now?'

'A fixer.'

Forge looked down and played with his tankard.

'Look, not that I'm mighty grateful to get some local support. But from what I understand, this city has a secret police that has watchers watching the watchers. If you start making noises, aren't they going to hear?'

'You are right. This city lives and breathes intrigue, but that is to our advantage. In the scheme of things, I operate far too low down the food chain, what I do is known and recorded but I have never done anything that is political or anything that was not obvious and clear. I have never given the authorities reason to follow me or look into my affairs.'

Forge heard the door open and watched a red-haired female swan in as if she owned the place. She was wearing a cloak and underneath figure-hugging leathers, a little unusual in this heat. She glided past them and went to the bar to speak to the owner, no doubt to see if there were any punters. He turned his attention back to Fudail.

'If that's the case, how did you get mixed up in this?'

'I said I have never done anything political, but my gang was sponsored by the Ashkent Embassy. Someone must have kept tabs on me when I left.'

'Sponsored?'

'You do not know about this?' asked Fudail, with a look of mild surprise.

Forge made a face and shook his head. He also made a mental note to give Nazar some shit for holding back.

'Karnak Karnassus is a big, big place, 'said Fudail. 'You go beyond the plateau and the houses of the wealthy and you start entering the territories of the gangs. There are dozens of them. Some rule just a few streets and lanes, others rule entire districts, especially if you go beyond the walls of the old city. The Red Skulls, the Drinkers, Aranag, the Bowed, the Cutters, the Blooded, Seven Devils, the Waybearers, that's some of the larger gangs. He pointed at his tattoos. I was a Drinker. A lot of business goes on that is far from legal or sanctioned. Goods are brought in without the proper permissions and deals are done that never come to the attention of the powers that be. It is all managed by the gangs. You want something moved then you have to grease the right palms. The City Watch might patrol the streets but the gangs rule them and the gangs enforce the peace,' Fudail smiled apologetically, 'though that peace is often disturbed by extreme violence. This is Karnak Karnassus and the politics of the world are played out within it. Each country that has any interest in gaining power or influence makes it their business to know what everyone else is doing. So they need foot soldiers, those who are expendable and can, if necessary, be cast adrift with no provable link back to the sponsor.'

'Deniability,' said Forge. He was beginning to understand quite clearly.

'Deniability,' agreed Fudail. He sat back in his chair and raised his hands up to his side, palms up. 'Of course, once this started, it escalated and everyone knew that the gangs were choosing sides and taking the money. It is an open secret. The Ministry of Relations know full well this is going on and is happy for this to happen. They would rather that intrigues and scores are settled by the scum of the city rather than the armies of aggrieved nations. And you can be sure that in every gang there are at least a dozen informants working for other sponsors. And one or two more who report directly back to the Ministry.'

'They know you worked for Ashkent?'

'They know I was once a member of a gang who was once sponsored by Ashkent. Gangs change allegiance like the wind changes direction, if one side can offer them more than what they are getting, then they switch. It's just part of the game.'

Forge shook his head. 'How the Hells does anything ever get done, then?'

'It works, after a fashion. There are some gangs, the older, larger ones, who have stayed quite steady in their allegiance. They make it their business to know who they can trust and who they can ally with. Sometimes they band together to deliver a message, sometimes they agree to look the other way.'

'It's messy,' said Forge. Yet, he had to admit, when he was a serving soldier, it wasn't all that different. He always knew who he was fighting, even if he didn't quite understand why.

'It can be messy,' agreed Fudhail. 'That is why I was contacted. It must have been felt you would need someone to help you navigate your way. It would be easy for you to trust the wrong people.'

No shit. 'You provide the local knowledge, I get that. Happy to have you. One question. How did they get you to agree to help me? What have they got on you?'

Fudail smiled. His teeth were a bright white. 'I told you I turned my back on the gangs. I wanted to do better, so I started helping people, those who couldn't do it for themselves. If I knew someone could help, I called in a favour and in turn earned other favours. Sometimes I had to use my fists. After a while, I had learned things, had gathered enough dirt on enough people that it was just better to let me carry on. Often my work benefits a gang, so they tolerate me. I have respect, I can move between many of the gang territories and

I'm left alone. I don't get involved in politics and I don't work for governments. Then Ashkent comes calling and reminds me of some of the things I did for them in the past. The killings, the disappearances, I was a very good foot soldier. It is why I left. I had grown sick of being another man's slave.'

'Yet here you are,' said Forge. He empathised with the man. They weren't so different.

'Here I am. I received a letter delivered by a gang member I knew had also worked for Ashkent. It provided details of my past history. Details that if given to the wrong gangs see me dead within a day. Some deaths go beyond the game, they stay personal. That letter also told me what I had to do to keep those details safe.'

'For what it's worth, I've done my fair share of killing,' said Forge. 'You think you can do your time, play the game and then you can cash out and move on. But you can't escape your past.'

'It would appear not. I do not have a choice. When I am done with you I will not stay here, I will leave and go someplace far away, where my past deeds matter for nothing. I will not be a slave.'

'Good luck with that,' said Forge. He doubted such a place existed.

'Do you have a plan, yet?'

'I was hoping you had one.'

'Me?' said Fudail, putting a hand on his chest. 'You have yet to tell me who it is I am supposed to be helping break out. Is it a political prisoner? Or just a criminal you have been hired to retrieve? If so, I know some people who owe me-'

'It's the Paternal.'

That stopped Fudail in his tracks. He went very quiet and very deliberately placed his hands, palms down, on the table in front of him. He took a deep breath in through his mouth and blew the air out of his nostrils. 'That's us both fucked then.'

'Now you're getting it,' said Forge.

Fudail shook his head. 'This won't work. It's suicide. I might as well run now and take my chances.' He stood.

'Hey, where are you going?'

'I am leaving. Good luck.'

Forge also stood. 'Wait.'

Fudail was already at the door. He took the handle and pulled it open, letting in the bright midday sunlight. 'You can tell your man, if he wants to watch your back, he should try and blend in.'

Right. Wenham. The guy was just supposed to bring him here. He guessed Nazar thought some back-up was a good idea.

'Look, Fudail. I know shit all about this place...'

Fudail raised a warding hand, shook his head and stepped out, blocking the light for a moment and then disappeared. Forge took a moment. This wasn't the best of starts. He still knew next to nothing of this place and the hired help had already decided to cut and run. At this rate, the best he was going to come up with was marching into the Paternal's palace, killing his guards and then marching the bloke out over his shoulder.

He opened the door, stepped out onto the street and crossed the road. Wenham was leaning against a wall directly opposite.

'Alright?' said Forge, by way of greeting.

'Yep,' replied Wenham.

'Decided to hang around did you?'

'Yeah, Nazar said I should.'

'Right,' Forge sighed, tucked his arms into his belt and looked up and down the street. 'Not that I don't appreciate it but next time let me know, huh?'

Wenham folded his arms. 'Sure, no problem.'

'Let's head back. I need to think about what I'm going to do next.'

Wenham and Forge made their way down the slope towards the harbour. They were only ten minutes away from the ship, and had not gone far enough into the city to get near the plateau. Nazar was sat on a stool next to the gangplank when they arrived and he waved at their approach.

'Good day, good day. Was it a useful meeting?'

'No. it was not,' replied Forge. 'I told him who I was here for and he decided to cut and run.'

Nazar's face turned grave. 'That is ill news.'

'Yeah, pretty shit.'

'What is our plan?'

Forge picked up on the 'our', it surprised him that Nazar appeared to be so amenable to this mission but he wasn't going to look that gift horse in the mouth.. 'Not sure yet, but Fahad Fudail was picked as a fixer, a local expert. He had knowledge I just don't have. I need to take the time to learn a little more about this place. I'll walk the harbour today then tomorrow I'm going to head into the city itself, try and get a sense of the geography and try and find Fudail.'

'Very good, but you must be wary of the going into the city. Trust me, you must tread carefully. Would you like Wenham to accompany you?'

Forge thought about it for a moment. Whilst he had no objection to Wenham, he'd rather be a free agent. Besides, he didn't want this crew getting into harm's way. 'No thanks.'

Nazar inclined his head.

'Then let me take you for a stroll. I'll show you my old property.'

Nazar led Forge back onto the wharf and they turned right, heading towards a gathering of warehouses that dominated the waterfront.

'So, Forge. I have never asked you before. You are a military man?'

'I was,' Forge acknowledged.

'But now you are retired. A sword for hire, yes?'

Sometimes he'd felt like that when he had been a professional soldier. 'No. This is a one-time deal. I don't fight anymore.'

'And what made you retire?' asked Nazar, in a casual, off-hand way.

Forge shot him another look. Nazar made an innocent face. 'I am just interested, Forge. You know my story. Now that we are locked into this adventure together, and have shed blood together, I was thinking we might trust each other?'

Trust. Forge supposed Nazar had earned a measure of it, and respect. 'I had just fought one battle too many. It happens to all of us. I was in Graves during the civil war. I ended up making a decision to put my mission before my men. That's just the job. We were betrayed. I had to do something to slow down an invading army of Harradan from surprising and flanking our forces. So we set up in an old fort. My command, some locals, we even drafted in our slave workers – Bantusai. Ever heard of them?'

'Oh yes. I saw one once, he was making ship timbers. Quite a skill. They might have made a fortune on the Jedah if they did not live so far south. But he said most have no interest.'

'They were quite something. And decent too. Better folks than most I've met.'

96

'You succeeded in your mission?' asked Nazar.

'Yes.'

'Then how was it a bad decision?'

'Militarily? It was a good one. But I lost almost everyone doing it.'

'And it weights heavily on your heart, yes?'

Forge grunted. Heavy was one word to describe it. 'After I got home, I resigned my commission.' Forge stopped and looked out onto the harbour. A large galley was maneouvering out towards the moles and open water. 'I took my pension and walked away. Went to pursue my dream of a better life making axes.'

'Ah, dreams. They are what drive us and then they shatter us,' said Nazar. 'I have known loss, but not in the same way as you, I think.'

Nazar touched Forge lightly on the shoulder. He flinched at the contact, just slightly. 'Follow me. You carry your burdens in here,' he tapped his chest. 'I myself have a more lasting monument to my mistakes. I'll show you my old warehouse.'

Forge followed Nazar. Not because he was interested but because he did not want to be alone. His thoughts and memories left unchecked might just drown him.

Chapter 10

Forge left the harbour, Old Karnak as he had taken to calling it, and headed inland, climbing the slope leading up to the plateau. It was only an hour after daybreak but already the city was alive and teeming. His foray into the harbour had been a short-lived and unproductive affair, although Nazar had taken him to a half decent tavern. The Gods only knew how he had made it back to the ship that night. He had awoken with a bastard behind the eyes and since then that bastard had been deliberately kicking his head in. Behind him, the harbour was busy with stevedores loading and unloading cargo and in the distance, beyond the moles, he had seen the fishing fleets already about their business and a dozen larger trading craft heading out into the main channel. They were using the tide to take them out to sea where they could catch the tradewinds and start a run north, stopping off at the Free Cities along the eastern shoreline.

The zig-zag street he walked along was just wide enough to accommodate two carts and it was the main route running up the slope towards the plateau and Karnassus. As such, he joined a fair amount of traffic flowing both ways. Those heading in the same direction as him tended towards the better off, with decent, well-tended clothing and an air of professional intent. Some wore wide-brimmed hats made of straw that looked a bit daft to Forge, but bearing in mind the lack of rainfall this place got, they kept their wearer's heads in shadow and protected them from the worst of the sun. The road did not follow a straight path to the high ground, rather it switched back once or twice, saving folk from having to cope with the steeper inclines above them. He saw any number of alleys, passageways and steps that he could use to cut short his journey but right now, without street-smarts, who knew what he might walk into.

He could see the dwellings here were built into the slope, their ground floors backing onto rock and earth and rising three floors higher, with small balconies standing out from doorways built into the upper levels. Many had sheets and washing hanging from them, while some others had neighbours leaning across conversing to each other. Forge passed a man applying whitewash to the wall of his bakery. He looked annoyed and was muttering to himself as he applied the paint over some graffiti. He could spot what looked like a bull with one hell of a hard-on trying to mount a man – it looked vaguely like the baker. It was something he had not really noticed before but by and large, these walls, all varying shades of white, were by and large clear of any defacement, except where it was clear the owner was advertising their business. Now if this had been anywhere in Ashkent, he wouldn't have given these walls one night before they had a host of views, opinions and insults applied. Folk back home thought it they had a Gods' given right to express themselves, and usually they'd get away with it. Perhaps the culture here was more respectful and, dare he say it, proud of their city. He thought it more likely that the city fathers practiced zero tolerance for such behaviour, a night in the cells and maybe a black-eye if they wanted to disagree. It was what he would do.

The street straightened and started to level out. Up ahead he saw the traffic slowing. Drawing near, he saw that they were joining a major thoroughfare that was coming up from the old walls, only a couple of hundred yards away to his right. To his left, heading in a north-westerly direction, the thoroughfare led on towards Karnassus proper. Twice the size of what he had just walked up, this was more like a boulevard than a street, and clearly designed to impress. The two lanes nearest him had horses, carts and people heading onto the plateau, and on the far side of a central reservation two more lanes took traffic towards the walls and the new city. The middle portion of the street was no simple dividing barrier, rather it was its own walking route, where small groves of trees and plants were tended by a workforce of gardeners, most of whom seemed to be engaged with watering. Obviously, keeping anything alive in the heat of the summer must prove a challenge. These patches of green were divided by large statues set upon marble clad platforms.

He looked left then right and decided that he probably needed to see the scene of the future crime first. He turned left, walking along a well maintained pavement, and soon had to join others in negotiating their way round a cart parked against the side of the street where two men were offloading barrels. Two more were rolling them into a tavern under the watchful eyes of the large, big-bellied tavern keeper wearing a stained apron.

As he walked, he studied the statues in the middle of the street. They all appeared to be of statesmen, wearing robes and carrying scrolls or books, or simply holding themselves in poses of authority. Not one warrior did he see among the procession. That was unusual. He couldn't think of a single other place that didn't like to celebrate their martial heroes. But then this was Karnak Karnassus and they had made it their business not to fight. If he was a betting man, and he often was, he'd put these guys down as all the previous Paternals.

Feeling inquisitive, he looked for a gap in the traffic and dodged his way to the nearest statue. There were a number of people walking along the paths that cut through the green and around the statue. There were even benches spread out along the way, and some were already occupied even this early in the morning. Forge stood before a statue of a man who looked around fifty, he was bald and had a long forked beard. He was gazing down, his hands clasped together, like he was deep in thought or beseeching some deity or another. There was a plaque on the plinth written in the local language with some dates, a period of five years, that were written in the same numeric symbols used throughout the Jedah, a shared legacy of conquest from years gone by. He walked on towards the next statue, this time a clean-shaven man no older than thirty, clutching a scroll with both hands as if his life depended on it. The date inscription was for another five-year period, this one just before the statue behind him. That answered the question; these were the Paternals, and by the looks of it, they were all in date order. By that reckoning he should come to the first Paternal at the end of this row. He continued along his way, checking statues as he went and enjoying the stroll, noting that those who shared the space round him were becoming less like a mix of local people and more like civil servants, functionaries and high ranking politicians. One or two of them eyed his sword belt with raised eyebrows as he walked by and he made an effort to scowl right back. After ten minutes, he came to the end of the procession. Directly in front of him was a weathered-looking statue, almost twice the size of the others. A man was sat on a throne upon the platform and he looked out with a stern expression, as if he were judging all those that came after him. He was well-built, with large hands and a full beard that covered most of his face. Upon his head was a crown of laurel leaves. In his left hand he carried a sceptre and in his right he held up as set of scales. Forge looked at the inscription. If this was the first Paternal, they had definitely done things differently that first time around. Judging by the dates, this one looked like he had been in play for ten years. They must have still been working the kinks out for this one.

The path ended behind the statute and facing Forge was a large building, fronted by columns and marble friezes set around the top of the walls. There were four sets of double doors at the top of a half a dozen steps, although only the middle two sets were open, a pair of guards standing by each set. He'd made a point of getting Nazar to give him a more detailed run-down on what the major sights were and had gotten him to draw a map - he'd never be able to remember half the stuff he'd been told. The building in front of him was the Crucible, the place where the ruling families of Karnak Karnassus met to govern. It might look angular from its front but within was a large amphitheatre open to the elements. Apparently, when the place wasn't being used for government, they used it as a theatre, and as such it was open to the public. He crossed over to the entrance, walking over a cobbled surface that was free of traffic, although a carriage was parked out the front of the building. Clearly if you were important enough you could cut across, everyone else had to loop round.

He turned left and continued following the flow of traffic heading into the plateau. The architecture here was a whole other level of filthy rich. Colonnades, fountains, plazas and well-to-do hostelries populated Old Karnassus. Quiet, tree-lined avenues split from the main street where grand houses and villas sat in well-tended, leafy gardens full of citrus trees. He cut down one avenue to have a closer look but it felt wrong for him to be there, armed and surly looking. This was a life he had never experienced and never would. He could never have dreamed the business of peace could be so profitable. A small party of children, each wearing a satchel and a simple white robe, was ushered on by a harassed looking man wearing spectacles. He gave Forge a look which was either one of disdain, disapproval or mild panic. Either way, the group moved on. A couple in their later years passed by Forge, the lady was carrying a parasol and wore a yellow silk dress and the man was wearing a blue toga, not dissimilar to that won by the Paternals. Their glances at Forge were much more obvious. He gave them his best shit-eating grin. Forge had seen enough of this place to know he didn't like it and there was very little reason to tarry, so he turned around and got back onto the main artery. There was still one place he wanted to visit and that was on the north side of the plateau. He found another street heading in that direction and trusted his instincts, and the dubious artwork of Nazar, to get him where he wanted to go.

That place was known as the Street of Artists and true to its name, the first hundred yards was a series of small shop frontages, some no more than cubicles, where men and women displayed friezes, busts and statues of people who Forge had no knowledge of, though he suspected several of them were probably Paternals. On the pavement, painters hawked their sketches and oils, and Forge recognised many of the scenes from his travels. There was even one that looked a little like the Mercy Mountains back home. Midway along the street, the shops got larger and the artists displayed their work inside galleries. Perhaps it was the higher quality purveyors not wanting their clients to be bothered by the skivvies. Or maybe it was the imposing building directly opposite – the Paternal's Palace. It was huge, and built in the customary style of white stone and marble, with columns, balconies and large towers with bulging rounded roofs set further back in the interior. Yet there was also something very functional about it, like it was a municipal building rather that the home of the most important political figure in a thousand miles. The central entranceway was on a grand scale, with a series of steps leading to a large colonnade, but on either side the two wings were identical, blocky and rectangular, with small wooden-framed windows and flat roofs. The wings looked like a later addition, add-ons to what had been a proper royal residence in the past. As he walked westwards, he spotted a difference in the second floor of the left hand wing; there was a corner with full-faced windows.

That meant something.

It meant that someone liked looking out on the street, and someone who could get a set of windows like that put in the Paternal's Palace had to be important and not someone Forge wanted to meet in a hurry. What had Nazar said? The Ministry of Relations was based in the Paternal's Palace and the Ministry was all about secrets and spies and snitches. He'd bet his life that Dav's fate was in some way linked to that organisation. A thought entered his mind, one that kept creeping in when he wasn't looking. *Just go in there and level the place. That would be the best way to honour Dav.* He found himself largely agreeing with the sentiment and it appealed to the part of him that like sticking two fingers up at common sense. He wasn't quite there yet though. If he was going to go down swinging, it had to be the right people he was landing the blows on.

At the corner of the Palace, a narrow street followed the line of the walls, wide enough to demarcate the Palace from the buildings around it but a wagon would be a tight fight. There were also two guards stood either side of the entrance which told him only those on official business went that way, or maybe it was security for the tradesmen's entrance. Still, it was good to know. He turned around and retraced his steps. He had a lot to think about. Even with just a cursory inspection, getting into that place was not going to be easy. Whatever way you cut it, there were armed guards to get by before you could even start looking for the Paternal and then what were you supposed to do with him? It would have to be at night, that was a given. After that, he didn't have a clue. He had no fixer, no inside intelligence but he had not given up on Fahad Fudhail just yet.

The smell of cooking meat brought him out of his reverie. He was back along the main concourse heading for the walls, and before him was a trader selling pieces of what looked like chicken suspended on wooden skewers over a brazier. Juices dripped from the cooking meat onto the coals below, causing them to sizzle and pop, releasing odours that made his stomach churn. He bought two sticks and took a bite of what he at least hoped was chicken. As familiar flavours hit his tongue, he started to feel a little better about life and his hangover started to dissipate. It was amazing how food could do that to you, as much as alcohol just seemed to make the problem worse. The thing was, he did so love the taste and if you drank enough, everything went away for at least a little while.

He finished the first skewer just as he was passing under the gatehouse of the old city walls. Now this was more like it. The stone here was undressed but the blocks were much larger, roughly a foot square. They looked chipped and worn but no less sturdy for all of that. A stout-looking door was built into the left-hand side of the gatehouse - that was where the defenders would enter to control the mechanisms and man the defences. The gatehouse passage consisted of a portcullis, the wooden gates and then another portcullis on the far side. The street had narrowed to two lanes of traffic, one in each direction, but the guards made no attempt to impede their progress. Karnak Karnassus was a hungry beast. He spied murder holes above his head as he approached the gates and more beyond as he passed through them. On the far side he looked up and studied the two towers that flanked the passage through. Three floors high with arrow slits all the way up to rounded, balconied roofs and battlements crossing between them. On this side the stone looked not only weathered but truly battered. In places, large ragged depressions suggested heavy artillery had taken chunks of stone away, and there were multiple little indentations left by smaller arms such as bolts and arrows. The walls stretched away to either side, demarcating the old city from the new, they looked just as battered as the gate. Yes, this place had seen wars alright, but all he had to do was look around to see how much has changed. The new city was vast. From his vantage point he looked out over a spread of humanity that must be three times larger than what was behind him. It was terrifying. He could map out a patch-work of different neighbourhoods just from the architecture and design, there were areas where there had been some planning and he could see small parks, ordered streets, and well-spaced houses, not unlike the plateau. In others, it was just a crazy riot of hotch-potch of dwellings of various sizes and shapes with curving lanes, random gardens, punctuated with larger buildings, which were possibly temples or theatres. Then, on the fringes, were the ghettos: shacks, sheds and hovels, all crushed together amidst a warren of alleyways, passages and dead-ends. If you got lost in there the chances were you weren't coming out again. More often than not, these neighbourhoods bled into each other, leaving no free space or lines of demarcation. The city continued on into a hazy vision of the hinterlands around the city. Did they even have any defences out there? The road he stood upon continued on through the city in an easterly direction, following a gentle slope down off the high ground. He was minded to continue on to the end, he wanted to get a sense of what would happen if you just kept on going and at what point you would no longer be in the city or under its control. He looked up at the sky. The sun was almost at its zenith and he wanted to try and locate Fudail well before it got dark. He did not doubt Nazar'a warnings of what happened when the sun went down.

He turned around and made his way back under the gate and along the parade heading towards the plateau. Turning left down towards the harbour, he negotiated his way back to *The Moon of Karnassus* and stepped through into its dark but cool interior. That proved to be a waste of time. Clearly Fudail's claim to make himself scarce had some substance. There was nothing else for it but to try the hard way. Fudail lived in the new city and he'd said something about the Nook. That was a district to the southwest, so if he made his way there, then as long as Fudail hadn't spun him a complete crock of shit, he ought to be able to get directions off somebody.

His initial optimism was quicky stymied after he had left the Old Karnassus road and struck out down a likely looking street. It was cobbled, wide enough for two carts and bracketed by long terraces of mismatched buildings of varying height and build quality. He continued on, following the street and ignoring any adjoining turns. After five minutes, Forge found a couple of urchins loitering at the corner of a non-descript alleyway. Grubby, with long tousled hair and wearing clothes that were too big for them, he had encountered their sort on a thousand corners in a dozen cities. He dug into his pocket and fished out a couple of copper coins. Forge walked directly towards them and they in turn eyed his approach warily. He squatted down, held the coins out in front of him and said in the trader tongue, 'Want to earn some easy money?'

The two of them looked at each other and then back at Forge. For a moment he thought they had not understood him, but then the one on the right held out a paw.

'You get this is you can tell me if you know where a man that goes by the name of Fahad Fudail lives. You know him? Fahad Fudail. Fah-Had Fu-day-al.'

The two kids shared another look and then the one on the right, a boy, pointed down the alley behind him.

'You go that way,' he said.

Forge looked down the alley, which continued on for a distance before turning right. There appeared to be no dwellings or doorways opening out onto it, perhaps that right turn just emptied out onto another street. As alleyways went he had seen more threatening ones but then either one of these little shits could stab him in the back. He ought to follow his own earlier observations about getting lost.

'You sure?' he said. 'Down there?'

The urchin on the right nodded and held his paw out a little further.

'Fine,' muttered Forge. He conjured a smile and placed a coin in the lad's hand. The urchin next to him, this one a girl, put her hand out. Forge placed the second coin into hers. He stood up and made his way down the alley. When he turned to look back, both urchins had gone. No surprises there. Forge whistled, rolled his shoulders and loosened his sword. He strolled down the alley looking as nonchalant as he could. The right hand turn was not a dead-end but a short switchback that did indeed spill him out onto another street running roughly parallel to the one he had been on. There were plenty of folk about and most did not give him second glance. He turned left, looking at the houses and shopfronts to either side of him. He was not sure what he was supposed to be seeing. He doubted a man like Fudail would advertise his work. A half-mile of walking produced no satisfaction. There was a street hawker selling fruit on the side of the road and Forge stopped to inspect his wares. He picked up a hollow shell containing a number of figs. He looked at the hawker and pointed at the fruit.

'How much?' he asked.

The hawker raised two fingers.

Without arguing Forge picked out two more coins and handed them over.

'You know a man called Fudail?' Forge asked.

The hawker tilted his head and narrowed his eyes.

'I know a few Fudails,' he replied.

'This one's called Fahad Fudail. Local guy.'

The hawker nodded.

'I know him. Just go down the street a little way. The road forks. Go left.'

'Much obliged,' said Forge. He raised a fig in salute and set off. The fig proved to be tough, chewy and without flavour. The road did indeed fork though the left hand route was smaller and less well travelled. He passed a small tavern where three men sat on a bench, feet spread wide, laughing at a private joke. Forge could not help but notice each one of them had purple-painted faces and hair that was spiked with some kind of thick, green gloop. As he came level with them he also got a glimpse of a mouth full of teeth that had been filed down to points. His eyes met the owner of the teeth and the man flashed a grim-looking smile. The other two did the same. Forge turned his head and increased his pace. That they were gangers was obvious, but he didn't want trouble. He carried on down the road, feeling their eyes on his back. Another time and another place, he might have considered staring them down. But not today. He kept his thoughts on the task at hand, looking left and right, hoping for some clue as to his Fudail's whereabouts. The quality of building was going downhill fast: ramshackle turning to shithole was the best description he could come up with. In fact, after only another fifty yards, the way turned into a dead end. A set of warehouse doors faced him, chained and padlocked.

Perfect.

He turned around and started back the way he had come. Approaching him were the three gangers. They were sauntering along, laughing and joking. One pointed at Forge, said something he couldn't hear and the others brayed even louder. The big question now was whether he rose to to this. He was trying to keep a low profile. *Hells, maybe they think I'm just a dumb foreigner who took a wrong turn.* But he was far too old to believe that bullshit. He slowed down a little, giving him a chance to size up the gangers. They in turn slowed down and took positions across the road, blocking his path. There was nothing special about any of them, the facepaint serving to hide any distinguishing features. They did not have any obvious weapons about them either. Their confidence was coming from their numbers. They stood, cocksure and easy, watching him, all pointed teeth and amused expressions.

'Help you with anything?' he asked.

He got silence back. Looking at these grinning, evil faces was a little disconcerting.

'You fellas know a guy called Fudail? I heard he was from around here.' Forge tried a friendly smile.

The one on the right pointed at Forge's belt.

'What? Oh, you want my money.' Forge placed his hand firmly and deliberately onto his sword grip and planted his right foot a little forwards of his left. 'Not going to happen, gents.'

The three painted faces smiled a little wider. They pulled knives from behind their backs and started to spread out. Forge didn't wait. He charged forwards, smashing into the middle ganger, knocking him to the ground. He turned and threw a haymaker at the nearest ganger to his left. His fist connected with a cheekbone and the ganger's head whipped round. Pain exploded in Forge's knuckle. He turned quickly, raising his left forearm high and blocking the downward stab from the third gang member. Forge jabbed with his right fist at the man's exposed throat and he staggered back, his knife dropping from his hand as he fought for breath.

A heavy weight slammed into Forge's back and he staggered forward. An arm wrapped round his neck and started to squeeze. The middle ganger was back on his feet and coming at Forge with a fang-filled snarl. As he closed Forge kicked out and connected with the ganger's stomach. The ganger doubled-over. The weight behind him shifted and a hand gripped his head and pulled it back. Teeth closed on his exposed shoulder, tearing into his flesh. Forge felt an explosion of pain.

'Fucker!' he shouted.

Growling in agony, he tried to reach behind him to get a hold of the ganger but he couldn't get a grip. He started to swing round, hoping the momentum would shake the bastard off. Forge glimpsed the other two gathering their wits. He was running out of time. He backed up and propelled himself and his passenger towards the nearest wall. As he connected his heard a grunt from the ganger. He took two steps forward then forced himself back against the wall again. Another grunt and the pressure about his neck lessened. He reached up, took a hold of the ganger's arms and leaned forward, hauling the ganger over his head and flipping him onto his back. Forge realised that he was no longer alone in the fight. Someone else was engaging the two other gangers but he had his own to deal with. The ganger on the ground before him was groaning, and his mouth and teeth were covered in blood. Forge's blood.

'Bastard!' growled Forge with an odd grace and sense of detachment. He aimed a kick at the ganger's head. His boot connected with the side of the ganger's temple. Forge changed his stance and followed it up with a stamp that smeared the ganger's nose over his face. Two more stamps and the ganger was done.

Forge finally drew his sword. One ganger, the middle one, was on the ground. The ground around his head was stained red. The third was facing off against a far bigger opponent. It was Fudail. The ganger held his knife straight-armed, trying to keep Fudail away from him. Fudail just stepped forward grabbed the wrist of the knife arm with one hand and drove his fist into stomach of the ganger. He then grabbed the gangers head and brought it forcibly down to meet his raised knee with a loud, satisfying crunch. The ganger dropped. Forge looked back up the lane, no one else was coming and no one appeared to watching. He sheathed his sword. 'Nice timing,' said Forge.

Fudail turned to look at him. 'You are a fool.'

'If you hadn't just saved my ass, I might be offended,' replied Forge.

Fudail shook his head. 'You came looking for me. I told you I was not interested.' He leaned over and picked up a knife. 'You should go.' He stepped over to the ganger he had been fighting, crouched before him and slide the blade into the ganger's neck.

'I wanted to try and talk you round,' said Forge. He watched as Fudail did the same to the second ganger. Fudail stood up and walked past him.

'I said no.' Fudail finished off the third ganger and left the blade next to the body. 'You bring nothing but trouble. Is this not evidence enough?'

'This wasn't my fault. They started it.'

'And they almost finished it. You do not know this city. You blunder about, asking foolish questions, drawing unwanted attention,' said Fudail.

'That's why I need you to help.'

Fudail shook his head. 'I just have. Now, I suggest you go back to the harbour. Think about what brought you here.'

Forge shrugged. After this encounter, he doubted Fudail

would be swayed. And the man had just saved his life. 'I could use a little help finding my way back.'

Fudail nodded. He turned and led the way back out of the dead end onto the street and past the tavern the three gangers had come from.

'Those guys are going to have friends,' said Forge.

'They have. Eyes will have watched five men enter and two men leave that road. The fact is you are lucky. The Devils have no friends among the other gangs. If you make it back, there is little risk they will come after you. They do not enter the old town – they are not welcome.'

'What about you?' asked Forge. 'They know you.'

'I will be long gone before they will try anything. I leave tomorrow.'

They walked in silence retracing the route back to the highway. Fudail halted some way before the street they were on emptied out into the bustle of the main route through the city. 'Do not leave the main highway. There is no protection for you beyond it.'

'Thanks,' said Forge. 'I'm going to be at the '*Moon* at midday tomorrow. If you change your mind.'

Fudail shook his head. 'I will not.' Forge watched him go and shook his head. *That was a fucking waste of time.* He looked at his right hand and winced as he flexed it. The knuckles were red, the skin grazed. He cricked his neck. It was starting to stiffen up and he knew there'd be some bruising. 'Fucking Karnak Karnassus,' he muttered.

Chapter 11

Forge entered the *Moon Over Karnassus* for the third time in as many days. The place, unsurprisingly, was almost empty. A woman with shoulder length red hair loitered at the bar, she looked familiar and he recalled her hanging around from his first meeting with Fudail. It could be she had a regular gig here keeping the residents happy. He nodded to the owner and went to the same chair he had occupied yesterday.

'You want two?' the man called over. Forge was practically a regular.

'Yeah, why not.' He settled down to wait.

The owner left two tankards on the table and scooped up the coins Forge had already dug out. Forge took a sip and made a face. Yep, same shit as before. He'd closed his eyes and sighed. His body ached and his right hand was swollen. They older he got, the longer it was taking for aches and pains to go away, so he'd suffer for the next couple of days.

The deep, sonorous peel of the noonday bell pierced his fragile sense of calm. This was it, time to call Fudail's bluff. Once the bell had stopped tolling, he looked at the door. It didn't open. He waited a few minutes longer. The door still didn't open. This wasn't going to work. He'd have to try a different tack. Maybe the owner knew of someone like Fudail.

It stood to reason; barkeeps always knew people. He turned to the bar and opened his mouth just as the door behind him creaked on its hinges and a shaft of daylight lanced into the room. A familiar shaped figure blocked the light for a moment then stepped inside. The door remained open as a second figure followed. Once the second one was in, they shut the door but did not move further into the room and Forge could not make out any further detail in the gloom. Forge tracked Fahad Fudail as his came up to the table, drew the second chair out and sat heavily. He looked miserable. Fudail laid his palms on the table like he had done yesterday and sighed heavily. It was only then that the second figure stepped away from the door. As they passed Forge experienced confusion. It was a woman, a curvy redhead wearing a long red dress, crimson against her hair's lighter tone. She smiled broadly at Forge as she swept past him and on to the bar to join the other redhead already there. Sisters? Forge looked back at Fudail, he was watching the pair of them with murder in his eyes.

'Why do I get the feeling you aren't here because you had a crisis of conscience?' Forge asked.

Fudail closed his eyes and took a deep breath. His hands didn't leave the table.

'When I younger, I had an anger about me, a rage, that was useful for the gangs,' he said, his eyes still closed. 'But I learned to control that anger, so that I could channel it and unleash it when needed.'

Forge knew what he meant. He had served with many men who had chosen the military life because it gave them structure and discipline; it was a way for them to control what they had inside and gave them an outlet for their rage.

'I have not felt this level of anger for many years,' continued

Fudail. 'And these two women, these harpies, these demons, they have unmanned me.'

'Oh tish,' said the women who had first been at the bar, her backed turned to them. 'He's being far too dramatic.'

'Quite right,' said the other, wearing the dress. 'We just explained to him that he needed to reassess his life choices.'

'It's important that one takes time to consider the options and weigh up the balances. It's often the case that the right answer is staring you in the face,' said the other, turning from the bar revealing a tray with four tankards on it. Beneath her cloak she wore a set of tight brown leathers. They didn't leave much to the imagination.

'Quite right, sister,' said the one wearing the dress. 'The proper application of motivation, encouragement and a certain level of mystery and doubt can do wonders for the decision-making process.

Forge didn't even know what that meant. Fudail opened his eyes and there was a look of desperation in them.

'You see? They talk like that all the time!' said Fudail, raising his hands and lifting them in supplication.

The woman in the leathers picked up the tray and walked over to them, taking the chair nearest the bar, to Forge's left.

'We'll join you,' she announced with a beaming smile, placing the tray on the table and putting tankards down in front of them all.

'Don't get up,' said the woman in the dress, as she walked behind Forge and took the chair to his right, her back to the entrance. 'I always prefer sitting with my back to the door,' she said conspiratorially. 'That way they don't know what I'm going to do to them'

'Whereas I prefer to see my targets as soon as they appear,' said the other one.

Fudail had gone quiet and was scowling, his eye darting between the two.

Forge did the same, making a quick assessment of the pair. They were twins, that much was obvious: red hair, green eyes and freckled, pale skin. The one in leathers was lean and muscular, whilst the one in the dress tended towards the buxom and her cheeks were rosy. They spoke with a delicate, lilting brogue. That put them from somewhere off the western coast of Cauker - one of the Isles.

'I take it,' said Forge, 'that you had a conversation with master Fudail, here?'

The one in leathers took her tankard and saluted Forge with it. 'That we did, did we not, sister dear?'

The one in the dress lifted her tankard and copied her sister. 'That we did, sister. It's OK, Forge, you don't have to thank us.'

Good. He wouldn't.

'You know my name. I don't know yours,' he said.

'True enough,' said the one in the leathers. 'My name is Taislin, this is my sister Taimsin.'

'And, lucky you, we have been commissioned to support you in this exciting endeavour that the four of us are all part of,' said Taimsin.

'We have been waiting for you for a couple of weeks and let me tell you, I have been getting quite antsy,' said Tailsin.

'Trust me, you have no idea how difficult she gets,' added Taimsin.

'I just don't like inactivity,' sniffed her sister. 'I lose my edge so quickly. It needs constant honing.'

'And that's why I chose the better profession. I'll be tip-top for years.'

'Not if you keep at those cakes you like.'

'I haven't eaten any of those for days!' cried Taimsin.

Forge rapidly felt he was losing his grip on this situation.

'Ladies, can we stick to the matter at hand?' he asked.

'Very well. We received a letter with a small advance fee saying we were to make haste to Karnak Karnassus, there to await the arrival of the *Crimson Shore* and liaise with a Captain Jon Forge, late of the Ashkent military,' said Tailsin.

'*Captain* Forge,' said Fudail, with a shake of his head.

'Fortunately we were quite close, just up in Achet having recently finished a contract. We got a couple of horses and had a lovely little trip down the coast,' added Taimsin.

'And those bandits were a boon, I had some nervous energy to let off,' said Tailsin. 'We were also made aware of a local contact who would give us the lowdown,' she pointed at Fudail. 'We didn't know who he was, so we waited for you to make contact with him.'

'Why didn't you meet me first?' asked Forge.

'Oh, no. That's bad policy. You have to know who you are dealing with before you meet them,' said Taimsin.

'Quite right, sister dear. We followed you, Forge, and then when we saw how poorly master Fudail reacted, we decided it was best to intercede.'

'What was that like?' he asked.

'Ever tried to punch a shadow?' asked Fudail.

'Never saw the point,' said Forge, drily.

'That's what it was like. I was packed and ready to go and the next thing I know, there was a knock on the door and she was stood there,' he said looking at Tailsin.

'We did try to reason with him,' she said.

'Oh, and that one, I didn't even see her get in. When they wouldn't take no for an answer, I tried to force my way out. Every time I tried to get her out of the way, she wasn't there.'

Tailsin was grinning. 'He was trying so hard, the look on his face.'

'Then she,' he was pointing at Taimsin, 'she stepped up right behind me, said a word and everything goes black. I wake up five minutes later with my hands tied behind my back and the pair of them are helping themselves to my larder.'

'You had some lovely grapes, really sweet and juicy,' said Taimsin.

'Anyway, once everyone had settled down, we had a chance to clear the air and have a nice chat,' said Tailsin.

'They convinced me that I should stay,' said Fudail. 'I was compelled.'

I bet you were. Forge had already seen and heard enough to know that Fudail had never stood a chance against these two, as big as he was.

'You two probably have a name you go by,' he said.

'That we do. We are known as The Sisters,' said Taimsin.

'What it lacks in originality it makes up for in accuracy,' said Tailsin, brightly.

'That it does,' agreed Taimsin.

'I haven't heard of you before,' said Forge.

'That's the point,' said Tailsin. 'Though we were known by that name, albeit informally, in the Pits of Coin.'

The Pits. Forge knew of the place though he had never been there. They were the arenas where youngsters taken from across the Jedah and beyond were trained to become fighters in a variety of martial arts, often including magic. It was rare that those from the Pits ever left the Oligarchy.

'We don't want just anyone knowing about us,' said Taimsin. 'I mean, we are pretty conspicuous as it goes. Especially down in these parts, and of course, my sister here didn't help any.'

'What, we tidied up after ourselves, didn't we?' said Tailsin, her face indignant.

'You had some trouble?' asked Forge.

'Nothing we couldn't handle,' said Tailsin.

Speaking of which. 'You two do specialist work, I get that. And the man I'm working for would have picked you because you are very, very good at what you do. You are going to need to be. Based on what I've already heard, I'm thinking assassin and mage. How am I doing?'

Tailsin slapped her hand on the table and hooted.

'He has our measure, sister dear.'

'At least we aren't working with an idiot. Which makes a refreshing change,' agreed Taimsin.

Forge felt that remained to be seen. Just agreeing to do this job wasn't the smartest of decisions. 'And you know who we are going after,' he stated.

'The Paternal,' said Taislin.

'Quite the target. Though breaking him out is not our usual sort of work,' added Taimsin.

'Are you sure you wouldn't rather we just killed him? It would be a hell of a lot easier,' said Tailsin.

'Hush, sister. This is a challenge, a true test of our skills. Just think about what it would do for our reputation.'

'I'm thinking more about what it will do for our purses. And our longevity.'

'You had much chance to scout the place out?' inquired Forge.

'A bit, we've kept ourselves to the harbour mostly,' said Taimsin.

'We wanted to wait for you before did anything too serious. It's your party after all,' remarked Tailsin.

Great.

'So, what's the plan?' asked Taimsin.

Good fucking question. 'I've been up to the palace, had a quick look. Place looks tight. But I've got next to no intelligence.'

'You've got us now, though,' said Tailsin.

Yeah, quite the crew. 'Let me sum it up for you all. We need to break out the Paternal, the most heavily guarded man in Karnak Karnassus, and we need to get him back to Ashkent alive. I have no idea how we are going to do that, but as of now we need to start building a picture. I need to know everything there is to know about the Palace: the routine, the safeguards, who guards the Paternal, who guards the guards, and what nasty little secret surprises are hidden around the Palace that not even the guards know about. I need to know who the main players are, where power lies, where we can apply leverage. I need to know who calls the shots and who is likely to coordinate any response when we initiate action. We treat this like a military operation, we assess strengths and weaknesses and we come up with a battle plan. But right now, more than anything, I need to know who the enemy is. I need to understand how they think. That way we can put together a strategy to wrong foot them.'

Tailsin clapped gleefully. 'Oh, this is exciting. We've never done planned a campaign before.'

Forge eyed her, he was seriously starting to doubt the woman's sanity, 'Fudail? '

'Hmmm?'

'Believe me, I get that you are here under duress. But I need to know you have your head in the game for this one. I need to know I can trust you to get job done.'

Fudail smile was rueful. 'I hardly have much of a choice.

You have a phrase, "between a rock and a hard place." I think that fits nicely.' His face turned grave. 'What do you need?'

'Let's start with the basics. Draw up a list of names, say what they do, where they live and we'll convene and discuss how we can use that. I also want some kind of floor plan for the Paternal's Palace and as much information as you can get regarding its security arrangements.'

'I'll see what I can do.'

'Good. Sisters? I want to get a picture of what's going on in the city right now. Are there any big delegations here or due in? Is the Paternal likely to be busy and is his Palace going to be full of strangers? Can you also have a look into what kind of surveillance we can set up on the Palace, bearing in mind there must be countless other countries that have tried something similar.'

Taimsin nodded. 'That we can do, we have plenty of ways of gaining information.'

'Very subtle, we are,' said Tailsin.

'Right.' Forge scratched his beard. 'We need a place to meet. Somewhere we can talk where we won't be bothered. We'll need a place to lay out drawings, maps and the like.'

'What about here?' said Fudail. 'We could hire a room out.'

'Won't the owner get suspicious?' said Forge. 'We aren't his normal clientele.'

'Don't worry about that,' said Taimsin. 'I can make it so he has no reason to complain.'

'I won't ask,' said Forge. 'Do we need to worry about any snitches or watchers around here, Fudail?'

Fudail shrugged. 'No more than is usual. Not much happens in this part of the city, it's just an overspill from the harbour. As long as you don't give anyone cause to notice you twice, we should be fine.'

'And I can keep an eye out for anyone acting shifty,' said Tailsin. She stopped and screwed her face up in concentration. It made her nose twitch, which Forge thought made her look quite cute. Then he quickly reminded himself, she was probably an insane killer. *Never trust the pretty ones.* She nodded. 'I just thought, we need to watch ourselves too. We normally operate as just two, doubling that means doubling the chances of getting spotted.'

To be fair, she was right. 'There's no reason to rush this, we can take our time,' said Forge. 'What?' he asked in response to a gentle cough given by Fudail.

'We have less time than you think. The current Paternal took his place during the festival of Rostos, the God of the Summer winds.'

'Let me guess, there has been four festivals already and this will be his last?' said Forge. It never rained but it pissed it down.

'Yes. The Festival of Rostos will begin in four weeks. The passing of the Paternal and the selection of his replacement is the highlight.'

'That explains why he wants go now,' said Forge. The Paternal's time was up, no more kingly living for him. No more any living for him. Forge looked at his tankard, it was empty. He hadn't even noticed he'd been drinking from it.

'We have four weeks to come up with a plan to spring the Paternal and get him out of the city without getting ourselves sliced into tiny pieces.' In a way it was good to have a deadline to work to. It helped focus the mind. 'Sisters, you get us a room sorted. We'll meet here at midday every day from hereon in. From what I can see, the city gets quieter when the sun is at its highest. We'll share information and decide our next moves. I am no expert in espionage but it makes sense that most of our work will get done in the wee small hours.'

'Always the best time,' agreed Tailsin.

'I'll sort that room out and get us all another drink,' said Taimsin, getting up.

'Not for me,' said Fudail. 'I might as well get started. It'll take me a little time to scare up some plans for the Palace. As you can imagine, just asking for them tends to raise the interest of the Ministry of Relations. There's never an innocent reason for wanting them.'

'Fair enough,' replied Forge. 'One more thing. I want you to find out where they buried Major Dav Jenkins.'

Fudail raised an eyebrow. 'Who's he?'

'He was the military attaché to the Ashkent embassy. He died here a couple of months ago. He was the man who the Paternal made contact with. I want to know how he died.'

'You reckon they were on to him?' asked Fudail.

'Probably. But that's not why I'm asking.'

'Oh?'

'He was my friend. I want to say goodbye.'

'Didn't mark you as the sentimental type,' said Fudail.

'We all got our problems,' said Forge.

'I'll look into it,' said Fudail then he turned and made for the door. Forge watched him leave, wondering if he would see him again. He felt a pat on his arm. It was Tailsin, she looked at him with something resembling concern.

'Don't worry. I'll keep an eye on him, make sure he stays on the straight and narrow.'

'Do I look worried?'

'Yep, your face is a picture. I know what you are thinking, will he go to the authorities and try and cut a deal in exchange for his own skin? He tries that I'll slice him a new arsehole and shove his own cock up it.' She said it with such a look of sincerity Forge had no doubt she would do exactly that - not a pretty image.

'All sorted!' said Taimsin brightly, she returned with three more tankards. She looked at the pair of them. 'What did I miss?'

'Your sister was just reassuring me that Fudail will stay on the straight and narrow,' replied Forge, reaching for a drink.

'Ah, yes. She has a way with words, doesn't she?'

Chapter 12

Calill left his room in the barracks to the rear of the Palace and exited from the postern gate. He handed over his round bronze marker to the guard in the gatehouse who placed it on the rack, a series of small metal hooks that went through the hole in the centre of the markers. There were another dozen markers already hanging on the rack. Once done the guard signalled to his colleague by the gate who raised the bar to the gate and swung it open.

Calill nodded to the guard in the booth and raised his hand to the man by the gate. Both men had their faces covered by their helmet masks but after a while you could tell who was who just by their shape and the way they held themselves.

'Thanks, Fizal. You off shift soon?'

'That I am. But it's straight to bed for me. I lost too much money to Siloh and Kareem last night and then I drank the rest of what I had left to forget it. When will I ever learn?'

Calill laughed. 'Fizal, I have known you for ten years. Every time you get paid, you tell me that finally your luck will change with the dice.'

'And in ten years I have consistently proved you wrong?'

'Yes! But you are consistent, my friend. That is a noble

quality.'

'I'd rather I was lucky. Have a good day.'

Calill passed through the gate, no larger than a normal doorway but twice as thick and reinforced by iron bands and shielding spells, and stepped into the dead-end street that ran parallel to the Palace. He passed the larger gatehouse that served as the entrance for goods, supplies and deputations that would rather not be seen. The gate was a set of large doors the same design as the postern, but flanked by two towers with arrow slits and wooden hoardings. Right now, they were both open. Two wagons were parked just before them and a guard was inspecting the contents of the wagons while another was examining a manifest. Nothing was allowed into the Palace without prior arrangement. They would not even have gotten this far without having been checked by the guards stationed at the turning off the Street of Artists. When he reached that post, he did not stop to chat to the men on duty. They was not allowed to fraternise in public. There was an image to maintain. Stepping onto the Street of Artists he turned east and made for the Parade of the Paternals. Away from the Palace he started to relax. Dressed in a simple robe with a brown leather belt and black leather satchel over one shoulder, he looked like any other citizen of Karnak Karnassus. He knew that his face and his name would be on somebody's list somewhere, a record for some future use by a third party. Almost all the Paternal Guard had been logged and marked by other agencies and groups, the little good it would do them. The Ministry of Relations would stamp out any attempt at subversion before it could gain traction. They also knew they could rely on the ingrained loyalty of the guards. All of them were local, most had families. The Paternal Guard were proud of their job, even if it was often dull, repetitive and uneventful. They all knew they were playing a small part in keeping Karnak Karranassus safe, they were party to knowledge from across the Jedah Sea and they learned just how dangerous it could be out there. It put things into perspective; the petty gang wars and low-level skullduggery enacted nightly on the streets of the city were a small price to pay. The City Watch might disagree and the Ministry might wish for a quieter life but at least you could set your course by it.

He strolled along the central path of the Parade and passed through the gate into the new city. He stayed on the main street for a short while before turning into the Farmers' District. At one time this had all been pasture but the city had swallowed it up, leaving small parcels of land that were either cultivated or grazed by little herds of cows and goats. Calill liked being here, the smells were different, the houses did not crowd into each other so much and he enjoyed the orchards and gardens that sat behind the buildings. However, these trips were now filled with a deep sadness and a hollowness in his soul. Calill had never felt sorrow or loss, he had never realised the sensation could be profound. He went to sleep with it in his mind and each morning it was his first thought. When was it supposed to end? He couldn't even talk to anyone about it - they would think him crazy or a fool at best. The worst could lead to something far more final. The far side of the district changed in character, a sombre mood prevailing even as the buildings fell away and the land opened out. It was here that growth and the renewal of life made way to the quiet remembrance of those lost and the resting place of the dead. He had arrived at the great cemeteries of Karnak Karnassus. Three square miles of land given over to the departed citizens of the city. It was not one single mass, rather many graveyards of varying sizes, shapes and importance. Large dividing walls kept paupers from princes, where the wealthy families maintained their own holdings and built mausoleums to house their kin. It was similar to how the city itself was divided. Many plots were old, overgrown, poorly tended and full to the brim with ornate and arcane gravestones, statues and markers. Others were full of tidy, well-tended rows of graves, each with small identical triangles of rock, upon which the names of the deceased were inscribed but little else. These were the most recent, municipal burial grounds, providing a service to the humbler citizens who could not afford a grander plot or a lasting legacy. It was the only way to maintain order amongst an ever growing population, either that or start burning bodies. That wouldn't go down well. Wood was expensive, simple linen shrouds were not.

The municipal plots were divided by district but only in as much as where the dead fell was where they ended up being buried. The city and its distinctive past-times that so many lost their lives to meant that many folk wound up in plots that had no bearing on where they lived or spent their days. He located the cemetery for the harbour, it was one of the oldest and largest, a concession to the history of the city, bordered by a high marble-faced wall with a wide gate made of wrought iron bars. A marble frieze above the heads of those that walked through was a tableau of the ancient god of the sea, a huge squid-like creature called Pleistelles, carrying the souls of dead sea-farers in its tentacles down, down into the depths. If you stopped to look, the dead had different emotions in their faces: shock, terror, laughter and serenity. It all depended on your point of view.

Calill had never thought much about death but now spent a

great deal of time wondering what it must feel like in the last moments. He wondered what he would feel, what he would think. He wondered what his love had felt when the waters had closed about him, even as the poison robbed him of his breath. Calill should have been there, he should have never let him die alone. But he had been forbidden. He'd had to let his love go, had to let him be found by some rogue who had beaten him senseless.

Calill had never been concerned about blood or violence. It was part of the job, the training yard was painted with his own and that of his colleagues, you had to learn to take it and give it. Yet he knew, right to his bones, he knew that he could not have watched his love die. So instead they said their farewells in a dingy, squalid room in a tavern that neither had ever had cause to use before. Then it was over.

It wasn't until a week later that he had overheard a conversation within the Ministry, just a normal, routine scrutiny of deaths and mysterious happenings in a city where the mysterious was considered routine and normal. Just a few sentences covering the discovery of a diplomat in the harbour, his death unusual, a murder definitely faked. It was flagged for the attention of the Minister but not considered to be of specific importance. For Calill, his world fell apart. It was a blessing his face was hidden behind his mask. Up to that point he had been living in hope, that perhaps it had never happened, that his love had changed his mind and found another way. In that first week Calill had daydreamed about a time, years from now, when a familiar face would appear from the crowd and together, without fear of discovery or punishment, they could make their escape from the city and go somewhere, anywhere. In the space of a moment that dream was crushed. He was still a member of the Paternal

Guard, an important and special role, and it defined who he was just as it had done for many years since he had taken the oath at the age of sixteen. But it wasn't *just* who he was, it didn't *just* define him anymore. He had changed, he had learned much about himself and who he was. You couldn't just deny that or turn away from it. He had tried, had made a real effort but it had made him feel even more miserable.

He walked along a path made of interlocking pieces of stone that were well worn and had weeds poking out from the gaps. On either side, palm trees provided shade and life; small brightly coloured birds flitted between the fronds making chirruping noises. To either side, graves stretched out in orderly lines. There were few people sharing the cemetery and of those, they were all ahead of him, where the newly dead were buried. Back here, nearest the entrance, where the first bodies had been placed, there was no one who cared about them, their families now generations and lifetimes removed from their ancestors. He passed by an old woman, carrying a small basket of handpicked flowers. Up ahead, a man was sweeping the path, the dust and dirt flying into the air and drifting away to settle on the nearest graves. He was almost at the point where he would turn right and walk along the rows to his destination as had become routine for him. It was why he almost did not notice that the space in front of the grave he had come to see was already occupied. He felt himself jump, and his heart skip a beat. He stopped, just off the main path and just stood there, examining the visitor. It was a man, on one knee, his left arm resting on upon it, his right hand clutching the pommel of the sheathed sword that sat against his hip. Questions tumbled through his head. Who was he? Was he Minsitry? Had they connected Calill? Was it too late to get away? Calill stepped back onto the main path and stood behind a palm tree to give at least a little cover. His breath quickened a little. He looked left and right, there was no movement, nobody was breaking cover to arrest him. What should he do? *Just act natural, you fool.* He stepped out from behind the tree and made his way down the path between the rows. Coming level with the row he wanted, he turned left and made his way along it, passing behind the man and continuing on for three more gravestones. He stopped and kneeled in front of it, the name of the man buried there a stranger to him. He placed a hand on the level top of the inverted triangle and bowed his head. After a few moments he tilted it to one side and risked a sideways glance at the man.

He was not a local, that much was obvious, his skin was weathered and browned but it was definitely a lighter shade, from somewhere north or west of here. Perhaps he was from the embassy, sent to check the grave. His hair was tied back in a short ponytail, flecked with grey, as was his beard. He looked muscular, there wasn't much running to fat he could see. He looked like someone who could fight, and it wasn't just the sword. When the man stood up, Calill could tell by his bearing that he could handle himself. Calill looked away as the man turned towards him. He tensed a little, waiting for a shout, a word or some kind of movement. When it didn't come, Calill risked another look. The man was gone, moving back up the rows to the main path. He closed his eyes and breathed out slowly. He allowed another minute before he stood up and walked back along the row. He slowed as he reached the grave of his love. He looked down on it for a moment, reading the words upon the stone:

Major Dav Jenkins. Ashkent.

It wasn't much. Next to nothing really, but it was all that was left. *I am sorry, I will visit for longer next time.* Calill returned to the path. A short way ahead the man had reached the entrance and disappeared from view. Calill was tempted to follow him but thought better of it. Nothing good ever came of following anyone in Karnak Karnassus. He might as well just walk back to the Palace and then try and get some sleep. He was on the early shift and had to be awake at an hour too early for any civilised man.

As Calill left the cemetery and turned towards the plateau, a figure stepped onto the path from behind a palm tree. The man strode out of the entrance and also turned west, keeping a respectful distance from the Paternal Guardsman.

Chapter 13

Forge placed his hands on his hips and surveyed the map that was pinned against the wall. It was a reasonably accurate rendition of the city Fudail had assured him. He had purchased it from a mapmaker in the artisan district, a shop of good repute. The maker had assured him that even the Ministry would purchase his work from time to time. Forge was happy to hear that, if it were true. At least he would be working with both the same detail and facts as the Ministry, though he could never hope to best them in local knowledge. This was their battlefield, their territory, and that gave them a massive tactical advantage over anything he was planning. He leaned in closer and inspected the area of the harbour. Forge liked maps. With a map there were always options and possibilities. With a map he could plan, make decisions and then act.

He located the main street leading up to the plateau and tried to follow his route to the Paternal's Palace. The streets appeared to mirror his route. He then backtracked, placed his finger on the map where the gatehouse was marked and moved it along to the cemetery where Dav was lain to rest. He thought he'd covered most of the city but if this thing was to scale, there was plenty more he had yet to see.

'Dav, what have you gotten me into?' he said quietly.

'You talking to yourself again, old man?' asked Tailsin as she sailed into the room.

'Less of the old, I'm in my prime,' replied Forge.

'Prime what?' asked Taimsin, following her sister in.

'He's saying he's past his prime, sister dear,' responded Tailsin before Forge could get a word in edgeways.

'Oh, well, that happens when you get to a certain age in your professions,' said Taimsin, pulling up a chair.

'Pfft,' replied Tailsin, and flopped onto the single bed, her back against the wooden rafters that ran down from the apex of the ceiling. They were on the topmost floor of *The Moon Over Karnassus,* a de facto attic that had been converted into another bedroom, but one that actually had a fair bit of space. With the bed pushed to one side they also had a table and four chairs and the far wall for Forge to put up what should be the first of many maps, drawings and sketches. He had yet to ask what Taimsin had done to the owner but the man barely noticed him when he had walked in on the first day and taken the stairs up.

'I was just thinking, I have to cover more ground,' he said.

'Why?' asked Tailsin.

'I want to know as much as I can about the terrain we are fighting on,' he replied. 'I've studied these maps, but now I need to see it all for real.'

'That will take time,' said Taimsin. 'Isn't this where local knowledge comes in... ' She stopped and cocked her head. 'And talk of a devil.'

Fudail opened the door and walked straight to the table, taking a seat and placing his hands in front of him, palms down. Forge had worked this particular mannerism out.

'Problem?' Forge asked.

'I have been trying to secure floor plans for the Paternal's Palace. It has proven difficult.'

Tailsin had pulled a knife from somewhere and started picking at a nail. 'Why can't you just ask someone?'

Fudail kept his gaze fixed on Forge. He wasn't going to forgive or forget the sisters anytime soon by the looks of it.

'Those who work in the Palace are trusted to keep its secrets. Those who have cause to visit the palace would surely baulk at such a request and likely report it.'

'I get that. What about the commercial concerns? The merchant cartels? They can't be so high-minded or worried about politics,' asked Forge.

'That is what I am thinking. Trying to contact an embassy or official delegation is already off the table, you have made that clear. There are no public records of the Palace, as you would expect, and no architectural businesses have any legacy drawings. That leaves us with less salubrious avenues to pursue. We would have to be careful about whom we approached and we would get fragments at best, never a complete picture.'

'Are you telling me that no one has been putting together a map of the place already? Surely somebody wants something like that in their back pocket?' mused Tailsin, still picking.

'I imagine the Ministry would have found them out?' responded Taimsin.

'They would bury that information deep,' confirmed Fudail. 'It is not just the Paternal himself who is protected, it is all the secrets and records that are held within his residence. That said, I am sure we could access some useful information, for the right price.'

And therein lays our first problem. Forge tapped the map

and took a seat opposite Fudail. 'We haven't got much to negotiate with. I have no cash to offer. So where's the incentive for anyone to tell us anything? You know, the more I think about it, we need more than just floor plans. We need eyes on the ground. One of us – that is, me – needs to get familiar with the terrain. Looking at plans is one thing but seeing a place for real shows you what plans can't - people, objects, walls where there aren't supposed to be. If it's tricky getting floorplans, then can you arrange it for me to get inside the Palace on official business? We can't afford to piss about on this one.'

Fudail reached up and ran a hand over his pate. 'Not an embassy mission. It would have to be something more mundane, something that would not draw attention to your nationality. I have some favours to call in. I know of one particular man who might deal with us. He is a member of one of the merchant cartels and I know he has been to treat with the Paternal many times. We have a small window of opportunity, but it may be worth a shot.'

'What will it cost us? Does he need anyone to... disappear?' asked Taimsin.

'It shouldn't come to that,' said Fudail.

'But it might do,' said Tailsin. 'Why not just offer our services? We can spend a week doing some cleaning up, that's bound to score us the information we need from a grateful scumbag. Everyone wins.'

'I'd rather we kept a low profile,' said Forge. The more they got involved with this city, the better the chances the authorities might take an interest.

'I agree,' said Fudail. 'Let me see if I can arrange a meeting with my man, give me a couple of days.'

'I can do that,' said Forge. 'Even with the visit, I still need to have a bloody great picture of the Palace stuck on the walls.'

Fudail shrugged. 'No easy answers.'

Forge debated whether he could tap Nazar for cash, maybe he had a secret stash somewhere on his boat, maybe he even banked here.

'Look, we are under some time pressure here, so can I propose another option?' said Taimsin.

'I agree, sister dear,' agreed Tailsin. 'Why don't we just grab a low level functionary from the Palace, I don't know, a servant or a guard, we can beat them senseless for information and then get rid.'

'I was thinking something less bloody, sister. I could manipulate details from them and then make them forget it ever happened. They go on their way and we have what we need.'

Forge had to admit, they made a strong argument.

'Fudail, why can't we just do that? It would save all the pussy-footing around,' he offered.

'A servant goes missing, that's a red flag for the Ministry. I am sure in any other place it would not be cause for concern, but here it's different. As for sorcery, I have no experience of how it works.'

Taimsin waved her hand and wiggled her fingers.

'It's all in the wrists.'

Forge raised an eyebrow.

'I hear tell they have some pretty powerful magic in operation up at the Palace,' he said.

'I've no doubt,' replied Taimsin, her face becoming serious. 'I have picked up on some of it on my travels. The thing you have to remember is that magic comes in different forms. Some of it is subtle, some of it all big and pretty damned obvious. We'll be mostly up against the former and the problem is the best sorcery is the kind you can't see, can't detect. Sometimes it's the simplest piece of magic, the smallest manipulation which will catch you out. If I was in charge of keeping a place safe, it would be through stealth and misdirection.'

'Damn, that was kind of the way I was hoping to do this,' muttered Forge.

'Don't worry, Forge, that's why you have us. We happen to be masters of stealth and misdirection,' assured Taimsin.

'And extreme violence, when that doesn't work,' added Tailsin.

Chapter 14

'Good evening, Forge, I trust all is going well?' asked Nazar, emerging from his cabin. Candlelight spilled onto the deck, a dirty orange glow against the wood.

'It could be worse,' said Forge, as he stepped aboard the *Crimson Shore*. There was no one else about, the crew were nowhere to be seen. Which meant either Nazar had relented and agreed to undertake watch duties or they had left the ship while was asleep in his cabin. With Nazar, Forge had learned that either option was possible.

'Then, by that deduction, things could be better,' said Nazar. He leaned against the tiller and proffered a bottle.

'Thanks.' Forge took the bottle and had three healthy gulps. The red wine it held was thick and sweet; they seemed to prefer it that way in these parts. He didn't hand it back to Nazar.

'Rough day?' asked Nazar, eyeing the bottle. 'Speaking of which, how many days do we have left?'

Forge had told Nazar that the window of opportunity was short and non-negotiable. He had also decided to be as upfront and honest with the merchant as possible. The man and his crew were as much in the shit as he was and as far as

Forge was concerned he had an obligation to them. You start keeping secrets from the men in your command and they start to lose trust and faith in you. It was a something he had always believed in, and that was probably part of the reason he had never been promoted. The higher you go, the more you have to hold back. That never sat well with him. He would rather he left this world with his conscience clear. You had to say this about Jon Forge, he was an honest bloody idiot.

'Let me see, the festival starts in three weeks. On the final day of Rostos, the Paternal is renewed,' said Nazar, answering his own question. 'That has always made me smile. *Renewed.* Try telling that to the poor bastard who is getting replaced.'

'Never wanted to live like a king? I thought you were all about that, Nazar.' Forge took another swig and passed the bottle back.

'You know enough about me to know that was once true, my friend. I have adjusted my position greatly since then. I've learned to enjoy the life I have, rather than the one I so long hankered for. I am getting old now, I know, that is hard to believe looking at my lithe form and exuberant lust for life. It's the little things that matter more: the comfort of my bed, hot food, the freedom of the sea. If I stay true to my course, I can think of no reason why I cannot live out my days aboard the *Crimson Shore* and, if my luck holds, I will die aboard her.'

Not a bad way to go, thought Forge. If that was what made you happy. *And what would make me happy?*

'And what about you, Forge?' asked Nazar, with uncanny coincidence. 'Is there a way you wish to go? Or does your retirement suit you?'

'Some fucking retirement,' said Forge.

'True,' smiled Nazar.

Forge paused for a moment, gathering his thoughts. 'I was glad to leave the Army. I'd had enough of the life, the bullshit. I had had enough of losing my friends. You make decisions, and sometimes those decisions mean that someone is going to die. When I was young I could square it but there comes a point when you question everything, when all you can think about is the mistakes you made, when duty is no longer enough to make you stay the course. I was done, I had to leave.'

'And did that give you peace?'

Forge held his hand out for the bottle and Nazar passed it back.

'Peace? Hells, no. To be honest, at the moment I can't see much of a future beyond the next three weeks.'

He took another long drink, held the bottle back and swished it. It was almost empty. *Oh well.* He finished it off and handed the empty vessel back to Nazar, who accepted it with a wry grin.

'Jon, if I may be so bold. You are a crotchety old bastard, but I can't help but think you enjoy this.'

'Then you are just as crazy as the twins,' Forge replied.

Nazar laughed.

'You might be right.'

Forge decided he'd had enough of the small talk. 'Nazar, I need to get into the Paternal's Palace. Fudail had been asking around, speaking to a man he knows in the Merchant and Traders guild.'

'Oh, a nefarious and corrupt organisation,' declared Nazar.

'Right. Fudail's man was able to tell him if any deputations are going in to the Palace to use the Paternal.'

'Ah, yes. That makes sense. The Guild members have many nationalities in their employ. You could go in as a deputation member without drawing too much attention to yourself.'

'That's the plan. Fudail says that there are two meetings scheduled in the next couple of weeks, two different groups. I wanted to run them by you.'

'Then be my guest.'

'The first one is a shipping conglomerate, The Southern Star. The second is a man called Aashiq Qadir, got his own company.'

Nazar hissed through his teeth and shook his head vehemently.

'The Southern Star are an old established concern, they stay on the level and, in the greater scheme of things, are legitimate in their dealings. It would be hard to convince them to allow a stranger onto their delegation. As for Qadir, he is a bastard.'

'OK. A little more?'

'Oh, there is plenty more,' Nazar almost snarled in a way Forge had not seen before. 'Qadir is a greedy, vain, selfish man. He gives all us honest traders a bad name.'

Honest? 'You had dealings with him?'

'Oh yes, I have had dealings with him. Several, in fact, and every time I did I ended up with less profit than was promised. But what could I do? Sometimes you have to make a deal with the devil to get ahead.'

'Dealing with devils appears to be our only option right now,' said Forge. 'You reckon I could get a meeting with this guy?'

'It all depends. What reason could you give him to grant an audience?'

'I guess threats wouldn't do any good?'

'Not really.' Nazar tapped a finger to his lip and sighed

heavily. 'I know where you will go with this. Yes, I know him well enough to make contact. Now, it appears I have run out of wine, but I...' Nazar looked towards his cabin. 'No, that was my last bottle, damn it. Forge, if I arrange a meeting with this man, you will have to provide a very good reason why he should consider allowing you on to his deputation. He is no fool. Anything you suggest must appeal to the worst aspects of his nature.'

'Money, profit, gain?'

'Yes, any or all of those will do.'

'Great, I have all of those in abundance. Nazar, Qadir is going into the Palace in six days. How soon could you get us in to talk to him?'

'If he is in the city, then we can go tomorrow. I know where his offices are. The mention of my name is sure to spark at least a mild interest in him.'

'Then we'll go tomorrow morning.'

'But not too early, eh? I doubt he would arrive until the sun is well on its way. Oh, Forge...' Nazar gazed into the heavens. 'I had such high hopes for this trip when I docked in Dunbar over the winter. Now look what luck has thrown me.'

'Tell me about it. I had my year all planned out. Fancy a drink? I'm buying.'

'I think I would,' said Nazar sadly. His brow furrowed as he inspected the deck. 'Where is everyone? Who is meant to be on watch?'

Forge shrugged.

'Thought it was you.'

Nazar placed a palm against his forehead.

'Have you ever seen such a mutinous crew than the one I am cursed to sail with? I turn my back for one moment and they abscond!'

'Knowing that lot, I think we'll find them at the nearest tavern,' Forge offered. 'We can always send one of them back.'

'Yes, yes. They are a faithful bunch of hounds. They never travel far from their kennel. Come along then, Forge. You may buy me a drink and perhaps between the two of us, we can concoct as story that the devious Aashiq Qadir will be so entranced by that he not only offers you a place on his party, but he also offers to pay me all the profits that he so cruelly denied me over the years.'

Chapter 15

The offices of Aashiq Qadir were located at the far eastern end of the harbour. They fronted onto the street overlooking the water and stood out amidst their less wealthy neighbours, many of which were just warehouses and storage buildings. The front of Qadir Trading was an immaculately constructed, well-maintained marble structure that was more in keeping with those found on top of the plateau. There was a small, pillared entranceway, several large glass windows on two levels, and running along the length of the roof was a brightly painted frieze depicting scenes of a pastoral life involving agriculture, dancing and the liberal imbibing of alcohol. A jolly and clearly hammered god wearing nothing but a wreath of flowers looked on benevolently as revelers danced, frolicked and fucked around him. However, as one passed through the portal into the double height atrium beyond, it became clear that the marble was just a façade and that the rest of the building was a wood-framed warehouse. The floor and walls were a well-polished hardwood, shipped in from the west, and a staircase climbed its way up to a balcony that sat above the far wall, overlooking the entrance. A surly-looking man kept station at the foot of the stairs and eyed Forge and

Nazar with equal measures of distrust and disdain. He did not look like a local, but his skin was still deeply tanned, Forge would guess he was from further north, perhaps the Oligarchy. A studded club hung off his belt and Forge could detect the familiar bulge of a knife behind the man's black leather waistcoat. In front of them was a waist-high counter that ran the width of the atrium. A leather-bound ledger resting in the centre of the countertop was the only adornment. A door behind the desk opened up and a man wearing a white robe, a large silver chain and a yellow skullcap emerged. Behind the man, Forge could just make out what looked like an office, with several other men bent over desks, one of whom was flicking the beads of an abacus.

'Gentlemen, welcome to the home of Qadir Trading. Do you have an appointment?' asked the man, a clerk by the looks of him, an ingratiating smile on his face. Forge noted the cuffs of his white robe were stained with ink.

'We have no appointment but my name is Nazar Ghali, also known as Nazar the Lucky. I and my associate were hoping to have a short meeting with your employer.'

'I can certainly look to give you an opportunity in a couple of weeks, if you could just explain to me the nature of your enquiry?'

'No, I am sorry that won't do. We are very keen to see Master Qadir today.'

The clerks' face fell and radiated disappointment.

'Oh, I am sorry. That will not do. Master Qadir is very busy.'

Nazar stepped forward and placed a hand on the counter and leaned across.

'Oh dear, that is very disappointing. You see, Master Qadir and I are very old friends and I am only in Karnak for such a short time. I wanted to share with him a very exciting proposition.'

Forge hung back and kept an eye on the muscle by the stairs. The man was stood a little more alert, a hand on his belt, resting next to the club.

The clerk shook his head.

'That is most regrettable. Master Qadir cannot possibly see anyone today. He simply cannot be disturbed.'

'Mmm. Well, I cannot deny I am deeply saddened. Master Qadir and I have had many successful dealings in the past and it is a matter of some personal affront that I am not afforded the chance to speak to an old colleague. Especially one who understands that to truly get ahead in the world often rests upon a moment of decision. He would, I am sure, be very grateful to you for showing foresight in this matter.' Nazar removed his hand and tapped a finger on the countertop. A gold coin lay where his palm had rested.

The clerk looked at the coin, then looked at Nazar. He tilted his head and flicked his gaze towards the guard. Forge watched the man shrug.

The clerk's arm shot out and the coin disappeared.

'I cannot promise you anything,' he made a show of inspecting the ledger. 'Master Qadir is a very busy man.'

Forge noted that the ledger was turned to a completely blank page.

'I'm sure he is,' replied Nazar evenly. 'Shall we wait there?' He indicted a padded bench against the right hand wall.

'Yes, if you want. I will go and inform Master Qadir he has visitors.'

'Very good,' said Nazar. He turned to look at Forge. 'Let's sit.'

Forge followed Nazar to the couch and sat on the right hand

side, his swordbelt hanging free over the edge. Nazar leaned back against the wall and closed his eyes, a slight smile on his face. The clerk walked up the stairs, then onto the balcony and after a gentle knock on the door, into the room beyond.

'You had better get comfortable,' advised Nazar.

'We expecting a wait?' asked Forge.

'I imagine so.'

'Right.'

Forge stood back up and leaned against the wall, side on, facing the stairwell. The guard copied his move, resting casually against the stair banister. A few moments later the clerk reappeared and made his way down the stairs.

'Master Qadir has been informed of your presence. If you would please wait, he will attend to you when his schedule allows,' said the clerk with a straight face and a false smile. He continued on back behind the counter and into the office beyond.

As they waited, there were two more visitors to the building. One passed straight through and into the office beyond while a second was met by a different clerk, and after a short discussion, the visitor turned around and left the building. The new clerk glanced their way, betraying no emotion and returned to the office. Forge estimated they had been waiting for half an hour. He knew what was going on, this Qadir was just fucking with them, trying to establish his dominance. That was fine. Forge knew how to be patient. He was also happy with anything that gave Qadir a reason to see them. He was under no illusion that they had to get Qadir onside, there was no other option on the table. Nor was he sure that Qadir would buy the story. He didn't.

'Nazar! You old seadog!'

A booming voice echoed down from the balcony. Forge

looked up at a man wearing a red robe beaming down at them.

'Aashiq,' responded Nazar, standing up.

'Well, well, this is quite a surprise,' said Qadir, coming down the stairs. 'I haven't seen you since...I can't remember! How long has it been?' he asked. The guard stood a little straighter as Qadir reached the bottom of the steps and strode over, arms wide and embraced Nazar.

'I'd say, ten,' said Nazar, extricating himself.

'Ten? No, no, you haven't aged a bit.'

'Neither have you, but then you were always old before your time,' replied Nazar.

'Ah, what can I do? I spend every day worrying.'

'About what? Look at you, still going strong, better than ever.'

'I try. I do the best I can. Now come along upstairs. Oh, my apologies, how rude of me. Who is this rugged-looking gentleman?' Qadir fixed him with a ready smile and appraising eyes. Qadir was a well-built man, with rather too much weight around the belly to be healthy. He sported a thick mane of hair that was swept back and oiled into ringlets, his face was broad, his nose hooked and framed by a full beard. Gold earrings hung from both ears and a thick gold chain was wrapped several times around his neck. The whole picture was of a man who wasn't afraid to put himself or his success forward.

'This is Master Jon Forge, from a long way west of here. You could call him my silent partner,' replied Nazar.

'It is a pleasure to meet you, Master Forge,' said Qadir, inclining his head in greeting.

'Likewise,' said Forge, trying to sound like he meant it.

Qadir looked back to Nazar and switched to the local

language, a fast stream of words that Forge could not follow. Nazar burst into laughter and clapped Forge on the back.

'Come, come,' said Qadir, beckoning them forward as he led the way up the staircase. 'Are you still in that ship of yours, Nazar? What was it called?'

'The *Crimson Shore*. Yes, still sailing her. She's done me proud.'

'Ah, that is good. It's important to hold on to the past, it reminds us where we come from, it keeps us honest,' said Qadir, earnestly.

They reached the balcony and followed Qadir into his office. Draped from the walls were thickly woven carpets bearing abstract designs of swirling curves and circles bordered with blocky angular shapes. Beneath their feet was another carpet and above their heads was a series of thin, light-blue linen sheets that hung in a random, wavelike fashion, hiding the wooden ceiling above. Qadir's desk was made of the same dark wood as the rest of the interior, with fluted, curving legs and ornately carved edges on the top. His chair was leatherbound and highbacked, carved of the dark wood and stylistically made as a companion to the table. The two chairs opposite him were simpler in design but packed with cushions.

'Please, sit,' Qadir urged, gently.

As Forge and Nazar arranged themselves amongst the cushions, Qadir fussed over a tray set to one side of his table that held a delicate glass decanter, pouring out a light green liquid into small, cut-glass beakers. He handed one to both of them and taking another, settled himself down in his own chair across from them. There was a period of silence as Nazar sipped from his glass and made a point of savouring the taste. Forge noticed Qadir doing the same so figured he'd better follow suit. He eyed his glass suspiciously, raised it to his mouth and let a small amount play over his lips and onto his tongue. A cool, bittersweet sensation registered, the taste was familiar.

'Mint tea, cool and refreshing,' said Qadir, watching Forge with a smile.

Forge made an appreciative face and downed the rest in one gulp.

Qadir frowned, his eyes narrowing, a dangerous glint to them, then it was gone and the glint returned to a sparkle.

'Master Forge has quite a thirst on him,' he said.

'Oh, you have no idea, my friend. And he has yet to learn many of the important customs and etiquettes that proper business requires,' responded Nazar, his tone apologetic.

'Then let us forgive him, just this once!' said Qadir.

'You are very kind, I take that as a personal favour, as is your consenting to meet with us today at such short notice,' replied Nazar, gravely.

'It is the least I could do,' said Qadir, spreading his arms wide. 'When such a man as Nazar the Lucky comes calling, there is always a good reason and that...' he tapped the side of his nose with a finger, 'usually means profit, yes?'

Nazar placed his beaker on the table, placed his elbows on the armrest and steepled his hands, closing his fingers and resting his chin upon them.

'Let's say, for now, that there is an opportunity that has presented itself. By chance to me but by design for you.'

Qadir leaned forward, copying Nazar's pose. 'Go on,' he said.

'Master Forge here requested passage on my ship so for a small fee I was willing to oblige. As we shared the travails of our journey east, we were able to make a bond of trust and understanding. He felt he was able to share with me the details of his journey. He represents a powerful group of individuals who wish to bring about a change in their fortunes. And that group are looking for allies.'

Qadir raised a hand. 'I am already intrigued, Nazar. Please allow me to fill your glass.' He stood and poured more tea. This time Forge left his beaker on the tabletop. He noticed that Nazar did the same. Qadir settled back into his chair clutching his tea and nodded for Nazar to continue.

'This group of individuals were on the wrong side of an...aggressive disagreement a few years ago. Since then they have been bidding their time. Rebuilding fortunes and influence, gathering resources and support. Yet they cannot hope to act alone. They need to get some serious backing before they can make a move.'

Qadir's eyebrow rose as he sipped his tea. 'Do I know this group?'

'Possibly. Do you remember the civil war in Graves?'

'Ah, yes indeed. There was some kind of coup attempt? Shifter was involved.'

'That's the one. It went badly for them after Ashkent got involved.'

'Bastards,' said Forge.

Nazar and Qadir looked at him in surprise. Nazar appeared annoyed at the interruption. Forge scowled and reached for his tea. Perhaps he should leave the play-acting to Nazar.

'Yes, well. The Regency in Graves was quickly re-established and everything went back to the way it was,' continued Nazar. 'But there were plenty of people left who were not happy with this intervention. The instigators of the coup found they had a core of new support. Folk of both low and high birth who sheltered them after the hostilities ended and the authorities looked to round them up. Instead of crushing the uprising for good, Ashkent simply fermented a stronger, deeper resistance.'

'Ah, I have long believed that interference can only ever lead to bad feeling. How often, Nazar, have you and I both fallen foul of yet another ill-advised trade agreement, tax or embargo? I have sympathy with you, Master Forge,' said Qadir.

Forge couldn't give a shit what Qadir thought of him but he continued to listen to the way they spoke to each other, their easy manner, like the friendship of old comrades. Nazar was pulling out the stops to be charming but there was something else. Yes, that was it - Nazar was focused in a way Forge had never seen before. The stories Nazar had told him of his earlier days as an aspiring merchant prince made a lot more sense now. Forge liked Nazar better as the bombastic, salty seadog than the negotiator, he was too good at it and it smacked far too much of politics. But then, Nazar was a child of Karnak Karnassus.

'Master Forge has been sent as an... emissary. I do not believe I speak out of turn when I say he is not exactly the most diplomatic of individuals. But that plays to our advantage. He was sent to find out whether there might be any opportunity, or appetite, for an audacious and gloriously outrageous plan. A plan that, I might say, is so incredible in its vision that at first I took Forge for a madman, a raving lunatic. But he was persistent and forthright and after time I decided that instead of throwing him overboard, he might just have something.'

'What is this something?' Qadir was looking at Forge and Nazar indicated that he should answer.

'My employers want to kidnap the Paternal,' said Forge.

Qadir, to his credit, did not balk, though he almost did spill his tea down his front as the beaker missed his mouth.

'Um. Ah. I see,' he responded. He was quiet for a moment, his eyes closed, his face a mask of neutrality. 'Nazar, I am struggling to see what possible advantage could be gained from such a thing. Could you please tell me?'

Nazar didn't miss a beat.

'Qadir, I see in you the same reaction that I had once our friend here announced his intentions. It is nothing short of madness. But, as they say, necessity is the mother of invention. Forge's employers are absolutely serious about this. They believe by taking control of the Paternal they have the ultimate bargaining chip, all of that knowledge just waiting to be exploited. The Paternal has been party to the discussions and negotiations of every important state, political group, trading concern and religious disagreement for the last five years. If anyone knows what conniving, devious and dirty dealings these groups are up to, it is the Paternal. Information, Aashiq, information!' Nazar made a fist and slapped it down onto the open palm of his other hand.

Qadir stroked his chin. 'I can see how that might prove useful. But, what has happened in the past is in the past. This is Karnak Karnassus, Nazar. People only care about what might be possible, what they can gain, in the days and weeks to come.'

Nazar leaned forward and pointed a finger at Qadir. 'Then why is it that the Paternal is replaced every five years? A man stores up so much knowledge, he can start to put together the fragments and see larger pictures, grander schemes A man who knows this much might start to believe they can manipulate things to their favour, start to work the system.'

'This much we all know, Nazar,' said Qadir, reclining back

into his chair with a shrug.

'And having a man like that, in the hands of a group that does not have a vested interest in maintaining the balance, provides an interesting challenge to all of us. It is fear, you see, fear that maybe, just maybe, he will say something, something that one side cannot afford to be said. What would be the price that someone would be willing to pay to ensure that information is kept secret?'

'You are implying that Graves wants to hold the whole region to ransom. What is then to stop everyone else descending on them from all sides?' asked Qadir. Forge was not at all surprised by his reaction. He would have been worried if it had not been so.

Nazar nodded in agreement.

'That is possible, but I doubt it would get that far. You miss the obvious, my friend. Who has the most to lose by the Paternal's disappearance? Let me tell you. It is Karnak Karnassus itself. If the city cannot be trusted to protect the secrets that the world chooses to bring to it, then what is its point? It becomes what it once was. A very attractive piece of land, which confers a strategic and commercial advantage to whoever owns it. Can you see the Families ever allowing that to happen, a hundred years of peace ended? If, by some sheer, insane chance, the Paternal was taken or escaped, do you think the Families would even admit to it? Not on your life. They'd bury the information, they'd hide the truth, they would play for time and try and get him back, or hope that the man never surfaced again or shared his information.' Nazar reached across and picked up his tea. 'The Families of Karnak Karnassus would deny to their last breath that the Paternal was lost and that anyone who claimed they had him was lying. Let's face it. Anyone smart enough to get the

Paternal in the first place would not make a song and dance about it. And as for the Families, they have deep enough pockets.' He looked across at Forge.

'If such a scheme were in play, I'd say that would be about the size of it,' Forge replied.

Qadir drummed his fingertips on the ends of his chair's armrests. 'This is quite possibly the maddest scheme I have ever heard and believe me I've heard a few in my years. None of which have paid off. More importantly, you have put me in a difficult position. Just being party to this conversation would ensure a long stay in the cells of the Ministry. I see no reason why I should continue to indulge you, Nazar. This is madness, even for you. This is wrong, whatever way you try and square it. Ah...' he shook his head, a look of frustration on his face and started to talk in the local lingo again. Forge glanced at Nazar, things didn't seem to be going well. The merchant raised a hand, the message clear: *just wait.*

'Qadir, please. We are all friends here and I trust your discretion, as you should mine. I have no wish to rot in a cell and you know that I have built a reputation based on integrity and good sense. Well, mainly.'

Qadir smiled at that comment.

'They do not call you "The Lucky" for nothing eh, Nazar?'

'I'm still sailing.'

'And yet here you are. Which tells me that you see an opportunity to change your fate. Tell me, Nazar, for the sake of our long and dear friendship, what could I ever hope to gain from such an enterprise?'

This was it. Even Forge could tell that they had reached the tipping point. For all his bluster, Qadir was interested.

'What would a man do if he suddenly found himself with the gratitude of an entire country? Why I imagine that gratitude might even go so far as to offer sole trading rights to that man. And if that man had a fleet of ships that he could use to move merchandise? Have you ever heard of such a thing? One man controlling all the flow, no doubt sub-contracting to help cope with the demand. I think a man like that would be wealthy beyond all our dreams. Of course, for such a situation to work, you'd have to give that country a little time to settle down, especially if it had been through a period of upheaval and change. Then it would be crying out for a predictable and trusted partner.'

'And why wouldn't you want to be that man?' asked Qadir.

'Because I do not have the resources or the reach. I tried that game once. And I am also one step closer to the conspiracy than you. My reward is significantly smaller, a sum of money that ensures me and my crew are comfortable for life. That is as far as my ambitions go these days. All I want is just one deal, one that means I can stop worrying about my future. This life takes most of us long before we have a chance to enjoy the fruits of our labours. I don't want that to happen to me,' said Nazar emphatically.

Qadir was watching him closely, his eyes trying to bore into Nazar's soul. Forge knew that every lie should have an element of truth. Nazar probably did want to enjoy the fruit of his labours, and he wasn't going to do that with McKracken ghosting him.

'You are telling me is that Graves is willing to offer me a complete monopoly on trade with them in return for services rendered.'

'Yes.'

'Then I should ask the question that you have yet to provide an answer to. What service would I have to provide that would guarantee such an outcome without immediately

159

implicating me in the plot?'

'You provide us with the one thing we cannot hope to achieve ourselves. Access to the Paternal's Palace.'

'Nazar, you wound me deeply, I thought you had chosen me above all others for our long friendship. Instead you have discovered that I am having an audience with the Paternal in two days.' Qadir made a clicking sound behind his teeth and shook his head. 'You are a cold man, Nazar, to use me so. Let me reason this through. You plan to liberate the Paternal from underneath the noses of his keepers just days before he is due to be replaced at the end of Rostos. For you to achieve that you need a means of scouting the Palace and also to contact the Paternal to let him know that an attempt will be made. I can provide the first by taking along who? Master Forge here? And you will try and get a message to him? Because believe me, I will not spend my time with him trying to pass a message or doing anything to incriminate myself and lead to my association with the plot.'

My association. Those words told Forge everything he needed to know – this bastard was actually considering it. Now to go in for the kill.

'I don't want you to pass any messages. I just need to get in the Palace. It was the Paternal who reached out to us. He knew the risk he was taking and I'm damn sure he won't try it again. When it happens, he'll go with it, what are his options? He's a dead man walking anyway.'

Qadir stroked his moustache. 'Just get you in?'

'Just get me in. I'll take a look around, and then I'm out and your job is done.'

'It sounds simple.'

'I wish the rest of it was,' admitted Forge. 'I wouldn't mind a look at the Paternal himself if that's possible.'

'It may be,' said Qadir. He put his head back, inhaled and exhaled loudly through his nose, then stared at Nazar.

'I do this one thing and, if you actually pull this off, I get the monopoly on all goods shipments from Karnak to Graves.'

'Yes. That is what you get,' said Nazar.

'And if you are caught. You will sing like the birds that cluster around an oasis and you'll drag me down with you.'

'We won't get caught,' said Forge. 'I have no intention of becoming a prisoner. If it comes to that, I'll take the poison I carry. Here,' he thrust his finger into his mouth and placed it on one of his back teeth.

Qadir craned his neck a little, trying unsuccessfully to see into the mouth. 'Serious business. Do you have one too, Nazar?'

'I do not. I might be in bed with Forge and his people but don't for a minute think I share his mission. I'm in it for the money, just like you. When this thing happens, if they are not back precisely by the time we have agreed, I am running up my sails and you'll never see me again.'

'Very wise, Nazar. And you, Master Forge, do you have other associates? Presumably you do not expect to pull this off by yourself?'

'I have a crew. But you won't get to meet them,' said Forge.

'Good, I have no desire to. Keep them away.' Qadir stood and walked around his desk and opened the door. 'Forge, you will be a new addition to my guards. It is not uncommon to see mixed races attending a delegation. Be back here one hour after dawn in two days' time. I have a dispute with two odious individuals called the Manseer brothers. I have spent the best part of two years starting up a new trade route with a settlement way out East. Now that I finally have willing suppliers and a means to safely transport my goods, the

Manseers say I have no legal right to stop others from exploiting my market. Needless to say your offer of guaranteed monopoly is dear to my heart right now. I will get you in, the Gods of all foolish endeavours help me, and then I will await the outcome of this folly.'

Forge and Nazar shared a look and stood up at the same time. Nazar led the way out of the office and they were halfway down the stairs when Qadir called down. 'Nazar. If anything goes wrong, there is nowhere in all the seas, charted and unknown, that I won't find you.'

Nazar was silent for a moment.

'Qadir, if it goes that wrong, I'll likely be dead.'

Without waiting for a response, Nazar turned and led them out. Forge gave the guard a look as he passed by and the guard looked back. As pissing contests went, it was short and unexciting, but the man wasn't likely to back down from a fight. Qadir could afford competence, at least.

'That went as well as could be expected,' said Nazar brightly, as they walked along the harbour front.

'We got what we came for. But I don't trust the guy one bit,' agreed Forge. 'You were right about him. I gotta say, I was impressed with your patter. Ice cool.'

'It comes with the territory, Forge. But you, that move with the tooth was inspired!' Nazar clapped gleefully. 'You don't actually have one, do you?' he asked, performing a similar neck contortion to Qadir's minutes earlier.

'Thanks and no, I don't. I have heard stories of agents who carry them.'

'The kind of agents who go on suicidal missions to break out very powerful people from heavily guarded palaces?' Nazar asked. He had a point.

Chapter 16

Forge and Nazar arrived back at Qadir's offices a short time after dawn. The meeting at the Palace was not due for another couple of hours but it was considered good form to arrive early. Qadir assured them that it was it was well worth it as visitors were treated as royalty and lavished with excellent food and wine. It was likely a clever ploy to get everyone in a pleasant frame of mind before negotiations. In which case, he approved. Forge wasn't sure he was in any mood to indulge. He was making a covert insertion into the heart of enemy territory and there was no easy way to get out if he got made. He had, in the past, forgotten his natural sense of self-preservation but right now it was at the forefront of his mind. He was out on a limb, trusting someone he had no inclination to trust and with no one he could rely on for back-up. It was, all things considered, shit.

'Good morning, my friends, good morning. It is a fine one is it not?' declared Qadir as he walked-down the stairs to greet them. He was wearing a fine red robe tied with a purple sash, his hair was freshly oiled and he had at least double the jewellery scattered about his person. He also smelled like a high class whorehouse.

'Good morning to you,' replied Nazar. 'I trust everything is in order?'

'As much as it can be,' said Qadir, as the door to the back offices opened and three clerks filed out, Forge recognised the one who had greeted them the day before. All of them wore clean, white robes and no ink stains on show. They carried a variety of ledgers, scrolls and books. 'As you can see, we have prepared our arguments and have documentary evidence to back them up. Of course, the Manseer's will have the same,' he leaned in conspiratorially. 'And you just know he would have had his people up all night fabricating them.'

'And you had yours working 'til when?' asked Nazar.

Qadir barked out a laugh.

'Hah, I had them all finished the day you came to visit!'

'You always did have the gift of thinking ahead, my friend,' acknowledged Nazar.

'It keeps me alive and successful,' observed Qadir. 'Now, Master Forge, are you ready to play your part?'

Forge nodded. 'The way I see it, I just keep my eyes open and my mouth shut. Should be easy.'

'Yes, it should. Three of my men will be joining us too. I think that four bodyguards should be enough, any more would be showing off and draw far too much attention to what is just a simple trade dispute.'

The same guard from the previous visit stepped through the door behind them and nodded at Qadir. He was no longer carrying the club. Instead he had a shortsword belted across his waist and a baldric of knives across his front.

'All is ready. Master Forge, just follow my man Goker's lead.' He indicated the guard. 'When we enter the Palace, I will not talk to you other than in the most perfunctory of ways. Please do not take offence. You will also have to divest yourself of your weapons, even the hidden ones. The Paternal Guard can get quite agitated by armed strangers prowling the corridors. When we are done, we will return here and then you'll be on your way. I trust at that point we will not see each other again?' he raised an eyebrow at Nazar.

'That is the plan,' said Forge.

'Very good.' said Qadir.

And no plan survives contact with the enemy. Forge decided he had better not mention that to Qadir.

The merchant adopted a sombre face, bowed his head slightly and went for the exit.

Nazar turned to Forge, smiled gamely and let out a deep sigh.

'Well, then. Good luck to you. Don't get caught snooping somewhere you shouldn't. It'll only end badly and we'll all die a terrible death,' he said.

'I'll try not to,' replied Forge. He slapped Nazar on the shoulder and followed the clerks out the door.

Outside he stopped and looked with a fair degree of surprise at the sight of a grand-looking litter. It was covered in white canvas and the woodwork frame was painted gold. Four bare-chested bearers stood to the rear and another four to the front. Qadir smiled at him as he pulled apart the canvas and stepped inside. There was a command from the lead bearer and, as one unit, they picked the two poles up firstly to the waist and then hoisted onto the shoulder. It was a smooth, well-practised movement. Once they were all settled, another command set them off, the three clerks trailing in its wake.

'We follow behind,' said Goker.

Forge duly did as he was told and brought up the rear as the litter made its stately way along the front and up the hill. Forge didn't envy the bearers one bit as the slope kicked in, though he imagined that after years of the job, their bodies were well used to the effort. He recalled the time when they had deployed up into the Mercy Mountains. By all the Hells that had been a fucking nightmare. They'd had to hump most of their stuff up small trails that weren't fit for mountain goats, let alone wagons. Perfect for Goblins, the little shits. Most of the locals had already fled the attacks but when the troops had made the settlements safe, they came back and started portering. Damn but they could fly up those trails. Life got a little easier after that, except for all the fighting and the deaths.

The crowds were getting busy as they crested the slope and turned west towards the plateau. Slotting into the traffic, the two guards at the front shouted and cajoled a route through pedestrians and found a place between a wagon full of melons and another litter sheathed in thin, red linen. The pace slowed down considerably and Forge took the time to enjoy the walk, grateful for the temporary respite.

'Your boss always travel like this?' he asked of his companion.

Goker didn't answer him immediately.

'My employer is a wealthy man, why would he want to walk when he can make others carry him?'

Forge wasn't sure how to answer that question. It wasn't his place to second guess, every culture did it differently. There weren't many men mounted on horses around him, and those were mostly military. There were plenty of litters of various sizes being humped by teams looking identical to their own, though he spotted one or two who looked to be labouring. Oh to have a thin employer.

As they moved forward, passing the Crucible on their right, Forge thought he could make a decent hired sword. It didn't appear to be a hard job, just lots of waiting, looking mean, and occasionally having to shout at people. Just like the military but less stressful.

Forge firgured it took them a good thirty minutes before they finally arrived at the Paternal's Palace. The sun was high in a sky that was bright and blue with no cloud cover. It had warmed up quickly, and Forge felt another bead of sweat roll down his back. To fit in better with his companions, he had elected not to wear his leather duster or his jacket. Instead he wore an open-necked off-white shirt and his black leather trousers. They were far from comfortable in this heat but he'd be damned if he was going completely native. At least he had his sword and his dagger, and the knife sheathed in his boot, at least for now. As they arrived at the Street of Artists, Forge felt his tension start to build again. The Palace hove into view and the litter stopped in line with the entrance at the top of the steps. There were plenty of folk around both on the street and coming and going from the Palace itself. Any number of them could be Ministry watchers or informants. Forge had to remind himself that he hadn't actually done anything yet. The litter bearers lowered it down to waist height once more and the material parted to reveal Qadir manoeuvring his legs out and onto the ground. Goker stepped forward and offered a steadying hand to Qadir who waved it off with an air of good-natured statesmanship. He adjusted his robe and took a moment to look around, as much to make sure that everyone else had taken note of his arrival.

He turned to Goker and looked at Forge. 'You two will escort me inside,' he pronounced, imperiously, then turned to the guards at the front. 'You two will remain with the litter.' With that he swept up the stairs, the rest of them in his wake. Forge fell in next to Goker and passed under the shadowed portico, immediately feeling the change in temperature, and on into the Palace.

The party entered a short hallway framed on either side by a procession of marble pillars of the same design as the ones holding up the portico. At the end stood a man wearing a yellow robe flanked by two guards. Behind them was a large table with a polished, black top. The man, clearly aged yet smooth skinned, bowed deeply as Qadir draw up before him.

'Master Qadir, you are expected and you are welcome. The other party has yet to arrive so I would like to invite you and your staff to take their ease while you await them.' The man indicated a corridor leading off to the right.

'Thank you, that will be acceptable,' replied Qadir.

'Good. If your men would remove their weaponry?' he indicated a table behind the two guards. 'They will be returned when you are ready to leave.'

Qadir nodded, raised a hand and pointed at the table. At that signal Goker walked around the guards, undid his belt and his baldric and placed it onto the table. Forge followed suit but was tempted to keep his boot knife, just to see if he could get away with it. However, a quick look at the two guards, who were paying close attention to what he was doing, suggested it wasn't worth the hassle. Forge took a moment to size up these guards. He had passed by the two on station at the entrance far too quickly to get a good look. Compared to what he had seen from the rest of the city, these guys looked like the real deal. Not that he could see past those facemasks but their bearing suggested they knew their business, and the smith in him could instantly see the quality of the amour they wore. The spearpoints looked sharp and the swords worn against their sides looked solid enough. Fudail had given him a little detail on the Paternal Guard and had assured him that they were a well-trained force. If so, Forge didn't want to get into a fight with them on their home territory.

Goker stepped back and returned to his position. Forge hung back just a moment longer, allowing him to see another yellow-robed man approaching from the left hand corridor.

As Forge took post, the first yellow-robed man gave Qadir a smarmy, toothy grin, bowed once more and started off down the corridor. The second had arrived at that point and was collecting the pile of sharp and dangerous weapons on the table.

They were taken halfway along the corridor and up a flight of stairs to the second level. At the top, they proceeded down another corridor heading deeper into the Palace, which continued on for some distance and was punctuated by small skylights in the ceiling spaced out every ten yards or so. The holes were less than a foot wide, certainly not big enough for a grown man to enter by, but big enough that the light they allowed in flooded the space. The man in the yellow robe halted by a set of doors. He gave them a gentle push and they opened inwards. He bowed deeply and indicated they should enter.

Forge followed the rest of the party into a large room that was full of long couches, comfortable chairs, pillows, cushions, flowing fabrics and other objects of luxury that Forge did not recognise let alone know how to use. There were murals and paintings on the wall, busts and statues in each corner. A long table against the left hand wall was laden with fruit, meat and bread. Opposite the door was an opening with a low, waist height balcony overlooking another, larger room or hall. Qadir walked over to the table, helped himself to a handful of grapes and looked out across the balcony railing. The clerks settled themselves in a corner on a group of couches and started to talk, their voices quiet and conspiratorial. Goker walked across to the low balcony, keeping some distance between himself and his employer. Forge followed him and gazed down onto what was an atrium containing a large, rectangular garden full of trees, flowers and flowing water. Their balcony was situated on one of the longer sides. Above, the atrium had no roof, just open sky. The light funnelling down from above filtered into their room but the ceiling above their heads gave them respite from the heat. A couple of small birds flitted by, one of them making an optimistic dart towards the table, only to be shooed away by Qadir. Forge was a little surprised to see the open ceiling. It seemed to him like the perfect access point which made him immediately suspicious.

'You can't get into the Palace that way,' said Goker, reading his thoughts. 'There are wards all around the edges of the opening and watchtowers have a line of sight to it. No way are you getting near it.'

That was more words than Goker had said to him all day. It was almost like he was initiating a conversation. On the far side of the atrium were a series of three more rooms, identical to theirs. Guessing a similar arrangement on this side, he leaned out a little farther and spied two more balconies to the right of them.

'These for other visiting groups?' he asked.

Goker grunted.

Great. Conversation over.

Forge turned at the sound of the door opening behind them and watched as three men in white robes entered. Each carried a musical instrument: a harp, a drum and a flute. Behind them followed two women. They wore diaphanous veils which did nothing to disguise faces that were young and very pretty. They also wore, no they didn't have enough to warrant that description, they *had*, covering key parts of their anatomies, gold and silver chainmail, linked together with larger metal circlets. They jangled a little as they entered and took up a position in the centre of the room, the three musicians going into a corner by the table. Everyone had stopped what they were doing and were now watching the two dancers take up a pose. The harpist played a cord and then the drums and flute took over, their tune slow and discordant. The women swayed in time to the flute, their limbs moving in waves, their hips moving in wide circles.

Forge glanced across at Qadir who briefly caught his eye and winked. The drumming started to increase in pace and the dancers responded, their movement becoming wilder and more erotic. The metal covering their modesty did a good job of staying in place but, as the women started to jump and twist and writhe, he couldn't help but catch brief glimpses of what was underneath. He now understood why Qadir wanted to get here early. The dance continued on, the music getting louder, the pace more frenetic, the dancers spinning. Then, with a single loud pluck of the harp, it all stopped. The women stilled, heads hanging low, chests quickly rising and falling with the exertion. Forge started to clap then noticed that nobody else was fallowing suit. He lowered his hands and felt a little embarrassed. Goker had a smirk on his face as he walked across to the table and helped himself to a pitcher of water. He then poured Qadir some wine from a fine-looking, jewel encrusted carafe into a silver goblet. The merchant took the drink without thanks and found a couch to settle into. The music struck up again, this time just the harp playing, a slow, gentle melody, and the women started once more, coming closer to Qadir. There was no energy to this dance, just graceful motion. Forge liked it better, it was calming. He

171

didn't need his heart to race any more than it was already.

Forge turned his back on the entertainment and studied the atrium once more. He started to map out in his head what he had seen so far and what their position was relative to the entrance. He'd needed to get as much of it straight in his head as possible. When they came back in here to get the Paternal, and just how they were to accomplish that was still far from being determined, he had to have a solid sense of direction. As soon as he returned to the room in *The Moon Over Karnassus* he had to get this all down on paper. He studied the gardens below, looking for the access to it. Whatever Goker had said, having such a bloody great hole into the Paternal's Palace was too good not to entertain. It took him a while to scan around the edges, and he had to lean out a little to see below. He could not get a clear view of any doorways beneath and he had spotted nothing on the far side or on the left. There was but one door, on the shorter, right-hand side. It was clear of foliage, surrounded by marble flagstones and had paths leading into the centre of the garden and around its edges. There were no guards to be seen but there was every chance they stood on the other side. Or perhaps the door just had one bloody great lock on it and was probably magically sealed to boot. It was a shame there was no way of knowing, having Taimsin on hand might have been useful. Distant raised voices made him look up. The balcony opposite was filling with people, at least a dozen or so.

'Ah, I see our esteemed competitors have finally arrived,' announced Qadir. He joined Forge by the railing and took a long drink of his wine. Two men came up to the far balcony and raised their hands in greetings. Qadir raised his goblet at them and nodded his head. He turned his back on them and walked away. 'The Manseer brothers. Always coming mob-

172

handed. As if that makes any impression on anyone. The Paternal always sees through that nonsense.'

Forge continued to watch the hustle and bustle on the far side. After a few minutes they got their own entertainment and the music drifted across the gardens, merging with their own. In response, the musicians on their side upped the volume, picking, blowing and beating a little harder. The Manseers didn't have long to enjoy the party as the doors opened once more revealing the man in the yellow robe. This time he was flanked by two guards. The music stopped immediately and the two dancers stepped to one side.

'Master Qadir. The Paternal is now awaiting you. If you would follow me to the Chamber,' said Yellow Robe.

'Yes. Let's get this over with,' said Qadir loudly. He marched purposefully out of the room, following the man. The clerks hurried along after him, Goker and Forge stepping into line at the back. One of the two guards closed the door once they had all excited and then joined the other in tailing the group at a discreet distance. Just far enough to give them room to react to any funny business, Forge noted. They carried on down the corridor, passing the two double doorways to the other waiting rooms. They reached a crossroads and carried straight on for what must have been another thirty yards. They then turned left, and after another short corridor they emerged into a large hallway. A doorway on the left was flanked by two more guards. Another corridor continued on opposite theirs. To their right was a row of plush benches built into the wall that was covered in small alcoves, each one holding a small bust. The alcoves climbed all the way to the ceiling, some ten feet above their heads, which had several more of the small skylights built into it.

'If your men will wait here?' said Yellow Robe. He framed

it as a question, but it really wasn't.

'At ease, gentlemen,' Qadir said to Forge and Goker.

'Yes, Master Qadir,' said Goker. He tapped Forge on the arm and pointed at the benches. He deliberately idled as Yellow Robe picked up a striker and sounded a gong hanging from a frame next to the doors. A deep gong echoed around the hall as it vibrated with the impact. The striker was replaced and the doors opened inward. Forge craned his neck to look as Qadir and the others headed in. The Chamber was a covered in what looked dull grey metal: the walls, the ceiling and the floor beneath. Another set of doors on the far side, were opening at the same time to admit the Manseer Brothers, had their backs covered in the stuff. Flaming torches hung from stanchions dotted around the walls to give the room light, though there was no reflection cast by the metal. The Chamber seemed to be completely sealed by it and it was obvious that there was something of magic about it. That would be what kept the place protected. The Chamber's interior continued on somewhere to the right of the doors and Forge could not see much from his vantage point, but it looked like there were two rows of chairs. The Paternal, if he was in there, must be sat further back. Once both groups were inside, the doors were closed once more. It looked like he'd have to wait a while longer before getting a peak at the great man himself. Yellow Robe kept his station by the striker, that smug smile still on his face. Forge turned to find Goker was sat on the bench, his back against the wall, his eyes closed.

'We allowed to get up and walk about?' Forge asked.

'Not from this room. There's food and drink over there,' he raised a hand and pointed vaguely at a small table in the corner. 'And don't try talking to the guards. That'll get you killed where you stand.'

'Thanks for the warning,' said Forge. He sighed heavily, placed his hands on thighs and drummed his fingers. He stood and walked over to the table and poured himself a drink of water, picked up a fig and took a bite. The two guards had not moved from their posts and looked like they were staring straight ahead but the eyes could be following him right now behind those faceplates. They bloody ought to be if they were any good. He wouldn't trust any bastard who came here to negotiate. He inspected the busts. It didn't take him long to realise that several of the faces looked familiar, the Paternals again, and a thought struck him. He had yet to get a description of what the Paternal looked like. He had just figured that it would be obvious when it came to it. Perhaps the current Paternal had a bust or statute already made. Then another thought struck him. *You are a bloody stupid fucker.* He could have just asked somebody. Too late now. He supposed he could ask Goker but he had no confidence he'd get anything like a useful answer.

Forge downed the water, wondering vaguely if they had anywhere he could take a piss and returned to the bench. He settled down and closed his eyes. He held that pose for almost two minutes before the effort of trying to be relaxed got too much. He shuffled down the bench to were the end met a pillar and leaned his shoulder into it. He stretched his legs out, folded his arms and put his head back against the wall. There was a time when he had found waiting easier. It was something you had to do in the military - hurry up and wait. He'd often hear the lads say it was the waiting that was the killer. Actually it was the other bloke with the sword, or the arrow you never saw, or the damn bugs and diseases that wasted your body away before you ever even got a glimpse of your enemy. Yet, he did get their point. As he had grown older, his sense of his own mortality had also grown. There was no such thing as old soldiers. Only because they got too slow, too weak to go toe to toe with a youngster who did not understand death and therefore did not fear it.

Suddenly the door opened and out strode Qadir, his face as much a mask as the two guards either side of him. That was fast. He and Goker stood together as Qadir made straight for the corridor they had entered by, with the clerks and Yellow Robe hot on his tail. As they passed the entrance to the Chamber, Forge risked a glance inside. For the briefest of moments he caught sight of a man wearing a gold robe, a close-cropped black-haired head bowed, contemplating who knows what. And that was it. The two guards moved away from the doors and fell in behind him. They carried on at a pace, almost a march, back the way they had come. Yellow Robe had caught up with Qadir and Forge could see they had a whispered conversation. Yellow Robe gave a curt nod and took post at the head of the procession. They gained the stairs, descended down to the lower level and back along the corridor to the entrance hall. Another pair of guards was coming the other way. As they drew closer, the two guards slowed and stepped to one side, waiting for Qadir's party to go past. As Forge drew level he could swear that the one on the right actually turned his head to watch him go by. Forge waited a few seconds and risked a glance behind his shoulder. *Shit.* One guard was moving off but the other was still at his place by the wall and his helmeted, featureless face was watching them. Forge instinctively went for his sword. *Shit.*

They entered the hallway and Qadir stopped. Forge spotted that Qadir's face had gone from neutral to scowl. Yellow Robe continued on down the far corridor and a few moments later the weapon collector returned with their gear and placed it with reasonable care back onto the table. Without waiting to be told, Goker started to arm himself once more and Forge happily took that cue. As he was buckling his belt, he watched Qadir tap his foot impatiently. Forge was tempted to take his time but swiftly remembered where he was and thought better of it. However, even when they were done Qadir still made no move to leave. They stood about, all looking somewhat sheepish, waiting for who knew what. Forge kept expecting a horde of guards to come charging towards them but happily only two more showed up and relieved the ones that were on station. Another two appeared, heading for the entrance. Clearly it was a change of shift and the two outside entered the hall and passed them by. Finally Yellow Robe returned, went straight to Qadir, bowed low and passed him a piece of folded paper. The merchant opened the paper, scanned it and handed it back to Yellow Robe.

'Come along. Time to leave,' he announced.

It was about bloody time and Forge was very happy to emerge into the dry heat of the day. The party exited the Paternal's Palace down the steps and met the waiting litter. Qadir climbed aboard and they were off, following the same route back. When they had passed by the Crucible, a hand emerged from the litter and made a beckoning motion. One of the clerks jogged up to it and then jogged back to Forge.

'Master Qadir wants to speak to you.'

Forge increased his pace but certainly wasn't going to run.

'Qadir,' he said, once he was level.

'Master Forge,' the litter's fabric parted though Qadir did not bother to lean out. 'The negotiations did not go well. The Paternal ruled that the Manseer Brothers had a legitimate claim and that I must allow them equal access to the market. I am not pleased. But the Paternal has spoken and it would be remiss of me to ignore his ruling. I have done all the work to open up this new trade lane and they get all the benefit! Ah, I have lost a lot of money on this enterprise. Did you get what you needed?'

'I know a little more now than I did before. That guy in the gold robe. He the Paternal?'

'Yes, that is him.'

'Right. How old is he?'

'Hmm, a good question. I think he is perhaps fifty? He was not a young man when he took the office.'

'You going to see him again?'

'No. I have no more business scheduled with him. Now leave me, I need to lick my wounds and decide what I can do to get even with the Manseers.'

The fabric twitched shut, ending his audience. That was fine with Forge. Qadir had held his end of the deal up and little did he know that he had been screwed over twice. Forge almost felt sorry for the man, and he also felt a little guilty. Subterfuge and double dealings weren't his style. That said, Qadir was a bit of a prick and he had messed with Nazir, a man Forge actually liked. All being well, he was sure Qadir would get over it when he realised there was no pay day or exclusive trade rights. Hells, Forge might arrange for McKracken to send some kind of recompense. After all, fair was fair.

Chapter 17

Calill returned to the barracks alongside his fellows, his mind racing. As they gathered in two lines in the square and waited to be counted off, he barely registered when they were all dismissed from their shift. He wandered vaguely over the flagstones trying to decide what to do. He was certain that the man that had entered with that merchant's party was the same one he had spotted stood beside Dav's grave. Yet what did that tell him? In short, nothing. It made no sense. What would someone who looked a like a hired thug want with Dav? How would he know him?

For a moment the thought occurred to him that perhaps he was a jilted lover, a past relationship, come to say goodbye. This was accompanied by a pang of jealousy. No, never. Calill quickly quashed that. That rugged, tough old man was not Dav's type. Besides, Dav had told Calill he had never had a relationship with anyone else before, he had been married to the Army, and Calill believed that. So what else?

'Calill? That you under there?'

'Hmm? What?'

'You still have your helmet on.'

'Oh, right.' He pulled off his headgear and ran a hand

through his hair. He smiled at the speaker. 'Sorry, Ansir, I was miles away. Pretty tired today.'

Ansir, a guard only a little older than Calill, sporting a trimmed beard and a friendly demeanour, smiled. 'Tell me about it. I don't care what they say, switching shifts always takes it out of you. Anyway, I'm for the commissary. You coming?'

'Later. I thought I'd go for a walk first.'

'OK, suit yourself. See you later.'

Calill watched Ansir go towards the kitchens along with most of the others, then made his way back to his block. It was another benefit of being a Paternal Guard, that each man had his own space within the barracks. It was good to have that privacy; he would have gone mad having to share with others. He handed his spear back into the armoury, walked down the corridor of his shifts' block and opened the door to his room. It was sparsely furnished with a bed, a wardrobe and a crude wooden manikin that a guard could use to hang their armour. It wasn't much to show for a life in the Paternal Guard but the pay wasn't bad and there was a good pension. And what did that amount to when all things were considered? What was the point of a life if it was just to survive? For a short time, he had discovered what that was. *Damn it all. This is for Dav.* If he was fast, he might still catch him.

Calill shrugged off the rest of his armour, leaving it where it fell. He grabbed a tunic and trousers threw them over his sweaty undergarments and ran out of the barracks, not even bothering to change his sandals. He ran across the courtyard and lobbed his disc at a startled guard and was out the Postern Gate and jogging down the side street. *Slow down, you fool.* He still had to remember where and who he was. He wished the two guards on duty a good morning and cut left. He angled up the steps to look inside the Palace's entrance. The hall within was empty, as he had expected. The man whose group he had passed was clearly a merchant, so the chances were he would be heading back towards the harbour and he was going to be borne by litter, especially with an entourage in tow. They wouldn't have gotten far. He walked swiftly along the Street of Artists and took the direct route back towards the Crucible. At this time of day traffic was relatively light. He saw several litters ahead of him but as he passed each one, there were no clerks following or the man from the cemetery. He had no idea what the litter looked like and it was entirely possible that the merchant's people would have left him. No, the guards would have stayed and what merchant worth his salt would not want to show off with followers. It occurred to Calill that he had no idea what he would do when he saw this man again. There was no evidence or suggestion of guilt of any kind. But perhaps he might able to find some if he looked hard enough. And then what would he do? He couldn't take this to his commander and he certainly couldn't speak to the Ministry about this without revealing his own relationship. He truly knew nothing but that would not stop the questions. They were very thorough. Whatever he had to do, it would be on him. If this man had any part in Dav's death, it was down to Calill to exact vengeance.

He was not long onto Viceroy Street when he spotted them. A white litter with a gold frame carried by eight bearers, with three clerks and four guards in attendance. He felt his heart ease a little even as he felt a new rush of energy. They were thirty yards ahead so he could afford to slow down and keep a decent space between them. As he predicted, the litter turned off the Parade onto the old Karnak road and took it slow and steady down the winding street. Hitting the harbour road, they turned east, heading for the warehouse and merchant districts.

The litter eventually stopped outside a building bearing the mark of an Aashiq Qadir. Calill had a vague recollection of the name, it would have been read out by the watch commander at the shift handover parade as a matter of course, and it was quite possible the man had visited the Paternal before. Merchants loved coming to see the Paternal, usually to complain. Calill carried on past the building and loitered at the corner of the harbour road and the next lane heading away from the water. The merchant climbed out of the litter and entered the building followed by the clerks and the guards. At a command, the litter was picked up, turned round and taken off back the way they had come. And that was it. There was nothing else left for him to do. He knew where the merchant worked and in likelihood where the man he followed worked. What to do next? There was little else for it but to scout out the building a little more closely. He started up the lane, trying to look as nonchalant as possible. He was very aware that in a city that thrived on subterfuge he probably stuck out like a sore thumb but perhaps that might work in his favour. He was too obvious and therefore not a spy or a thief - at least that's what he told himself.

The frontage of Qadir's offices gave way to a large red brick warehouse that ran back some fifty yards from the road. Another lane turned left and ran along the back of the building and he turned down it. The lateness of the day meant the lane was mostly in shadow though there was just enough light to see by. He considered his next steps. If the man worked for this merchant then he would have to stake out the place, wait for him to leave and follow him to wherever he called home. It was possible that he had lodgings within the warehouse. If so that would make it harder to confront him and, if necessary, subdue him. Calill's training as a Paternal Guard meant he could go toe to toe with any bravo or mercenary in Karnak Karnassus. He was part of the best equipped and trained force within the city, far better than the city guard and, in a straight fight, the agents of the Ministry. Even in hand to hand combat he could hold his own. He was young and his body was honed after hours of combat in the training yard. He was smart and he was also, usually, sensible in his decisions. As long as he could get to the man someone where quiet and alone, he could get the answers he needed, even if he still wasn't sure of all the questions.

The lane behind the building was just wide enough to allow a cart to go by although. Midway along, he could just make out the almost black rectangular outline of what must be a rear entrance. He reached the corner of the lane and stepped out onto another thoroughfare running up along the western edge of the building. The sun was falling below the horizon and in the shadowed gloom of dusk lights were appearing in the harbour. He walked back down the road towards them. Just as he was reaching the junction, a band of men appeared from around the corner. He stepped out of their way, expecting them to be either stevedores or employees from another merchant business. As they passed him by it became obvious they were neither. They were wearing a mix of clothing but hidden underneath tunics and cloaks were leather bracers, padded jerkins, sheathed swords, knifes, clubs and at least one axe. In ones or twos such a sight would not have been unusual down here. Even a half dozen might have suggested they worked for someone local or that they had just come off a ship. But he counted at least a dozen men. There was a confidence and a sense of purpose about the way they walked. He was also sure he recognised a few of them, even in the failing light: Ministry. These were men who did the dirty work, men who were called in to watch persons of interest. They were paid good money to be on call for the Ministry deliver reports, gather assignments and assist in certain direct negotiations. They were men who blended into a crowd, whose faces were unremarkable. To have so many in one place meant somebody was going to have a very bad night.

He hung around, watching them continue on their way, when a large door opened up in Qadir's warehouse about midway along its length. Light spilled out onto the road as the whole party went inside and then the door was shut behind them. Calill felt a surge of excitement. What the hell was going on? Something much bigger was in play and if the Ministry was involved, then it started to give meaning to Dav's death. It also complicated matters. If his love had been involved with anything to do with the Ministry, there was little hope that Calill could do much to avenge him. He could not go to war against his own masters. He jogged back up the road and found a darkened alleyway just a little further along from the doors and on the opposite side of the road. He could hide there and wait for the men to conduct their business. As he stood in the shadows watching the doorway, which was more like a gateway, high and wide enough to take goods deliveries, his mind raced with possibilities. He tried to construct a theory around what he was seeing and what he knew. The one that stuck was that Dav had been involved in some subterfuge with this merchant and that, having met the Paternal, it had become clear to the Ministry that they had had a part in it. They were now looking to clean up and shut down whatever scheme Dav and this Qadir had been undertaking. Calill had a feeling that whatever business was going down tonight, this would be his last chance to get answers. He certainly couldn't go asking questions with the Palace. He had to act now. Maybe he could get inside...

He stepped out from the alleyway and halted as a short sharp whistle came from behind. *Who the?*

'Now, now, lad. Don't do anything stupid like shouting or any shit like that. Just step back into the shadows and you and me can have a quick chat.'

He tensed his body, ready to fight his way out before he was made. He could still get out of this.

'And don't try that either. I have an arrow pointed at your back and at this range I won't miss. Oh and if you try and take me on I'll bust your nose and shove my knife somewhere the sun don't ever shine.'

Chapter 18

'Welcome back. How did it go?' asked Nazar.

'Poorly,' responded Qadir, as he entered the dimly lit hall. Forge followed the clerks inside and went to join Nazar. A couple of candles burned in brackets on the walls and a three pronged candlestick sat to one side of the counter.

'And are you well, my friend?' Nazar asked Forge, soberly.

Forge nodded. 'It went as well as could be expected.'

'I'm glad somebody got something out of this,' said Qadir, sourly watching his clerks were entering the office behind the counter.

'You did not get the ruling then, Qadir?' asked Nazar.

'No, I did not. And I am very unhappy about it. It makes a man lose all faith in our system of arbitration. Now, if you'll excuse me, I need to have a moment with my clerks. After that I will come and talk to you about our agreement. Goker? I'll have a word with you and your men as well. It's late and I want to make sure our security is up to scratch before I dismiss you all.' With that Qadir went into the offices, followed by Goker and the other guards. As the door shut behind them, Nazar turned to Forge and smiled. 'Between you and me, it fills my heart with joy to see him like that. The arrogant rogue deserves some bad luck. From what I understand, he had quite a strong case, but there you go. That's life. Now then, to business. How was it?'

Forge puffed his cheeks and blew. *Good question.* 'I got a sense of the Palace, I now know where the Chamber is. It's a start and I even reckon we could get inside from the front. I still don't know how we'd get to the Paternal, his quarters are further back inside. I don't suppose you know anyone who has any giant eagles or tame dragons handy?'

'Sorry, no. That said, I did know of a local sorcerer who was rumoured to have a flying carpet.'

'Really? That might do it. We'd just need something to anchor a rope ladder to and a good shielding spell to stop the arrows...'

'Um, Forge, are you serious?'

Forge shrugged, he wasn't discounting the idea. Hells, a flying carpet could come in handy. 'I don't know, I just figure at this point we need anything that gives us an edge.'

The door to the office opened again and Qadir stepped out followed by Goker who moved across the hall and took his usual place between the stairs and the entrance. Qadir smiled, his teeth white and his eyes glittering in the candlelight. He held his hands up in an act of apology. 'Forgive me my mood, Nazar. As you can imagine, it has not been the best of days. I find myself out of pocket, having invested a great deal and having to share in the returns. Such is our world, eh, Nazar?'

'Quite so, Aashiq,' said Nazar. 'I hope that the partnership you have with us will provide you with a better outcome.'

'As do I.' Qadir turned and walked back around his counter. 'You know what they say, out of every crisis comes an opportunity. Your presence has not changed what that would be, but it does present me with a chance to at least come out of this with a little...credit?' He opened the door to the clerk's office and a number of armed men bustled in.

'What is this?' blustered Nazar, taking a step back against the wall. Forge knew. His sword was already out.

'Come on!' he grabbed Nazar's arm and pulled him towards the exit. If he kept them busy he could get Nazar out onto the street and away. All he had to do was hold the doorway, fight them one on one and then leg it before they outflanked him on the street. Goker blocked the door, his sword out and levelled at them. Forge made to engage him just as the door opened and the other two guards stepped inside. The outflanking had already happened.

Forge raised his free hand in the air and lowered his blade.

'Wise decision, Master Forge,' called Qadir, as the room continued to fill up with men. 'As I was saying, your visit and subsequent threats to my person, and my staff, left me with no choice but to risk it all and send a brief cry for help. Fortunately the Minister's clerk was on hand and authorised this rescue.'

These were Ministry men? Forge rapidly concluded they were very likely fucked.

'Qadir, how could you?' hissed Nazar.

'How could I? You see? You see how they try and implicate me?'

The man next to him, a swarthy balding man, nodded.

'I see. We'll take them back to Orlaise. He is waiting in a safe house not far from here. We'll get the facts from them,' said the Ministry man.

'You will ensure Orlaise and the Minister know how I and my men cooperated with you?'

'I am sure he'll want to speak to you himself. To thank you in person.'

'I am just glad I was able to get a message to him, as scant and lacking in detail as it was.'

'Qadir, you are a bastard son of a whore. I hope you burn in all the nine Hells for this,' spat Nazar.

'If I do, I will see you there, Nazar,' replied Qadir. 'Your treachery to our city will live in infamy. Please take them away.'

'Time to go,' said the Ministry man, nodding to two of his men. 'Your sword,' he said to Forge.

Forge knew the game was up. Time to go down swinging. 'Like fuck I will!' he roared, raising his blade and charging toward the Ministry man, who took a step back, a look of shock registering on his face. Suddenly there was a flash of bright blinding light and a sound like thunder echoed through the room. Forge was carried forward by his own momentum smashing into his target. The pair of them fell to the floor, arms and legs flailing. Forge had the breath knocked out of him and lost his grip on the pommel. Without trying to find it, he did the next best thing by getting onto his knees and raining blows on the struggling body beneath him. He went for the face, feeling the pain of impact as his left knuckle connected with a cheek bone and then the satisfaction of a nose crumpling underneath his right fist. That would do for now. He rolled off the man and carried on for a couple more turns before hit something hard and unyielding. He got into a crouch and pulled his dagger out.

Sounds of struggle, men swearing, shouts and screams filtered through his ringing ears. Dark shapes flitted past his vision as the afterimage of the light faded away. No one was coming at him yet so he allowed himself a moment to take stock. There was a fight going on, but he had no idea who was fighting who. He felt a hand grasp his arm and pull him up.

He went to stab with his blade before a loud voice cut him short.

'Easy Boss, don't go ruining a perfect rescue.'

The voice was male and sounded familiar, and with nothing sharp being hurled at him, Forge accepted the assistance and took a moment to get steady. His back was still against the wall.

'Hang on,' the voice said, and Forge could make out the swift movements of a bow being drawn followed by a loud 'twang'. A body collapsed not three feet from him. His vision was getting better now and he saw another form engaged in a dance with three others. They swung and hacked at the first one, who just seemed to sway, duck and dodge out of the path of their weapons. Then an arm would shoot out and a body would fall to the ground. He had never seen such grace. If he was a betting man, and he frequently was, that had to be Tailsin.

By the stairs he saw Fudail. With one hand he had a thug pinned to the wall by the throat and was punching him repeatedly in the kidney with his other hand. Finally he looked towards the entrance as one of Qadir's men made a break for it. Another figure, robed and hooded, appeared in the doorway, stuck out hand palm first and Qadir's man flew backwards like he was nothing more than a leaf on the wind, crashing into the wall behind the counter. Three more got to the door to the back office and were through it before anyone could stop them.

'I'm on them,' shouted Tailsin, and she leapt away from the pile of bodies that had surrounded her and was through the door.

'Scream if you need any help, Sister,' called Taimsin as she pulled back her hood and stepped inside with a look of mild distain. 'Always so messy, my sister.'

'Gotta say, love her knife work,' said the familiar voice next to Forge. Recognition dawned and he shook his head.

'Jonas, you son of a bitch,' he said with a laugh, as he turned to look at his rescuer.

'She wasn't that bad, according to dad,' said Corporal Jonas, of the Ashkent 7th Mounted Infantry Regiment. Forge clapped him on the shoulder and looked over his old comrade. He had not aged one bit, lithe and supple, and no doubt still with the ability to drop a man at a hundred yards with a bow. And of course there was the long blond hair and brown, almond eyes that betrayed some elvish blood that ran within his veins, not that he ever cared to admit it or talk about it. He was dressed in baggy green trousers and shirt over which he wore a brown sleeveless leather jerkin. Over one shoulder was a quiver and in his hand his old longbow, worn through years of use yet lovingly maintained. Only Jonas would think he could get away with using a weapon like that in a close-quarters fight.

'You got my message, then?' asked Forge.

'Yeah, I got it. Just got back to the garrison when it arrived, so I didn't bother unpacking.'

'You get permission to come?'

'Like shit I did. Just didn't bother telling the new captain. Guess that means I'm AWOL.'

Forge grinned. By the Gods, it was good to see a familiar face.

'The new captain, huh? I've been gone a while now.'

'He ain't earned his spurs yet,' Jonas said, with a shrug. 'Besides, not many of us old ones left now. You gotta look after your own.'

Forge had been banking on that when he had sent the letter. He knew he needed someone he could trust on this mission.

191

'How's Kyle? Still climbing the career ladder?' he asked. Kyle was one of only a handful of his men who had survived the defence of the River Rooke, all those years ago.

'Kyle? Yeah, some idiot has gone and made him a First Sergeant, if you can believe that shit. He's running a training company in Ashkent City.'

'Good for him. You wearing any more stripes yet?'

Jonas snorted. 'Like that's ever gonna happen. Besides, I'm happy where I am.'

'Sorry I had to get you into this. You might lose your job over it.'

'They can shove it if they want. But they won't because I'm still the best damn scout they got.'

Forge gave Jonas another squeeze on the shoulder then turned back to the carnage behind him. There'd be time to catch up properly later. Fudail stood watching them with his hands against his hips and a sour look on his face. Taimsin was wondering amongst the bodies, giving the occasional one a prod with her foot.

'Thanks for weighing in,' Forge said to them both.

Fudail shrugged. 'Thank her. I just got dragged in for the ride.'

'Oh, no need to thank us,' said Taimsin, as she knelt down and rooted through the pockets of a dead Ministry man. 'Just protecting our interests. I had a little friend watching this building and he spied this crowd heading towards it. I took an educated guess that they might be up to no good, as is the case with most folk in this city, so I gathered up my sister and Fudail here and hightailed it over. Your man stepped in just as we were about to make our dramatic entrance.'

'Good thing you did, I was going to go down in a blaze of glory. Speaking of which, where's Nazar?'

'He took off up the stairs after Qadir. His man tried to stop him so I thought it best to intercede,' he pointed at the bloodied mess of a man he'd had pinned to the wall moments earlier. Forge could see now that it was Goker. The door on the balcony above them opened and Nazar came out of Qadir's office and looked down at them.

'Everyone alright?'

'Yeah, you?' Forge asked.

'Yes,' Nazar stepped back from the balcony's railing and made his way down the steps. 'I was caught a little off guard by all the excitement.' He was wiping his hands with a piece of material. It was the same colour as Qadir's robe. 'As Qadir was fond of saying, I spotted an opportunity and decided to take advantage of it.'

He reached the ground floor and threw the rag on the ground. Even in the dim light of the candles, the dark bloodstains were obvious.

'Qadir no longer a problem then?' asked Forge.

'Not for anyone,' agreed Nazar simply. 'I've been waiting to do that for a long time.'

'What about this place? And what about the Ministry?' asked Fudail. 'If they know about us, we need to be somewhere else very quickly.'

'How much do they know?' asked Forge. At the worst case, they had maybe an hour or so before someone started asking where the crew they sent out was.

'It's possible they know nothing more than there is a plot. It would be excuse enough to send these men. As long as they don't have names we are safe enough, I suppose,' said Nazar.

'My sister will find out the truth of it. She can be very thorough. I say we torch this place and head back to base,' said Taimsin.

'Best way to hide the evidence for a while,' agreed Nazar.

'You gonna use your magic?' asked Forge.

Taimsin shook her head. 'Best not. I've used too much already. It was one of my specially prepared packages. Magic leaves a scent, a signature if you will. I don't like the opposition to know who they are dealing with and it may be that Karnak Karnassus has some half decent practitioners who might recognise my work. Until I know for sure, I'd rather keep a low profile.'

'Fair enough. We can do it the old fashioned way. Corporal Jonas?'

'No problem, Boss. Might want to leave off the Corporal bit though, don't want our cover blown,' suggested Jonas.

Forge shook his head. Funny how he just fell back into the old military etiquette.

'Good point. Come on. Let's see what we can find to burn in the warehouse. I want to make this a pretty mess.'

'What about us?' asked Nazar.

'You head back to *The Moon*, we'll regroup there and discuss next steps.'

'Do you mind if I stop by my ship first? I want to warn the crew we might be leaving in a hurry,' said Nazar.

'Good idea, go ahead, but let's hope it doesn't come to that,' said Forge.

'Come on then, gentlemen,' said Taimsin, 'I'll see you back safe. Oh and Forge, I'll keep an eye on you from above, just in case you need bailing out again.'

'Thanks,' said Forge, drily, not wanting to rise to the bait. He'd already learned it was best just to let the twins' arrogance wash over you.

As they filed out, Forge followed Jonas through to the office. The place was a wreck, with overturned chairs and scattered documents all over the floor. Clearly the clerks had left in a hurry except for the one behind a desk lying in a pool of blood, his throat slashed open, eyes wide in shock. Jonas was poking his head through another doorway.

'The warehouse is back here, loads of crates and some bales of fabric. Oh and there's a couple of dead guys in here. One looks like a clerk. The other is one of those Ministry shits.'

Tailsin was cleaning up fast.

'I'll make a pile in here,' Forge said. 'You get another one going in the warehouse.'

'Right.'

Jonas disappeared while Forge worked quickly, gathering a huge heap of papers then breaking up some of the chairs and putting the pieces on top. He picked up a still flickering candle, lit another document and used that to start off the pile. Just for good measure, he also set a flame to two racks of scrolls that stood against one of the walls. He stopped to admire his handiwork for a moment.

'Done,' said Jonas, coming back into the office.

'Good, let's go.'

They retreated into the entrance hall and went for the door. Forge stopped and looked up the stairs.

'We'd better see to Qadir too.'

They jogged up the stairs and got to work. Two minutes later they were out the front door. Another fire was burning merrily on Qadir's desk. Nazar had done quite a number on him the stab wounds were all over his body, back and front. He must have bleed out fast. As they worked, Forge had bought Jonas up to speed on what this whole mess had been about. Jonas listened quietly while Forge had outlined the mission objectives. Once Forge finished, Jonas shook his head. 'It's a fucked up job boss, but Dav deserves a proper ending, if we can give it to him.'

'That's the plan. Come on, time to go.'

The heat was rising in the entrance hall and smoke was coming through the open office doorway. They had to move fast, somebody would start taking an interest soon. Forge ran out of the door and made for the harbour street. Jonas clapped him on the arm.

'This way.'

Jonas turned right, ran across the road and cut into an alley.

'Jonas, why this way?' Forge asked.

'When I got into the city and found out where you were, I hung back, like you suggested. Found a bloke was tailing you but not reporting in to anyone. He was watching you at the cemetery as well, and he came here tonight. You said we were going to have trouble getting inside. I reckon he can help.'

'How so?'

'The guy is a Paternal Guard.'

'Shit.' The moment when Forge had sworn he had been found out started to make a lot more sense. Were they already on to him? But why use a Guardsman when agents were better?

'That him over there?' said Forge, spying a large shape in the shadows.

'Yeah.'

'He still breathing?'

'Probably. Hang on.'

In the dark, Forge watched Jonas bend over the shape and fiddle with something.

'Gag's off.'

Forge knelt. He couldn't make out much.

'Who are you?' he said quietly.

There was no response except for the sound of deep, angry

breathing. They didn't have time to piss about with this, he had to make a decision on what to do right now.

'Let's start again. Depending on what you say next this might be a short night for you so I'll give you something. Dav Jenkins was my friend. I came here to find out what happened to him. All I need to know is, why are you following me?'

There was a pause.

'Because I thought you might know who killed him,' came the gruff reply.

It was not necessarily the answer Forge had been expecting.

'I haven't a clue. All I know is that he was taken out because he got wind of something that he couldn't afford anyone else to know about. Why does the Paternal Guard want to know about it?'

'They don't. I do.'

'Why?'

'Because I loved him!' hissed the voice.

Oh. That definitely wasn't the answer he was expecting.

'Look,' said Forge, 'I don't know you and I don't trust you. But you saw me in the Palace, didn't you?'

There was a pause.

'Yes.'

'But you didn't stop me?'

'Why would I stop you? Anything I do, I do for myself. Do you know what would happen to me if anyone found out what I had been doing? It is forbidden for Paternal Guard to have relationships, let alone with a member of a foreign power. I would be dead.'

'True,' mused Jonas.

Forge chewed his lip. He was having trouble processing all this information. 'Okay, tell you what. We are going to take you with us. When you find out what we are doing, you may not be best pleased. But I guarantee I won't kill you, unless you give me no choice. What's your name?'

'Calill.'

'Calill. Dav Jenkins was my oldest friend. I don't have many left now. I'm here to finish what he started, to see it done and damn the consquences. Are you good with that?'

Another silence.

'Is your name Jon?'

'Yes.'

'Dav talked about you. He said you were a grumpy and sour faced son of a bitch who was getting worse with age.'

Forge smiled despite himself.

'That sounds about right.'

'Then I will come with you.'

'Jonas? Cut his bonds.'

'Yeah.'

Jonas leaned down and used a blade to saw through whatever it was he had used to tie up the man. He replaced his knife and hauled Calill up. Forge knew he was taking a risk, that maybe this Calill was just playing him for time and a chance to get away. Yet here they had someone who knew the Palace intimately. It was an opportunity the likes of which would not present itself again.

'We really need to go. Now,' said Jonas.

They returned to the mouth of the alley. A few figures were gathered on the road pointing excitedly at the smoke pouring from the roof of the warehouse. Flames could be spied flickering behind the small windows.

'Too late to go along the harbour road. Too much attention,' said Forge.

'I can lead you. Where are you going?' asked Calill.

And if I tell him he'll know where to send the authorities to incarcerate our asses.

'Tell you what, let's work on the trust angle first. Let's meet tomorrow, say a bell past midday. We'll talk then.'

'Where?'

'You know where.'

'Yes, I think so.' said Calill.

Now they had a little more light to work with, Forge could see the man a little better. He was young, mid-twenties perhaps. He had the shadow of stubble on his face and short cropped black hair.

'We'll talk more then. Try and screw us and one of my people will finish you,' he warned, knowing he had people he could trust to do just that.

'I understand,' said Calill. He turned right out of the alley and walked over to join the crowd that was forming. Just another bystander.

'Guess we should go left,' said Jonas.

'Crack on. But let's take it easy. I'm too knackered to run anywhere.'

Forge shot Jonas a meaningful look. Jonas hefted his bow and rested it on his shoulder. It all looked casual enough but at a pinch, Jonas could let fly within moments. If it came to that tonight, it would probably be too late.

Chapter 19

'Hello, sister dear, I am back.'

'Yes, I know you are. I knew that about three minutes ago,'

'Of course you did. It was just a greeting.'

'And you have that look on your face. You are pleased with yourself.'

'As a matter of fact, I am. I thought we pulled off an audacious rescue.'

'That's true.'

'Forge, what do you think? You were there, in the balcony seats as it were. Impressed?'

Forge had been studiously ignoring the exchange but it was only a matter of time before he got drawn in.

'Not bad. But to be fair, I didn't see much of it,' he put two fingers to his eyes. 'I couldn't see anything.'

Tailsin made a sympathetic face.

'You know, I get that. Taimsin loves her little fireworks but they do tend to backfire if you are not prepared.'

'The whole point is that you are not prepared, it's called the element of surprise!' said Taimsin, flinging her arms up into the air.

'Yes, but the surprise needs to be on the enemy's side, sister dear,' admonished Tailsin.

Taimsin sniffed. 'Collateral damage. Perfectly acceptable in the circumstances.'

'Either way, you have my thanks,' said Nazar firmly. 'We all got out of it in one piece. I would call that a success.'

'Agreed. Now if you could find a place to sit or stand, we need to talk about next steps,' said Forge.

They were all gathered in the top room of *The Moon Over Karnassus*. Fudail and Nazar sat on one side of the table with Taimsin on the other and Forge standing against the wall next to his maps and plans. Reclining on his own piece of wall was Jonas, nonchalantly cleaning his nails with his knife. Tailsin grabbed the remaining free chair beside her sister, turned it around and straddled it, resting her arms on its back.

'Did you get them all?' asked Fudail.

'Oh yes, I got them. The last two blokes made me work though. One of them actually had the affront to turn round and try and hit me. The other got another thirty yards before I had him,' replied Tailsin.

'How did that work out?' asked Forge.

'Like the rest but not before I had a chat with him. He claims that all they were told was to arrest and detain whoever Qadir fingered as conspirators. They had no prior knowledge of who or how many there might be. He also said that you were to be taken to a safe house to be questioned.'

'So they were Ministry?' asked Fudail.

'Seems that way. I got the location of the safe house and went to have a look. There were four guys outside trying their best to look like they weren't there to hurt somebody, and inside there were another half dozen.'

'You got that close?' asked Nazar.

Tailsin shrugged.

'I just took a quick peek. There was another man, looked like some kind of authority figure, not like the rest. He looked official.' She raised a hand and bent two fingers to emphasise the word.

'Impressive,' said Nazar.

'Oh don't tell her that!' groaned Taimsin.

Tailsin beamed.

'Moving on,' said Forge, anxious that time might be against them. 'What does everyone think? Do we believe that Qadir did not reveal any of our identities?'

'I think he was telling the truth. He didn't have much option,' said Tailsin.

'We haven't been hit here yet,' said Taimsin. 'I can't spot anyone coming either.'

'So maybe they just know names,' said Fudail.

'Then they only know me and Nazar,' said Forge.

'He is right,' said Nazar, worry clouding his face. 'It is something I had not considered. I should get back to my ship.'

'You probably shouldn't,' said Jonas.

'He's right. If your name was mentioned then they are likely already there. You'd be better off waiting a wee while,' said Taimsin.

'I am minded to think we might have gotten away with it,' said Forge. 'They weren't expecting the attack and their information was sketchy at best.'

'But now they know somebody wanted and gained access to the Palace,' said Fudail.

'Ah, there's plenty who have done that. But I think the fight might have exacerbated things,' said Nazar, gloomily.

'What about the one that got away?' asked Taimsin

'Who got away? No one got away. I would have killed them

already!' declared Tailsin in a fit of outrage.

'No, sister. It was someone else. This gentleman caught him,' said Taimsin, indicating Jonas.

'And you let him go?' asked Tailsin.

'I let him go,' said Forge. 'Let's say I decided I could trust him. He is called Calill and he's a Paternal Guard. And he was a...friend of Dav's.'

'A friend?' asked Tailsin, with a glint in her eye.

'Yes. A friend,' repeated Forge. He shook his head. There was no need to be circumspect. 'They were lovers.'

'Now who'd have thought it? Your man setting a honey trap,' said Tailsin, grinning.

Forge opened his mouth to bite back but Fudali raised a hand.

'Forgive me, but now that we have gotten round to it, why do we have a member of the Paternal's Guard on the loose who knows all about us?' asked Fudail.

'It was my call. This man had an opportunity to call me out at the Palace. He chose not to. Instead he followed me back to Qadir's because he was trying to gain some measure of vengeance for Dav's death. As it stands, the only two people he has seen are Jonas and me. I'll hold off from letting him meet any of you just yet.'

'That's a relief,' said Fudail, sarcastically.

'That doesn't change the fact that somebody is going to have to ensure he doesn't let on,' said Nazar.

'Presumably, you are not going to tell him what we've got planned?' asked Fudail.

Forge leant across to the table and helped himself to a jug of ale that someone had thoughtfully brought up to the room. 'Actually, I was thinking that having someone on the inside would dramatically improve our chances.'

'They'll be able to fill in the blanks, certainly,' said Nazar.

'Are we going to have to torture him?' asked Taimsin. 'If so, don't let my sister do it.'

'Why not?' complained Tailsin.

'Nobody is torturing anybody,' said Forge, exasperated.

'But I will if you want me to, boss,' said Jonas. It was the first words he had said since returning to the inn.

'Thank you, Jonas, but I'd prefer to keep you honest with your killing. No torture. Not until I'm persuaded of the need for it,' said Forge, before he took a long drink of the ale. A very long drink. He refilled his mug.

'I'll see what I can do about that,' said Tailsin. 'Nice moves with your bow by the way,' she said looking at Jonas, with a smile and an approving glint in her eye

'Thanks. All appreciation welcomed,' Jonas replied, with a flourish of his hand and a small bow.

'You two know each other, then,' said Taimsin, to Forge and Jonas.

'We served together for a few years,' said Forge. 'He's the only man I trust to watch my back.'

'What about us?' asked Tailsin, indignantly.

Good point. 'I haven't had a chance to thank you all yet. That was quite a piece of work you all pulled. You didn't have to, but it finally showed me who I'm working with. It gives me faith that we can pull this off.'

'That's the spirit!' said Taimsin, raising her own mug of ale in salute.

'What's our next move?' asked Nazar. Forge was surprised how strongly the merchant had become committed to the mission. He guessed that after tonight, he had a far stronger personal case for seeing it through. He admired the man for that; Nazar could have cut and run, especially with the

Ministry sniffing so close, but he was clearly made of sterner stuff.

'I've arranged a meet with Calill tomorrow. It'll just be me. We'll talk and if it looks like he is honest and there's no trace of backup or surveillance, then I'll tell him what we need and what we plan to do. If he truly was Dav's, er, lover, then I get a feeling he is not going to risk his own skin exposing that particular piece of info.'

'Not if he wants to keep his job he won't,' said Fudail.'Soon as they even get a hint that he was linked to a foreign national, he's done.'

'The fact that he admitted to it tells me he is either lying his teeth off to get close or he is down the line. Right now I'm minded to believe the latter.' He leaned across and refilled his tankard, 'we'll know more tomorrow. Jonas, you'll be coming with me. You keep back and see who's watching us.'

'Right.'

Forge looked across at the mage. 'Taimsin, your little friend?'

'Hmm?'

'Just what is it?'

'Oh, hang on.' She stood, went to the window and whistled. A small bird, covered in orange and yellow feathers landed on the sill. Forge had seen plenty of these around the city. Taimsin reached out a hand and the popped hopped onto it. She turned and smiled at the group.

'It's the easiest way to keep an eye on what's going on and the simplest of magics. So low level that most wouldn't stop to consider it. You just take what you find around you, make space to implant a few commands and hey presto, you have a bird's eye view of your surroundings!'

'She loves saying that. Tickles her, so it does,' said Tailsin, drily.

Now that was an interesting trick. Forge could see a lot of uses for that. 'Can we get that bird overhead tomorrow?'

'No problem.'

'Good. And how about the Palace? There's an open garden, right in the middle of the place. Plenty of other birds around.'

'Hmm. Is it magically shielded?' she asked.

'Probably.'

'Then we'd have to think carefully about using my friend like that. Flying around the city is one thing, you'd never have enough mages to scan everywhere, but in a tighter space like the Palace they'll have alarm bells on the alarm bells just primed to pick up even the faintest whiff of unauthorised magic.'

'Well, it was worth thinking about,' said Forge, taking another long drink.

'Oh, don't get me wrong. I'm sure we can rustle something up. It's just likely to be a one-time deal,' she added.

'Like this mission,' said Jonas. He sat down next to Forge and leaned in close. 'Boss, I know we've just been in a fight, but since when did you start drinking so much?'

'Huh?' asked Forge.

'That's your second jug you're working through.'

'I almost had my arse handed to me back there. Are you surprised I'm a little thirsty?'

Jonas shrugged. 'Just saying. You used to keep a handle on it when we were in the field.' He pulled at an earlobe. 'I remember when we got back from Graves. After we'd finished our business in Shifter, you were drinking more than I'd ever seen. And then you quit...'

Forge kept quiet. He wasn't sure what Jonas expected of

him. He shrugged. 'A man's gotta have a poison.'

'Your poison was always coffee.'

'Not much coffee in Littlebury,' said Forge. He raised his mug and drank deep. 'Besides, we aren't in the field anymore.'

'Aren't we?' asked Jonas. He stood up and walked away.

Forge felt a flash of anger. Where did Jonas get off saying that to him? *I was his commanding officer. I get to decide. And I'm bloody retired.* Nobody had the right to tell him what to do. And if he wanted a drink, he'd bloody well have one. It helped. And if it helped, what was the problem? If he didn't drink he couldn't sleep. He'd tried and every time the nightmares had come. His friends screaming in agony, his men dying. And they all blamed him. With their last breaths they cursed him for being a fool and wasting their lives in a pointless fight. And he couldn't blame them. But he also couldn't face them. Not again.

Chapter 20

'Enter,' Minister Swarbreck responded to the firm knock on his door. He already knew who it would be. No one else ever knocked that loudly. The door opened and in stepped Orlaise.

'A good morning to you, Minister,' said Orlaise.

'And to you.'

'Have you had an opportunity to read the report from last night yet?'

'Yes. And I must admit, I am unhappy with the lack of detail.'

Orlaise stood before Swarbreck's desk and placed his hands behind his back.

'I must apologise for that. This kind of event is unusual enough that I felt it warranted a more personal and vocal briefing. I wanted to make sure we had clarity.'

'Quite so. Tell me then, Orlaise, why it is we lost...how many?' he scanned the document even though he was well aware of what it contained.'Fourteen members of our Ministry in what should have been a straightforward arrest and detain operation.'

'It was rather short-notice in its implementation, I am afraid, Minister. We had the scantest of information to work from.

Little more than a summons for assistance. You were unavailable so I decided that we must act swiftly. I despatched what I felt would be sufficient manpower to achieve the task.'

Swarbreck was deeply annoyed at the situation but, having been away at the Crucible at the time, the decision of his deputy was indeed the right course of action to have taken. He doubted he would have authorised anything different himself.

'It should have been. Any more than that and I would have believed us to be quelling a gang or going to war. Now, tell me, this merchant, Qadir?'

'Yes.'

'This Qadir had met with the Paternal and, after the audience, was able to get a message to you speaking of a plot. There was a member of his party who was not what he appeared?'

'Yes. Qadir intimated he was being coerced. I established his office's location, and told him to expect our men to arrive. He was to allow them access by a side entrance to his property.'

'And then Qadir and his party left and you contacted our men?'

'I did. I personally went to meet them at one of our safe houses so I could take receipt of any prisoners and return them to the Palace for questioning.'

Swarbreck stood up and turned to look out of the window. He watched a troop of litter bearers labour along the street, their load clearly of an unusual heft.

'At which point, the next thing we know for sure is that there was a fire in Qadir's warehouse and inside was a slaughterhouse, or so we assume.'

'Assumed, yes, many of the bodies were too far gone for

identification or means of death,' Orlaise added. 'There is no way of telling how many if any of them were part of the plot. Yet we know that at least one member of this group must have gotten away because three more bodies were discovered not far from the building. One looked like an employee of Qadir's and the other two were our men. Their throats were cut.'

'A professional, then?' mused Swarbreck.

'I believe so.'

'I will summarise what we have. We have a group who are intent in gaining access to the Paternal's Palace. That group had an encounter with our people leading to significant loss of life, including the merchant and his people?'

'Yes.'

'And we know that at least one of this group survives.'

'And one of our mages detected magic. Not much and not enough to indicate who or how powerful they are.'

'Excellent, good. So we have to presume that a professional killer is still on the loose. Now, the answer which eludes us is why the individuals want access to the Palace. It is either that they wish to do harm to the Paternal or that they wish to steal some of the secrets we have stored.' In all his years of service, there had never been a move made against the Palace. The game had always been played outside, amongst the backalleys, drinking dens and secluded parks. Yet it was required of him to consider the impossible, that an attempt was going to be made to enter the Palace. Indeed they had already succeeded in that endeavour. But would they try again, now that they had been compromised?

'It would seem a pointless exercise, trying to kill the Paternal at such a late stage of his incumbency. Unless they wish to prove some kind of political point?' said Orlaise.

Swarbreck shook his head. The litter bearers had disappeared from view although the man who was heading in their direction was taking his time, looking interested in everything but the litter itself. He was one of Swarbreck's and the Minister was a little disappointed that he had spotted him so easily.

'I doubt very much they wish to do that. No, I suspect they want information. Either way, we cannot have it.' He turned back to look at Orlaise and leaned onto his table his hands placed wide onto the top to give him support. 'Orlaise, I want you to convene a meeting of the City Watch commanders, the Ministers of Defence and Trade, and our own Guard. I will represent the Ministry, with your aid of course. I will not take the risk that this group has been effectively neutralised. We have to prepare for the worst and assume nothing.'

'Very well, Minister. How far do you want to take this?'

'I want to put the City in a start of high alert. Or at least those elements involved with its security. We already know what the target is so we concentrate our focus on that. I want our agents drawn into a tighter ring around the plateau and I want an increased presence both outside and inside the Palace.'

'Won't that be an obvious sign that we suspect an attempt?'

'Exactly the point. I want to send a message to anyone out there with an interest in this affair. They were almost caught once, they must realise that with our increased vigilance we will brook no second chances.'

'The embassies will know we are up to something.'

'Good for them. With Rostos starting soon it provides us with cover and an excuse. They can speculate as much as they like but they will have nothing concrete.'

'How long will this go on for?'

'At least until we have a new Paternal in place. I know we cannot maintain this for an extended period so we will have to call in extra support. I want the City Watch to provide the extra manpower needed to secure the Palace. We will merge them with the Paternal Guard shifts. That way we can control them and ensure we have reliable people on side.'

'Yes, Minister.'

'And send message to the gang masters. I want to know if any of them have been involved with parties that may be linked to the incident. General amnesty of course. Also, spread the word that the blaze and loss of life was down to a hired mage in the employ of Qadir. An unexpected turn of events. Oh and call in all our mages and get them to put together a plan for providing extra safeguards on all the entrances. And yes, they will have to pull shifts alongside everyone else.'

'They'll love that,' commented Orlaise.

'That's because they are all arrogant and self-obsessed. I also want you to run a check on all the licensed magic-users in the city and see if any of them are behaving oddly.'

'Anything else?' said Orlaise, without the slightest hint of sarasm.

'I want the meeting in one hour.'

Orlaise's face dropped a little.

'Yes, Minister. I shall get onto it right now, if you will allow me?'

'Hop to it, Orlaise. This is why we are here. To deal with matters such as this. We cannot, must not, be found to be wanting. The Families would have both of our heads.'

'That I don't doubt,' remarked Orlaise. He bowed low and left.

Swarbreck retook his chair, placed his arms on the rests and gazed up into nothing. He could not remember a time when the Ministry of Relations had suffered such a grievous challenge to its power. Irrespective of what had happened last night and whether the group planning the incursion had been stymied, it was a matter of principle and sound common sense. There was a clear and present threat to the foundation stone of Karnak Karnassus and he had a duty. He would not allow anything to go wrong on his watch. It was not a matter of pride, that didn't come into it. It was a matter of survival.

Chapter 21

Forge took a rag from his pocket and wiped the back of his neck. The sun was behind him and low in the sky and the shade provided by the wide-brimmed reed hat didn't reach that far. He felt like a fool wearing it but he'd hadn't gotten round to getting a keffiyeh, the distinct headscarf that you could wrap around your whole head. He'd seen a lot of the local workers on the docks wearing them and it would be a lot easier to move about without his face on show. He'd pick one up later, if this meeting didn't go south.

He looked down at Dav's gravestone and shook his head.

'Hey old man, this is the second time I've visited you in the space of a month. That's twice as many times as I've done in the last three years. Sorry about that. It was good of you to write to me though. And I apologise for being crap in never writing back to you but I guess you knew that would happen. I wish I could have been here, Dav. You needed back up, someone you could trust. I owed you. And I let you down.'

He went quiet, struggling with his emotions. He felt like he'd let a lot of people down over the years, each one of them now deep in the earth. Several dozen birds passed overhead, making happy, chirruping noises. One of those could be Taimsin's. He wouldn't know unless one deliberately landed on the gravestone. That was the signal to run. It didn't escape him that it was just as likely that another one might take a fancy to perching there and give him cause for an unwarranted heart attack as he tried to get away. It was too damned hot to run anywhere.

'You know what the worst part was?' said a quiet voice.

Forge whipped his head around to look at Calill. The guard was wearing the same clothes as the previous night. He hadn't heard him coming. He took a moment to regain his calm and returned his gaze to Dav's gravestone.

'I couldn't be there to help. He wouldn't let me but I might have been able to help. Or if I couldn't do that, at least he wouldn't have had to die alone.'

'Knowing Dav, he wouldn't have wanted that.'

'No, he wouldn't.' Calill fell silent for a moment. 'Where's your man, Jonas?'

'Oh, he's around,' replied Forge. He had no clue himself but the scout would be in bowshot range, of that he was sure.

'I suppose you were expecting to be arrested?'

'I was expecting the worst and hoping for the best.'

'I have heard that phrase before. My old shift commander used to say it.'

'Army man was he?'

'Yes. I came alone.'

He hadn't seen any birds racing at high speed to the gravestone yet so Forge had to take his word on that one.

'There is a bigger game being played,' said Forge.

'There always is. This is Karnak Karnassus.'

'I was sent here to finish what Dav had only just started. But I *came* here to honour my friend's memory and get some payback.'

'And what is it that Dav had to die for?'

'If I tell you that, you might not be pleased with what you hear.'

'I saw you in the Paternal's Palace. That means that you were doing something that is likely to get you killed.'

'True enough,' Forge turned to look Calill right in the eye. 'We are here to steal the Paternal.'

To his credit Calill didn't lose his cool. Though he did blink a few times.

'Why?'

'Because he asked us to.'

'Huh?'

'Somehow he got a message to Dav and Dav got that message out of Karnak. But he must have gotten spooked, maybe he knew they were on to him, maybe he felt he couldn't risk his part being discovered. Maybe he was protecting the country he served and those he cared about.'

Calill shook his head. There were tears in his eyes. 'He came to say goodbye to me. He said that he knew he had a tail and that one way or another he was going to get found out. I knew what happened to him and I did nothing.'

'Dav was always a patriot, loyal to the cause. And he was killed for it in the end,' said Forge.

Calill's bloodshot eyes flashed. 'And do you think I am not loyal too? I would gladly give my life to defend the Paternal.'

'I don't doubt you. But who would you choose? If it was Dav or the Paternal?'

Calill angrily shook his head and turned away.

'Dav. Every time. Dav.'

'I fought and killed for Ashkent for years. Didn't always approve but never doubted my duty. Things change. I'm not here for them. And I think this is as close to a suicide run as I have ever been and trust me, I've been close before.'

'You want the Paternal?'

'Yes, he asked to be smuggled out.'

'It makes sense. His time is almost up. You know he lost his family? His wife and two young children in a stupid sailing accident. There was nothing anyone could do. He lost his reason to be compliant at the end.'

'He can't be the first Paternal who has had a change of heart,' said Forge.

'No, I'm sure he isn't but he is the first where the Families have no leverage over him.' Calill turned around and smiled sadly. 'Perhaps he has become like us, he no longer feels the sense of loyalty to his nation he once had.'

'That's how I figure it. He's a dead man anyway. What's he got to lose?'

'What have you got to lose?'

Forge laughed.

'Me? I got shit all but a crappy cabin in a crappy village a thousand miles from here. I'm still attached to living, but even then I do have my off days.'

'I don't have much and without Dav, there doesn't seem any point to it.'

'That'll probably change with a bit of time. You carry the burden, you don't forget but you do move on.' *Mostly.*

Calill nodded. His face was set in a grim expression, his eyes determined.

'I have served Karnak Karnassus faithfully, I believe in what it stands for and the stability and surety that the institution of the Paternal provides. But the Ministry took away something far more important. It took away my future and my hope. I want to hurt them, I care nothing for what they do to me. I cannot bring down the Ministry nor do I want to destroy the peace of Karnak but like you, I want Dav's death to mean something. You want information about the Palace. Its layout, guard schedules, security points and what magical protections are in place. You want to know where the Paternal can be located and you want to know the best way of getting in and out.'

'Pretty much.'

'I can give you all of those things but they won't do you much good. There's no way you could get in and out without discovery, not now. They know there is a plot. You'd do better trying to assassinate the Paternal than breaking him out. Either way you'd all still die in the process.'

'I know that, but I got a good crew, I've pulled off a few things I never should have in the past.' It was true but Forge was not sure who he was trying to convince.

'Even so. You would be better off if you had an army at your back...' Calill stopped and held a hand up. 'Wait. I have an idea.' He barked out a short laugh and shook his head. 'The world is a truly strange place. After last night's excitement, we have just been placed onto a new footing. The Ministry were quite put out by losing so many men in one incident and more importantly they are worried that they have also failed to eliminate the threat. The security of the Palace has been increased. Our shifts are being augmented by the men of the City Watch, mages have been called into heighten our magical protections. All these things work against you. Yet, I believe we can make them work in our favour.'

'Colour me intrigued,' said Forge.

'There was no way we could have gotten you into the Palace before Rostos. Not in any official capacity – you blew that chance with Qadir. But I believe we can get you inside now. By tomorrow the Palace will be full of new faces. The City Watch is efficient and professional but we the Paternal Guard do not mix with them. We do not know many of them or what their names are. We certainly do not know their faces,' he said slowly enunciating each word, a sly smile on his face.

'You want us to go in disguised as City Watch?'

'Yes. Why not? As long as we can get you inside the Palace then no one will question who you are. As long as you have a member of the Paternal's Guard with you.'

'Huh,' said Forge. Funny how things worked out. It looked like going in with Qadir proved to be a good call, even if it almost was a clusterfuck, but that pretty much was the tone for this mission. 'Alright. I like the sound of that. What do we do next?'

'I'll need to find out a little more about how the security arrangements are going to work. Then we can work out the best way to get you in. We'll have to work fast.'

'I'm used to that,' said Forge. He smiled. He liked this lad. 'It looks like I'm going to take a leap of faith and bring you into the circle of trust. Are you free again tomorrow?'

'I should be. It depends on the new arrangements, but our shifts are usually protected. They they don't want tired guards.'

'Okay. Get yourself to *The Moon Over Karnassus* at midday tomorrow, I am going to introduce you to the rest of the crew. Then we sit down and plan this bastard through. It might take a while.'

'I understand,' said Calill, with a nod. 'I will be there.'

'Good. Look, Calill, I know what you are doing for us. I appreciate it. Your neck is on the line. If any of us get caught, then it's probable that you'll be exposed.'

'I know that. And you know why I am agreeing to it. Let's just make sure it works.'

'Agreed. Um. Are you going to stay here for a bit?'

'Yes, I'd like that.'

'Right. In which case, I'll see you tomorrow,' said Forge, awkwardly.

'Tomorrow,' said Calill, quietly.

Forge stepped back and took his leave, heading for the path out of the cemetery. Glancing behind he saw Calill with his head bent low, both hands clutching the gravestone. Dav had been a lucky guy, that one was carrying a seriously broken heart. Forge returned to *The Moon Over Karnassus* two hours later. He had taken it slow, going a roundabout route and even stopping at a friendly looking tavern for a drink. They now had to take every precaution in the wake of the fight. The Ministry was on the lookout and would be displaying extreme paranoia. On his travels he bought himself a keffiyeh but he would need someone to show him how to wear it. Occasional glances into the sky provided sightings of birds flying overhead but he still couldn't be sure which one was theirs.

Fudail was sat at a side table downstairs in the bar when he entered. Another precaution for when they were out and about. He'd wait for a short while to see if anyone followed Forge in. There was an open book in front of him and a half-drunk ale to one side.

'What are you reading?' asked Forge.

'Hmm? Oh, no idea. I don't understand the language it's written in, but I found it left in our room. I thought it would be a useful prop,' replied Fudail. 'I am not much of a reader.'

'Me neither. I always fall asleep when I try. I'm a better drinker. Say, Fudail, we got the makings of a new plan. What's your connections with the City Watch like?'

Fudails eyebrows furrowed into a pained expression.

'I might have one or two acquaintances I maintain, favours

for favours and such like.'

'Good. When you come up, I'd like you to have put some thought into how we go about acquiring a set of City Watch uniforms. Ones that fit.'

Fudail did that thing with his hands and sighed.

'Very well.'

Forge tapped the table. 'Good man.'

He continued on, up the stairs and into their top floor room. Taimsin and Tailsin were rolling dice. A gentle trilling sound drew his attention to the windowsill and the small, brightly coloured bird perched upon it.

'Nope, nobody seen following you,' said Taimsin, her attention focussed on the three cubes in front of her.

'Scrying?' asked Forge. It had occurred to him on the way back that there were other, magical means to watch him, not just by using birds.

'I'm impressed. Finding a scryer, is no easy task. The energy is generated at a distance, not in the immediate vicinity. I'd have to cast a wide net to locate a scryer and would get picked up by the second mage looking for my signature.

'Scrying's a waste of time anyway,' said Tailsin. 'It takes a lot of energy and as soon as you lose sight of a target then it's damn near impossible to acquire them again.'

'Doubly impressed with you, sister. She is quite right. Scrying is all about focussing on a particular spot. If it disappears then you have to focus on something else.'

'See, sister dear? I do listen to you when you have something useful to say.'

'And at that point, we move on. You did follow our protocols?' asked Taimsin.

Forge nodded. 'Yeah, I took my time, merged into crowds, stopped off for some shopping and a drink. I ditched that stupid hat, too.'

'Then you should be fine.'

Jonas opened the door and wandered in. He looked across with interest at the two twins. 'You dicing?'

'Wh? Do you want in?' said Tailsin.

'Don't, she cheats terribly,' warned Taimsin.

'That's alright. So do I,' said Jonas, pulling up another chair. 'Didn't see anybody, boss. I kept some distance, double-backed a few times. If anyone was following either you or me, then they are very, very good.'

'It's possible they might be,' said Forge. He folded his arms and watched them play. In the five minutes that followed he saw Jonas lose a pile of scraps to Talisin who then lost it all on one roll to her sister, prompted a tirade of insult and abuse. Taimsin clapped her hands jubilantly and winked at Forge.

'Curses,' Tailsin scowled hard at her sister. 'That's it. I'm thirsty. Who wants a drink?'

'Gone on then – make it wine. Good stuff if they have any. I feel like celebrating,' replied Taimsin.

'There's a surprise,'said Tailsin. 'Forge?'

Forge shook his head. He remembered what Jonas had said to him. Maybe it was time he started doing things a little differently. 'I'll just have some water. If they have any.'

Tailsin raised an eyebrow. 'I doubt that but I'll ask.'

As she left the room Taimsin leaned back on her chair and stroked her chin. 'You listened to your friend, then?'

Forge nodded.

'He has a point. I guess I've been relying on the drink too much for a while now.'

'It's easily, done. It starts as a support, becomes a crutch and you never end up dealing with the root problem. I can help with that if you like. Give you something to help with the nightmares.'

It was Forge's turn to stroke his chin. The nightmares. *How did she know about them?* 'You two ever been in the military?'

Taimsin smiled. 'It's not something we like to talk about, but yes. We spent a couple of years in the Ashkent army. Not mounted infantry like you and Jonas – he told us by the way – marines.'

'Damn,' said Forge. The Ashkent military had an equal opportunities approach to recruiting. They'd take anyone from any nation as long as they had talent and knew how to follow orders. It occurred to Forge that was why they had been picked for the mission. It all made sense now. McKracken had probably used them before. 'Tough crew, the marines.'

'Indeed. We saw our share of fun. My sister and I formed quite a team, they used us for operations that required a fair degree of autonomy.'

'Left on your own to sink or swim, huh?'

Taimsin smiled. 'We kept treading water, at least. The issue was that Tailsin got it into her head that if we were doing this stuff anyway, then why not do it for ourselves and make some money in the process. She always preferred working without shackles.' She raised her hands. 'And my sister is no good by herself. She gets into all kinds of trouble. So I agreed to go with her and become freelance.'

'You don't look happy about it,' said Forge, noting the wry look on Taimsin's face.

'I liked the military. It gave me structure and a sense of purpose. We'd learned our trade the hard way back in the Pits but we were both used and abused. That's why we left. In the military I had support from people who I could trust.

Being a battlemage takes everything out of you but you had colleagues to share the load.'

'And the lads always appreciate the back-up,' said Forge, noting the times an aerial shield had saved their bacon or a well-placed fireball had cleared the way for an advance.

Taimsin nodded.

'I liked that. It felt good. But where my sister goes, I have to follow. She has too much of the crazy in her. I have to remind her that a contract has to be honoured, that agreements have to be abided by. Otherwise our reputation would turn sour. Call me old-fashioned, but if I say I'm going to do it...'

The door opened once more and Fudail walked in carrying a fresh jug of ale. Tailsin trailed behind also holding a jug.

'The bar is quiet. One of the regulars came in but that's it,' he said, placing the jug in the middle of the table.

Tailsin followed suit. 'Your lucky day, Forge. I had a quick look and I couldn't spot anything larger than tadpoles swimming inside.'

Forge inclinded his head and helped himself. 'I know Nazar isn't here but I can keep him in the loop later. Fact is this next stage is purely down to us. The meeting with Calill went as well can be expected. For what it's worth, I trust him.'

'That's worth everything,' said Tailsin. 'If you didn't we'd be, well, buggered right now.'

'True. As it stands, he's on board all the way. He'll be here tomorrow after his shift and he'll be bringing his knowledge of the Palace.'

'Good stuff. I knew it would all work out,' said Taimsin.

'He's also come up with a plan for getting us in. Thanks to the mess we made of the Ministry boys the other night, they are adding extra security to the Palace and are calling in the City Watch to help.' He allowed a pause, waiting to see if anyone got the idea.

'I always thought I'd look good in uniform,' said Tailsin.

'I've always looked good in uniform,' said Jonas.

'Remind me, do they have women in the City Watch? Because there is no way I am going to be able to hide these puppies behind a breastplate,' said Taimsin patting her ample bosom.

'They do,' confirmed Fudail. 'Only in the new city, but I expect they'll be making exceptions now.'

'Good. I'd hate to miss all the fun.'

'Fudail, you come up with any options?' asked Forge.

'Yes. I know where I can acquire some uniforms. There is a something akin to an armoury that holds the kit for new recruits. I know the man who runs it, I helped him out with a personal problem a couple of years ago.'

'Won't he be suspicious of you going in and taking a half-dozen sets?'

'He can be as suspicious as he likes but he isn't going to say anything that puts me in front of an officer of the law or a judge. The city turns a blind eye to many faults but one thing it will not tolerate is men with a penchant for young boys.'

There was a pregnant pause. Forge coughed. 'That sounds pretty cut and dried. There is nothing else we need to talk about. Fudail, you go and chat to your man. The rest of you, we'll meet back here tomorrow. But let's play it careful, I'll arrive first, the rest of you can find places to hide and wait for Calill to arrive. Then we give it a little soak time. I might trust him but I am also an old fool.'

'I wasn't going to mention that,' said Jonas.

Chapter 22

'There are only three entrances to the Palace,' said Calill. He marked these on the blackened board with a piece of chalk, adding to his crude rendition of the Palace and its grounds. 'You come in via the main entrance off the Street of Artists or you go around the side. In via the double gates if you are delivering or by the postern gate at the far end if you happen to be a member of the Paternal Guard. That's where we are going to go.'

'Right past the roadblock at the start of the lane, which you said has now got ten men manning it?' said Tailsin.

'Yes. If they let you in there, then the Postern gate will be easier, they'll ask no questions as long as you are with me,' said Calill.

'Why can't we be Paternal Guards?' asked Tailsin. 'Surely they have the best access and the least questions asked.'

'Because we are all tracked going in and going out. We all carry a marker that is handed into the gate guard. They only hand it back to the man who gave it to them,' said Calill patiently. 'There are not enough of us to pull more than our shift allowance each day and our masters know better than to overwork us. That's why City Watch are being used, but they will never go anywhere without a Paternal Guard escort.

'Fair enough. Continue,' she said imperiously.

Calill raised an eyebrow. 'They've already started with the reinforcement of the Palace, the first units of City Watch are in place. From what I've been briefed, they will have a rotation of manpower over the coming weeks until after Rostos. City Watch will be attached to and take orders from the Paternal Guard, increasing the footfall within the Palace. Where pairs normally walk we will have whole squads.'

'Mages?' asked Taimsin.

Calill shook his head.

'I do not know where they will be, only that they will be on hand. No doubt somewhere in the west wing of the Palace, where the Ministry is located. They believe you are trying to access the records so it makes sense they are placed there.'

'Where will we find the Paternal?' asked Forge.

'His private quarters are in the east Wing and the Chamber,' Calill tapped his chalk against a rectangular room in the centre of his drawing, 'is located in the central portion of the Palace. He only goes there when he is mediating. We will pass it on the route I intend to take.'

'And what will the security be like in his chambers?' asked Jonas.

'He has guards on the entrance to his chambers but inside he only has servants and officials attending him. The place is a little empty without his family,' replied Calill.

'Is there any way we can talk our way past them to get inside?' asked Forge.

Calill shook his head. 'Not without a member of his staff and certainly not at that time of night.'

'Then those will be the first we have to take out,' said Tailsin.

'I don't want any of my brothers hurt,' said Calill firmly. 'I am helping you get the Paternal out, not slaughter my family.'

'I'm not sure this one grasps the reality of our situation,' said Tailsin to Forge.

'Calill, I can't guarantee that,' said Forge. The last thing he needed was for Calill to grow a conscience right now. 'All I can promise is that we want to keep things as quiet as possible. Getting into a fight isn't part of the plan. Tailsin, this is your territory, you can knock them out, right?'

Tailsin smiled indugently. 'I am the best. I can probably manage something,'

'If not, I can sort it,' added Taimsin.

'Can you risk using magic inside?' Forge asked. 'I thought that was a big no no.'

'I can use some low level stuff that won't get noticed, until they go looking for it. Best I hold it back and let my sister do her thing until she realises that she needs me to bail her out.'

'Which will never happen, sister dear.'

Forge fixed his gaze on Calill.

'Will that work for you?'

Calill met his eyes and matched his stare.

'It will, if she's good enough.'

'Good enough?' spluttered Taimsin.

Her sister burst into laughter and pounded the table.

Fudail shook his head in disapproval but Forge couldn't hide the smile that crept unbidden to his face. He was starting to warm to the crazy twins.

'I haven't asked yet – but I need to know. I've seen you in action, but how long can you keep that up for?' he asked Taimsin. Knowing she'd spent time as a battle mage had given him a fair degree of confidence in her powers. But magic was a fickle and dangerous weapon. He knew that well enough.

'Magic is wielded at a price. It feeds off life energy. Use too much and it will kill you. Each user's power is defined by how much they can draw on before it exhausts them. That's why you see a lot of magic used on objects – they can be made and used later. By all accounts I am considered to have a high level of magical endurance. It means I can keep a couple of glamours on the go almost indefinitely. But you can ask any battlemage who has been in a fight, and they'll tell you that they are out for the count for a couple of days afterwards, at least.'

'Unless they weren't pulling their weight,' interjected Jonas.

'True,' agreed Taimsin. 'When we go in, I'll have a few surprises on me. But hold me back from using my power unless it's to counter their mages or we have no other choice.'

'Let's take that as a yes,' replied Forge. 'Moving on, we get into the Paternal's quarters, give him the good news and then we smuggle him out again. Fudail?'

'As well as uniforms for you, I have a spare set for the Paternal roughly matching his size and shape. Unlike the facemasks his Guard wears, there is nothing I can do to hide his features, but context is important. I imagine no one would ever give a City Watchman another look,' said Fudail.

Forge nodded at the fixer. 'Good work. We march him out of his quarters and we haul our asses in a calm and collected fashion back to the postern gate, Calill goes back to his post and we walk away. We head down to the harbour and board the *Crimson Shore* and pray for a stiff wind.'

Taimsin whistled and Tailsin scratched her neck.

'You know, it all sounds pretty simple.'

'That's what I'm afraid of,' said Forge.

'When are we doing this?' asked Jonas.

'Calill? When does your shift change?' asked Forge.

'Tomorrow.'

'Tomorrow it is, then. I want this done,' said Forge.

'Happy with that,' agreed Jonas.

'Fudail, can you get your gear here tomorrow?' asked Forge. Fudail nodded. 'No problem.'

'In which case, we'll call it quits. Let's gather here at midday. Calill, we'll meet you at the Palace tomorrow night. How does the tenth bell sound?'

'That works. I will see you there,' said Calill.

With that the Paternal Guard nodded to Forge and took his leave.

The twins shared a look, Fudail looked sour and Jonas was looking out the window and was shaping to spit.

'We all happy with this?' he asked to the whole crew.

'If he's going to stab us in the back, it'll be when we walk out this door or tomorrow night,' said Fudail.

'Not tonight,' said Taimsin. 'There's no one watching us. Leastways no one who's within a hundred yards of this place.'

'We'll leave first and do a sweep,' said Tailsin. 'If you hear explosions and lots of screaming, I'd hightail it while you've got the chance.'

'You two take care,' said Forge.

'We always do,' said Taimsin with a wave, as the sisters followed after Calill.

Fudail hadn't moved, he tugged at his right ear and then pushed himself off his chair. He was his normal brooding self but Forge knew that out of all of them, Fudail was the most exposed.

'Fudail?'

The man stopped.

'Hmm?' he looked distracted.

'When we get out, it won't take them long to work out that it was City Watch that were involved. They'll trace it back to your man and then you.'

'Yes. That is exactly what is going to happen. It doesn't matter. That man can burn in all the hells for his crimes, I always regretted helping him out. As for me, I'm leaving, just like I was going to before those lovely ladies of yours talked me out of it. That die was cast the day I met you.'

'Look, Fudail. For what it's worth, I am sorry. It was never my plan to drag you into this shit,' said Forge.

Fudail smiled. 'I know and I don't blame you. We are all slaves to a higher power. Now that we are committed to this course, let's make sure we see it through. It will be one hell of a story to tell, years from now.'

'If anyone believes us,' said Jonas.

Forge grunted his agreement. *If we're alive to tell it.*

Fudail walked to the door and opened it.

'That is true, my friend. At least we will know.'

When the door closed behind Fudail, Forge looked across at Jonas.

'What do you think?'

Jonas rubbed a hand over his head.

'Happy lad there needs to lighten up. It's not like he's going in with us.'

'Neither are you,' said Forge.

'Like fuck I'm not!' said Jonas.

'I want you on the outside, giving us some cover. When we get the Paternal out I want you ghosting us. You're my ace in the hole.'

Jonas looked at him, clearly unhappy. 'I can't argue with that but I don't like the idea of you going in there without backup, real backup.'

Forge knew what he meant, backup in the form of a fellow soldier of Ashkent, someone who'd fought in the line with you, who wouldn't turn and run. Forge trusted Jonas with his life but if things went south in the Palace, one more sword wouldn't do any good.

'Those twins might be a little crazy but they are effective. As for Calill, I think he'll come through for us.'

'He'd better do.'

'Come on, let's find Nazar.'

They found Nazar and his crew in the tavern on the docks. Having gone first to the *Crimson Shore*, they had discovered young Hassan keeping watch. He was a game lad but not exactly the best choice if anyone decided to actually board the ship. The crew were gathered in a corner of the crowded room and there was an amiable hubbub about the place. Forge caught Nazar's eye and beckoned him over to where he and Jonas had found a free spot by the bar. Forge laid a few coins on the countertop.

'Jonas, get 'em in for everyone.'

Jonas nodded and waved at a woman wearing a corset that was not fit for someone of her age and girth.

'Forge, my friend, how are you?' asked Nazar.

'Been better, been worse, leastways things are moving.'

Nazar nodded.

'When is it happening?'

'We are going in tomorrow night.'

Nazar's eyebrows raised a little.

'Really? You are not messing about.'

'I want to get it done and us on our way. Since the skirmish I've been feeling antsy.'

'Oh, I heartily agree with you on that one. We'll be ready to go as soon as you make an appearance. We won't make much headway until we reach the moles and get out into the channel of the Green River. Once there we can run up the sails and start putting some distance between us and the city.'

'Can we outrun their ships?'

'No, not a chance. We need to get out without raising any alarms. If they see us going then they will run us down and either sink us or board us.'

'If they board us then we can fight our way out of it.' If they had the Paternal, the Ministry wouldn't risk using any artillery or magic on them. They'd want to board and, in a hand-to-hand fight, he'd back his people to win.

'That may be so, but I would rather not risk the lives of my crew any more than is necessary.'

'I understand that,' replied Forge. 'If this goes according to plan, we should have at least an hour before any message gets down to the dockyards.'

'Hmm. Very well, that should be enough, as long as we don't dawdle.'

'Thanks, Nazar. I appreciate what you and your boys have done. Things haven't been easy so far, but we are due for a change of luck.'

'Now's the time. Let's hope I can live up to my name for once,' chuckled Nazar. Forge detected a slight quaver in the sound.

'Ale's up,' announced Jonas, gathering several tankards.

'Let's get these over to the lads,' said Forge.

The three of them joined the crew at the table, Wenham shoving over to accommodate Jonas.

'Lads,' said Nazar. 'This is our last night in this fair city of my birth. Tomorrow we will set sail for new adventures and new fortunes, with a little luck!'

There was a cheer from the crew and Medjhi leaned back and sighed theatrically.

'Thank the Gods, my barnacles were starting to grow roots.

233

I've been too long on solid ground.'

'That's because there are no whores left who'll agree to bed you,' said Rabi, loudly.

'Ah, I'm looking forward to seeing the girls from fair Misbah' sighed Benji.

'And the boys are looking forward to seeing you, brother,' retorted Bors.

As Nazar and his crew traded insults, Forge clapped Jonas on the back.

'Been a while since we've done this.'

Jonas snorted.

'Been more than a while. Last time any of us hung one on was way back before we set sail to Shifter.'

'I remember!' exclaimed Forge. 'We made old Tarney open his bar at nine in the morning and he didn't shut it 'til nine the next day. We had the place all to ourselves 'cos Tarney said he couldn't risk his usual punters getting hurt.'

'We didn't trash the place, much,'observed Jonas.

'No windows broken at least,' agreed Forge.

'You remember Thom? He was showing everyone his arse. There was still an almighty welt where that troll had smacked him.'

'He should've watched where he was sitting. You don't park yourself in front of a cave that smells of rotting flesh.'

'It was a good thing that troll had been hibernating, it wasn't thinking straight, or it could have been a lot worse,' said Jonas in a rare display of equanimity.

'Dumb shit couldn't ride his horse after that. Mac made him walk all the way back down the mountain.' Forge smiled as he recalled his old friend.

It was easy to laugh now. The morning after that session, he had never experienced pain like it. He had never wanted to die so much, anything to get rid of the feeling that someone had embedded an axe right in the middle of his forehead. Instead he was summoned to the Regiment to be told by Dav that they were all shipping out at the end of the week to Cauker. That's when things had started to go downhill. Forge had never really found a way to get back from what had gone down. Too many scars.

'What are you going to do when we get back?' he asked Jonas.

'I wasn't thinking much beyond tomorrow really, boss,' replied Jonas.

'I suppose so,' said Forge. He took a long drink.

'Reckon I'll head back in to the unit. See if they still want me,' mused Jonas. He didn't sound that bothered either way.

'If it helps, I can vouch for you. After this, McKracken will owe me a bloody favour or two.'

Jonas's right eyebrow rose. 'McKracken was it? That makes sense. I heard that bastard had retired.'

Forge shook his head. Gods, he hadn't gotten round to telling Jonas who had started him on this trip. 'He came and found me. After he told me about Dav, he hadn't left with me with much of a choice.'

'Using you because you're an expendable asset, huh? Sounds familiar,' said Jonas, sourly.

'I never thought I'd end up doing McKracken's dirty work. I feel like a Godsdamned mercenary.'

'Pretty much what we all are if you think about the crew we got for this. Except me, I volunteered.' Jonas paused for a moment and looked thoughtful. Not something you saw much of in Jonas, his opinions usually came fully formed. 'Are we getting paid for this?'

'I reckon so. Everyone here seems to have been given some

kind of incentive. You're getting fuck all,' he bantered. 'Like you said, you volunteered.'

Jonas downed his ale.

'No fucking surprise there then. Just like being in the Army. You want another?'

'Oh, yeah.' Forge looked down into his tankard. He hadn't noticed he'd finished it.

'Stop!' announced Nazar, as Jonas shaped to stand. 'Sit yourself down. Never let it be said that Nazar does not stand his crewmates a round. What do you want?'

Forge shared a look with Jonas. Jonas looked at Nazar. 'We'll have two ales and two bottle of red.'

Chapter 23

Calill stood by the barrier and looked down the Street of Artists. Lights blazed along its length from braziers specially put in place to keep the approach to the Palace illuminated. Above him, lanterns and torches drove away the many shadows that gathered upon the ornate rooftops and towers of the Paternal's home. It was a hot night but a gentle sea breeze had gained access to the top of the plateau and provided welcome relief. A swirl of wind gathered around the nearest brazier and pushed a blast of heat into his face, his mask taking the brunt. So much for the welcome relief. He rose up on his toes and then slowly lowered himself back down. Paternal Guard did not fidget and fuss, but the tension was getting to him. He glanced sideways at his brother Guards; their attention was focused elsewhere. There was still a great deal of footfall along the street as most of the shops remained open until late. There had been some discussion of sealing the Street off and Calill could see the merit, if not the personal advantage, in having done that. But for all that they had increased security, they did not want to send a message to the local populace that there was a problem. A patrol of City Watch approached and for a moment he thought Forge and the others had arrived. He felt a rush of excitement through his body. Yet they passed him by and, on counting, he realised they were only three strong. He pursed his lips and closed his eyes. The last thing he wanted to be doing was getting jumpy and giving himself away.

After the watch commander had issues their assignments, he had gone to Nishtuq, another Guard on his shift, and requested that he swap with him, citing ill health. After the expected good-natured insults and questions about his manhood, he had gained the switch with a promise of favours and several bottles of wine. That swap gave him the single duty of manning the armoury. It wasn't unheard of, there were some better jobs during a shift and the men of the Guard often horse-traded when they fancied an easier time of it. The night-shift within the armoury was always quiet. The men gathered their weapons at the start of the night and they handed them back at the end. Even the watch commander seldom bothered to visit – there was no risk and no danger. It was the Palace that needed protecting, not the armoury. If all went as planned, no one would ever know his part in the breakout.

Calill waited a further five minutes before he spied a patrol of City Watch walking toward him along the street. They looked purposeful if a little out of step. He counted three, not the four he had been expecting. A moment of doubt hit him before he recognised Forge at the head the trio. The man came straight to him, his face all business.

'We are the replacements you requested.'

Behind him, the twins looked pretty convincing in their armour. He could see they had applied some kind of lotion to darken their light, freckled skins and their red hair was tucked well underneath their helmets. Tailsin winked at him.

Calill was glad his mask hid his exasperation. He nodded, beckoned them forward and started down the side road. They walked in silence back towards the postern gate. The Guard stepped to one side to let them through. Calill had already sowed the cover story that these were late additions to the newest batch of City Watch and he'd been sent to collect them. The Paternal Guards had already seen so many through the gate that three more wasn't a cause for concern. Calill removed his faceplate as another Guard came out and handed back his token.

Calill nodded his thanks, replaced his faceplate and continued on. Neither guard had given any of them a second glance. Calill felt conflicted. Had the Guard became so lax, even in this state of heightened security? Perhaps they were just confident in the measures that were in place and their own abilities. *Or maybe it's just that they all trust me.* The guilt was stronger than he had expected. He was betraying a brotherhood that had been his life since he was sixteen. It was going to continue to be his life after tonight as well. At least, that's what he had told himself. But would things ever be the same again? So much had changed.

As they walked across the square towards the entrance to the Palace proper, he took a moment to check there was anyone else nearby. Satisfied they were alone he stopped by the door and turned to face his companions.

'Is everything well? I thought there would be four of you?' he asked.

Forge shook his head. 'I just made a small change. Nothing to worry about. We are good to go.'

'Very well. When we get inside, stay behind me and do nothing to draw attention to yourselves. I'll try and keep us away from any of the other City Watch patrols but I cannot guarantee it.'

Forge nodded his understanding and Calill looked at the twins. Tailsin was studying the Palace walls with professional interest and Taimsin was giving him an encouraging smile. He hadn't noticed it before but somehow they had given themselves stubble. It was quite unnerving.

He turned, pushed the door inwards and stepped through. Beyond the portal was a small entrance hall with two doors other side and a passage leading deeper into the Palace. He immediately took the left hand door which revealed a small, winding stair leading up. He led the way up the steps and quickly gained the second floor, a small landing facing another door. The steps continued up two more flights to a small observation tower that Calill knew to be manned. Once they were together, he led them through the door and left down the corridor that was on the other side. From there it was a series of short passages, halls and atriums that carried them closer to the Paternal. He wondered whether his companions were committing this route to memory. He had drawn it on the board yesterday, but it was not the easiest to follow. As they approached the final corridor, the route took them through the rearmost reception room of the Chamber and into the path of the two Paternal Guards and two City Watch that happened to be already passing through it. Calill swallowed and felt his forehead go cold. They marched on past, keeping them to their left. For their part, his brothers did the same, sticking to their protocols of silence and anonymity. The City Watch just trailed in their wake, looking bored. They disappeared from his limited vision and he held his breath, half expecting a breezy "good evening" from Tailsin.

He breathed a silent prayer of thanks when no such

exchange occured. They carried on down another series of corridors, lit by torches set in brackets every ten metres. The skylights above their heads revealed clear skies and a hazy glow - the rooftops of the Palace displacing the ambient light with dozens of man-made ones.

'Here we go,' he whispered, mostly to himself, as finally the entrance lobby to the Paternal's quarters came into view. The lobby itself was a rectangle, its longest sides stretching away to a set of ornate double doors inscribed with gold filigree weaving across the surface. Above them was a glass ceiling, criss-crossed with steel reinforcing bars. He knew those reinforcing bars were themselves reinforced by powerful magics that made the glass ten times stronger than normal. All around the sides of the hall were small marble pillars painted with very realistic green vines weaving their way around the circumference. In the spaces between each pillar was a tall amphorae-shaped pot with flowers spilling out of the top.

Calill was more concerned about the two guards at the end by the doors. He knew who they were and they'd soon recognise him when he started to speak. As he drew near, movement from his left side turned into one of the twins marching forward, raising her hands high and bringing them down palms first towards the ground. As she did so both guards slumped surprisingly quietly to the floor. The other twin leapt forwards and somehow gathered up both spears before they clattered onto the marble. Taimsin turned round and smiled.

'That's how we do it,' she said, smugly.

Calill pushed on past her to the doorway. He gripped the handles and pushed inwards, the doors opening easily and without a sound. He stepped through, saw no one coming to investigate and then beckoned the others through. Taimsin took the spears and Forge and Tailsin each hauled a guard through the doorway, laying them against the wall to either side of the entrance, Taimsin then placing a spear by both men. Calill closed the doors and took a moment to breath. He had stopped doing that at some point. He looked around and took in his surroundings. He had never actually been in the Paternal's Quarters before. Strangely, no Guard had. Only servants, members of the ruling Families, and of course high-ranking officials of the Ministry, were allowed access. He was absolutely convinced that many of those 'servants' were not as they seemed and were very probably well trained in the martial arts.

The room they were stood in was a large reception hall, similar to the one found outside the Chamber. There were comfortable chairs and sofas set around the sides and a large marble table set in the centre which supported three shallow pots filled with yet more flowers. There were two small doors leading off to either side and a wider opening directly opposite, draped with thin, almost diaphanous curtains. Calill pointed at them and looked at Forge. He gave him a look to suggest that he lead on. When Forge had acknowledged the gesture, Calill cricked his neck and moved towards the curtains, pushing them gently apart. Within was a bigger chamber which contained a large dining table that could seat at least twelve. The walls were covered with portraits and pictures and this room had an ornate plastered ceiling. The group fanned out as there were at least two doors and two more curtains leaving the room. The curtains to the left of him were billowing gently, as if a breeze was playing against them. He moved across and pulled one aside, stepping out onto a balcony. It looked remarkably like those used by the delegations and was full of comfortable sofas, couches and cushions. There were yet more of the flowerpots but the smell here was stronger. He walked to the balcony edge and looked over. Beneath was a garden full of trees rustling in the night air, buzzing insects and the gentle splashing of a fountain somewhere in the middle of it all.

'Another one of these open air delights,' said Forge.

'I didn't know this was here,' said Calill. He was genuinely shocked. How did he not know about this place?

'You never been up any of the lookout towers?' asked Forge.

'Yes, but I never saw this. I have never entered this room before. Look, it has no roof, how could I not have seen this?'

'Illusion,' said Taimsin. She had joined them on the balcony and stood with her hands on her hips looking up with interest.

'What?' Calill asked, feeling foolish.

'A very good one at that. Takes a lot of power to maintain this. There must be some lodestones buried in the walls surrounding it.'

'Lodestone?' he asked.

'It's used to focus magical energy. It amplifies it. Very hard to come by,' said Forge.

Taimsin whistled softly. 'Hey, colour me impressed, Captain Jon Forge.'

'This illusion makes it look like another part of the roof of the Palace?' Calill asked.

'I'd imagine so,' said Taimsin.

'Gang? Could you come back inside a minute please?' said Tailsin, poking her head round one of the dividing curtains.

Calill led the way back into the dining room then drew up short next to Tailsin. A man stood in the doorway. He wore a simple robe of blue linen. In one hand he carried a goblet, in the other a book. He was looking expectantly at all of them. Calill felt his throat go dry.

'My lord Paternal,' he croaked out.

The Paternal cocked his head and took several steps into the room.

'I assume you have a reason for coming into my quarters?'

Calill nodded. He felt his face grow hot and a bead of sweat tumble down his cheek. He had never spoken to the Paternal and years of training and protocol were hard to ignore.

The Paternal placed his book on the table and took a drink from the goblet. He looked surprisingly calm.

'Perhaps you should tell me then?' the Paternal prompted.

'My lord-' said Calill. Forge stepped in front of him.

'My name is Jon Forge, we are here to get you out.'

The Paternal placed his goblet next to the book and folded his arms.

'Get me out of where exactly? Are we under attack? I'm sure I would have heard of it.'

Forge took his helmet off. 'Real deal.'

'Hmm. You are not a son of Karnak, but the City Watch does draw from a wide pool. Is the Ministry concerned that I am not well protected? Where else can I go?'

'Paternal. You gave Major Dav Jenkins a message. You asked for help. He died. So they sent me,' said Forge.

The Paternal paused to examine Forge closely and then closed his eyes and nodded. 'Very well. I did not expect anyone to truly come for me and so I must still play my role. I would not put it past the Ministry to lay a trap for me.' He sighed deeply. 'In a matter of days I am due to die. It is my required fate.' He opened his eyes and stared right at Calill who had to fight the urge to step back. 'I have lost everything that truly mattered to me. But I don't want to die.'

'Join the club,' said Forge. He looked at Calill then the others. 'Let's get to work.'

Calill stepped back and watched as the others started to pull items of clothing and armour that had been secreted about their person. A helmet from a sack that had been hidden underneath Tailsin's cloak, Taimsin removed a chain shirt that had been worn over her own, Forge took off his gloves.

Calill tensed as the Paternal came and stood next to him, his attention still on the activity in front of them. 'These people are obviously not of the city. But you are,' he glanced briefly at Calill. 'You are Paternal Guard. Your loyalty is absolute. What did they offer you to betray your sacred trust?'

'Nothing,' said Forge. 'He volunteered.'

'Then that makes me even more intrigued.'

'I was offered nothing,' said Calill hotly. 'It was what was taken from me, by the Ministry.'

'Taken?'

'Someone I cared about.'

'Ah,' the Paternal nodded. 'That I can understand. Loss can change your perspective, re-evaluate your choices.'

'No different to you then, eh?' said Tailsin unbuckling her swordbelt and handing it over to the Paternal. He took hold of it with an uncertain look. 'Congratulations, you have just joined the City Watch.'

'Do you not need this weapon?' he asked.

'I've got my blades,' Tailsin replied, pointing at a second belt she had been wearing underneath her first. On either side were two long, thin knives with forked handles.

'Paternal. You need to get yourself into this kit. Do you have any trousers matching ours?' asked Forge.

'Yes, I believe I have something similar.'

'Then go get 'em. We are mixing and matching a little but

nobody should notice.'

'I will need to go to my dressing room,' said the Paternal.

'No problem. Go with him,' Forge said, looking at Calill.

'Very well' Calill replied. He was not enjoying this at all.

As he followed the Paternal towards another door, Forge called after them.

'We are leaving in three minutes.'

Calill entered a short corridor that opened out into a plush, and very grand sleeping chamber, lit by several candelabras. The bed was big enough for three people, four-postered, covered in cushions and draped in fine silks. The room opened out onto another balcony although there was a series of shuttered doors that currently sealed off much of the view.

'Wait here,' ordered the Paternal. Calill did as he was bid and stood to an awkard attention as the Paternal crossed the room, opened another door and stepped through. He heard some rustling and the sound of something dropping to the floor. A minute later, the Paternal emerged where sturdy yellow breeches and a white tunic.

'This should do,' he said as he passed Calill by. 'I should be very worried about my Guard, if I wasn't trying to abscond.'

Calill didn't agree. *You won't find any others like me.*

Back in the dining room the Paternal set about putting on the uniform, and Calill helped with buckling the sword-belt and buckling the helmet securely on the Paternal's head. The Paternal looked by and large just like any other watchman, plain and forgettable, as long as you didn't dwell on the eyes. They were far too knowing and intelligent and radiated a certain presence. Forge nodded his head in approval. 'Good enough for government work.'

Calill wondered what that phrase meant.

The Paternal looked down at himself and shook his head.

'Although I can guess most of it, what is the plan, may I ask?'

'We get you out of the Palace and onto a waiting boat,' said Forge.

The Paternal nodded, a wry smile on his lips.

'The simple plans are always the best. I look forward to its smooth running.'

'So do I,' said Forge. 'How long before someone comes to check on you?'

'I have already dismissed my servants for the evening. I can expect to be alone until dawn, when they return with my breakfast.'

A bit of luck there, that should give us time. He pointed towards the entrance hall. 'Come on.'

Forge led the way back and Calill brought up the rear. Waiting at the doorway were the sisters. Tailsin was just closing one of the doors. 'All clear,' she said.

'Good,' said Forge. 'Let's go. Paternal, you stay at the back, next to me. Calill, you go first. Take us out of here.'

Calill shot him a furious look and hissed. Forge had named him! If something was to go wrong and the Paternal was taken and questioned, then his identity would be revealed. Now, more than ever, Calill felt that he had lost his way, his certainties. But there was no going back now. Forge had the grace to look ashamed at least. Calill hefted his spear, turned and walked to the doors as Taimsin opened them both, allowing him to pass. Her face had a curious look of sympathy; it had not escaped her either. As he passed beneath the threshold and out into the Palace proper he took a deep breath. He could not remember a time when he felt so damned afraid.

Chapter 24

Damn me for a bloody idiot. Forge was pissed at himself. He had dropped Calill in the shit. There had at least been a chance that Calill could have gotten away with helping them, but if it all went south then he'd get fingered. As they started back down the corridor away from the Paternal's quarters, it took him a few moments to figure out how he could make amends. In the end it wasn't that difficult. If the shit hit the fan he would have to kill the Paternal. It meant failing his mission and letting McKracken and Dav down but in the cold light of day, the last thing Dav would've wanted was for Calill to be drawn into this. He'd apologise to Dav for that when he caught up with him in whatever place they had reserved for dead soldiers. At least he could protect Calill's identity. It was all he could do, if it came to it. And it would all be for nothing if they couldn't get out of this bloody place first.

They retraced their steps at a brisk pace but it still wasn't fast enough for Forge. He was fighting every instinct to run hell-for-leather. This cloak-and-dagger shit was really not for him, he was far too long in the tooth. He risked a look at the Paternal who was matching his pace stride for stride, keeping his face forward, a hand resting on the hilt of his sword. He was a cool customer, this one. It probably came with the territory. But still, it was damned odd just how calmly he'd taken it all. For a man in fear for his life, a little more relief would have been in order.

They made it back to the Chamber's reception hall without incident only to find that the patrol they had encountered earlier were now on their way back. There were also two men dressed in the same robes worn by the functionaries he had seen on his earlier visit. They were fussing about the flowers and fruit bowls, no doubt preparing for a new set of visitors, absorbed in their own small world. As they passed the patrol, still on their left side, Forge noticed out of the corner of his eye movement, a head lifting up, looking at the Paternal who was but six feet away. There was a gasp, an arm raised, a finger outstretched, pointed right at him. Time slowed as realisation hit both Forge and the Paternal that he had been recognised. 'Fuck it,' said Forge. Instinct took over.

He reached out and pushed the Paternal towards the others, the man stumbling into Taimsin. Forge spun, his sword sliding from the scabbard, as he took his first few steps towards the other patrol, who by the looks of their faces, were still trying to understand what had just happened. That was all he needed. He levelled his blade at chest height and used his moment to thrust the blade underneath the rim of the Paternal Guardsman's faceplate. He pulled the sword out and a gush of dark red blood followed in its wake. The Guard's companion had taken a step back and was lowering his spear for a stab. Forge brought his sword into a high port, stepped inside its reach and brought his sword around and down in an arc, slamming it into the Guard's head. The man crumpled to the floor. The first was on his knees, a hand clutching his throat in a fruitless effort to stem the tide. Forge readied himself to receive the charge of the two City Watchmen but

Tailsin had got there before him, her twin knives drawn and bloodied. Both of them were down and truly out. The two functionaries were a bloody mess - dark red smears against the walls marked where they had been picked up and bodily hurled. Taimsin's back was turned and she was facing the way they were headed, one hand raised palm first. The Paternal was stood rooted to the spot, his face switching between the various pieces of carnage.

'That was fast,' he observed, with a hint of awe.

'Best way,' muttered Forge. 'Calill...'

Calill had not moved from his position at the head of the group. He was looking at Forge but was saying nothing.

'Calill. Sorry, I had to do that. We had no choice.'

'They were my brothers,' said Calill.

'They were. The moment you agreed to help us that changed,' said Forge, trying to keep his voice calm, even as energy was coursing through his body. 'We need to go.'

Calill nodded and started off. The twins hurried in his wake, getting back into formation. Forge grabbed the Paternal by the arm and hauled him along until they all got into a walking rhythm, somewhat faster than before. Forge thought through their options. If they were quick and lucky, they might still get out of the Palace before anyone found the bodies. They went past the doors leading to the balconies, Forge knew his way from here. They continued on, back into the maze of corridors and passages. A horn sounded, it blew again and again, its echoes joined by distant shouts.

'Calill,' Forge said. The Paternal Guard kept walking. 'Calill, wait!'

Calill stopped. 'What?'

Forge pushed to the front of the group.

'Get going. We'll take it from here.'

'But you need to get out the gate.'

'Too late. Too difficult. We are heading out the front,' said Forge.

'Really?' asked Tailsin.

Calill shook his head.

'You won't make it.'

'Not your problem. You've done enough. Get your arse back to the armoury before someone sees you. Go!' Forge pushed him away with one hand and Calill staggered back. Forge turned his back and pushed to the front. 'Tailsin, you and me to the front, Taimsin you are at the back with His Highness. I'll lead us out.'

'Out the front?' said Taimsin.

'Out the fucking front,' repeated Forge. 'You ready?' he asked of the Paternal. The man nodded, his face grave.

'Right.'

He led his small group back the way they had come. He drew his sword. If the alarm was sounding, it would look just as convincing to have it out as in. He marched them back towards the Chamber and the steps leading down to the ground floor. Whatever else happened now, at least he had done right by Calill. It might be the last thing he would do. Several armed men ran past them all as they gained the bottom of the stairs. No one looked up at them. It was a good start. He led them on towards the entrance lobby. There were lights blazing ahead, it made sense. As they drew near, Forge made out several Paternal Guard, a few City Watch and a bunch of guys dressed in robes. Forge entered the hall and made a smart left turn, taking his squad towards the exit. They were almost halfway to the open portal and no one had yet thought to close the doors.

'Damn, we've been made,' whispered Taimsin.

'How?'

'Those guys back there are mages. They've just picked up my scent. Watch out!'

Forge turned just in time to see Taimsin clap her hands together. A loud roar accompanied the faintest shimmer of air and the gaggle of armed men and mages were blown from their feet. A shout from behind forced him to turn once more as several men came at them from the entrance. Tailsin ran to meet them waving a hand and pointing at her sister.

'It's them, they got the Paternal!' she said in a passingly gruff and manly voice. A couple of them hesitated in their stride but continued on towards Forge.

'Get behind me!' he shouted at the Paternal, pushing the man back with one hand.

Tailsin stuck a leg out as the last guardsman drew level with her. He careened forward into the man in front causing both to clatter to the ground. She was upon them immediately, finding exposed flesh and driving her knives deep. Of the two remaining guards one turned to face this new threat, leaving just one to have to deal with. Forge preferred those odds. The Paternal Guard had a spear and a shield, held in a defensive posture, shield out in front protecting his torso and legs, the spear held tight against the shield, ready to thrust. There was one sure way to handle this one. Forge yelled and charged at the Guard, looking to force the man off balance. As he collided with the shield, he felt the wind go out of him, the guard holding his ground. The shield was pushed hard against Forge, forcing him backwards against a pillar. The shield moved away from covering the body, allowing the Guard room to follow up with the spear. Forge readied to bat the thing away with his blade, if he could. The Guard gave a grunt and fell to his knees. Tailsin stood over him, a knife dripping with blood.

'Come on, old man, you're slowing us down. You too, sister dear.'

'Tish,' said Taimsin, running past Forge with the Paternal in tow.

Forge pushed himself away from pillar and stumbled after them. He would have liked to have made a comment about his age but right now he was having trouble breathing. He looked back to check for pursuit. A few of those struck by Taimsin's spell were trying to get up. Several more guards had arrived and were moving towards Forge and his people. He gained the exit and was out onto the portico and down the steps. As they hit the street, another half dozen men were approaching from the side road of the Palace. Tailsin did the same trick again, pointing back up the steps.

'Quickly, we need more men, they are coming through!'

The approaching Guards and City Watch slowed down and looked up the steps to the entrance where their brothers had appeared. One of them looked at Forge then back at the men advancing down the steps who were pointing and shouting their hearty disagreement of Tailsin's suggestion. At the back, one of the mages was shaping to create something unpleasant.

'Nice try, sister,' said Taimsin, withdrawing a small wooden ball from a pouch. She crushed it in one hand and flames burst into life, licking over her fingers, and yet she did not register any pain. She flicked her wrist, opening the hand and releasing a small, angry-looking fireball. It landed on the steps right in front of the advancing guards, exploding outwards and engulfing them in a wave of searing heat. Forge shied away from the blast, covering his face.

'It's a shame it only ever works the once,' agreed Tailsin. She spun and drove a knife into the neck of a Guard and kicked a Watchman in the balls. Feeling like he wasn't pulling his weight, Forge smashed his sword down onto a Watchman's head then parried an overhead swing from another. He pushed the blade away, stepped in close and drove his mailed fist into the Watchman's open mouth. He punched again just for effect and left the Watchman reeling. A Paternal Guard was charging him, spear levelled. At the last moment, Forge grabbed the watchman and threw him into the path of the Guard. There was a scream as the spear hit something soft. The Watchman fell to the ground as the Guard tried to steady himself. Forge didn't give him the chance. He swung his sword and connected with the Guard's unprotected spear arm, shattering bone and severing flesh. The Guard cried out in agony, dropping his spear and shield. Happy that the threat was removed, Forge looked for another target, but they were all down - dead, dying or wishing they were. By the steps, Taimsin was weaving a complicated pattern with her fingers. At the entrance to the Palace he could see several strands of glowing light forming within the gap, attaching themselves to the frames. More were added until a web-like structure blocked the way. Even as she lowered her hands a booming noise sounded, causing the web to shudder and bow outward.

'Let's go. That's bloody powerful magic I'm holding off. They'll keep sending more and I'm buggered if I'm killing all of them,' she said.

'Spoilsport,' replied Tailsin, but she sheathed her blades.

Forge assessed their situation. There was nobody close who looked dangerous so now was probably their last chance to get moving. 'Lead on,' he said and they started back along the Street of Artists. He looked at the Paternal. In all the excitement he had forgotten to check him over. 'You alright?'

'Yes. I appear to be. Perhaps I should help you. I haven't drawn this sword yet.'

'You know how to use it?'

'No, not really.'

'Then best not.'

'We heading straight back?' asked Tailsin.

'Yes. We stick to the plan,' said Forge. There was another boom.

'There goes the barricade,' said Taimsin looking over her shoulder. 'They must have some serious users back there.' She coughed, hacking up phlegm. 'I had to put everything into that barrier.'

They were almost at the end of the street now and all they had to do was get out of sight and then look to blend in. With the shit storm they'd started, there would be plenty of City Watch cutting about the place.

'We got some more angry looking men with swords coming after us,' said Tailsin. 'Want me to turn back and deal with them?'

'No need,' said Forge. 'We've got covering fire.'

From somewhere just above their heads, they heard a familiar twang. Forge looked up. He could see nothing but shadows and what appeared to be an open window. The Gods knew how Jonas had gotten up there without being seen. Hopefully he could get out again. A moment later another shaft was loosed.

They rounded the corner. Forge rolled his eyes in the relief. They were alone. It wouldn't last. 'Back in formation everyone. We're just another patrol. Look mean and surly.'

'Easy in your case,' quipped Tailsin.

They got a hundred yards before encountering another patrol. Their leader hailed them as they drew close.

'What's going on?'

It was the Paternal who spoke up first.

'There's a ruckus at the Palace. Someone tried to break into the records room, I heard. They want the City Watch to fan out and try and catch them. We're going to set up a road block here.'

'Right. We'll head that way,' the Watchman said, pointing at a street running at right angles to their own. 'Come on.' His men followed him away, the sound of the boots hitting the cobbled stones fading.

Forge nodded at the Paternal.

'Nicely done.'

'One thing I have experience of is giving suggestions and direction,' he replied with a wry smile.

Forge noticed a bead of sweat running down the man's cheek.

The group pressed on. Taimsin produced a brand from within her cloak, spoke a single word causing it to burst into flames, and passed it to her sister. It added to the picture of a patrol going about its business. They took a roundabout route, following streets and lanes off the main routes as much as possible. It meant more time in the open but ensured less prying eyes.

A thought struck Forge. 'Can you use some kind of misdirection spell on the Paternal, make so that folk don't really recognise him?'

'I could,' said Taimsin. 'The problem is, they'll have mages looking for any magic. They'll be able to identify me and depending on what I do, be able to locate it. I haven't much left in the keg if you know what I mean. I'll use it if I think somebody might get too close.'

They had cause to use it five minutes later when they

arrived at the Parade. The Crucible was aglow with lights and there were hundreds of people milling around on the streets circling it. Just by looking at the number of litters and armed guards, the Families must have gotten wind about the Palace. City Watch were gathered around in great numbers at the multiple entrances to the Crucible, holding back the crowds and letting only a few, obviously wealthy, individuals through.

'Everyone be cool and just keep walking,' muttered Forge.

'The big man is covered,' said Taimsin.

Forge glanced at the Paternal. It was obvious the man was there, he could see him and hear him, yet even as he looked, he couldn't quite get a fix on his features or the clothes that he wore. It was like he was looking at him through a pane of thick, cloudy glass.

They carried onto the Parade, moving along the central path, passing by the statues and gardens. There was plenty of traffic, all of it heading onto the plateau. Another large squad of City Watch marched by but no one thought to stop and question them. They soon turned south, heading back down the slope towards old Karnak. The route to *The Moon Over Karnassus* already had plenty of twists and turns but Tailsin threw in a couple more just to be sure. News had yet to filter down this far and old Karnak looked no busier than any other night. Folk went about their business, fishermen went by carrying rods, nets, and baskets of the day's catch, stevedores stinking of sweat were heading towards taverns and other hostelries. There were even a couple of speculative suggestions from whores hanging out of brothel windows.

They reached the inn and hurried round to the back door and up the stairs to the top room. Their passing drew puzzled looks and quiet alarm from the clientele they encountered but no one dared to question them. They were City Watch after all. Fudail stood when they entered, his face sharing both relief and concern. To Forge's own relief, Jonas was already back and in his usual spot, back against the wall.

They piled in and started removing helmets and kit. 'Any problems?' Forge asked Jonas.

'Not really. After you lot legged it I shot a couple of locals. That kept their heads down for a wee bit. I got out when it looked like someone was going to throw a fireball my way.'

'Nice. Taimsin, you got your eyes out there?'

'Yes. She's doing circles around this building, two hundred yards out. Nothing unusual going on.' She had dropped into a chair, he arms and legs spread-eagled.

Forge smiled. As breakouts went it could've been a lot worse.

'Tough night?' he asked.

'Yeah, I'm pretty beat,' acknowledged Taimsin.

She'd done well, thought Forge. He'd seen enough battle magic to know the toll it must have taken. 'Jonas, haul ass down to the harbour. Let Nazar know we are on our way.'

'Yes, boss.'

Jonas picked up his bow and strode out of the room.

'Leave the guard uniforms. We shouldn't need those now. We are leaving in two minutes.'

Fudail joined Forge. He looked at the Paternal, who was being helped in unbuckling his armour by Taimsin, and shook his head in wonder.

'Jonas told me that there was some "excitement" as he called it.'

'We had to fight our way out.'

'And you made it out alive?'

'Yeah. Crazy, huh? Turns out the last thing they were expecting was us going out the front door.'

Fudail pointed at his face. 'You have some blood on your cheek.'

'Ah.' He spat into his palm and rubbed at the indicated spot.

'And now you are heading for home?' Fudail asked.

'Damn straight.'

'Mind if I come with you?'

'I thought you were heading in the opposite direction?'

'I was, but the more I think about it, your way may well prove to be the faster exit from the city.'

Forge thought for a second as he removed his chainmail and shrugged on his leather jacket.

'Can't see why not. You got everything you need?'

'All that I value is in that knapsack,' he said pointing at the black leather sack next to the table.

'Fine.' Forge looked across to the Paternal, now divested of armour. Taimsin was good to go, Tailsin was putting herself into her leathers. Forge caught sight of more than he had intended and got a blown kiss for his troubles. 'We all set?'

Forge collected his sword belt and led the way back out of the room, down the stairs and out onto the street. The party of five walked purposefully towards the harbour. Forge felt calmer, less on edge. Perhaps it was the atmosphere, the warm night skies and the benign neighbourhood.

'You are from Ashkent,' said the Paternal, walking next to him.

'I am. But strictly freelance on this one.'

'I see. Naturally the Assembly wanted to keep their involvement debatable at best.'

'They can still trace me back to them. Although, if put under torture, all I could honestly say was that I was chosen for a black op by a retired general.'

'In this world, that is enough to give Ashkent a defence. After all, they cannot control the actions of one rogue ex-general can they?'

'I guess not.' They walked in silence for a moment. 'You gave that message to my friend, Major Jenkins. It got him killed. Why him?'

'I see now the reason for your presence. Why him? I had only met him on two occasions but he struck me as an honest man. That and it was simply opportunity. I am watched by day and I am never alone except for when I am in my quarters or within the Chamber. Once there, I could of course plead for assistance, but why would anyone help me? The ruling Families want me mediating not running off with a thousand secrets and lies. Further to that, no one would consider it a worthwhile proposition to attempt to free me. The Ministry knows that a Paternal might consider escaping, but as I am sure you know, I have little left to lose. What life I do have left, I want to spend it on my terms. I passed Major Jenkins a note as we stood to leave the Chamber, it was nothing more than a desperate gamble. I did not even know he was dead. I am truly sorry for his loss and truly thankful he acted on my plea. I presume the Ministry were following him?'

'Yes.' Forge felt a deep bitterness welling up inside, that sense of frustration and rage that men should die because of random acts of chance, good men that deserved better after a lifetime of service.

'When they get a scent, they are like dogs,' said the Paternal. 'They are adept at rooting out schemes against the city. I have never known them to fail.'

'They didn't get it their own way this time.'

'I agree. Your plan was simple and audacious, even if it

didn't work quite as you intended. Getting that Paternal Guardsman on your side was a masterstroke.'

'He had his own reasons.'

'I am sure he did.'

Up ahead, Taimsin stopped.

'What?' asked Forge.

'We got trouble,' she replied. 'My little friend has just flown over the main street leading down to the harbour. There are about a hundred City Watch heading that way.'

'The Ministry moves fast. They will want the harbour sealed off,' said the Paternal.

That much was obvious and it had been expected, but Forge had hoped he would have more time.

'Can we get to the ship before them?'

'No chance,' said Tailsin. 'Unless you want us to fight our way through. I'm not averse to the idea.'

'There'll be mages on their way, if they aren't already in that lot,' said Taimsin.

'Shit!' spat Forge. 'Let's get as close as we can. There might still be a way through.'

Even as he said it, he wasn't sure he believed it. More importantly, where was Jonas?

Swarbreck marched down the corridor towards his office. Orlaise and several others were waiting for him by his door. One of them carried a lighted candle.

'Just you,' he said, looking at Orlaise while reaching out for the candle. The others bowed their heads and returned back along the corridor. He frowned. It was an unusual breach of protocol to have so many gathered. It was not how it was done. Things must be bad. He raised his eyebrows at Orlaise.

'Tell me. Do not wait until we are inside. Talk plainly.' He fished into his pocket and retrieved his key.

'The Paternal has been taken from the Palace,' said Orlaise.

Swarbreck swore. He placed the key into lock, leaned in close and whispered. The lock clicked.

'Taken with extreme prejudice, I might add,' continued Orlaise, as he followed Swarbreck inside.

'Explain,' said Swarbreck, walking across to his desk and lighting the three candles upon it. Orlaise closed the door.

'Whoever they were, they gained entry via the barracks. No alarms, no questions. They silenced the guards outside the Paternal's apartments and got as far as the Chamber before things changed.'

'What changed?' asked Swarbeck blowing out the single candle and settling down into his chair.

Orlaise face looked a little redder, his eyes seemed bigger. He was clearly agitated. 'It would appear they were confronted and challenged, so they changed tack. They fought their way out wreaking havoc as they did so. They went right through the main hallway!' He shook his head. 'The audacity of it. They had a sorcerer too. Blew chunks out of our mages who tried to intervene and positively ruined the décor.'

Swarbreck drummed the fingers of his right hand on the table. 'Let me get my facts in order. They went out the front way? The most heavily guarded route. Where all our eyes were facing? Our roof was well covered and those damned gardens were sealed off. So they went out the front way.' He was still trying to imagine the events of the last two hours. It wasn't too hard, one just had to walk through the bloody mess in the entrance hall.

'They were wearing City Watch uniforms,' added Orlaise.

'Yes. That would make sense. We invited them inside, after

all.'

'We knew something was going down, Minister. It was the right call. The prudent call.'

'And they used it against us,' Swarbreck muttered. *Audacious indeed.* 'How many people did we lose?'

'Not including the wounded, all in we think about thirty. That includes two mages.'

'Who did they lose?'

'Not a one.'

'Of course. And there we were believing we had removed the conspiracy.'

'And all we did was scratch the surface, Minister. They even had archers on the street to cover their exit. This was well-planned.'

Swarbreck looked at the carafe. He was feeling thirsty. The city was in an uproar, the palace was chaos and not all of it organised. Things had to be done, decisions made, people organised.

'Orlaise, I assume the city is on lock-down?'

'That it is, Minister. I have all our people out on the ground, the City Watch is fully mobilised and, without your leave, I have sent our mages to join the hunt. They have a scent and I'd rather they followed it.'

'Quite right. Send the Paternal Guard out too.'

'Minister?' Orlaise's face was a picture. It was as if Swarbreck had just ordered the slaughter of the firstborn sons of all the Families.

'The role of the Guard is to protect the Paternal. They have failed in that task and now there is no Paternal to guard. I sense they will have a measure of mortification about this. They also happen to be the best fighters we have. I think we'll need them.'

'Minister, I have men on their way to the harbour. Word has already been sent to the fleet. There will be no escape by water. The old town gate is shut, the walls patrolled. I cannot believe they have already made it beyond our reach. We moved too fast.'

'I understand, Orlaise, but think on this. Think about how they got in, how they got out. They used stealth, guile, foresight. Then they used brute force, skill at arms and powerful magic. This is a momentous event, my friend, and we must rise to the challenge, we must use every asset at our disposal. Flood the streets with anyone you can muster. We must force this group to cut a bloody swathe through our city, give them no place to hide, no safety. We must wear them down until, one by one, they drop. Then we will have our Paternal back and our pride restored. Nothing less than a complete and total response will do.' Swarbreck sat back and studied Orlaise. 'Are you alright?'

'I am sorry, Minister, I do not think I have ever seen such passion in your face.'

Considering the circumstances, it would be difficult for him to not betray some emotion, but he had his position to consider, he had his role to play.

'Orlaise, an unthinkable thing has happened on my watch. I must move heaven and earth to ensure that we contain this incident. This is not just about damage to our reputations. Our very lives depend on it.'

Orlaise turned deathly pale. 'The Families are demanding answers, even now they are gathering in the Crucible.'

'Then I will have to go to them and report what we know. And that is precious little. I know what they will ask. Is this a prelude to a war? Some kind of foreign intervention? Or is the motive simpler and we must pay a ransom for the

Paternal. I know which one I'd prefer, it is the former. Better that they think we are pitted against a nation than a band of fortune hunters. It would make us look like fools.' Swarbreck stood. It would seem that the carafe would have to wait. 'I will go to the Crucible directly.'

'Here is a short report I have prepared for you, Minister. It has all the facts as we know them,' said Orlaise, handing over a scroll. 'I have already issued a statement to the delegations and embassies informing them of an attempted break-in to our records vaults.'

'Thank you.' Swarbreck walked around his desk and stopped when he drew level with Orlaise. 'A thought. We must treat these kindappers with a measure of respect. Let us assume that they reach the outer city before we apprehend them. Are our chances increased or lessened at that point?'

'Lessened. But only from the position that they have more places to hide. But they still have another city wall to contend with. And if they escape, our mages can track them just as easily.'

'I don't want them getting out of the city,' said Swarbreck.

'Then I would suggest we open our coffers and call in all our favours. We have an army waiting to be mobilised, with the proper incentives.'

'You mean the gangs. Yes. I agree with your assessment, Orlaise. It will free up our people to cover the main arteries and walls. They know the ground better than we.'

Orlaise nodded. 'I will start the process. Messages and promises will be sent. I'll send some small downpayments too.'

'I will leave that to you, Orlaise. Do what you must, coordinate our forces as you see fit, do not underestimate these people.'

'There is no chance of that, Minister. I'll do whatever it takes to root them out and protect the safety and legacy of our city,' said Orlaise.

Swarbreck detected an almost fervent tone to Orlaise's voice. The man truly was a dedicated servant of the city and its masters. There was no doubting his ability nor the lengths he would go to get things done. But the Families would be looking for people to blame for this whole crisis. *And I will gladly give my life in service to the greater good. But I'd hate for it to be a waste.* He led the way out of his office, closing the door behind him. Turning the key and saying the warding words. His greatest challenge lay ahead of him: facing the ire of the Families.

Chapter 25

Nazar leaned against the tiller and chewed his lip. Tonight was the night. And he was damned glad to be leaving this city. In a way, he was quite excited to be part of such a stupendous act of insanity. He planned to dine out on it in his dotage, weaving tales to any who would be willing to listen of the time he and the intrepid crew of the *Crimson Shore* stole away the Paternal of Karnak Karnassus.

'Everything alright, Captain?' asked Medjhi. He came and leaned against the tiller from the other side. 'You look thoughtful. I don't see that face much.'

'Very funny. How are the crew?'

Medjhi looked along the deck.

'All fine. Anxious and eager to be away. Benji has fallen foul of a local who objects to his dallying with his wife. He is particularly keen to be off. No sign of anyone yet?' Medjhi asked.

'It would appear not. But they ought to be here soon. Their timings were quite specific. Unless of course they are all dead. In which case, we'll be leaving within the hour.'

'Nice of Forge to give us the option.'

'He is an honourable man.'

'A bit sour if you ask me,' sniffed Medjhi.

Nazar laughed. 'Oh, he's been through the wars, he has the right to be a little grumpy.'

'He likes his ale, though, I'll give him that,' announced Rabi, coiling some rope for want of anything better to do.

'And he gets the rounds in,' shouted Bors, from the front of the ship.

'You see, my old friend. Everyone loves Forge!'

'Huh,' said Medjhi, shaking his head in disgust.

'Nazar!'

Everyone turned at the panicked shout. It was Hassan, running hell for leather along the quay, pointing back towards the city. They gathered at the gangplank.

'What is it, Hassan?' asked Nazar.

'Nazar!' he shouted once more. His face was flushed, his eyes wide.

'Calm down, lad. Breathe easy,' said Wenham softly.

Hassan took a gulp of air. 'City Watch. Hundreds of 'em. They are spreading out all along the harbour front.'

Nazar and Medjhi looked at each other, sharing a single thought.

'Shall we set sail, Captain?' asked Medjhi.

Nazar shook his head.

'No, let's brazen this out. If we try and leave now, they'll just send word to one of their ships and run us down anyway.'

'They're coming, Captain,' said Bors, indicating some lights that had appeared at the end of the quay, bobbing and swaying as the approached.

'Everyone, stay calm and stay steady. I'll go and speak to them. Remember, we are all just humble sailors, getting ready to continue on our way. We have nothing to hide.' Nazar took a breath and marched down the gangplank and onto the quay to await their arrival. He put on his best smile and waved as the men, at least ten of them, approached. Two carried flaming brands, one more carried a lantern fuelled by whale oil. 'Good evening friends. What is happening? We don't get City Watch coming along here often.'

One wearing the crest of an officer upon his helmet stepped forward. His face was grim and his eyes suspicious. 'There has been an incident within the city. We have been ordered to seal off the harbour and allow no one leave to exit by land or water.'

'Oh, but that is precisely what we are planning to do. Our ship is loaded with goods, our business is done and we must be away.'

'Not now, you are not.'

'Good sir, I beseech you. If I miss the tide then I miss a whole day of potential trade opportunities, my competitors will steal a march on me and all my crew will be the poorer for it.'

'Not my problem. We've had a bad night tonight. We have lost a number of City Watch, friends of ours. We are in no mood to piss about.'

Nazar considered the man's words. There had been a fight, lives lost. Clearly the breakout had run into difficulty. But the very fact that they were looking at stopping anyone leaving the city suggested that at least some of Forge's party were still alive. That in turn meant they would be seeking a means to get back to his ship.

'Very well. I understand and feel your loss. We shall stay here and await further news.'

'Good.' The officer pointed at several of his group. 'You four, search the ship.'

'But why?' protested Nazar. 'We have nothing to hide.'

'Then this will be quick. We were told to search any ship

that was manned and making ready to sail. That means you too. Now stand back and let us do our job.'

Nazar relented. Better to get this over with quick. He watched as the four City Watch climbed up the gangplank and boarded the *Crimson Shore*, their swords drawn. Medjhi stepped back to allow them access. Two went to his cabin, the others demanded of Rabi that he open the hold. He looked at his crew: Medjhi looked calm, Hassan frightened, Benji and Bors stood close together sharing a similar scowl, he could no longer see Rabi, and Wenham was... stood by his cabin, his face was clouded, Nazar could see his fists flexing, his forehead screwed up tight. *Steady, Wenham, steady...*

The commander of the Watch turned his back on Nazar to talk to another member of his group. This one was wearing a cloak, his face obscured. In fact, Nazar was surprised he had not noticed it before, but the cloaked fellow was not even a member of the watch. The commander leaned in close, listening to the whispered words coming from the cloak. Nazar tried to listen in but he could hear only the barest of rasps coming from from the shadowed face. The commander nodded and turned back. He drew his sword and pointed it at Nazar.

'You are under arrest. Tell your men to come ashore.'

What was going on? Nazar raised his hands, 'Please, what have we done? We have nothing to hide!'

The cloaked man reached up with arms covered in bandages and pulled back the hood. The face revealed was a mess of raw and swollen fire-touched skin and dark, purple bruises. Even with all the mess, Nazar still recognised the man. It was Goker.

The thug raised a crocked finger towards Nazar. 'He's one of them. They torched all it all.' His voice was a whisper, each breath he took was pained. *Curses, how do I get out of this?* Nazar looked to his crew, their faces registering the encounter, knowing just as he what deep trouble they were in. There were no options, they had to surrender peacefully.

'All of you. Come along down,' said Nazar quietly.

Wenham spat and started making his way to the gangplank. The Watchman nearest Wenham prodded him in the back with the tip of his blade, and that was all it took. Wenham rounded on the guard and threw a punch into the startled man's face. He staggered back, clutching his nose. Nazar looked on, his heart sinking.

'Fuck you!' screamed Wenham, pushing the Watchmen away. The man collided with partner and fell to the floor, smashing the oil lantern. Then all hell broke loose. Benji and Bors charged at one of the other Watchmen, fists flailing. He heard a scream, it sounded like Rabi.

'Get up there,' ordered the watchman in charge, and another one of his men ran up the gangplank. With a roar, Medjhi leapt to meet him, a small fish knife in his hand. He landed hard against the Watchman and together they fell off the gangplank back onto the quay. Wenham was using a small cudgel to hammer the head of one the guards, the other was rolling around on the deck trying to put out the flames that had caught on his cloak from the oil that was burning unhindered around him. Of little Hassan there was no sign.

Nazar stepped forward his hands held up in front of him. 'Stop, wa-' Nazar felt a sharp pain on the back of his skull and lights flashed before his eyes. He fell to his knees, aware that he had been struck by something. He tried to stand, only to be kicked in the back and forced to the floor. It took him a few moments to regain some of his wits. He could feel something warm running down his neck. He turned his head, a man was stood over Medhji, driving a sword deep into his friend. On the ship the fire was still burning, spreading, licking up his cabin walls. Another fire had somehow started at the mast, and the sail was now alight too. He could make out figures still struggling in the flickering light, but his vision was starting to blur. It was clear what was happening. All was lost. He crew were dead or dying and his ship would soon be their casket. He looked ahead of him, the edge of the quay was just there, and beyond it was clear, open water. He started to crawl, he needed to keep moving, no matter what they did to him. He was going to die, but he would die as he wanted, on the water, not on land. His legs were weak, his arms weaker, but he kept on, expecting a final thrust of steel into his back. *Please, let me be lucky, just once more.* He heard someone near to him grunt and then felt the vibration of a body thump down next to his. *Ignore it, keep going.* There was a shout, a ring of metal on metal, then silence. His hands closed on the edge of the wooden walkway, his fingers felt the water lapping against it. Just one more pull and he was home.

A hand landed on his shoulder, pulling him back. He tried to struggle, to kick out. Instead he was hauled up, back on to his legs.

'Steady on, for fuck's sake,' said a familiar voice. 'This has gone to shit.'

'Jonas?' asked Nazar, his head swimming.

'Who else?'

'What, where?'

'No time.' Jonas threw an arm underneath him and the started back down the quay.

'My ship. My crew,' said Nazar, trying to turn his head, trying to stop his feet dragging.

'They're gone. You're alive,' said Jonas. 'We need to get

away from the harbour before they close it down. That lot was just the first.'

Another group of lights were making their way along the harbour wall. They were trapped. Jonas stopped for a minute, looking around at the other ships tied up against the quay. Nazar thought perhaps Jonas was thinking they could hide? Little good it would do them. The City Watch would see the fires and the bodies and they would hunt them down. Better to jump in the sea.

'It would have to be, wouldn't it?' said Jonas dryly.

'What do you mean?' said Nazar.

Jonas hefted him upright. 'Come on. I know where to go.'

Chapter 26

'We can't go down there,' said Taimsin. They had gone no more than two hundred yards before she had stopped them all. 'There are dozens of Watch on the waterfront.'

'There must be a way,' said Forge. 'We can handle the numbers.'

'We might, but they have at least three mages with them. I'm good but if I'm busy holding them off that leaves you with just my sister watching your back.'

'Wonderful vote of confidence, sister dear.'

'You know I'm right, Tailsin,' said Taimsin. 'I am running at a low ebb in case you hadn't noticed. Any more excitement and someone will have to carry me.'

Forge had never seen her in such a serious mood. He was minded to believe her assessment but he still had people down there. 'Then we go back, get changed into the City Watch uniforms and bluff our way through,' he suggested.

'Forge, it's no good. My bird's just seen something. A ship is ablaze. There's been fighting, we've lost them. Hang on...oh, you bastards.' She staggered against the side of the empty warehouse the group had taken shelter within.

'You OK?' asked Forge.

'Yeah,' said Taimsin, clutching her forehead. 'They spotted my bird, torched her out of the sky.'

Then they were blind. Any advantage that they'd had was lost. Forge was enough of a realist to know that no plan ever survived contact with the enemy and things had already gone tits up. He had lost Nazar and his crew, for all he knew Jonas as well. He would grieve later and it would probably destroy him. But right now he had a mission to finish.

'Forge?' asked Fudail.

'Yes?'

'What do we do now?'

'I'd like to know that too,' said Tailsin, poking her head back from her position by the doorway.

'We still need to get out of the city. We need another route out,' Forge said.

'One that doesn't involve a great deal of violence and destruction? I don't think that's likely,' said Tailsin.

She had a point.

Forge looked at Fudail, 'Tell me. How do we get out?'

'You are kidding, right?' said Fudail. 'We have just put the entire city on high alert. Every man and woman armed with a sword is looking for this man.' He pointed at the Paternal.

'Getting the city riled gave us the chance to get him out in the first place. Let's roll with that,' said Taimsin.

'Fudail. We are going back to the *The Moon* and then we are going to walk out of the city. Can you make that happen?' asked Forge.

Fudail shook his head and laughed. 'We have to get through the old city gate and then we have to get through the new city. You know what that means?'

'We have more room to manoeuvre, more places to hide,' said Forge hopefully.

Fudail spat. 'I know what this means. The Families do not control the new city like they do the old. They guard the main roads and the gates but the places in between, the districts? I have told you about this, is is the gangs.'

'That's better, right?' said Tailsin.

'No, it is not,' said Fudail. He sighed heavily and ran his hands down over his face. 'The Ministry will pull in all its favours and will spread its wealth. They will buy as many of the gangs as they can. Any loyalty they might have to any one embassy or nation will disappear in a heartbeat. They will be looking in their hundreds and they'll be looking for us.'

'Not yet, though,' said Forge. His was thinking hard and fast. He was on a roll and he was damned well not going to stand still and wait to be found. *When in doubt, act.* 'They can mobilise the City Watch quickly but it'll take time for them to get all the gangs onside. Let's take this one step at a time. We get out of the old city and into the new, we put those City Watch uniforms on, do whatever we have to do get through and then we find a place to hole up and plan the next move. How about your place, Fahad?'

Fudail threw his hands up in the air. 'Wonderful. Why not?'

'Good, that's decided.'

Five minutes later they were back in the attic room. Forge called the group together. 'Everyone, get changed. We are heading out again. When we get to the gates, Taimsin, we'll need you to cover the Paternal again.'

'I'll give it a go, if I have to. Like I said, they'll be looking out for magic but I might be able to lay a few false scents, keep them guessing for a bit.'

'Fine, do what you can. Come on people, hustle.' Forge undid his leather jacket and picked up the chainmail shirt. He looked across at the Paternal. For the first time, the man was looking a little uncertain. 'You OK?'

The Paternal smiled. 'I am still alive. However, the irony has not escaped me that by trying to save my life, I may have ended up shortening it.'

Forge dropped his tunic to the floor and set to helping the Paternal dress.

'If they were to get you back, what would they do?' Forge asked.

'To me? Oh, nothing really. They'd keep a tight watch on me and then wheel me out at the end of the festival to end my life and declare a new Paternal.'

'They must have had others die early. How do they get round that?'

'You wouldn't believe it if I told you.'

'Hands up,' Forge threw the chain shirt over the Paternal's head. 'Go on.'

'They fake it. They just wait until the next festival and announce that the Paternal is to be replaced due to ill health. It's all illusion, a spell. A convict is selected, a glamour put on him by the best mages the Ministry have and then they allow the man to die in the place of the old Paternal. And the Families are told that, at the pain of the death, they had better damn well keep the secret to their graves.'

'Well, bugger me,' said Forge, cinching the sword belt tight around the Paternal's waist. 'How do you die, by the way?'

'It is quite civilised, actually. We are allowed to take a poison. It works quickly and is quite painless, I hear.'

'That's nice of them. Right, you can finish off the rest yourself. I need to get sorted.' Forge picked up his own chain and manoeuvred it over his head, wondering about the games that states and nations played. In a way, everything was an illusion, power was where they told you it was, but you never really did see who was pulling the strings. Mostly, he'd been fighting for the puppeteers. At least, he thought he had.

They reached the old city gate twenty minutes later. As they marched along the Parade, they might as well have been moving in daylight. There were torches, beacons and braziers scattered along the route. In the middle pedestrian lane, oil lamps were suspended on the poles that Forge had spotted on his earlier travels. And the streets were busy. That was unusual. Forge had thought that some kind of curfew might have been declared but, as both Fudail and the Paternal pointed out, the Families of Karnak Karnassus took the security of their city very seriously. If there was an incident, they wanted to know who, how and why they did it. The Crucible would already be full and there would be loud and pointed questions being asked.

As they approached the gatehouse, things started getting very interesting. The gates themselves were, inevitably, shut. Forge counted at least twenty City Watch clustered before them, of which a dozen were engaged in trying to hold back a crowd of people. They were a mix of locals both wealthy and poor as well as a smattering of foreign-looking types. Those individuals were being weeded out and held to one side, each one being questioned closely and searched. In the towers of the gatehouse and upon the walls, yet more lights blazed and figures prowled along the parapets, some looking out, others in.

Fudail, who was now dressed in some of what was to have been Jonas's uniform, leaned in close to Forge. He had taken care to remove all of his jewellery and adornments. 'They won't open the gates again. Not for anyone without official business and a Ministry seal or letter to prove it. I know the procedure they have in place. The gate commander's life would be forfeit.'

'I don't suppose you know him, do you?' asked Forge.

'It is possible, but not until I get close,' Fudail replied.

'Alright, then. We'll do it the hard way,' announced Tailsin.

'What hard way?' asked Forge.

'I'll give you an excuse. You just make sure you get through the gates. I'll meet you at Fudail's. Sister, dear? Might I borrow one of your little surprises?'

'Of course, sister,' replied Taimsin. She produced a small clay ball and handed it over. 'Do be careful.'

'Hey, it's me!' replied Tailsin. She turned away and crossed the Parade, disappearing into the crowds.

'Um. What's she doing?' asked Forge.

'Diversion,' replied Taimsin. 'You'll see it in a minute. When she kicks it off, we need to be ready to move.'

Forge was happy to roll with that. 'Let's get closer, look as if we should be here.'

The group moved nearer to the gate, pushing aside folk who got in their way and generally trying to look mean and in a bad mood.

'Hey,' Fudail shouted out to a nearby Watchman. 'Any news? We've just done a sweep along the Parade.'

'Nothing. We heard there was a fight down by the water but nothing's come this way. All we know is nobody is getting out. Hey, just get back!' the Watchman shoved a very agitated woman away.

Fudail eyed Forge. Whatever Tailsin had in mind, she had better hurry up. Forge was not happy stood in the middle of a bunch of people who might just notice that there was a foreigner, a woman and the Paternal all masquerading as City

Watch.

There was a shout of surprise followed by as scream. Forge followed the sounds to the northern half of the city walls. He saw a figure fall from the heights, swiftly followed by another. More watchmen were heading along the wall. Then there was a blinding flash of light and an almighty boom just a moment afterward. Forge had to look away, his vision disrupted. The crowd erupted and the noise was almost as loud as the crack of Taimsin's surprise.

'They are going over the wall! Open the gates!' shouted the Paternal with authority.

'Come on, bloody open them!' added Fudail. The pair of them started pushing forwards, getting free of the crowds and heading towards the gates.

Forge looked at Taimsin, who raised her eyebrows and grinned. They hurried to join them.

'I can't open them. Not without orders,' a Watchman bearing the crest of an officer in his helmet was shouting back at Fudail.

'I am giving you your bloody authority. They are over the walls. If we don't give chase, we are going to lose them,' retorted Fudail, angrily.

The officer looked momentarily confused then nodded his head. 'Open the gates. Get them open!'

Several of the City Watch ran forward and removed the bracing beam from its brackets and pulled the gate inwards.

'Come on. Quickly, before they get away!' ordered the Paternal. Together Forge and his crew led the charge under the gatehouse and into the new city. Behind them the crowd surged as the City Watchmen lost control and they streamed through. Taking advantage of the confusion, instead of heading left to cut off Tailsin they carried on down the main street before cutting right into a small lane, Fudail leading the way. Away from the walls and the main streets it was darker, the houses crowding around them, and Forge quickly lost his bearings. After a while Fudail slowed his pace and all of them became watchful as they got deeper into ganger territory. They passed figures in the shadows, feelings eyes tracking their movements. Forge leaned in close. 'We need to get off the street and out of these uniforms. We're attracting too much attention.'

'You are telling me that?' whispered Fudail. 'These are my people. Can you imagine what they'd think if they recognised me? There are some who I trust but plenty more who will report us straight to the authorities.'

They continued on for roughly another half mile before they reached Fudail's home. It was a two-storey tenement sandwiched between a butcher's shop and some kind of hardware store sporting a sign proclaiming that anything would be bought for a good price and sold for a better one.

Fudail produced a key from around his neck and unlocked the door, ushering them inside. Forge took a moment for his eyes to adjust. They stood in a room which was comfortably furnished. Rugs covered the floor and there were two leather chairs sat to either side of a small wooden table that held a hookah pipe and two glasses. Fudail busied himself with a lantern and, once lit, the gentle glow revealed more. There were stairs facing the front door winding up the side wall to the second floor and underneath them a door set into the corner of the far wall. Covering the bare patches of wall there were paintings and even a mirror. The place was generally very clean, tidy and quite homely in a way that had never quite happened for Forge's little shack. A small table on the opposite corner to the door contained a bowl, bottles and above it, shelves of vegetables, crockery and clay containers. Facing the table and chairs were more shelves containing scrolls and books.

'You can undress here,' said Fudail. 'Don't worry about making clutter, I had not thought to return.' He started to undo his sword belt and remove his gear.

'Why didn't we just make a run for the city limits?' asked Taimsin. 'There aren't any walls in the way.'

Forge guessed he knew why but let Fudail explain.

'The stunt your sister pulled may have worked for us, but word travels fast. A cordon will be set up, watchers posted around the outskirts of the city. It may sprawl but even if we made it through, which would be extremely unlikely, then what would we do? We have no transport, no supplies. We have to prepare. Otherwise we will die of thirst or be hunted down like dogs.'

'We would have managed,' protested Taimsin.

'Or not,' said Forge. 'Fudail is right. The city is a bloody big place and we have gotten out of the hardest, most well-guarded part of it. We are safe for now. Let's take a moment to plan our next move.'

'Trust me,' said Fudail, shrugging off his chainmail. 'It will not get easier. I am heading back out. I will see what the lay of the land is, what the gangs are saying, and I will try and procure items for our journey. I will leave the key. Lock the door behind me and stay quiet.'

'Where does that back door lead?' asked Forge.

'There is a small yard out back and beyond that an alleyway.' He opened the knapsack he had been carrying on his back and retrieved a number of items of jewellery. 'I must look the part,' he said.

'If we wanted to stay discreet, why didn't we go down that

alley way before?' asked Taimsin.

Fudail stopped for a moment and snorted.

'Because I clean forgot. I guess it happens when you are running for your life.'

He handed the key to Forge and left the house. Forge inserted the key in the door and locked it.

He turned, puffed his cheeks and blew out a gust of air.

'I presume we wait?' said the Paternal. He had taken off his cloak and his swordbelt and now dumped himself into one of the chairs with a sigh.

'Yes. Let's see what the city does next. Where's that sister of yours, Taimsin?' asked Forge.

'Oh, she'll be along. No doubt leading folk a merry dance and leaving a trail of destruction in her wake,' replied Taimsin. She sat down on the other chair and removed her boots. 'I really hate having to hurry,' she muttered. 'Forge, is there any wine?'

He looked across at the small counter in the corner and spotted a bottle. He was sorely tempted but thought better of it – Jonas would be pissed at him.

*

Almost an hour later there was a knock at the door.

Forge reached for his sword, but Taismin raised her hand nonchalantly. 'That's Tailsin. Three knocks a pause then two more.'

Forge unlocked the door and Tailsin strode into the room, she was back in her leathers, having kept them on under her uniform. He looked up and down the street outside. It looked quiet. The sky was looking brighter, a false dawn presaging the arrival of the sun. He didn't believe in omens, good or bad. Shit just happened. He locked the door behind him.

'That was fun,' Tailsin announced.

'What's that, sister? Blood?' asked Taimsin, sitting up from her chair.

Tailsin arched an eyebrow. 'What? Oh, yes. I caught a bit of a lucky blow. Bastard blindsided me.' She raised her hand to her forehead where a mass of blood had dried and congealed within her hair. 'You should see what I did to him.'

'Any real problems?' asked Forge.

'Not really. Good thing the idiots allowed people to build right up to the walls. I just made the distance onto a roof and scurried around up there for a bit, making sure they caught sight of me and started chasing. After a while I ditched the outfit and made a long circuit round coming to this place from the east.'

'What's the security like?'

'There are a fair few City Watch and other types making their way along the major roads. And when you get off them, there's a fair few gangers abroad. It's a little early for them so I guess Fudail was right, the Ministry is starting to grease palms. Speaking of which, where is he?'

'Gone looking to get us a way out,' said Taimsin.

'Lovely,' said Tailsin. She tapped a finger to her lips. 'Sister, is it me or are your teeth stained a little red? Is there wine?'

Chapter 27

Fudail pulled a scroll off one of the shelves and unrolled it on the counter. It proved to be a hand-drawn map of the city, very precise and with immaculate lettering.

'I don't know how the Ministry worked so fast but I've spent the last three hours watching every gang in the vicinity come to life and put all their people on the streets. They are prowling around, knocking on doors - busting them in if they don't get a response – and generally being a pain in the ass. They are setting up roadblocks and asking questions of everyone they meet. I saw a bunch from Aranag start beating up on a young couple just because they weren't local to the district.'

'Are they really that easy to buy off?' asked Forge.

'It's a special situation,' said the Paternal. 'All hostilities will cease. This is not about loyalty to an embassy or a cartel. This is about an attack on Karnak Karnassuss itself.'

'Do they know what they are even looking for?' asked Taimsin.

'The gangers claim all they know is that a number of foreigners tried to break into the Palace. They've just been told to stop anyone suspicious looking or who are not from their neighbourhoods; if there is trouble then try and catch them but killing is fine too. The only places being patrolled by the City Watch and Ministry people are the main arteries out of the city.'

'Then we have an opportunity. We just have to continue pretending to be what we are not,' surmised the Paternal.

Fudail shook his head.

'It might work, but it's not just gangers. I spotted others with them, men and women who I know aren't from the local patches. I reckon they are Ministry people, higher level operatives, those who can be trusted with a secret. And I think some of them might be mages too. They'll be looking out for the Paternal.'

'Let me guess. We have to fight our way through?' said Forge.

'I'd like to avoid that if possible,' said Fudail. 'I may have burnt my bridges but as yet nobody knows I've thrown in with you. I still have friends and favours. I believe I can chart a course through to the edge of the city. When we get there I will have to look to you to get us out before the arrows, artillery, mage fire and cavalry charges all converge on us.'

'Has anyone ever told you that you are not a very optimistic person?' asked Tailsin.

'I used to be, I'm sure I did,' responded Fudail, somberly.

'How long will it take you to sort this out?' asked Forge.

Fudail pointed at the map again. 'Other than my contacts, we have one other advantage. The gangs will not stray into each other's territories. To do that is considered a massive insult and a power play. In the past it only happened when one gang had declared war on another.' He traced a line along the map. 'If we head through the Nook to the Knife then we can skirt the boundaries of Oasis – there's no way we can walk through there - and look for a way to enter Traveller Fields. I will have to negotiate directly with the gang leaders of the Waybearers. They are very independently-minded and have scores of members. Once we are in their territory, I can get us to the Supplicant Gate. There are a number of caravans that camp out there waiting to ship goods into the city. We might be able to find some mounts we can use.'

Forge nodded his agreement. Right now any plan which involved stealth and eventual escape was something he was more than happy to entertain.

'You start greasing the palms, Fudail. We'll be ready. When are we going?'

'Night seems appropriate?' said Fudail.

'Works for us, eh, sister dear?' said Tailsin.

'It does indeed. It will give me time to get some strength back,' replied Taimsin. 'Yesterday's excitement took more out of me than I thought.'

'And that's your problem, you always need time. I am always ready.'

'Good for you, sister. It must be very tiring, being perfect.'

'I'm going before I am driven insane,' said Fudail. 'You might as well get some rest. Eat and drink whatever you can find. I see you've already started that, Forge.'

There was a knock at the door. Forge tensed. Taimsin stood and Tailsin's knives appeared. Forge tilted his head towards the door. 'Go on, Fudail. Might as well answer it. Everything is normal after all.'

'Who is it?' Fudail asked.

'It's Calill.'

Everyone looked at each other.

'Open the door,' advised Forge.

Fudail reached out and pulled the door open. Calill stepped inside. He was wearing his Guard uniform but around his waist he carried a short-sword. Forge had to do a double take.

'That's Ashkent military issue.'

Calill nodded.

'It was a gift. A strange one you might think but it meant something to me. It was Dav's.'

'That's one weird love token,' remarked Tailsin.

'How'd you find me?' asked Fudail.

Calill smiled. 'I asked. I overheard you say what district you lived in, I took it from there.'

'And why are you here,' Forge asked.

'We were told that there had been a fight in the harbour and that a ship had been torched, its crew all killed. That was your way out. Then I heard somebody had been seen escaping over the wall. My brothers have been sent onto the streets so I decided to break away.'

'Quite a risk, you didn't know who might be waiting for you,' said Forge.

'All things considered, it is a small risk,' smiled Calill.

Forge smiled back. 'You get into any shit from last night?'

Calill shook his head. 'Not at all. I was lucky to have made it back to the armoury just in time. They called out all of the Paternal Guard to seal the Palace but of course, at that point, it was too late. And now we are patrolling the city.'

'Unusual and unprecedented,' observed the Paternal.

'No one has ever escaped before, Paternal,' said Calill. He suddenly took the smallest step back and turned his eyes down, his cheeks gaining colour.

'You have never spoken to me before,' said the Paternal, not unkindly. 'The Paternal Guard are the faceless, silent watchers. But I believe you can stop thinking of me as your Paternal.'

'That might take some time,' replied Calill, his eyes flicking to the Paternal then just as quickly away.

'Why'd you come anyway?' asked Fudail, hovering by the door.

'I wanted to see this through to the end. Perhaps I can still help.'

'All help gratefully received,' said Forge. He looked at Fudail. 'Carry on, get stuff sorted.'

Fudail nodded and left.

'Come on, sister. I'll clean that wound of yours,' said Taisim, pulling Tailsin towards the counter where a bowl of clean water rested.

'Oh stop making a fuss. I think it adds character,' complained Tailsin, but she went just the same.

Forge reached out and clapped Calill on the shoulder. 'It is good to see you, Calill. We are a little short of friends right now. Sorry we had to drag you into this.'

'I believe you are,' replied Calill. 'That is why I am here.'

'And I also owe you a debt of thanks,' said the Paternal. 'One I did not have a real chance to express before. I know you serve the city and the institution of the Paternal, if not the man who holds the office. But without you, I would not have had this chance.' He held out his hand. Calill looked at it and recoiled in horror. His years of training and beliefs sorely challenged. The Paternal did not take his hand away. 'My name is Neruh Malik and I thank you, Calill.'

Calill swallowed hard then reached out and gripped the hand.

A small part of Forge appreciated the moment, but the larger, older and grumpier part would have none of it. 'OK. All friends now? Tailsin, tell me you haven't drunk all the wine.'

Chapter 28

They left at dusk. This time they exited by the rear door, through the small, carefully tended rear yard cum garden and out into the alley. Fudail led the way then Forge, the Paternal and Calill, with Taimsin and Tailsin hanging back to watch their rear.

Fudail had returned a few hours earlier, carrying two knapsacks both packed with dried meats and cheeses along with several leather canteens of water. For all his pessimism, at least he was planning ahead. He led them on a roundabout route through small lanes, quiet roads and several alleyways, where the buildings to either side crowded so close that often the space between them shrunk to the point where Forge and Fudail, being the bulkiest, could barely squeeze through. But it was the only way. Fudail had made a deal with a low-level ganger lieutenant from the Drinkers and they had to get to where that man and his crew were patrolling. If they encountered anyone else, their journey would have to take a violent and possibly permanent halt.

They reached the end of another tight alleyway which opened out onto a wider thoroughfare running at a right angle to it. On the far side was what looked like a smithy, Forge throught, spying a horseshoe sign.

Fudail turned his head slightly. 'We cross here and go through into the farriers.' Forge had been half right, then. Fudail raised a finger. 'We will be stopped before we make it. Let me handle it.'

Fudail stepped out into the road and Forge followed him out, confident as he could, looking like he had every right to be there and keeping his hand well away from his sword. The door to the farriers opened as they were halfway across. A man stepped out. He wore a purple waistcoat over a bare chest. His trousers were blood red and cinched by a wide leather belt through which several knives were either tucked in or hanging from sheaths. His face was tattooed on the right side with a symbol of a circle split in two with two dark colours filling each hemisphere. As he got closer, he spied purple in the top half and red on the bottom. No prizes for guessing that he took his gang allegiance very seriously. As did the four others that filed out and flanked him, two to a side, armed with clubs and other blunt objects. Fudail moved towards the man, spoke a few quiet words and then shook the other man's hand. Forge wasn't sure but he thought Fudail had given him something within that meeting of hands. Then the man stepped to one side. Fudail turned and said, 'Come on.'

Forge followed him inside. As he did, he eyed the gangers. They looked on with various expressions of amusement, watchfulness and dangerous arrogance but they did not make a move. In any other circumstances he would have liked to have seen them try. Inside, the farriers was lit by a single candle. They wound their way through a small forge, with an anvil and a pile of coal heaped high. Forge ducked his head to avoid several hammers hanging from pegs on the low-lying beams. Another door led them into a back yard which stank of horseshit and sweat. Fudail stopped at a crude wooden gateway and pulled up the small retaining bar.

'There is a short alleyway outside, it leads to the Knife district. The leader of those gangers is my cousin. He was willing to listen and let us through here. To either end of that street we just passed through are much larger groups blocking our way. There is no way we could have gotten past them.'

'What did you give him?' asked Forge.

'You saw that, did you? That will be the keys to my house.'

Forge grunted quietly. 'Really have burnt your bridges, haven't you.'

Fudail raised his eyes to the heavens and shook his head sadly. He opened the doors and looked out. 'All clear. Come along, now, we have to find a way past the Oasis.'

'How do we do that?' asked Taimsin.

'I know this one,' replied Calill. 'We're getting dirty, right?'

'Yes,' replied Fudail. 'Though it'll be the smell that gets us.'

He opened the door further, revealing an alley, quite a wide one at that. Forge counted the crew through, closed the gate behind them and tracked along after the others. They reached a dark T-junction and took the right hand turn. Looking left, Forge could see a larger, well lit street about thirty yards away and figures moving along it. Some looked armed, but it was unlikely those on the street could see them. The right turn was along another, tighter alley, opening out into a small square, little more than a convergence of lanes and other alleys. In the centre of it was a large round, metal disc embedded in the ground.

'Ah, the sewers. Wonderful,' said Forge.

'Right, sister dear, turn around. We are going to fight our way through the city because I'm not going down there,' said

Tailsin.

'Since when have you been afraid of a little smell, sister?' asked Taimsin.

'It'll be hell to get out of my leathers.'

'I thought you'd be used to entrails and the like spilling over your gear,' remarked Forge, pushing through to Fudail and Calill, who were engaged in lifting up the cover.

'I'm too fast to get splashed,' remarked Tailsin, archly.

'OK - quietly now - just lay it down over here,' whispered Fudail. The metal scraped softly over the stony soil as they dragged the disc away, revealing the hole beneath. 'This is it,' said Fudail, wiping his hands.

'What's down there?' asked Forge.

'A route through to Travellers Fields' Fudail replied.

'You know, a thought occurs,' said Tailsin.

'And to me,' agreed Taimsin.

'No such luck,' responded the Paternal. 'I know of this system. And of the other sewer runs that snake underneath large parts of the city. This section is closed off to the others. A separate route. If I recall, it empties out into the Green River but at a height that makes it impossible to leap or scale down from.'

'That's about the size of it,' said Fudail. 'That's why your nascent plan of just working our way through the sewers is flawed. Trust me, the rest of the system will be watched and guarded. There is no chance we could get through to the gate. This is the safest route and even then I am not certain that it will be free of danger.'

'Fighting in the dark - not the best environment,' said Forge. For years since, he had tried not to dwell on his days fighting in the goblin tunnels. They were hard times. The inky blackness, the claustrophobia, the endless sense that eyes were watching and the constant worry that with a word the whole damned passage could come tumbling down on top of you.

'I'll go first,' said Taimsin. I can produce a little light, just enough for us to see by. Down there it won't be noticed unless they have mages.'

'I'll stay behind you and give directions,' said Fudail.

'I'll take the rear,' said Tailsin.

Forge felt a little surge of panic. He really didn't want to have to go down there. He hadn't realised just how much the Mercy Mountains had affected him. *Add that to the list.* But there was nothing for it. He went down after the Paternal, dropping his legs into the hole and finding a series of metal bars forced into the rock that resided under the thin layer of the dirt and rubble that passed for topsoil in these parts. The bars took him down about ten feet before his legs found no more purchase, just an open space. He continued to climb down the last few bars, just using his hands until he was almost folded over.

'You'll have to drop down,' said Fudail.

Forge released his feet, letting them dangle free, letting his arms take the weight. He let go and he fell another six feet or so, landing with a gentle splash and into the supportive arms of Fudail. Forge could just make him out thanks to the light coming from above, but that small circle did not extend far.

'OK?' asked Fudail.

'Just perfect,' said Forge, curtly. He stepped away to allow the Paternal space to drop. 'Taimsin? You there?'

'Yes. I'm just sending out a few feelers to see if we are alone,' she replied.

Forge took a step towards the voice, hearing an 'oof' behind him which announced the arrival of the Paternal.

'Seems fine,' said Taimsin. 'Let's try this.'

Just in front of his face the faintest of glows appeared. As it gained strength and form, more shapes revealed themselves. In the middle of it was a small, glowing orb, levitating over Taimsin's outstretched hand. The light it gave off was dirty, almost grey, like the dawn of a winter's day when all is covered in mist and the sun is just a brighter smudge in the sky. Forge could see the sides of the sewer walls and reached out a tentative hand. He felt rough rectangles that crumbled slightly to his touch. The floor beneath him was mostly dry, a few pools of water, piles and lumps of things he didn't care to dwell on were scattered randomly about his feet. Gods, he needed a drink.

'This will give us enough light to see by but won't travel much beyond our little circle,' said Taimsin.

'Good enough,' said Forge. He had worked with less. Forge counted two more splashes. That should be all of them.

'It doesn't smell too bad,' announced Tailsin.

'Trust me, it'll get worse,' said Fudail. 'Now we need to head along this channel. Taimsin, go first, I can direct you.'

'It's my dream job,' replied Taimsin, as she stepped into a tunnel. Everyone fell in behind her and perhaps it was just his own insecurities, but Forge could swear they all crowded that much closer together.

'Where will this spit us out?' asked Forge.

'Eventually we'll come to a dead end, at least one which we can no longer traverse,' replied Fudail. 'Then we find a cover, lift it up and we'll be in Waybearer territory. That'll prove interesting.'

'How so?'

'I am going to have to speak directly to their leader and appeal to his better nature.'

'That sounds like a cluster from the start.'

'I'm not sure I completely understand your meaning but I hope to convince him. He and I grew up together.'

'A cousin?' said the Paternal.

'No. But I did him a favour once.'

'Gives us something to work with, I guess,' said Forge, more to help his own confidence than anyone else's.

'Hey Fudail, tunnel forks ahead,' said Taimsin.

'Go left.'

'You sure? I see movement.'

'It shouldn't be a problem. Beggars and the like live down here. They won't get in our way.'

'They had better not,' said Tailsin, from the back of the line.

As they continued there was a light, faint and flickering, that was quickly snuffed out. They saw signs of life. Pictures, usually of genitalia and large-breasted women, had been crudely scratched into the brick and highlighted with white chalk. Occasionally there were some words, but none that Forge could recognise. The smell of tallow briefly helped mask the underlying odours, much to Forge's relief. Up ahead the dirty light showed what looked like a series of openings, about halfway up the walls on both sides. As they drew closer, he saw these openings, no more than the size of casket, contained rags, blankets, bits and pieces of tat. And in one or two, pressed far back against the stone, were people. He had a sense of eyes tracking his passing. It was a proper little community down here in the dark.

'Those dwelling here have had to carve out their niches over time,' said Fudail. 'When they pass on, someone else will move in.'

'They ever got flooded out?' asked Forge.

'Not during the summer months but during the winter sometimes storms come and overwhelm the systems. They always lose a few. Sometimes you find the bodies have been collected by the City Watch and left above surface. If they don't do that, the dead block up the smaller channels. They putrefy and disease spreads.'

'It doesn't already down here? Perhaps it would be better for all if they weren't allowed to live in here,' said Calill.

'Says the man who doesn't have to toil every day down in the new city,' said Fudail. 'You make do with what you can find. At least these folk have carved out a place for themselves. We are all just trying to survive and get by. You find a place and you make it a home.'

'As have I,' said Calill, testily. 'Yet look at us. Are we all not just reduced to survival, no matter what our previous station?'

'I suppose so,' consented Fudail.

They passed two more sets of cells built into the sewers but none thought to challenge them, the denizens content to let them pass without incident. They finally arrived at another confluence, a mirror of the above-ground entrance back at the start of their underground adventure. The small rivulet that had been flowing around their feet joined others and formed a larger channel, heading away to the right down another passage. Forge could hear the faintest of noises, the irregular sound of waves striking the shore.

'If we had a boat and a long enough piece of rope, we might have tried for an escape that way,' said Fudail.

'Now you tell us,' muttered Taimsin.

'We go up here,' he continued, pointing to another ladder built into the wall opposite, one with rungs reaching down to the floor. 'Who's got the strongest back?'

Forge looked over his crew. Calill could probably do it

but...'That's you, Fudail,' he said feeling a little bloody-minded. 'You are the biggest.'

Fudail gave him a sour look but did not argue the point. He climbed the ladder and encountered another metal disc. There were several holes it in that allowed soft beams of light to come through. He manouvered his back against the disc, his head bent forward at an uncomfortable angle and forced up with his legs, the disc giving way almost immediately. As it moved, he continued with his upward motion, using his body to create a wider gap. He twisted and used his hands to push the disc away before climbing out of the hole. Everyone waited a few moments before Fudail called down. 'It's clear.'

'Sisters, you go first. I'll bring up the rear,' said Forge. He was making this a point of principle, the sweat had been rolling down his back for the last five minutes and his breathing had become faster and ragged. He was damned if he was going to let his fears get the better of him. He watched the sisters climb out, then Calill, then the Paternal. Once they were all clear of the ladder, he grabbed a rung and made to haul up. He stopped and looked around. He smiled and spat on the floor. *I beat you.* Another small voice in the back of his head whispered that it would have been better if he could have had that drink. Just a nip of something to take the edge off. Forge shook his head. When had this started? When had he started needing rather than just wanting a drink? Jonas was right, it was different now.

A hand reached under his shoulder and helped him out of the hole. He nodded his thanks at Calill. They were in another small area, similar to the one they had entered by, but this one had just two exits leading from it.

'Fudail, we in the right place?' asked Forge.

'I believe so. If we take this alley, we'll arrive right in the heart of Waybearer territory. Then it's just a short walk to the walls. There is a postern gate that the master of the Waybearers has the key to. He bribes the guards to look the other way at the dead of night. It is how they smuggle contraband in and out.'

'Nice gig,' said Taimsin.

'Very much so. It has made him one of the wealthiest of the gang masters. There have been small wars fought over the possession of that key by both gangers and their sponsors.'

'Do the Ministry know about it?' asked Forge.

'Probably, yes. But it suits them to know it exists and that they can monitor who is trying to use it and for what purpose. Crime exists, criminals will always exist, better to contain their activities than waste time and resources trying to stamp them out.'

'It is a pragmatic approach that has guided our path for many decades,' added the Paternal. 'It is for the greater good.'

'I've heard that before,' said Forge, sourly. 'Come on. Let's get this done.'

Chapter 29

They emerged into a sizeable square, a market place by the looks of it though it was currently empty of any stalls or signs of trading. Forge counted close to a score of gangers, several carrying torches, loosely spread across the width of the square, with a tight knot in the centre where a man stood a little way forward of the others. They were all dressed in a similar fashion, black leggings tunics and turbans that wound across their faces, showing only their eyes. It reminded Forge of a group of assassins he had encountered many years ago. If these blokes were anywhere near as good as them, they should already be ruling the city by now. But they were let down by their choice of weapons: clubs, axes, swords of all kinds. Behind the gangers, another lane continued on, no doubt to the city walls.

'Wait here,' said Fudail.

Like before, he walked forward with his arms raised high and went to talk to the apparent leader. Forge strained to listen but could not hear the quiet conversation between the two, though the nodding of the leader suggested progress. He then raised a hand and the conversation stopped. He turned his head to look directly at Forge and the others. He nodded once more and said something else to Fudail. Fudail bowed his head.

'Please, all of you, come forward. We are to be allowed passage.'

'You heard the man. Almost there,' said Forge.

They formed a tight group as they entered the square and approached Fudail and the leader. Forge noted that as they drew close, the gangers fanned out a little more, starting to form a semi-circle around them.

'Forge, I hate to worry you and everything but another bunch have just appeared behind us,' said Tailsin, casually.

'Uh huh,' replied Forge, allowing his hands to drift to his sword hilt. The leader raised his hand to halt the group. He reached up and unwound the cloth from around his face. Underneath was a chin tattooed with the symbol of an octopuss. He looked first at Calill with an amused expression then at the Paternal.

'I like your escort. It is important that men are loyal to their masters.' He said and looked at Fudail. 'Very well.'

Fudail smiled at Forge, the relief plain on his face. It turned to shock and horror as his body spasmed forward and a blade forced its way out of his stomach. The blade was withdrawn and he collapsed to his knees. One of the gangers stood behind him, carrying the bloodied shortsword. The other gangers clustered around, their weapons held ready. Forge already had his sword out, Calill his spear levelled and the sisters were in a battle stance. The Paternal looked on in shock, his eyes fixed on Fudail's final death throes.

The leader looked at Forge. 'Why should men be loyal to a master who has already chosen to give up their power? Men need to find better masters to be loyal to. Ones that pay better. We will take the Paternal and his Guard. The rest of you do not need to live but I will give you the chance to surrender.'

'Like fuck you will,' said Forge and he stepped forward to smash his blade into the leader's face. His swing was checked by the ganger carrying the shortsword and Forge stepped in close and drove his first into the ganger's face. As the ganger staggered back, the square lit up and Forge felt a search of heat against this back followed by 'wooshing' burning sound. Taimsin was letting rip. Another ganger came into view and Forge stepped forward and down into a lunge, sweeping his blade in a low arc, cutting through leg and smashing into the next, the ganger collapsing in a screaming heap. 'Kill 'em all!' he roared.

Calill registered Forge's battlecry and felt a surge of energy run through him. He had been taught to fight calmly and with focus. The Paternal was to his back, and Taimsin was protecting their rear with a display of light and sound. A ganger charged towards him, an axe raised. Calill stepped forward and thrust calmly, piercing the stomach. He raised his spear and batted a sword to one side, then sweeping around with the butt he brought it in between a set of legs and flicked a ganger back onto the floor. He then smashed the butt into the masked face. He raised the spear and blocked a downward swipe forcing the blade back and pushing the ganger away. He quickly regained his posture and used the momentum to drive the spearpoint into the ganger's throat. He was dimly aware that he was barely thinking about his actions. It was all automatic, months and years of drills and sparring, hours of hard lessons, of blood and sweat, all for this moment, the first time he had ever had to fight for his or

302

anyone else's life. He was glad it had not been a waste.

'Watch out!' cried the Paternal. Calill turned his head to see the Paternal stepping between him and a ganger coming up on his left side. The Paternal brought his sword up, blocking a downward strike from the ganger. The man followed it up by forcing the Paternal back with a push of his hand. Calill was already moving, jabbing his spear into the ganger's midriff. He registered that they were not actively engaging the Paternal, their orders were clearly to capture him alive. He put an arm out to steady the Paternal. 'Thank you, now stay behind me. Keep watching my back,' he ordered. The Paternal nodded, his eyes wide.

There was a respite in the fighting around them. Calill counted at least twenty dead. Forge was by himself, wading in to a small group in front. Behind them, the gang master stood, exhorting his troops. To their rear Tailsin, was engaged with the gangers who had come up behind them. It looked like she was driving them back down the alley, they were falling back and falling down around her feet. He was impressed she was able to keep her footing.

'Heads down!' shouted Taimsin.

Calill crouched instinctively, reaching behind him and pulling the Paternal down too. A sheet of flame passed over their heads. Calill watched it splash and spread against some kind of invisible barrier in the air. A moment later he saw that barrier was flickering as it countered the fire. Beyond the barrier were two men, their hands raised in concentration. Neither was wearing the same ganger uniforms, just dressed in simple robes. Mages. The sheet of flame abruptly stopped. Calill looked back at Taimsin, her arms dropped to either side, her head cocked, like she was listening to something. One of the mages lowered his hands, cupped them then pushed them outwards like he was forcing something away. As the same time the other mage lowered his hands, presumably dropping the shield. Calill felt another surge of energy pass above him. Instead of blocking it, Taimsin ran towards them and raised one hand at an angle, the other she forced out, level with her head, fingers splayed, a green light emanating from the tips of each one. There was a flash of light against her angled hand and that surge of energy literally bounced away, impacting against a nearby wall with a loud crack and a spray of dust. Simultaneously, five bolts of green lightning jumped from her fingers and stabbed at the two mages. They were picked up and thrown away before smashing to the ground. The lightning continued to snake over their writhing bodies for several more seconds. Neither man stood back up.

Taismin walked past Calill and the Paternal. She looked down at them and winked. 'Second rate spell slingers. I'm almost insulted.'

Calill would have been very impressed were it not for the beads of blood dripping from her nose. She was clearly exhausted. Calill helped up the Paternal. The sounds of battle had grown distant. He picked his spear, ready to help Forge. As it was, that particular fight was already over. He jogged across to the soldier, and found him stood clutching his left arm. There were a half dozen gangers on the floor around him, including the gang master.

'Are you alright?' asked Calill, removing his facemask. He examined the nasty gash at the top of Forge's left arm, near his shoulder.

Forge looked at him with unfocused eyes. He was breathing heavily.

'What? Yes, yes. Fine. I got whacked by a club. Hang on.' He bent down, wincing, and retrieved his sword from where it stood embedded in the stomach of a ganger. He tried to move his left arm, it felt numb. 'It's buggered. I'll have to look at that later. Do me a favour and search the leader. See if you can find that key.'

Calill knelt down to do as he was bid. 'Taimsin's in a bad way,' he said, quietly.

Forge nodded. 'We all are. Taimsin? You seen Fudail?'

'He's gone,' Taimsin called back. She coughed and hacked up something dark.

'Right,' said Forge.

Calill placed his hands in the pockets of the gang master's trousers and searched around his neck and his waist for any pouches.

'Nothing here,' he said.

'Not surprised,' grunted Forge. 'Paternal. Get over here. We need to move on. That little fireworks display is going to bring people running. We don't have much time. Where's Tailsin?'

The Paternal put his arm around Taimsin and helped her stumble across the square. She jerked a thumb back towards the street behind them. 'She's coming.'

True to her prediction, Tailsin jogged into view. Her knives were back in their sheaths.

'They broke and ran. I thought I'd just keep up the momentum and give them a reason to keep going,' she said.

'They coming back?' asked Forge.

'I shouldn't think so,' said Tailsin. 'There were only two left by the time I decided to stop.' She drew up just behind Taimsin and placed a hand on her sister's shoulder.

'That was fun wasn't it, sister dear?'

'I was expecting something a little more challenging. They only had two mages,' she replied. Oh...' Taimsin looked down and placed a hand against her stomach. It came back glistening red in the scattered fires burning around the square. The Paternal let go of Taimsin and took a step back, shock registering on his face. Calill could not believe what he was seeing. Tailsin held a knife. One she had just stabbed her sister with. It made no sense. He looked at Forge, the man's face was clouded with confusion and shock.

'I didn't want to have to do this myself. You are family after all,' Tailsin said.

'Sister?' gasped Taimsin, as she collapsed to her knees.

'Because I knew you would never agree to this,' she smiled at Forge. 'Our employer gave me very explicit instructions. No loose ends. The less people who know about who took the Paternal, the better. My poor sister is far too honourable, she has a very soft spot for her old Ashkent comrades. And she is no an assassin. Considering our current situation, I had to make a decision. Quite frankly, she's been holding me back.' With her spare hand she withdrew another knife. 'I was told I had to bring the Paternal back alive. Everyone else was a nice to have, but certainly not necessary. My sister is all used up, and the rest of you are beat and of no use in a fight. I'd rather not have the hassle of trying to keep you all alive.' She took up a fighting stance. 'No doubt you'll want to contest this.'

Calill watched Forge, he looked terrible. He was shaking his head, his smile was grim. 'Fine. Just gimme a minute to get my breath back.'

Calill wasn't going to wait. He leapt at Tailsin, his spear levelled right at her stomach. She twisted out of the way at the last moment. He had expected this and used his speed and torso strength to whip the butt of his spear round, aiming to drive it into the side of her midriff. Instead she carried on twisting out of the way and he carried forwards, his feet slamming up against the corpse of a dead ganger. He fell sprawling, his head meeting the ground hard.

Forge watched this play out. Good for Calill for giving it a try but the assassin was always going to be too fast. Be that as it may, he might as well give it go. He was almost out of the nervous energy the fight had given him and soon his left arm would no longer function. He took a two-handed grip on his blade even as his left arm screamed at him. He shaped a decapitating swipe at her head, trying to catch her off-balance as she was turned to watch Calill careen by. She looked back, saw him coming and dropped low, her leg sweeping out in an arc and knocking his feet from under him. He went crashing to the ground, a sharp pain flaring at the back of his head as he connected with something hard. 'Fuck,' he groaned as he tried to focus through the flashing pain. Tailsin stood over him.

'Nice try, Forge. I'll make this quick.' She crouched, a knife ready to cut his throat.

Taimsin's arm shot out and grasped her sister's ankle. Tailsin gave a short, surprised squeal and tried to shake it off. Taimsin's head raised a little. Blood dripped from her mouth as she smiled. 'All used up am I, sister? You never appreciated my talents.'

Forge saw her eyes gleam like two pools of flame. These flames grew, replacing her orbs and then bursting outwards covering her face and racing along her arms. Tailsin reached for one of her daggers and started to hack at the wrist. The hands spasmed and gripped tighter. Her squeal turned to a scream and Forge swore her heard bones crunching. These screams continued as the flames jumped from Taimsin to

Tailsin. She lit up like a beacon, the fire eating at her flesh.

Arms reached under Forge's armpits, pulling him away and lifting him off the ground. He grunted as a surge of pain travelled up from his wounded left arm. He felt a trickle of something hot run down it. 'Shit, that hurts.'

'I think we should go,' said the Paternal, releasing his grip of Forge.

'Good idea,' said Forge, still mesmerised by the display. Tailsin continued to struggle even though she was already done. There was no coming back from that.

'This way, I can get us to the wall,' said Calill, using his spear to haul himself back onto his feet.

The Paternal tugged at his arm, Forge shook his head and turned away. 'Here,' the Paternal handed over his sword.

'Come on,' urged Calill, jogging down the alleyway. Forge stumbled after, the Paternal continuing to support him. Half of him still felt numb but he was starting to get some feeling back in his legs. They carried on blindly, following Calill, Forge having lost all sense of direction. He had to clear his head and work out what they should do next. There was no way through the postern gate and he was damned if he could start climbing walls. He couldn't think of a way out. He could barely get his breath back and now too many parts of his body were starting to ache. The path they followed led them down an alley at the end of which was a high, stone wall. A light burned from a brazier sat atop the parapet. Calill turned and held up a hand.

'We are not far from one of the gates. I think we can get through. On the other side are the caravan camps. From there, we steal some horses and ride north.' He started to reattach his facemask. 'I'll lead the way in.'

'What do you have in mind?' asked Forge, pushing the

Paternal away and trying to stand up straight.

'I'm still a Paternal Guard. That carries weight and authority. I'll make sure they let us through.'

Forge dropped his sword into its sheath. 'I'm pretty much beat. If you reckon we can still get through, then crack on.' Forge never liked admitting defeat but they had been screwed over left right and centre, he had lost all of his crew, and their best bloody fighter had turned out to be a backstabbing bitch anyway. Leaving the alleyway, there was little traffic moving along the walls. The route they followed was little more than a path, six feet in width. Already the city was starting to bulge at its new seams. This new city wall was roughly twenty foot high, not as thick or as well built as the old wall, but it had not been designed to withstand the sieges of the past. Apart from the occasional fires on the walls that barely reached to the ground below, much of the way was in shadow. They passed a couple of travellers who were more interested in Calill and his uniform than the two older men who struggled in his wake. Forge had to admit a stark truth. He was now the one holding them back. If it came to it, then he'd have to act as a diversion. He could give Calill and the Paternal a chance to get away. There was an irony that it would be a Paternal Guard that saw the mission through and got his master away from the city. Forge flexed his right hand. He could still wield his sword. He was still good for one last fight.

Chapter 30

After a couple of minutes, Calill spotted the Supplicant Gate. It was about thirty yards away and was within a bright circle of light. He stopped his advance and pushed against the wall. Unsurprisingly, this was far better manned than the heights above. He was convinced that the battle they had fought against the gangers would have drawn the City Watch, irrespective of territorial rights. That manpower would have come from the walls, not the gate. He also spotted several men clustered by a brazier. The gatehouse itself was similar to the one leading to old Karnak Karnassus. The city might not have invested in the walls but the gate was well built and solid with a mechanism to control both the doors and portculli within the top chamber over the passage. This would play to their advantage if his plan worked. He turned to his companions. The Paternal was covered in dirt and blood. Forge looked worse, something dark dripped away from his left hand but his face was set hard.

'Both of you wait here. I'll clear a path for you. When I do, make for the gate and keep running.'

'What about you?' asked the Paternal.

Calill smiled behind his facemask. 'I'll be along.'

Forge took a step forward, an eyebrow raised.

'You should tell me what to do. I can cover you.'

Calill was sorely tempted by the offer yet he knew it would not work. 'I'm going to get the gate open. With the best will in the world I doubt you would make it to within ten yards of the gatehouse before they were all over you. Best you get your breath back.' Calill turned to go. He stopped and sighed. *I might as well.* He held his hand out to Forge. The man looked a little taken aback but took it. Calill saw a range of emotions run across Forge's face before settling on a grim smile and a knowing nod. He held the grip for a few seconds then let it go and looked at the Paternal. This was harder, he didn't know what to say and he certainly did not want to shake the man's hand again. The Paternal was responsible for everything that had befallen them. Yet he could hardly hold it against the man for wanting to live. Instead he drew himself upright, snapped to attention and bowed his head. He turned smartly and marched off, gathering his thoughts as he did so. He was a Paternal Guard. That meant something, it meant he was someone to be respected.

He entered the circle of light surrounding the gatehouse and saw that the City Watch had already spotted his approach. One of them, his markings on his helmet indicating he was an under-officer, stepped forward, flanked by two Watchmen.

'Guardsman. What are you doing here? Are you alright?' the under-officer asked.

'Does it look like it?' replied Calill. 'My squad were caught up in the battle.'

'We saw the mage fire. I sent six men to help.'

'I didn't see them. They may already be dead. I got out while I could, it's a bloodbath back there. Is the gate secure?'

'It is. Everything is locked down tight.'

Calill looked up, studying the towers and parapet to either side. 'Not many men up top.'

'Those were the ones I sent.'

'Then I suggest you put more up there. I believe that those we are hunting plan to scale the walls.'

'We are a stretched thin. If I send men up top I risk leaving no one to guard the gate below.'

'It is sealed tight, is it not?'

'I suppose so, but-'

'Enough. Send some men up top and along the southern stretch. In fact, you can show me the inside of the gatehouse, while you are at it.'

The under-officer looked a little flustered. 'I'll need to-'

'Do as you are told!' snapped Calill. It was easy to inject the right kind of irritation in his voice when he was feeling it anyway.

The under-officer stood up and saluted. 'Yes, sir! You three, with me.' The under-officer led the way through the bottom door of the gatehouse, leaving the remaining three men behind. Calill smiled. If he'd known commanding men was so easy, he should have tried for promotion much earlier. Too late now. He climbed up the steep, dimly lit set of stairs to the gatehouse chamber. The Watchman ahead knocked on a door.

'It's me, open up.'

There was the sound of a bolt being drawn back and the door opened, letting out a little more light. They all marched inside into a high-ceilinged rectangular room that was lit by a few torches and featured several small arrow slits built into the walls looking outside of the city towards the mainland. Spaced out on the floor were a series of hatches - murder holes where hot oil, rocks and spears could be thrust downwards onto the heads of attacking forces. A door on the far side and another next to the one he had entered by led to the parapets. A set of ladders led up to the next two floors of the towers built into either side of the gate. The place was a little fortress and could be expected to hold out long after the walls around it were breached. Calill counted two more men inside.

'Send your men south,' he ordered, pointing at the far door. The three City Watch pushed past Calill and exited through the far door.

Calill walked further into the room, studying the two mechanisms controlling the portculli. Both were in the raised position.

'You have not lowered these?' he asked, very pleased there were not.

'No. We were told just to seal the gates.'

'Hmm. And how many men in the towers?'

'One man in each. We are overstretched. We have people all across the city.'

'And yet the ones we seek are in the neighbourhood. The gates. They are not braced?'

'You see those bars?'

Calill saw two vertical iron bars that dropped through small circular holes in the stone floor of the chamber. On the top of each bar was a horizontal crosspiece about a foot long.

'Yes?'

They drop down into the frames of the gates and then on into holes in the ground. They act as braces. We only use wooden beams in the case of a siege engine and there has not been one of them used on us for several generations. Controlling the gates here, in this room, is far more secure.'

'Good. Let us go back outside.'

The under-officer went first and was two steps down the

stairs when Calill reached out and pushed him forward. Calill closed the door to the gatehouse chamber and slid the bolt back into place. He turned to look at the two gatekeepers.

'Don't just stand there. Lock the doors to the parapets!'

The pair of them stood there, staring at him then at each other.

'We have to seal this room now!' he shouted.

One of them turned and started to pull the bolt across the door. The other ran towards the door opposite. Calill could hear footsteps and raised voices coming from the stairs below. This was accompanied by loud banging on the door. The Watchman, his hand raised to the bolt, hesitated and looked at Calill again, doubt and uncertainty in his eyes. *That's the best I'm going to get.* Calill pulled his dagger from its sheath and thrust it into the Watchman's neck. He let go of the blade and readied his spear. The other Watchman, sword drawn, was running at him.

'Help us!' the man screamed as he closed. Calill took two steps forward and thrust his spear forward before the Watchman could strike. He withdrew his weapon and looked round as another Watchman appeared from one of the towers, jumping down from the ladders. Calill jabbed backwards, his butt connecting with the Watchman, forcing him backwards and off balance. Calill turned and slashed in an arc but the Watchman leapt back. Calill recovered his pose as the man drew a shortsword. Calill lifted his spear high, blocked a downward strike and stepped in close, driving his helmeted head into the Watchman's nose. A cry of pain and a satisfying crunching noise was the result. Calill felt a deep, sharp, burning pain in his left shoulder. He cried out and threw himself backwards against his attacker, the one from the other tower. They careened back and both lost their footing, falling to the ground in a heap. Calill pushed himself up and twisted off.

He picked up his spear and drove it deep into the chest of the Watchman. There was a bloodied dagger on the floor, the blood was his. He scooped it up and through it at the final Watchman whose nose he had broken. The man had only just regained his feet and slumped back against the wall, the dagger embedded in an eye socket. Wincing at the searing pain coming from his shoulder blade, Calill stumbled across to the first of the iron bars in the floor, he got both hands on the cross piece and hauled it up, going hand over hand when the crosspiece was too high for him to continue holding. The bar was not thick but it was heavy and he swore as his muscles and bleeding back started to fight against him. That dagger had gone in deep. He moved to the second, ignoring the loud banging coming from the door leading to the stairs. It should hold for some time. They'd need a mage to blow it off its hinges if they wanted in. Once more he hauled. He got halfway before he heard the gate swinging out. Forge must have worked out what he was doing. Thank the gods for that, he didn't think he had the strength to lift the bar any further.

He let go of the bar and sat heavily on the floor. The doors leading to the parapets started to vibrate as the Watchmen on the walls realised something was amiss. Calill sighed and rolled his shoulders. 'Ahhh,' he hissed. He pushed himself back until he hit solid stone, then he removed his mask and helmet. Breathing deep he rested his head against the wall.

'There, Dav. I've done everything I could. Your man is out and away. The rest is up to him. I hope you are happy. I did it all for you.' The banging coming from one of the parapet doors was getting heavier, more like pounding. They must have found some kind of ram. Calill decided what he should do next. He ought to take his own life, just cut his wrists open and let it all flow out. He felt tired, he wanted to be with Dav. But there was a part of him that did not want to go, did not want to die just yet. He was still a Paternal Guard, he was proud of who he was and what he had done. In his own way, he had fulfilled his duties; he had protected and served the Paternal to the end. He didn't want to die but when the Ministry got hold of him, they would make him suffer. He regretted many things. But he had fallen in love. And things could never have been the same after that. The pounding got louder. He heard something crack. That wasn't good. Last chance. He reached across and hooked a foot round his spear and pulled it towards him. He gripped the shaft and pulled himself up. He smiled.

'I'll see you soon, Dav.'

Chapter 31

'I think he has their attention,' observed the Paternal.

'You think?' Forge watched the excitement as first a Watchman came out the doorway almost falling ass over tit, then the same Watchman charged back up the stairs followed by the others left standing guard by the gates. 'Come on, that's us.' He and the Paternal left the shadows and jogged to the gatehouse. Forge looked back along the parapet. He had heard footsteps go past above them and was expecting them both to be spotted. But their luck held. They got underneath the gatehouse and out of sight. The banging and shouting coming from the open doorway was getting quite agitated. Forge inspected the gate, he spied brackets for a wooden brace and two horizontal iron bars fixed to the two halves of the gate. He pushed at one but met very firm resistance.

'I don't see a lock. Is it braced from the outside or something?' he asked, looking up at the curved stone passage above their heads, the murder holes loomed dark above them and the sharp spiked teeth of the portcullis threatened to snap down and trap them.

'You won't,' replied the Paternal. 'Look at the doorframes where they meet in the middle. See how they are thicker?

Inside are metal bars that run down and hold the gates in place. Look at the bottom.'

Forge crouched, his bones protesting, and looked closed at the ground underneath the gates. He could just about make out a small circular depression and something sat within it.

'How does Calill get it open?'

The Paternal raised his hands. 'He has to lift.'

'Right.' There were new voices, drifting in from the parapets. They were running out of time.

'Wait. Listen,' said the Paternal. Forge cooked his head. There was a metallic scraping sound, coming from the gate on the right. He stepped closer and pressed his head to the wood. He could follow the sound as it moved upwards. 'It's out,' he announced. He pushed at the door, it gave a little but was damned heavy. 'Give me a hand,' he ordered and the Paternal leant his shoulder. The door opened a crack more, six inches, then a foot. 'Get through,' he ushered the Paternal out with a push then followed suit. He thought for a moment. 'Let's close this.'

The Paternal stopped. 'But Calill...'

'Isn't coming. We need to close this. That way they won't notice we've got through, buy us a couple more minutes.' The Paternal rejoined him and they pushed the gate shut again. Forge had considered just for a moment trying to clear a path for Calill. But it was too much of a risk. They had no time to waste. Calill was still alive for now but with all the racket and the Watch trying to get in, Calill had nowhere to go. He'd known this was how it would pan out when he offered to get the gates opened.

'This way,' said the Paternal. Forge followed him away from the gates. There was a paved road leading to the North, along the coast. It was empty of traffic, a hundred yards off to the right, towards the river, was a sea of campfires, tents and pack animals. Forge's left arm was aching like a bastard. He clutched it tight; it was moist and warm to the touch. He kept looking behind at the walls. Expecting a shout of recognition or at worst an arrow in the back. He saw several shapes moving behind the battlements, gathered at the gatehouse, their attentions fixed squarely on Calill's diversion.

'Here!' the Paternal pointed at several horses picketed at the edge of a cluster of tents. No one was about, though there had to be a guard at least.

'You ride a horse before?' Forge asked.

'Yes.'

'Know had to saddle one?'

'No.'

'Great.'

'Hey!' someone walked around from the side of one of the tents.

Great. Forge reached for his blade.

An old man, toothless with a scraggy white beard, walked up to them and put a hand to his cheek, picking at something or other. There was a moment of awkward silence.

'You Fudail's lot?' the old man asked.

Forge and the Paternal looked at each other.

'Yes?' ventured Forge.

'Thought so, you look like it. Thought there would be more of you. Come on.' The old man turned and walked back around the tent. Forge, with no better ideas, followed him. 'Got five horses. All saddled. Food and water for a day or two,' said the old man indicating a gaggle of horses, tied against a single wooden pole driven into the ground.

'Fudail squared us away,' said Forge. For all his complaining, the poor bastard had still planned like it was going to work out. 'You know where we are headed?'

The old man shook his head. 'Don't know. Don't want to know. I'm heading east now. Was told to disappear for a couple of weeks. Works for me.'

'Me too. Paternal, pick a horse and mount up and let's get out of here.'

'We taking all of them?' asked the Paternal.

'Spare mounts and the provisions they carry? Damned right we are.'

*

Forge wiped his brow and glared up at the sky. He had left that damned stupid-looking hat back at *The Moon* and was regretting that decision. His head was baking.

'We should have stayed at the last village,' said the Paternal. Forge glanced behind him. At least the man had the sense to wear a hooded robe. He didn't reply, he'd said it already. They had ridden at a gentle pace all night, changing horses at regular intervals, following the coast road rather than strike out into the badlands. Forge had no confidence in his ability to survive in these conditions and by using the road, the signs of their passage would merge with the traffic. They did not see anyone else moving along the road but passed some camps and several fishing settlements. Forge was hopeful no one had noticed their passing. With a good twelve hours of travel behind them, he estimated they had sixty, maybe seventy miles to play with. It was just a question of how quickly Karnak Karnassus got its act together and sent people out to hunt them down. They next major port was Creed and they should make it by nightfall. It had no special relationship with Karnak according to the Paternal so that should give them a chance to get inside. Unless of course the Ministry offered them some serious cash or money to apprehend them. In the hot, blazing, bastard light of day it was going to be a significant problem. He was not in any condition to bash heads. But he did still have a large portion of the coin given to him by McKracken.

'Paternal. How do you feel about lying in the back of a wagon covered in horsedung?'

'Right now, I'll take any suggestion you care to make,' he said drily.

'If we're lucky, it might just be figs...or fish.'

'Both sound wonderful.'

Good. That was decided again. They'd steal into the city having bribed a friendly local. Simple. And he was sure there'd be no probing by spears or halberds.

'Forge?'

'Yes?'

'There is a party of riders coming our way from the south.'

Forge turned and squinted. It took him a moment to register a dust cloud, and several dark specs. It could be nothing, could be something. It was still a busy route but no one rode that hard if they didn't need to.

'Let's take a canter down towards the beach shall we?'

Forge turned his mount to the left and led them off the road and up steep and rocky slope. As they came to the top, the sea, blue and surprisingly inviting spread out before them. He looked back and saw the group was drawing near and at speed. He counted six riders. Sunlight gleamed from metal. A lot of metal. He kicked the flanks of his horse, nudging it towards the water, a hundred yards away. The scrub and rock gave way to a long stretch of sand running down to the water. It was slightly off white, soft with no rocks or pebbles, the hooves kicking up small sprays as they left firm imprints in their wake. They were out of sight of the riders. In the distance to his left Forge could see a ship tacking towards the coastline. It's sails were coloured bright orange. A gentle breeze played against his face, bringing relief from the heat if not the burning from its rays.

'Forge?'

'Yeah?'

'The riders.'

He looked back. The six were arrayed at the top of the rise and were now urging their horses down into the sand. They appeared in no hurry. Forge eased his horse round and tired to roll his shoulders. His left side complained bitterly. He reached down and eased his blade a little way out of its sheath.

'No need for that,' said the Paternal.

Forge squinted at him. The Paternal was smiling.

'We had a good run. And I must say, I have not felt so alive in years.'

'Ain't over yet,' grunted Forge. Though he was pretty much out of ideas.

'You see that one,' the Paternal pointed at the rider in the middle of the group. He was the only one of the six dressed in flowing white robes and a keffiyeh. The others were armed and armoured in different fashions, not one of them alike. They also looked grim and deadly serious. 'That is the Minister of Relations.'

'Nice of him to come in person,' said Forge.

'That is his style.'

The Minister drew up in front of them. The other five riders kept back a respectful thirty paces, their horses grouped together in a pack. Forge debated trying to take the man hostage, but knew he couldn't defend against those five. They looked far too competent. The Minister appraised Forge for a brief few moments and he locked eyes with the man. He wasn't a local or at least his ancestors weren't. The skin tone was lighter, the features less hawkish, more rounded, like someone from further north. The Minister looked towards the Paternal and bowed deeply.

'Paternal. I am pleased to see you are healthy and unharmed.'

'Minister Swarbreck. I am likewise pleased to see you are hale.'

'You led us a merry dance, I'll give you that. Though I fear your rescuers are much depleted.'

'That is so. They gave much to see me this far. A feat that, were it not for the outcome it brought, should be acknowledged as quite remarkable.'

'Yes. But then, we were assured that such a thing could indeed happen.'

'To live through it is a very different experience. One starts to doubt the wisdom or the sanity of such a plan,' mused the Paternal

'I don't doubt it. Things were sticky at my end too for a time,' agreed Swarbreck

'Hang on a fucking minute!' Forge shouted. He was having a real problem working out why these two were having such a friendly chat. Both men stopped and regarded him. Swarbreck with something like amusement and the Paternal with sympathy. 'What the hells are you two talking about?' Forge asked.

'Forge, you are a clever man and I am sure even now you start to fathom just what has come to pass here,' said the Paternal.

'I'm starting to get whiff of something that stinks,' agreed

Forge.

'Sir,' Swarbreck looked at Forge. 'I am the Minister of Relations. I have served my city for many years. Do you know why?'

'The pay is good?' said Forge sourly.

'No,' replied Swarbreck patiently. 'I serve it because I love it. I serve it because I love its people and the good that has come out of decades of peace. But the city has a rotten core. One that has corrupted too many, that spreads and taints everything. It touches all and leaves us diminished. It encourages lies, deceit, pain and manipulation. All these things are done not for the benefit of the many, but the few. This city welcomed my family with open arms. I owe it for that. But as I grew from childhood I started to see, to understand that what had been a dream to save all and help the people of Karnak Karnassus thrive, had turned into a tool of the ruling Families to hold onto their power. They have created a state where the elite watch from their seats high on the plateau and encourage those around them, the gangs, to fight and squabble and kill.

'It is an illusion, a construct. By keeping the masses at each other's throats, by allowing other states to use our people as foot soldiers, they can sit by and rule unchallenged, knowing that their Ministry watches all and ensures the game is played as we wish it. If anyone steps out of line, then we intercede.'

'Forge,' said the Paternal. 'I had grown sick of playing this game. When my family died, I no longer had any reason to. I was ready to join them and I told the Minister that I would not continue to support this way of life, this most bloody and twisted of poltical systems. Imagine my surprise when he agreed with me.'

'You two *planned* this?' Forge said. *By all the Gods, the audacity!* 'Who else knew?' he growled.

'Outside of the Paternal and myself, almost no one,' said Swarbreck. 'Not until the scheme was afoot. Even then the organisation I had helped to maintain was almost too good to beat. My assistant, Orlaise, is a loyal servant but always to the families and the status quo. I know not how but he started to get a sense of something wrong. He almost destroyed our plans when he got hold of one of your people, the major. And it appears he all but succeeded in wiping you out by mobilising the city against you. When I was informed of his actions, I could wait no longer. These men,' he indicated the riders behind him, 'and others like them, have been long in my employ and mine alone. I finally brought them into play and in so doing, Orlaise and other key officials have been...removed from their offices. I personally saw to Orlaise while he was attempting to question your man we found at the gate. He was somewhat shocked. As was your man.' He turned and made a beckoning gesture at the riders behind them. The group split, and the rider at the rear of the group rode his horse towards them. Forge took a closer look at this one. He wore ornate armour that was stained with blood. The man unwrapped the cloth that covered his face. It was Calill. He nodded, his face neutral.

Forge nodded back. He was pleased to see the lad but it still didn't resolve matters. He scratched his head and wiped some sweat from his eyes. 'What happens now? You going to kill us?'

'Kill you? No, not at all,' said the Paternal. 'Nothing would be served by that and quite frankly, there has been enough death. This escape was genuine. We could not afford to have this incident traced back to us. If we had tried a coup, there would have been greater bloodshed across the city, far in excess of the carnage you and your companions wrought. As it stands, you have done us a service in wiping out one of the more 'independently-minded' gangs. I will now return to the city protected by Swarbreck and his men, and I will speak to the Families who have been gathered. I will tell them that my kidnap has shown that our system is flawed and cannot be maintained. I will propose a new way, where instead of secret deals and hidden plots, the city will no longer be used as a battleground but as a place for all nations to come and debate openly. I believe the Crucible should be that place.'

'With the City Watch and Paternal Guard reeling from their wounds and the destabilising nature of the last few nights events, I will personally call off the festival,' added Swarbreck. 'There will be no ritual slaughter of the Paternal, no replacements. Instead I will throw my weight behind the Paternal's words. I believe the people of the new city will be with us and the Families will have no iron fist to persuade the people otherwise.'

'You think all the embassies are going to go with that?' asked Forge, sceptically.

'No, not all,' admitted Swarbreck. 'But there will be some. Enough, I hope, who will support us and will not attempt to sow discord. I know who the real troublemakers will be and I'll keep a watch on them.'

'Forge,' said the Paternal. 'You were an unwitting pawn in this. I am sorry for all the deaths, particularly of your companions. Truly. But there is a greater good to be found here. I know you will not see it that way but, for what it is worth. I thank you.'

Forge grunted. 'One question. Why us? Why did you choose Ashkent, why Major Jenkins?

The Paternal looked across at Swarbreck to answer. The

Minister shrugged. 'I said there was virtually no one who knew about the plot. Ashkent was a nation we knew we could deal with, pragmatic, not adverse to underhand dealings, but more interested in stability and prosperity. They take the broader view, they play the longer game and we know they don't leave their allies hanging in the wind. I set up a situation where the Paternal could get a message to Major Jenkins, I knew him to be a man of honour, who would do the right thing. We believed he would get the message back to your Assembly, and then we would let the game play out.'

'Big risks,' said Forge.

'Yes, but we had faith in you.'

'Fantastic,' muttered Forge.

'We have to go now, Forge. Captain Forge, I believe,' said the Paternal.

'Retired,' corrected Forge.

The Paternal inclined his head.

Swarbreck pointed at the spare horses. 'You may keep those. And him,' he said, looking at Calill. 'He has expressed a desire to leave my employ.'

The Paternal smiled.'I can hardly have a Paternal Guard who has divided loyalties.'

With that he and his men swung their mounts around and headed back over the slope and out of view. Forge watched them go. He was still coming to terms with what had just happened. *Now how did he know I was a captain?*

'Good to have you back,' he said to Calill.

'It feels good to be back,' acknowledge Calill. 'Orlaise had a mage ready to rip me there and then.' He sat back on his horse and sighed. 'What do we do now? I have never been so far from the city.'

Forge looked up and down the stretch of beach. For the

first time in many weeks he had run out of steam. He had no sense of purpose and very little motivation. He figured he had to head home but it didn't feel like much of a victory march. And when he got there? Maybe there was something to deal with after all. He looked out to sea. The sun sparkled off the wave tops and the water lapped gently against the shore. He ought to carry on north and look to see about getting passage. Now he was out of danger there was no reason to be covert about it. He noticed that the craft with the sail had drawn closer to the land. In fact the sails had been gathered in and it appeared to be stationary. And there a small boat coming towards him, four oars dipping in and out of the water. He leaned forward and placed his hands on the saddle horn and watched it approach. Fifty yards out one of the figures in the boat raised an arm and started waving at him. He squinted. The figure looked familiar.

'Fuck me,' said Forge. What the fuck was Nazar doing in an elf-ship?

Epilogue

Forge stepped out of his home and placed both hands on his belt. He wore his leather jacket although the nights were still warm, autumn having just started to exert its grip.

'I missed you at Dunbar,' said McKracken, as his dismounted. He had two companions, who stayed on their horses. The one on the left had blond, short-cropped hair, the one on the right long black hair slicked back and tied into a ponytail. Both wore black leather and chain.

'I wasn't going to hang around. I fancied getting back to my own bed. Besides, Red wanted his horse back.'

'Fair enough,' said McKracken. 'I did have a man waiting for you. He said you came ashore alone. No, the merchant was with you, Nazar.'

'Yeah. He lost his ship and crew.'

'Lost the Paternal as well, by the looks of it,' said McKracken.

'I didn't lose him, I had to hand him back.'

'Uh huh. Anyone else of your crew make it out?'

'No. Just me and Nazar.'

'Hmm,' McKracken nodded and craned his neck, looking past Forge towards his home, then made a show of inspecting the clearing.

'Anything else you need?' asked Forge.

McKracken raised an eyebrow.

'I suppose not. It didn't quite work out as planned, did it?'

'You tell me,' said Forge, folding his arms.

'Karnak Karnassus isn't the same place anymore. Things have changed a bit since your heist and it seems the Assembly is content with that. Happy to support the new regime, such as it is. A pity we didn't get the Paternal but we've got a place on the inner circle, a standing council of nations. Those that want to take part at any rate.'

'That's nice. Got a question for you.'

'I thought you might.'

'Did Dav know what he was getting into?'

McKracken shook his head.

'No. He was just in the right place at the wrong time.'

'Tough luck, huh?' said Forge.

McKracken sighed expansively and shook his head.

'All my life I have had to make the tough calls, the hard decisions. I have always had to put my men on the line, their lives in the balance. No different to you, Forge.'

'At least my men always knew what they were fighting for,' said Forge, hotly.

'That's a luxury I didn't always have. Sometimes, Forge, if you knew half of the real reasons we fought for things, you wouldn't have been so happy to do it. Dav was a man who I knew I could trust to do his duty. Did I want him dead? No. I just couldn't afford for him to know it was all a set-up. We had to be able to break the chain if he got caught. We had to protect ourselves. Hells, I took a risk using you.'

Use. Now there was a word. 'General, you got my friend killed. I'm pissed at you for that.'

McKracken smiled. It wasn't arrogant, it was just very knowing. 'Welcome to my world, Forge.'

'Not mine. Not anymore.'

'Fair enough,' said McKracken. He turned for his horse and stopped. 'Shame about the sisters. Did they mention me at all?'

'Enough,' said Forge. 'Enough to know that we were just expendable assets.'

McKracken didn't move for a moment then tilted his head to one side. The rider with long hair raised his hand and Forge felt a crushing pressure build around his his body. *A fucking wizard.* Try as he might he could not move his arms or his legs. He went to open his mouth but his lips were stuck to each other. He felt a tightness across his chest and he could barely draw in air.

'I'm sorry, Forge. But this mission is over. And no one can know about it. You were a good soldier. We'll make it quick.' The second rider dismounted and walked towards Forge. He drew a short blade from his belt. Forge wanted to swear, to scream at McKracken. He felt the muscles of his face strain as he tried to form the words. The knife man was steps away from Forge. There was no smile on his clean-shaven face, no amusement in his blue eyes. The man was a professional killer, and Forge just another target. McKracken had started his walk back to his horse. The bastard didn't even have the balls to watch him die. The knife-man stepped onto the porch and raised his blade. Suddenly the wizard on the horse jerked backwards as an arrow buried itself in his neck. McKracken swore in surprise as another hit the wizard in the chest. The knifeman turned his head. Forge felt the crushing pressure on his body disappear. He kicked out and connected with the man's knee. He fell to the floor with a grunt. Behind Forge the door opened and Calill emerged. He charged forward with a cry, levelling his spear and thrusting into the open mouth of the knifeman and the point burst through the back of the head with a spray of bone and blood. Forge stepped past the transfixed killer and walked towards McKracken who ran to his horse and pulled a shortsword from a sheath tied to the saddle. Forge continued walking towards him. The wizard on the horse had slumped forward, a third arrow protruding from his side. McKracken turned and raised his blade. Forge stepped in close and punched him in the face. McKracken staggered back. Forge grabbed his shoulder with his left hand and drove his fist into the general's stomach. He felt McKracken's air expel from his body as he sagged forwards. Forge shifted his next punch and aimed three jabs into the kidney. McKracken had dropped his sword. Forge released him and bent down to pick it up. McKracken took a few steps back and raised himself up. Blood was dripping from his nose.

'What are you going to do? You kill me, nothing changes. Others will take notice. People will come for you,' he said, through ragged breaths.

Forge inspected the blade. It was Askent military issue. Nothing special, just a simple short, stabbing sword made for hard living and hard fighting. It was a fitting weapon. He followed McKracken as he backed up, his hands raised in a warding gesture. Forge did not stop. He buried the blade deep into McKracken's belly. The general's hands grasped Forge's own, trying to push it back out. Forge leaned in with his body and the strength in McKracken's grip lessened.

Forge put his mouth next to McKracken's ear. 'You get a soldier's death looking the enemy in the eye. More than Dav got. But you'll die slow at least.' He released the blade and stepped back. McKracken swayed a little and looked down at the weapon the returned his gaze to Forge. He opened his mouth to speak but blood spilled from his mouth. He collapsed to his knees and fell to his side.

'Bastard,' muttered Forge. He heard rustling in the trees to his right. Branches parted and Jonas emerged, bow in hand.

'You left that late,' said Forge.

'I was waiting for your signal,' protested Jonas. 'I could've taken them all down before they'd had time to shit themselves.'

'Even so,' said Forge. '*I* almost shat myself.'

Calill walked over to join them, his spear resting lightly on his shoulder. He nodded to the pair of them.

'What now?' he asked, as Jonas hauled the dead wizard off his horse and started to check his pockets.

Forge shrugged. 'You heard him. Might be others will come looking. But maybe not. McKracken was working off the books. Either way I don't want to go to war with the Assembly. So I reckon we take Nazar up on his offer.'

'A life plying the seas,' said Calill, with a slight smile.

'You said you wanted to travel,' said Forge.

'Yes. It was Dav's fault. He fired my imagination for far off places and people.'

'You tend to find that wherever you go folk are pretty much the same,' observed Forge. 'But I like the idea. A life as a smith was far too boring.'

'Just as long as we don't have to deal with any elf-ships,' said Jonas. 'Made my bloody skin crawl. Ah, here we go.' He pulled a pouch from around the wizard neck. He opened it up, peered inside and nodded. 'McKracken paid well, I'll give him that.'

Forge turned to Calill. 'Go check that one for money. I'll

search McKracken. I reckon we can help Nazar out with buying our cargo.'

Calill nodded and jogged back to the dead knifeman. Forge watched him go. He was a good lad. It reminded him of another man he'd met back in Graves. There was a spark of vitality in him, even though he still mourned for Dav. He'd do well.

'Hey, boss,' said Jonas, tapping him on the shoulder. He jingled the pouch in front of his face. 'Before we go. Fancy heading into the village and getting hammered at Red's? We got a bunch of people need toasting and remembering. And an old friend who needs a proper soldier's send off.'

A drink. He'd weaned himself off that habit since Karnak but this time he knew it would be different. Scores had been settled and some burdens weighed less heavily. Forge smiled.

'Sounds good to me.'

ABOUT THE AUTHOR

Alex is an ex-Regular Army officer having served in both the Royal Engineers and the Education and Training Services. He is now in the Army Reserve and is a lecturer at Cambridge Regional College. He has also written for computer games such as the BAFTA nominated *Merlin: the Game*.

He lives in Saffron Walden with his wife Siobhan and his ancient cat, Fluffy.

He enjoys rolling lots of dice and moving things across tables.